THE
MIDNIGHT HUNT

Applause for L.L. Raand's *The Midnight Hunt*

"Thrilling and sensual drama with protagonists who are as alluring as they are complex."—Nell Stark, author of the paranormal romance *everafter*

"An engaging cast of characters and a flow that never skips a beat. Its rich eroticism and tension-packed plot will have readers enthralled. It's a book with a delicious bite."—Winter Pennington, author of *Witch Wolf* and *Raven's Mask*, the Kassandra Lyall Preternatural Investigator paranormal romance novels

"'Night's been crazy and it isn't even a full moon.' Who needs the full moon when you have the whole of planet Earth? L.L. Raand has created a Midnight otherworld with razor-cut precision. Sharp political intrigue, furious action, and at its core a compelling romance with creatures from your darkest dreams. The curtain rises on a thrilling new paranormal series."—Gill McKnight, author of *Goldenseal* and *Ambereye*, the Garoul paranormal romance series

"L.L. Raand's vision of a world where Weres, Vampires, and more co-exist with humans is fascinating and richly detailed, and the story she tells is not only original but deeply erotic. A satisfying read in every sense of the word."—Meghan O'Brien, author of the paranormal romance *Wild*

Acclaim for Radclyffe's Fiction

Lambda Literary Award winner *Stolen Moments* "is a collection of steamy stories about women who just couldn't wait. It's sex when desire overrides reason, and it's incredibly hot!"—*On Our Backs*

Lambda Literary Award winner *Distant Shores, Silent Thunder* "weaves an intricate tapestry about passion and commitment between lovers. The story explores the fragile nature of trust and the sanctuary provided by loving relationships."—*Sapphic Reader*

Lambda Literary and Benjamin Franklin Award Finalist *The Lonely Hearts Club* "is an ensemble piece that follows the lives [and loves] of three women, with a plot as carefully woven as a fine piece of cloth."—*Midwest Book Review*

ForeWord's Book of the Year finalist *Night Call* features "gripping medical drama, characters drawn with depth and compassion, and incredibly hot [love] scenes."—*Just About Write*

Lambda Literary Award Finalist *Justice Served* delivers a "crisply written, fast-paced story with twists and turns and keeps us guessing until the final explosive ending."—*Independent Gay Writer*

Lambda Literary Award finalist *Turn Back Time* "is filled with wonderful love scenes, which are both tender and hot."—*MegaScene*

Lambda Literary Award finalist *When Dreams Tremble*'s "focus on character development is meticulous and comprehensive, filled with angst, regret, and longing, building to the ultimate climax."—*Just About Write*

By L.L. Raand

The Midnight Hunt

By Radclyffe

Romances

Innocent Hearts

Love's Melody Lost

Love's Tender Warriors

Tomorrow's Promise

Passion's Bright Fury

Love's Masquerade

shadowland

Fated Love

Turn Back Time

Promising Hearts

When Dreams Tremble

The Lonely Hearts Club

Night Call

Secrets in the Stone

The Provincetown Tales

Safe Harbor

Beyond the Breakwater

Distant Shores, Silent Thunder

Storms of Change

Winds of Fortune

Returning Tides

Honor Series

Above All, Honor

Honor Bound

Love & Honor

Honor Guards

Honor Reclaimed

Honor Under Siege

Word of Honor

Justice Series

A Matter of Trust (prequel)

Shield of Justice

In Pursuit of Justice

Justice in the Shadows

Justice Served

Justice for All

Erotic Interludes: *Change Of Pace*
(A Short Story Collection)
Radical Encounters
(An Erotic Short Story Collection)

Stacia Seaman and Radclyffe, eds.:
Erotic Interludes 2: *Stolen Moments*
Erotic Interludes 3: *Lessons in Love*
Erotic Interludes 4: *Extreme Passions*
Erotic Interludes 5: *Road Games*
Romantic Interludes 1: *Discovery*
Romantic Interludes 2: *Secrets*

Visit us at www.boldstrokesbooks.com

THE
MIDNIGHT HUNT

by *Radclyffe* writing as
L.L. Raand

2010

THE MIDNIGHT HUNT

ISBN 10: 1-60282-140-2
ISBN 13: 978-1-60282-140-8

This Trade Paperback Original Is Published By
Bold Strokes Books, Inc.
P.O. Box 249
Valley Falls, NY 12185

First Edition: March 2010

Credits

Editors: Ruth Sternglantz and Stacia Seaman
Production Design: Stacia Seaman
Cover Design by Sheri (graphicartist2020@hotmail.com)

Acknowledgments

As this is a new adventure in my writing career, I must thank all those who said "do it!"

First and last and always, my partner Lee, without whom none of what is best in my life would be possible, for always believing in my stories. *Amo te.*

Editors extraordinaire, Ruth Sternglantz and Stacia Seaman, for finding the wrong turns—those that remain are all mine.

First readers Connie, Diane, Eva, Friz, Jenny, Paula, Robyn, and Tina, for embracing the dark even when it was "scary" and learning to love the "others" as I do.

Sheri, after ten years and two hundred–plus outstanding covers, I am still amazed at how truly gifted you are.

And finally, to the readers who continue to support and inspire me—my everlasting gratitude.

L.L. Raand, 2010

Dedication

To Lee, my mate

CHAPTER ONE

Sylvan hungered to free her wolf. After three days in the city, encased in a steel-and-glass building fifteen hours at a time with nothing but concrete under her feet at night, she needed to fill her lungs with the scent of warm earth, sweet pine, and rich, verdant life. She needed to run with her wolves and lead them on a kill. The insistent pressure between her thighs and the shimmer of pheromones coating her skin reminded her of another critical need, one not so readily satisfied. She'd gone too long without sexual release, but she couldn't risk even a rough-and-ready tangle with a willing female when her wolf seemed insistent on claiming a mate. That she would never do.

Never long on patience, she was edgy and amped on adrenaline and hormones. Even knowing she could be in her Adirondack Mountain compound in thirty minutes didn't curb her temper while she sat at a desk in the New York State Capitol Annex building listening to a politician patronize her. But she needed to do the job that had fallen to her when she had ascended to Alpha shortly after the Praetern species had stepped out of the shadows for the first time in millennia. As head of the Praetern Coalition representing the interests of the five Praetern species—Weres, Vampires, Mages, Fae, and Psi—she had been charged with convincing the senior senator from New York to push PR-15, the new preternatural protection bill, through his committee.

"We'd like to bring the bill to a vote this session, Senator," Sylvan said into the phone, careful not to allow her frustration to bleed into her voice. She spun around to face the view of the Hudson River six blocks away. A breeze through the open windows of the twelfth-floor office carried a teasing hint of the river on a raft of summer heat, reminding her that her imprisonment was only temporary. "The bill has been tabled for the past six months and the Coalition members are asking why."

"We all want the same thing, Councilor Mir," Senator Daniel Weston said, "but we have to remember, this is all very new for the human populace. We have to give the voters a chance to get used to the idea."

The senator's patrician tone grated, and Sylvan growled softly, her right hand tightening on the leather arm of her desk chair. The wood creaked, protesting the crushing pressure, and she consciously relaxed her fingers. No one knew better than she that for some humans, there would never be enough time to accept those who were *other* as equals. The nonhuman races had hidden their preternatural essence for centuries in order to survive in a world where they were greatly outnumbered. Eventually global culture expanded until isolation was impossible, and the Praeterns learned to hide in the light, forming uneasy coalitions while building a formidable economic power base. Sylvan's father had finally convinced the Praetern leaders to make their presence known to the world, arguing that the benefits of visibility outweighed the dangers—their corporations could compete openly in international markets, their scientists and doctors would have access to greater research opportunities, those in politics who now had to work behind the scenes could actively advocate for their rights. And most importantly, they could demand protection under the law for future generations.

Shortly after Antony Mir had spearheaded the Exodus, he had died, leaving Sylvan to assume the mantle of leadership. She had been twenty-six years old, a year out of law school. Her father had been her Alpha, her mentor, her friend, and her greatest champion. She'd had no time to mourn because the Pack needed a leader, especially in the midst of the chaos the Exodus had incited. His absence remained an agonizing void in her heart.

"Over a year now, Senator—and several million dollars in campaign donations. That's a long time to wait for basic protection from those who would destroy us for simply being different." Sylvan couldn't help but think of her father's death and how little progress she'd made in achieving security for those whom she had been born to protect and defend. Anguish and fury frayed the last remnants of her temper and a low rumble resonated from deep beneath her breasts. Her skin tingled with the ripple of pelt about to erupt and her claws sliced through her fingertips. Her wolf shimmered so close to the surface that her slate blue eyes, glinting back at her from her reflection in the window glass, sparked with wolf-gold. Her dusty blond hair took on the silver glint of her pelt. Along with the impending shift came an exhilarating surge of power and raw sensuality.

The door behind her opened and a husky alto voice inquired, "Alpha?"

Sylvan swiveled to face Niki Kroff, her second and *imperator*—the head of Pack security. One of Sylvan's *centuri*, her personal guards, Niki was also her best friend—they'd grown up together, tussled and played dominance games as adolescents, sparred together as adults. Tonight Niki wore her usual uniform—a formfitting black T-shirt, cargo pants, and lace-up military boots. Her compact muscular form looked hard and battle worthy, despite the soft swell of her full breasts and the luscious fall of thick auburn curls that touched the top of her shoulder blades. Niki had sensed the rise of Sylvan's wolf, stirring Niki's instinctive need to guard her Alpha against any distress. Sylvan didn't find Niki's sudden appearance in the office an intrusion on her privacy. Pack members had very few physical or emotional boundaries. In fact, Sylvan hated having the *centuri* stand between her and the rest of the Pack, forcing her into even more isolation than her status as Alpha demanded. But since her father's death, the Pack would have it no other way. She was too important to them not to be under constant guard.

"I'm fine," she *sotto*-voiced, too low for Weston, who continued to try to placate her with platitudes, to hear. Niki, though, could hear her easily, and after one last searching look, backed out of the room and closed the door. Sylvan reluctantly brought her wolf to heel, promising her freedom soon. Breaking in on Weston's monologue, she said, "Some of the Coalition leaders are beginning to question if our friends in Washington are really friends at all."

"Now now, Councilor," Weston said almost jovially, "I'm sure you can explain things to the Coalition and your own…uh…followers."

"Pack. My Pack," Sylvan said softly. She wanted to point out, not for the first time, that the Adirondack Timberwolf Pack was not a cult or a religion or a social organization. They were a community, connected physically and psychically. She was their Alpha, their leader, but she was part of them as well. But she was too weary and her wolf was too anxious to roam for her to repeat what she had been explaining publicly for months. "The Mage and the Fae have never been as solidly behind the Exodus as the Weres. I don't think I have to remind you how strong a force those two groups are in industry and international commerce. I don't think you want to lose their support."

"Of course not. Of course not. The committee plans to convene within the month, and I assure you this matter will have priority on our agenda."

Sylvan could tell she'd gotten as far as she was going to get with him that night. Human politics were fueled by money, and until the money train carrying funds from the Praetern Coalition to Capitol Hill ground to a halt, the laws to protect them would be slow in coming. Hopefully, once humans began to appreciate that Praeterns had lived and worked among them for centuries, and not only performed many essential functions within society, but were their friends and neighbors and, sometimes, even relatives, popular opinion would swing in their direction.

"I look forward to hearing from you soon, Senator," Sylvan lied, and put down the phone. Almost ten thirty. Traffic on the Northway would be light this time of night. She couldn't wait to shed her pale gray linen shirt and tailored black trousers, a necessary concession to her high-profile persona as the head of U.S. Were Affairs. If she and her *centuri* left now, they'd be home before full moonrise. Running under the moon was her favorite time to hunt—the forest took on a primeval glow and the very air seemed to glitter with moon dust. She preferred to run in moonlight whenever she could, even though most Weres had evolved to the point they no longer needed the pull of the moon to shift. She and her Pack could shift at any time, although she alone could shift instantaneously. Even her most dominant *centuri* needed a minute or more to accomplish the change. Her singular ability to call her wolf at any time, to shift partially or totally at will, was one of her greatest joys and helped balance the price she paid in loneliness for being the Alpha.

"Niki," she said quietly as she packed her briefcase. The door opened and her second slipped inside. Niki's forest green eyes took in the unfinished meal she had delivered earlier in the evening and narrowed in displeasure. Sylvan ignored the look. "Have Lara bring the Rover around. Let's go home."

"You didn't eat."

"Do I look like I need a den mother?"

Niki folded her arms beneath her breasts and spread her legs, an aggressive stance. She met Sylvan's eyes for a second before looking away. "More like a mate. If you won't look after yourself—"

"Niki." Sylvan gave a warning rumble. She knew many Pack members were anxious for her to take a mate, not because of pressure to produce an heir—she had decades for that—but because she would have more protection. The Pack Alpha could accept intimate care and safeguarding from a mate, whereas she couldn't from anyone else. She had her reasons for ignoring the not-so-subtle hints that Niki and those close to her had been making, especially the last six months. She did not want a mate. She had seen the desolation in her father's eyes after the death of her mother over a decade before. He had fought his desire— the innate drive—to join his mate in death until Sylvan was old enough to take her mother's place, but he had been broken, an empty shell of who he had once been. Sylvan had lost her mother, and in many ways, her father, all in a few moments of betrayal and blood. She would not allow herself to be that vulnerable. Ever. "We've had this discussion. I don't want to have it again."

"You've been working twenty hours a day for six months and ignoring your needs. It's not going to help the Pack if you're too weak to stand a challenge." Niki was a dominant Were at the top of the Pack hierarchy, and one of the few who would dare incite Sylvan's ire in order to protect her.

Sylvan cleared the desk so quickly Niki barely had time to put her back against the door before Sylvan towered over her. Sylvan didn't touch her. She didn't have to. Niki dropped her chin and turned her face away. Sylvan brought her lips close to Niki's ear, and when she spoke, even the Weres outside in the hall, who could hear a mouse in the walls three floors below them, did not hear her. As their Alpha, she could speak to them mind-to-mind as effortlessly as she could with words. *Do you question my ability to lead, Imperator?*

Niki shivered and tilted her head, further exposing her neck. A Were as powerful as Sylvan could crush the windpipe or tear open the great vessels in seconds. "No, Alpha, I do not doubt you. But I am responsible for keeping the Pack safe, and for that, we need you."

Am I not always here for you?

"Yes, Alpha," Niki whispered, her eyes nearly closed, her gaze still averted. "But many in the Pack fear what will happen if the humans decide to hunt us. You give them the strength to fight the fear."

Sylvan sighed and pressed her mouth to Niki's neck, grazing the bounding pulse with her fully erupted canines. Sylvan's caress was possessive, not sexual. Niki was her wolf, as were all the wolves in the Pack, and Niki needed Sylvan's touch, her heat, her strength. Isolation was a form of death for a Were. Niki arched subtly against her, taking comfort from Sylvan's reassurance. Sylvan growled and bit down gently until Niki whined, her shiver of fear turning to pleasure. Gradually, Niki relaxed against Sylvan's body, at ease and content. Only then did Sylvan release her.

"Do not worry, my wolf," Sylvan whispered aloud. "The Pack will always come before all else in my life."

"I know," Niki murmured, grateful and saddened at the same time.

"Come on." Sylvan squeezed Niki's shoulder. "Keep me company tonight on a run?"

"With pleasure, Alpha." Niki reached for the door and then abruptly stepped in front of Sylvan. "Wait."

Sylvan felt it too. Waves of tension streaming toward her from the guards outside the door, but she could sense no immediate threat. No scent of enemies. "Open it."

Niki did, but continued to shield Sylvan's body with her own. "What is it, Max?"

Max, a barrel-chested male easily six inches taller than Sylvan's own five-ten, filled the doorway, his grizzled face tight with strain. "We have a problem. Several of the young slipped our perimeters and left the Compound. We just found out."

"Where are they?" Heat flared in Sylvan's eyes. The northern extent of Pack land bordered the Catamount Clan territory in Vermont. The cat Weres were mostly feral and as territorial as the wolves. They would not give safe passage within their territory, even to foolish wolf pups.

"Here, in the city," Max replied.

"Who?"

"Jazz, Alex, and Misha."

Three teenagers, two brothers and a dominant young female, all in military training at the Compound—Sylvan's home and Pack headquarters. The adolescents had strict curfews, not only because they were still too immature to control their shifts in the face of rampant hormonal changes, but because like all young wild animals, they craved excitement and had no sense of their own mortality. Sylvan cursed.

"That's not all," Max said grimly.

"What else?" Sylvan fixed him with a hard stare and he dropped his gaze to her shoulder.

"Alex was the one who called us. They're at Albany General Hospital. We don't know what happened, but Misha's injured."

Sylvan shouldered him aside and was halfway down the hall before he even finished speaking. Niki, Max, and the third guard, Andrew, ran to keep up. Sylvan didn't bother with the elevator but loped into the stairwell, grasped the metal railing, and vaulted over the side and onto the landing one floor below. She leapt down, floor by floor, until she reached ground level seconds later. When she went through the door into the dark, she was racing on all fours. The others couldn't shift while moving, and she didn't wait for them. She was the Pack Alpha, and one of hers was in danger.

Sylvan ran alone through the night.

❖

"Jesus," Harvey Jones exclaimed, "what the hell is that racket?"

Drake McKennan listened to the steady cacophony of snarls emanating from behind the closed curtain at the far end of the ER. "Wolf Weres. I paged the Were medic already."

"What are they doing here? I thought they were indestructible or something."

"They're extremely long-lived, I understand," Drake said, "but not immortal. They can be hurt. Killed."

Her fellow medic didn't even bother to hide his disgust, and Drake had to work not to make a caustic comment. He wasn't the only medic who didn't seem to think the oath they took extended to Praeterns, even though most of them had probably taken care of a witch or a lesser Fae at some point in their careers without knowing it. Probably not a Were, though. Harvey was right, the Weres rarely showed up in the ER. Their Packs or Prides had their own medics. Just the same, if she'd had the slightest idea how to treat the young female Were who'd arrived with a stab wound to the shoulder, she would have. Assuming the adolescent males with the pretty young brunette would let her get close to the girl without a fight, which she doubted. Just the same, she would have tried if she'd thought she could do any good. The six-foot-tall boys had a few inches on her and more muscle, but she was a pretty solid fighter. She'd had to learn quickly how to defend herself in the series of foster homes and state facilities she'd grown up in. The problem was, she didn't know much about Were physiology—just one of the many secrets the Weres protected.

"Well, I wish to hell they'd quiet down. They're making the real patients nervous."

"I'll see if there's anything I can do." Drake had seen the girl when the boys had brought her in. She was scared and she was in pain. The boys looked scared too, but they put up a tough front, snarling at anyone who approached, demanding a Were medic look at her and no one else. Drake's instinct had been to help her, but she'd put in a call to Sophia Revnik, the medic who had worked in the ER for five years and who, after the Exodus, had announced to everyone she was a wolf Were. Drake liked the plucky blonde, but some of their colleagues had given Sophia the cold shoulder since discovering she was a Praetern.

"Why bother with them," Harvey scoffed.

"Because that's why we're here," Drake said, realizing that at the next ER staff meeting she'd have to bring up the schism developing around treating Praeterns. The bias had been subtle at first, but as each day passed, the prejudice was growing. The heated public debate over allowing Praeterns the rights of full citizenship hadn't helped. Some, more each day it seemed, argued that the constitution only protected humans.

"Watch yourself," Harvey grunted as she walked away.

She stopped in front of the cubicle, not foolish enough to surprise the boys when they were obviously upset.

"Hey," she said to the curtain. "I'm Dr. McKennan. Can I help you at all? Can I come in?"

"No," a rough male voice snapped back.

"Look—I can start an IV, maybe give her something for pain."

"No one will touch her."

Drake took a breath, kept her voice calm. "Someone's going to have to." She debated sliding back the curtain, but the sound of a commotion coming from the direction of the ER entrance diverted her. A blonde strode toward her, but it wasn't Sophia Revnik. This woman was taller and leaner than Sophia, with dusty blond waves that just brushed her collar in place of Sophia's shoulder-length platinum locks. Keen blue eyes that took in everything around her in one sharp sweep dominated her strong, angular face. Even dressed in jeans and a plain navy T-shirt, she exuded an unmistakable air of authority.

Everyone in her path backed away, hurriedly averting their gaze, but as the blonde bore down on her, Drake couldn't look away. When the slate blue eyes fixed on hers, an unexpected wave of heat coursed through her. She had seen Sylvan Mir, the Special U.S. Councilor on Were Affairs, on television but the cameras had not done her justice. They had made her look older than she obviously was and had muted her untamed beauty and charisma. She smelled wild too—burnt pine and cinnamon, with an undercurrent of tangy sensuality.

"Are you responsible for them?" Drake said, holding up one hand. "I need to see the girl but they won't let me in."

Slowing, Sylvan studied the woman standing almost protectively in front of the closed curtain. Her thick, collar-length black hair contrasted sharply with her ivory skin, as if her face were bathed in moonlight. Her carved cheekbones and slightly square jaw reminded her of the stark beauty of sweeping mountain peaks. She wore scrubs the color of warm blood, and she blocked Sylvan's path with unwavering courage. This stranger should have been afraid—of her and of her nearly out-of-control adolescents behind the thin curtain—but her charcoal gray eyes radiated only calm. A calm that slid over Sylvan's skin like the brush of warm lips. Sylvan shook off the unfamiliar urge to let down her guard, to rest for a moment in that seductive peacefulness. She could smell Misha's pain, the boys' rising aggression. They were hers to protect, and this human had put herself between her and her wolves. A very dangerous and foolish thing to do.

"Who are you?" Sylvan demanded.

"Dr. Drake McKennan."

"You're a human physician."

"Yes. You're the Were Alpha, aren't you?"

"Yes," Sylvan said, impressed with the human's use of the terms. Many humans preferred to avoid a direct reference to her species or her status. "Sylvan Mir."

Drake finally broke free of Sylvan's hypnotic gaze and took in the whole of her long-limbed, rangy body. "You're barefoot."

For just a second, Sylvan's full, perfectly proportioned lips flickered, as if she might smile, but then her expression cooled. She moved forward so quickly, Drake barely had time to get out of her path.

"You'll excuse me." Sylvan reached for the curtain. "I need to see to my young."

"Can I help you?"

"No." Sylvan pulled the curtain aside.

Drake stayed where she was. The Were Alpha hadn't said she couldn't watch.

"Alpha!" one of the boys exclaimed. Both boys, handsome dark-haired teenagers with startlingly beautiful dark green eyes, immediately ducked their heads, seeming to shrink in on themselves. The equally beautiful brunette girl on the stretcher whimpered.

"What happened?" Sylvan growled.

"Rogues," one of the boys whispered. "They attacked us in the park. We fought them, Alpha, but—"

Drake jerked in shock and barely stifled a protest when Sylvan Mir grabbed the boy by the collar and yanked him up onto his toes, shaking him so hard his thick black hair flew into his face. The Alpha and the young male were nearly the same size, but she handled him as if he were half her weight.

"You brought Misha out of the Compound and then failed to protect her?" Sylvan roared.

The boy trembled in her grasp and the girl, to her credit, forced herself upright on the stretcher, even though she was in obvious pain.

"I don't need males to protect me," Misha cried, her dark brown irises circled in gold. "I am strong enough—"

Sylvan whipped her head around and silenced the girl with a glare. "And you? You followed these brainless pups against my explicit orders? You want to be a soldier, yet cannot obey a simple command from your Alpha?"

The girl's pale face blanched even whiter and she shuddered.

"She was attacked," Drake exclaimed, instinctively wanting to shield the injured girl. There'd been a time when she had been the defenseless one, and no one had stood for her. She had stopped hoping for, stopped needing, that kind of caring a long time ago, but she couldn't erase her bone-deep drive to defend the defenseless. "She's hurt and in no condition—"

"This is none of your concern," Sylvan snarled, rounding on Drake, lethal-looking canines flashing. Her eyes were no longer blue, but wolf-gold. "These are *my* wolves."

Drake stiffened, the memory of bruises inflicted by older, stronger youths in a group home suddenly as fresh as if the blows had been delivered yesterday. She heard a low rumble and her skin prickled, the fine hairs on her arms and neck quivering. Forcing herself to think, not react, Drake assessed the scene as she would an unknown clinical situation. The boy was limp in the Alpha's grasp, the way Drake had seen young kittens and puppies go boneless in their mothers' jaws. The teenagers did not appear frightened or abused. Chastised, yes. But not afraid. In fact, all three of them looked at Sylvan Mir with something close to adulation. Drake realized that no matter how human they appeared, these Weres did not live by human social and moral conventions, and she was out of her element.

"My apologies, Ms. Mir," Drake said softly. "I meant no offense."

Inclining her head infinitesimally, Sylvan said, "None taken."

Sylvan was impressed with the human's fortitude. When Pack Alphas went dominant, they exuded a complex combination of powerful hormones that triggered a deeply ingrained flight instinct in the primitive brain centers of every species. Any other human, and even the most dominant wolves, would have cowered in the face of her rage. But Sylvan had no time to ponder why this human female seemed able to absorb her fury without fear. Misha needed her.

Sylvan released Jazz and turned to Misha. When she stroked the girl's cheek, the teenager nuzzled her palm.

"Where are you hurt, Misha?" Sylvan inquired softly.

Misha lifted her chin, seeming to take strength from Sylvan's touch. "My shoulder."

Drake watched the exchange, struck by the tenderness that passed between the Alpha and the young Were. Anyone who wasn't looking closely would have missed the small signs of caring, but to Drake the subtle gestures said everything. The deep love that existed between these Weres and Sylvan Mir was unmistakable.

"Did any of you shift?" Sylvan asked, taking in the three teens. The two boys had crowded around the stretcher now, each of them stroking the girl, comforting her.

Misha shook her head. "I wanted to, because I thought it might heal my shoulder, but I was afraid to try. You said we couldn't, without permission."

"So you did remember something," Sylvan murmured, rubbing her knuckles along Misha's jaw. "Turn over, let me see."

Obediently, Misha rolled onto her side and Drake eased into the cubicle for a better look. Misha's shirt was in tatters and Sylvan swept it aside, revealing a long gash in the trapezius muscle, beginning high on her back just to the left of her spine and extending diagonally downward for six inches. The wound didn't look like any knife wound Drake had ever seen. The edges were blackened and already beginning to fester. Angry red streaks extended outward from the gangrenous margins for several inches. Something was very wrong.

"That wound is infected." Drake pushed closer. "Let me at least take a loo—"

"No," Sylvan lashed back.

Then Drake heard a sound unlike anything she'd ever heard before—not a snarl, not a growl. A deep, resonant rumble filled with pure animal fury. The air around Sylvan Mir shimmered, and a surge of energy skittered over Drake's skin. Her breath caught in her chest as Drake tried to make sense of what she was seeing. Sylvan held Misha facedown on the bed with one hand clamped around the back of her neck. Her other hand was no longer a hand, but an elongated appendage with inch-long, razor-sharp claws. Before Drake could force her own limbs to move again, Sylvan plunged her claws into the girl's shoulder.

Misha screamed.

CHAPTER TWO

Drake shoved her way in front of the boy at the head of the stretcher. "Back up, let me get to her."

She briefly registered a look of confusion in his emerald eyes, then something like acquiescence. He made room for her, switching his grip to Misha's arms. Drake grasped Misha's shoulders to prevent the thrashing girl from throwing herself off the stretcher. Whatever Sylvan Mir was doing, Drake had to believe it was necessary. "I've got her."

"Be careful, don't let her bite you," Sylvan ordered.

The Alpha's voice was an octave lower than it had been and so rough Drake had to strain to make out the words. When she comprehended the warning, she bent down to see Misha's face. Her eyes were wide and wild, a red-gold eclipsing the brown irises. Sharp canines extended beyond her blood-flecked lower lip. Bones grated, muscles bunched and rippled beneath Drake's hands. The young girl emitted a terrified whine, bucking and writhing, the flesh on her fingertips tearing as she flailed at the table. A brackish black fluid welled from the laceration in her back, bubbling out over her smooth golden skin, an obscenity of putrefaction and decay.

"What is that?" Drake asked.

"Poison," Sylvan snarled, forcing her claws deeper into the wound.

"Is she shifting?"

"She can't—the poison is paralyzing her."

Rivulets of sweat ran down Misha's face. The flesh beneath Drake's hands was blisteringly hot.

"She's becoming hyperthermic." Drake railed inwardly at her helplessness. She didn't understand Were physiology. Pre-Exodus the Weres had hidden their biologic differences to prevent discovery, and they still safeguarded that information. Some theorized the Praetern species feared their enemies would develop bioweapons to be used for their selective termination. Right now, Drake didn't care about politics or power games. She cared about one teenaged girl who was going to die.

"What's causing it? What's the toxic agent?" Drake demanded. Misha's lips were covered with pink froth and her breathing was labored. An ominous crackling sound accompanied every breath. "Her lungs are filling up with blood. Maybe I can administer an antidote. Let me help her before she drowns."

"You *can't*." Sylvan dragged a two-inch triangular object from the depths of Misha's wound. It looked like metal of some kind.

Drake registered a babble of voices behind her in the hall, shouts and snarls morphing into an incomprehensible roar of anger and panic. The next thing she knew, she was thrown against the wall and pinned there with an arm across her throat. Acting on instinct, she shot out her fist and connected with flesh and bone. Someone cursed. The pressure on her throat lessened for an instant, and Drake wrapped both hands around a forearm that was smaller than she had anticipated but as hard as sculpted iron. She managed to suck in a breath.

"I'm a friend," she gasped, focusing on the fierce hunter green eyes that bore into hers. "A doctor."

The only response was a threatening growl from the auburn-haired female who restrained her. Drake responded with a near growl of her own. She'd tried negotiating. Now she'd fight. Even the warning flash of canines couldn't stop her. She let go of the arm across her throat, but she hadn't counted on the inhuman speed of these Weres. Before she could even begin to throw a punch, her arm was slammed against the wall and held there in a granite grip. The constriction on her throat tightened again and her vision started to dim.

"Niki!" Sylvan shouted. "Let her go!"

Instantly, Drake was freed. She fought the urge to slump down as she struggled to fill her lungs with air. Her throat was raw and her wrist throbbed, but she refused to give in to the shadows that crept over her mind. Stiffening her spine, she stared at the female who stood between her and Sylvan with an expression in her eyes like nothing Drake had ever seen before. She had no doubt this Were wanted to rip her limb from limb, and probably would have had she continued her fruitless struggle.

Drake was aware of a crowd gathering outside the cubicle, but she didn't care about anything other than Misha. To her astonishment, Sylvan reached down and lifted the unconscious teenager into her arms as if she weighed no more than a child. For the first time Drake noted the changes in Sylvan's face—an angular elongation and sharpening of the bones that seemed to be disappearing even as she watched. The Alpha's limb had reverted to a hand as well.

"She's too unstable to move," Drake warned.

Niki growled softly. Drake ignored her, her focus on Sylvan. "At least let me check her before you leave. If her temperature is still elevated, she could seize. Her lungs are already compromised."

The Were Alpha seemed not to have heard.

"Max," Sylvan said. "Take Jazz and Alex out to the Rover." She gave the boys a brief glance, her expression softening for an instant. "Go. I have Misha."

The teenagers obeyed instantly. As they trooped out behind the enormous, craggy-faced Max, Drake tried to approach Sylvan, only to find Niki firmly in her path. She hadn't even seen the Were guard move.

"Excuse me," Drake said, meeting Niki's gaze but attempting not to transmit any kind of challenge. She wasn't interested in fighting, but she intended to speak with Sylvan.

Niki's expression remained completely impassive, but her green eyes flared in warning.

"It's all right, Niki," Sylvan said with surprising gentleness.

Niki hesitated and Drake could feel her reluctance, sensed her agonized compulsion to follow two dictates. She pictured how it must have looked to Niki coming upon the mad scene in the cubicle—Misha thrashing in agony, the Were teenagers almost out of control, the enraged Were Alpha. Drake had been standing so close to Sylvan *and* with her hands on one of their young. No wonder she'd ended up against the wall. Niki had been trying to protect Sylvan, and Drake respected that.

"I'm no threat to your Alpha," Drake said, her anger dissipating. "I give you my word."

Niki's brows rose in surprise. Her harsh glare softened, but she said quietly, "If you make one wrong move, I'll rip your throat out."

"So noted."

Apparently satisfied, Niki stepped aside.

Sylvan frowned at Drake. "Are you hurt?"

"No," Drake replied.

"What you did—getting that close to Misha, to me—was very foolish." Sylvan stroked Misha's hair and the girl whimpered, burrowing her face against Sylvan's neck. "We're very protective of all our young, but especially the females. When one is threatened, we become—aggressive."

"What I did was as natural for me as what you did was for you."

Sylvan shook her head. "I don't think so."

"At least tell me what happened here," Drake insisted. She understood enough of Were culture to know they were driven more strongly than humans by physical instincts, but her instincts to care for the injured were just as strong. "I've seen something like this before."

"That would be very unlikely," Sylvan said.

"Just explain—" Drake hesitated as Sophia Revnik, the Were medic, slipped through the crowd and into the cubicle.

"Alpha," Sophia said, dipping her head briefly before glancing at Niki. Her gaze seemed to catch as it passed over Niki's face. *"Imperator."*

"Sophia," Niki said, her tone low and rough.

"I'm sorry, Alpha," Sophia said to Sylvan. "I was across town when I got the call. I came immediately. How is she?"

"Better." Sylvan cradled Misha's head against her shoulder, her blood-streaked hand on the back of Misha's neck. *This might not have been an isolated incident. I need you to check the records for other rogue attacks.*

Sophia nodded.

Drake sensed the silent communication. The Weres had never admitted to having any kind of telepathic ability, but it was clear Sylvan was addressing Sophia in some way. While she appreciated the need to prevent knowledge of Were biology from being turned into a weapon against them, she resented being excluded. Irrational, but there it was. These Weres shared something unique with Sylvan Mir, and Drake envied the intimacy.

"I want to know what kind of emergency treatment I should institute next time," Drake repeated, shrugging off the emotional reaction that made no sense to her.

"Niki, Sophia," Sylvan said, "wait outside."

Sophia immediately retreated to the hall, but Niki whipped her head around, muttering something too low for Drake to hear.

"I'm fine," Sylvan said. "Go, I'll be right there."

With one last warning snarl in Drake's direction, Niki disappeared.

Sylvan regarded Drake with a penetrating stare. "If this happens again—or anything like it, you should not interfere."

"I won't stand by and watch a patient die."

"You don't understand the repercussions. What kind of danger you'll be in."

"Then why don't you tell me."

"I don't know you, Dr. McKennan. And even if I did, I wouldn't tell you."

"Why not?"

"You're not Pack," Sylvan murmured, wondering why she was bothering to explain. Revealing their presence to the human population had been risk enough. She would not expose her Pack or any of the other Praeterns to potential genocide. She didn't even know why she lingered to talk to this human doctor. Misha, although not in immediate danger, was exhausted from her instinctive struggle to shift and expel the poison. The toxin leaching into her system had blocked her shift, and she was at risk for more serious complications. Complications Sylvan had no intention of revealing to a human. Sylvan needed to get Misha home so the Pack *medicus* could monitor her.

Drake frowned. "What happens the next time a Were comes in like this, and you're not here?"

"I will be."

"You can't be everywhere," Drake insisted, her temper rising. She did not suffer impotence well.

"I will be where I need to be." Sylvan started toward the hall, then stopped and turned back. "I apologize for any pain we may have caused you. The Pack is in your debt and you may call on us for repayment at any time."

Drake straightened. "No debt is owed, Ms. Mir. I would do the same again."

"Beware that your bravery does not lead you into harm, Doctor." Sylvan stepped into the hall where Niki and a redhead nearly too beautiful to be male fell in on either side of her.

Watching them glide down the hall, their long strides fluid and graceful, Drake noted that all three wore T-shirts, jeans, and no shoes. The big male Max, who had escorted the teenagers out, had been dressed the same way. Another secret she would not have the answer to this night. Sylvan Mir and her wolves disappeared, leaving Drake feeling oddly empty.

CHAPTER THREE

Y ou worthless mutt! Your orders are to capture females, not kill them!" Rex clubbed the young male on the side of the head, knocking him to his knees, and kicked him in the midsection. "I should gut you for letting them escape."

"Please, Rex, I'm sorry." The Were moaned and curled into a ball as the tall, muscular blond known only as Rex loomed over him. Rex was decked in leather from head to toe, and was as much feared in his human shape as wolf. He killed ruthlessly and efficiently in either form. "We didn't expect them to resist—they're only pups. But they fought, and the struggle was beginning to draw attention, so we retreated. We thought—"

"I don't pay you to think." Rex kicked the sniveling underling again. "I pay you to do as I command."

Rex paced the length of the abandoned warehouse situated on the banks of the Hudson, his anger a black miasma threatening to snap his control. Bare bulbs swung from exposed beams, and the smell of rotting fish and decaying wood assaulted his acute sense of smell. He was forced to make his headquarters in a decrepit, derelict building while Sylvan Mir's expansive compound occupied thousands of acres within the even vaster territory owned by the Timberwolf Pack. He should be the leader there, not her. Pivoting sharply, he stalked back to the pathetic, cowering runt who had let a prime female escape. He'd promised delivery and now he would have to find a plausible reason for the delay.

The male scuttled back against the wall, drawing his knees up to protect his body. Blood dribbled from the corner of his mouth. He glanced at the ragtag assortment of rogues clustered in the shadows, hoping for some support. No one came forward in his defense and his voice rose as he babbled, "We've been watching their perimeters, Rex. The pups are restless and often stray outside. We'll get another one."

"You'd better," Rex growled through gritted teeth. He kicked the huddled youth into unconsciousness, then turned on the rest of the pathetic group shuffling uneasily nearby. "What are you still doing here? Don't you have product to move out on the streets?"

"Yes, Rex," they replied in unison before fleeing.

Alone in the dank darkness, Rex raged at the injustice and bad fortune that had left him with nothing but a handful of decent soldiers and a pack of worthless rogues to carry out his orders while Sylvan Mir played at being Alpha. Her Pack was promised to him. *Promised*. Now that she had been appointed Special Councilor, the other Alphas were afraid to move against her. As if her negotiations with the humans really mattered. Weres should never negotiate with humans or any other species. Weres should take what they wanted—and he would. Starting with the Adirondack Timberwolf Pack.

CHAPTER FOUR

H ow is she?" Niki slid onto the bench next to Sylvan in the rear of the heavily reinforced Rover. They'd removed the seats and bolted benches along each sidewall to make transporting Weres in pelt form easier. Lara, the youngest of the *centuri* at just twenty-three, drove while Max rode shotgun. Andrew and the two boys sat on the floor, while Sylvan held Misha.

"She's weak, but there's no sign the toxin is spreading." Sylvan skimmed her hand over Misha's cheek. "No indication of cellular breakdown."

"You're sure it was argyria poisoning?"

"Yes." Sylvan's voice was still rough with fury. "I've got the proof in my pocket."

Niki sucked in a breath. "What is it?"

"A knife blade, coated in silver. It must have struck bone and broken off when they stabbed her. I dug it out from under her shoulder blade. Another three inches and it would have been in her heart."

And the beautiful young Were would have been dead before Sylvan could have reached her. Sylvan snarled her rage.

"You shouldn't be carrying it," Niki said, looking panicked. "Let me."

Sylvan swiveled her head and narrowed her eyes. "And risk you getting cut?"

"Alpha—" Niki's tone was agonized.

"Niki," Sylvan chided, cupping Niki's jaw in her palm. She leaned closer and kissed Niki's forehead. "Stop worrying. I'm in no danger."

"You're not impervious to the poison. Damn it, Sylvan, you're not immortal."

Sylvan grinned. "Trying to scare me?"

Niki rolled her eyes. "As if I could." Her expression suddenly grew serious. "What if Misha develops the fever?"

"She'll fight it. We'll help her." Sylvan breathed out a sigh. "She's young and strong. The anaphylaxis stopped as soon as I got the silver out. She should heal the injury rapidly as long as the dose of toxin isn't too high." She tightened her arms around the young Were who slept so innocently in her arms. "If the paralytic had spread much further, she might have been permanently damaged."

"Her shoulder." Niki shuddered. "If the muscles are destroyed, she won't be able to run."

For a wolf there was nothing worse than being chained, being unable to run, unable to hunt, unable to breathe free under the moon.

"Misha will be fine." Sylvan rubbed her cheek against the top of Misha's head, then wrapped an arm around Niki's shoulders and pulled her close. Niki laid her cheek on Sylvan's chest and threaded her arm around Sylvan's waist. The boys crowded closer, one wrapping his arm around her calf, the other laying his head on her thigh. Andrew braced his back against her other leg.

"Rest, my wolves," Sylvan murmured, tilting her head against the window and closing her eyes. "Everyone is safe."

She didn't sleep as the Rover turned off the highway onto an overgrown, unmarked trail that led deep into the forest to the Compound. Instead, she mentally replayed the scene in the ER. She dealt with humans on a daily basis and unlike many of her Pack, she didn't think that humans were weaker or less honorable than Weres just because they lived by a far more ambiguous moral code. Still, she couldn't afford to trust them—she couldn't put her Pack, or any Praetern species, at risk by confiding in a potential enemy. But she had allowed Drake McKennan to witness more of their vulnerability than any human ever had, believing instinctively that Drake would hold their secrets. This human female had slipped through her defenses, and that made her very dangerous indeed.

CHAPTER FIVE

Drake found Sophia in a small conference room tucked into an alcove in the ER. The Were medic sat alone, filling out charts. Ever since Sylvan and her Weres had left, the ER staff had been giving Sophia a wide berth, and some had been casting curious glances in Drake's direction. She'd even heard a few disgruntled comments about *those kind* going somewhere else for emergency treatment. Tonight, for some reason, the thinly veiled prejudice bothered her more than usual. She kept seeing the pain and terror in Misha's eyes.

Drake poured herself a cup of coffee and when Sophia glanced up from the charts, pointed to the pot. "Want some?"

"No thanks."

"You know, I don't think I've ever seen you drink coffee." Drake sat down across from the blonde at the small round table that bore the stains of many leaky paper cups and spilled take-out food containers. "I didn't think it was possible to be in medicine and survive without coffee."

"Most human drugs, even caffeine and alcohol, don't really have much effect on us," Sophia said softly, appearing curiously shy. "Something about our metabolism just counteracts them."

"I guess that can be good or bad, huh?"

Sophia smiled, and Drake was struck by the subtle similarity in her appearance to Sylvan and Niki. Like the other two Were females, the muscles in her bare arms below the short sleeves of her scrub shirt were subtly enhanced, the sweeping arch of her cheekbones bolder than that of most women, her eyes slightly up-tilted. And the edges of her deep blue irises flickered with gold. That was as far as the likeness went, however. Both Sylvan and Niki exuded an air of confidence that might have been construed as arrogant if it hadn't seemed to be such an innate part of their personalities. Sylvan was several octaves higher on the aggression scale than even Niki. Sophia, while outgoing and friendly, lacked that aggression—for want of a better description. One feature they all shared, however: they were each extraordinarily beautiful.

"Is your baseline temperature higher too?" Drake grimaced at the burnt aftertaste of her coffee and set the mug aside.

"Almost two full degrees. How did you know?"

"Misha's temperature was shooting through the roof. A lot more than that two-degree difference could account for."

Sophia looked away uncomfortably.

"She didn't seem to be febrile when the boys brought her in. Is it okay to call them boys?"

"Boys works fine. We also call them pups," Sophia said softly, "or young."

"Pups seems about right." Drake laughed and Sophia grinned.

"She was on the verge of Were fever, wasn't she?" Drake asked.

"I didn't examine her. I couldn't say."

Drake knew she was being evasive. "If human medics knew more about Were physiology, we could take care of these emergencies when one of your medics wasn't around."

"We're not all that different. Organs in the same place, more or less. Same skeletal structure when we're in skin form—" Sophia sighed. "Obviously there *are* differences, but they're not readily apparent."

"And you can't tell me?"

"That's for the Alpha to decide."

"Sylvan."

Sophia flushed. "The Alpha, yes."

"She knew you on sight. Are you friends?"

"With the Alpha?" Sophia stared at Drake as if she had just said something terribly amusing. "No. She's the Alpha. She knows all our names."

Drake wanted to keep Sophia talking. She wanted to know more about Sylvan Mir. She couldn't stop thinking about the way Sylvan had handled the teenagers. Her combination of discipline and tenderness had struck a chord in Drake, whose own adolescence had mostly been one of indifference bordering on neglect. The way Sylvan had attacked the poison in Misha's body, as if it were a lethal enemy to be destroyed with claws and teeth, had taken Drake's breath away. She'd been brutal, fierce, stunning in her wrath. The Were Alpha was an intriguing contradiction, and Drake was fascinated.

"I read there are hundreds in your Pack," Drake said, figuring if she referred to public knowledge Sophia would be more comfortable. "That's a lot of names."

"We are the largest Pack in North America—only the Russian White River Pack rivals ours worldwide," Sophia said proudly. "The other North American packs were hunted almost to extinction and are just now coming back."

"Hunted." A cold chill flashed along Drake's spine and she leaned closer. "By humans?"

"We have not always had to hide, but we have always been hunted." Sophia flushed again as if realizing she'd said too much. She stood up abruptly, averting her gaze. "I should get back to work."

"I'm sorry." Drake rose, recognizing Sophia's posture as similar to the way the boys had reacted to Sylvan's anger. She hadn't meant to intimidate the medic and wasn't sure how she had. "I didn't mean to make you uncomfortable. Your Alpha made an impression on me. When she was treating Misha—her power was amazing."

"You felt that?" Sounding surprised, Sophia busied herself with collecting the charts.

"Yes. How could anyone not?" Drake hurried on before Sophia disappeared. "Why do you all seem to trust her so much?"

Sophia frowned, giving Drake a cautious look. "She's the Alpha. Our leader. Without her, the Pack couldn't function. There would be power struggles, rebellion, chaos. Many of us would not survive."

"I understand the importance of her position, but the trust part?"

"She'd die for us." Sophia spoke with simple conviction and absolute certainty.

Drake tried to comprehend the kind of strength and personal sacrifice required of one individual to safeguard an entire community, and couldn't. If she hadn't seen Sylvan with her wolves, she wouldn't have believed it possible. But she *had* seen her, and her blood still raced from the excitement of their encounter.

❖

Sylvan paced the small room in the infirmary where she'd brought Misha directly upon arrival at the Compound, three hundred square miles of fortified mountain ranges deep in the heart of Pack land. Her mother had built the protectorate almost a century ago when she had consolidated the many small, scattered enclaves of wolf Weres in the Adirondack Mountains of New York and the Green Mountains of Vermont into one cohesive Pack.

The nerve center of the Compound consisted of an enormous hard-packed earth courtyard ringed by a dozen log buildings, all enclosed within a twelve-foot-high fence. The main building was a massive three-story timber and stone lodge with Sylvan's headquarters on the second floor. The barracks, a long two-story building, housed the young males and females who were in military training, two to a room. A breezeway connected the barracks to the mess hall. Tall antennae and rooftop satellite dishes for long-range surveillance marked the communications center. In the center of the Compound, protected by an internal perimeter guarded twenty-four hours a day by some of Sylvan's finest fighters, was a heavily fortified single-story building with two wings housing the infirmary and the nursery. Underground tunnels connected all the structures and led to escape exits in the surrounding forest. Sylvan's private den was five miles farther into the forest, a simple three-room single-story log cabin whose location was known only to her personal guards.

"Any change?" Sylvan halted abruptly, fists on hips, and confronted Elena, the Pack *medicus*. The sight of Misha helpless and hurt was making Sylvan's wolf rip at her insides in a mad fury to protect her own. Sylvan wanted to lash out, wanted to loose her claws and shred whoever had dared harm one of hers. She shuddered and silver pelt glinted beneath her skin, her wolf breaking free. Ignoring the pain, she held her back. "Elena?"

"She's not going to wake up for a few more hours at least." The petite brunette, perched on a stool next to the bed where Misha lay beneath a colorful knit afghan, cast Sylvan an appraising glance. Her lips thinned in concern. "You look on the verge of frenzy. Why don't you take care of it?"

Sylvan narrowed her eyes, emitting a barely audible rumble.

Elena raised one dark brow in Sylvan's direction. "Don't growl at me, either. I whelped you, and I remember when you were just a mewling scrawny pup."

"Is there any sign of the fever?" Sylvan chose to ignore Elena, knowing she wouldn't win an argument with her. Their chief medic was barely two decades older than Sylvan, and in the centuries-long lifespan of a Were, that was negligible. Their relationship was as close to that of siblings as Sylvan could have with anyone in the Pack. Elena would never undermine that closeness by challenging her in front of others, but she didn't shy away from nagging Sylvan in private.

"No sign of fever yet. In another few hours I can say for certain that she's safe." Elena traced her fingers tenderly along Misha's pale cheek. She shook her head, her dark eyes filling with sorrow. "Who would do this to a child?"

"Jazz said they smelled like wolf Weres, but not Pack. Rogues."

"But why would they poison her? It makes no sense."

"I'm not sure they meant to kill her." Sylvan regarded the broken knife tip she had dug out of Misha's body. Elena had placed it in a safe, sealed container to be delivered to their technicians at Mir Industries— their medical and pharmaceutical research facility—in the morning. While they needed a complete analysis of the chemical nature of the poison impregnated into the knife blade, she didn't need a scientist to tell her it was silver-based. Only another Were would know that silver was lethal, even in very small doses. "Jazz said the rogues tried to separate Misha from the boys, and when all three of our adolescents fought back, the rogues panicked. Misha was accidentally stabbed in the chaos."

"They intentionally targeted Misha," Elena echoed bleakly, keeping her hand protectively on Misha's shoulder. "Misha would make three, Sylvan. Three dominant females. It can't be a coincidence."

"No," Sylvan said darkly, her canines lengthening as her wolf howled in rage. "Someone is abducting our females."

Two young Were females had disappeared in the last half year— the first had been believed killed in a landslide while hiking alone, but her body had never been recovered. The second had disappeared from a local campus after leaving a note in her dorm room saying she and a male from another Pack were eloping. The girl's parents swore she would never have kept a serious romantic relationship from them, especially not one with a non-Pack male. Sylvan had ordered an investigation, but her *sentries* had found nothing. Although young wolves, males and females, frequently roamed before mating and settling down, Pack and family ties were central to every Were's life. Runaways were almost unheard of. These females did not disappear willingly.

"Why? What kind of wolf would do such a thing?" Elena's voice shook with outrage. "You've let it be known that any rogue is welcome to join us if they swear allegiance to the Pack. They don't have to live like feral *cats*."

"I don't know," Sylvan said grimly. "But I'll find out."

Sylvan knelt on the flagstone floor by Misha's bed and rested her forehead against Misha's. Closing her eyes, she murmured, "Sleep, little one. Sleep and heal. All is well."

Misha whined contentedly in her sleep and nuzzled Sylvan's cheek. Sylvan rose and, feeling Elena's worried gaze on her face, stroked Elena's ebony hair. "Don't worry for me."

"If I don't, who else will you allow?" Elena caught Sylvan's hand and entwined their fingers. "You should at least take a lover."

"Elena, don't push me," Sylvan warned, her tone turning Alpha.

"I'm the Pack *medicus*. It's my responsibility to attend to your well-being," Elena insisted.

"My *well-being* is fine."

"Your wolf runs close to the skin. She needs calming. So do you." Elena gave Sylvan's fingers a squeeze. "Rena would tangle willingly. So would Anya or Lara."

"Lara is one of my *centuri*," Sylvan protested. Her guards swore a blood oath to her, and she to them, a bond as unbreakable as a mating bond. For her to take one of them as her lover would disrupt the unity of their cadre. Any hesitation, any uncertainty in rank or order, would leave them all vulnerable in a fight. Sylvan's voice dropped dangerously low. "You would have me risk their lives for empty pleasure?"

"Pleasure is never empty when there is caring, and they love you. We all love you."

"I know," Sylvan whispered, skimming her lips over Elena's knuckles.

"Your father was *centuri* to your mother," Elena pointed out. "That did not stop her, why should it stop you?"

"We will not speak of them," Sylvan said, and this time it was a command. "My *centuri* are not my bed partners."

"As you wish, Alpha," Elena said, "but Rena is not even a soldier. She has the look of a *mater* through and through. She would set your bed afire and give you strong, sturdy pups."

"Ever since you and Roger mated, you've become an incorrigible matchmaker," Sylvan teased, hoping to deflect Elena from a topic she had been trying to ignore. She hadn't tangled with anyone for weeks, and for a Were, more than a few days was a very long time. Physical contact—touch, sexual release—was essential to Were physical and emotional well-being, and the more dominant the Were, the greater the need. Without a physical outlet for their intrinsically high levels of endorphins and adrenergic hormones, especially if augmented by stress, the delicate balance between beast and reason broke down. Unrelenting sex frenzy could push Weres to become feral, and going feral was a death sentence.

As a natural counterbalance, all Weres were highly sexual, and since there were no social sanctions against casual sexual encounters, unmated Weres often had multiple partners of both sexes simultaneously. Abstinence for an Alpha was unheard of. Their innate super-aggression heightened their sex drive, and without frequent venting, their untamable wolves pressed for dominance. Sylvan's wolf had been riding her hard the last few weeks, enraged by the escalating dangers threatening the Pack, demanding the freedom to hunt and destroy their enemies. Sylvan knew she was walking a dangerous path. She needed all her control at the best of times to keep her wolf in check. Negotiating with the human politicians, containing the constant infighting among the Praetern alliance members, and providing stability for her Pack strained her reserves to the breaking point. She was agitated, sleepless, hypersexual. But every time she thought she had to take a female for a night or surrender to wolf madness, she resisted, knowing she would remain unsatisfied. Her body craved sex, her wolf craved a fight, but her heart, despite all of her attempts to deny it, craved a connection. So she denied herself the sex, denied her wolf the release, and refused to acknowledge what she really wanted.

"Rena wants a mate," Sylvan grunted.

"And you need to release before you find yourself in full frenzy."

Elena pointed a finger, stopping Sylvan's protest. "Even I can feel your call, and I have a mate who satisfies me quite nicely. If my urges are triggered this much, before long, you'll throw the females into heat—"

"I won't let that happen." An entire Pack of females in heat would drive the dominant males and females crazy. They'd have chaos as the dominants fought for bedding rights. If Sylvan couldn't dampen her pheromones enough to prevent the females from cycling to her, she'd need to have sex just to settle the Pack. "I've got it under control."

"For now," Elena sighed. "Stubborn wolf."

"I must go." Sylvan kissed Elena on the mouth, a brief brush of lips. "I need to double the border guards on the Compound, and we have unmated females in the community who need to be warned and protected. Call me if there's any change with Misha."

"Promise me you'll sleep at least."

"I'll sleep," Sylvan said as she closed the door to the sickroom behind her. She would sleep when her enemies were dead and her Pack was safe.

She loped through the empty halls of the Compound and out through the massive double wooden doors onto the deck that wrapped around three sides of the building. The moon was well past its zenith now, and storm clouds slashed across her face. Sylvan breathed deeply, sniffing rain in the air and the scent of deer moving through the trees. She sent a silent message to Callan, the captain of her *sentries*.

Reinforce our outer borders. Double the guards on the inner perimeter. Give no one safe passage on Pack land.

She pulled off her T-shirt, unzipped her jeans and pushed them off, and left the clothes in a pile at the top of the wide stone stairs. Running naked toward the trees, she shifted in motion, gliding into the forest as invisibly as a wraith. She lifted her face to the moon and howled, the pull in her loins and the longing in her heart for a mate to run with her under the night sky so strong she ached. Scenting another wolf following her, she circled back on her own trail and crouched in the underbrush, waiting until the sleek red-gray wolf drew near. Then, as silent as a ghost, she exploded from her hiding place and caught the wolf's neck in her jaws, dragging her down. The she-wolf snapped at her, closing her powerful jaws millimeters from Sylvan's foreleg. Sylvan growled and shook her powerful shoulders, forcing the gray onto her back. She pressed down, belly to belly, then let her go. The gray jumped up, snarled, and they circled one another, lunging and snapping, rolling and thrashing. Eventually when the gray began to slow the slightest bit, Sylvan caught the other wolf's muzzle in her jaws. The wolf went limp, allowing Sylvan to mount her. Sylvan clasped the wolf between her legs and growled. When the wolf whined and licked her face, Sylvan released her and settled on the ground. Panting, the gray wolf inched closer until their shoulders touched. She rested her head on her paws and gazed at Sylvan.

Elena sent you, didn't she?

Niki rubbed her nose under Sylvan's jaw.

Did she tell you I needed a tussle?

Niki flashed a wolfie grin.

Sylvan sighed. *Come, hunt with me. If you can keep up.*

Surrendering to her wolf, Sylvan jumped up and tore off into the woods, Niki hard at her shoulder. Sylvan loved Niki, loved running with Niki at her side, but still her heart ached.

CHAPTER SIX

"Mmm," Anya murmured, arching her back and rolling her hips as her orgasm ebbed, "I do love it when you run with the Alpha."

"Why is that?" Niki nuzzled the small redhead's neck, licking the spot she'd bitten earlier just as she was about to explode all over Anya's gorgeous ass. Anya turned her head and nipped at Niki's jaw.

"You're always wild for a long, hard tangle after."

Anya was right. Running with Sylvan, awash in the Alpha's power, always left Niki excruciatingly aroused and ready to tangle with the first willing female she found. Tonight, the burning in her loins was greater than she could ever remember, the fire so hot she hurt. The sex glands buried on either side of her clitoral shaft swelled and pulsed, reminding her she wasn't done yet. She caressed the svelte muscles in Anya's back and when Anya raised her ass in invitation, Niki straddled her and fit her stiffening clitoris into the tight cleft between Anya's buttocks. She groaned when Anya squeezed down on her. The clitoral core went rigid and she wanted to come.

"Be careful how you tease," Niki gasped, her canines lengthening as Anya's motions stripped her control. Like most dominants, she could extrude her canines and claws at will, but they would emerge involuntarily when she was enraged or sex frenzied.

"Tonight you're even hungrier than usual." Anya tightened and released her powerful muscles, milking Niki's clitoris and making her growl. "You're still ready and you've already come three times."

"Four, but who's counting." Niki bit Anya's earlobe and dragged her clitoris free before the frenzy claimed her. She'd already been selfish enough. She was dominant to everyone in the Pack except Sylvan, and Anya would have been more than willing to couple with her at any time. But that wasn't the reason Niki had come to her tonight. Anya did not think of her as a potential mate, so she could tangle with her without any guilt later. She'd shown up naked at Anya's door, waking her from a sound sleep, panting and dripping with sex sweat. The dominance scent she'd exuded would have instantly readied any unmated Were in her vicinity.

I need you now, she'd snarled.

Anya hadn't said a word, only dropped to her knees and sucked her to release within seconds. She'd come a second time straddling Anya's thigh while she fucked her on the floor. Anya had screamed through her orgasm, clawing at Niki's shoulders and back. When Niki had finally been able to focus through the frenzy, she'd carried Anya to the bed and taken her a third time from behind, thrusting hard inside while she stimulated Anya's clitoris with her other hand. Her primal need for dominance had been so great, she'd refused to release Anya's clitoris after Anya came, forcing release after release from the keening female. Now that she had regained a little control, she scented that Anya was still ready and Niki wanted to satisfy her. Anya's appetite for sex was always strong, but tonight she seemed particularly needy. Niki stroked the inside of Anya's thigh and cupped her high between her legs. She was hot and wet.

"I'm not the only one who's still ready," Niki whispered, caressing the underside of Anya's firm clitoris where her sex glands rested. "You're burning."

"The craving's been riding me so hard for two days." Anya whimpered and pumped herself against Niki's hand. "Even when I release it doesn't quiet." She reached back blindly and dug her nails into Niki's forearm. "Oh God, please just fuck me. Make me come. I need it so much. I hurt."

Niki registered a warning somewhere in her clouded brain, but the frenzy hit too fast for her to pay attention. She rocketed to her knees and pushed deep between Anya's legs. Slick blazing muscles gripped her fingers. She found the thickened internal ridge that connected directly to Anya's clitoris and massaged it with each stroke. The deep-seated sex glands were hard as stones. Anya panted and moaned, clawing at the mattress as she struggled to crest.

"Harder, oh God, I am so close and I can't…"

"Massage your clit," Niki growled. Anya's hand flew between her legs. Niki fondled Anya's breasts. "That's right. That's good. Keep doing that." Sweat matted Niki's hair and her stomach muscles spasmed. Her glands were about to burst. She spread her legs and crushed her clitoris against Anya's tight ass. Groaning, she pounded them both to the edge. Her sex glands throbbed viciously. They'd empty soon.

"It's coming," Niki gasped. "It's coming."

Anya drove herself up and down on Niki's hand and frantically manipulated her clitoris. "Help me. Help me. *Make me come.*"

Niki wrapped her arm around Anya, jerked her up against her chest, and sank her teeth into Anya's shoulder. The dominant bite flooded Anya with pheromones and spiked her release. Niki spent when Anya cried out, pleasure pain ripping her apart.

Long moments later, they collapsed. Niki shuddered as she lay protectively over Anya's back. Anya made contented sounds when Niki stroked her arms and turned her face for Niki's kisses.

"All right now?" Niki nibbled gently on Anya's swollen lower lip, then licked the spot.

"Mmm." Obviously struggling to stay awake, Anya flicked her tongue over Niki's neck. "You need more?"

Niki chuckled. "If I do, I'll be back."

"Good." Anya's lids fluttered closed.

Moving carefully, Niki eased from the bed and let herself out. Dawn was not far off. The summer heat had given way during the night to mountain coolness, and the chill felt good on her heated skin. Her craving had been eased, but want still rippled under her skin. Fortunately, she was close to her own quarters. She needed a cold shower and a few hours' sleep. But first, she needed to check on the Alpha. Sylvan had remained at the Compound instead of returning to her own den after their run, and Max and Lara were standing guard.

She retrieved her clothes, along with her phone clipped to the waistband of her cargo pants, from the bench where she'd left them earlier and hastily dressed. If Sylvan had needed her, she would have reached her mind-to-mind. And if the Alpha had been in danger, she would have sensed that no matter where she was. The only thing that could have pulled her from her sex frenzy would have been Sylvan's call.

The Compound was waking, and Niki nodded to *sentries* heading to their stations, adolescents making their noisy way to the mess hall, and a number of mated pairs emerging naked from the forest after an early morning run. Niki acknowledged the mates in passing but was careful not to let her gaze linger. Skin was as natural a covering to the Weres as their pelts, and nudity was ignored other than for the appreciative glance of one healthy animal to another—providing the Were being "appreciated" was unmated. Mated pairs were sexually exclusive, aggressively territorial, and violently possessive. Even a nondominant Were would attack a dominant if he or she felt the mate bond was threatened. And a dominant Were in mating frenzy could not be contained short of death—logic and reason giving way to the far more powerful and primitive instinct to preserve the mate bond.

Niki vaulted up the steps to the main lodge and crossed the broad porch. The entrance opened into a grand hall, with the library and Pack archives on one side and the gathering room with a huge stone fireplace, sofas, and chairs on the other. Sylvan could often be found there when she wasn't in her office on the second floor. Lara stood guard at the top of the sweeping, central wooden staircase. Max was just outside the closed, carved double doors of Sylvan's office. When Niki reached the second-floor balcony that circled the grand hall below, she motioned for them to follow down the hall and away from Sylvan's door.

"Has she slept?" Niki asked.

"No," Max grumbled. His eyes narrowed and his nostrils flared as he surveyed Niki. "Looks like you didn't either."

"Jealous?" Niki grinned, knowing both Max and Lara could scent her pheromones and traces of Anya's. Because she and Anya weren't mate bonded, she didn't carry the unique third scent—the chemical fusion of two Weres' hormonal signatures that branded them as a pair for life.

"Damn right," Max snarled. Lara grimaced in agreement.

Niki looked them both over, picking up on something other than the usual sexual rivalry that was natural among unmated dominants. She remembered how she'd felt after the run with Sylvan, a craving so intense she'd been nearly mindless. Max and Lara would have borne the full force of Sylvan's pheromones while they guarded her, since there were no other Weres around to help absorb it. Lara's whiskey brown eyes were wolf-flecked and her skin was sex-sheened. Max had an admirable bulge in his jeans.

"I'll get Andrew over here," Niki said. "We'll stand guard. You two go find someone to tangle with."

"I'm fine," Lara snapped, clearly insulted that Niki was relieving her from her post.

"So am I." Max's canines lengthened.

Niki growled, pushing into their space, making them both back up. They were compatriots, but there could be only one leader where Sylvan's safety was concerned, and she was Sylvan's second. "I need your heads clear or you won't be fit to guard the Alpha. Now *go* before I make you go."

Silence fell while Niki stared them down.

"You're right." Max shrugged and grinned, his grin the only concession to Niki's supremacy. "The craving is riding me harder than usual."

Lara shivered. "I thought it was just me. I'm so hungry Max is starting to look good."

Max laughed. They were close friends but both too dominant to tangle. He tried to put her in a headlock. Lara blocked his arm and punched him in the stomach. Max laughed again and the tension broke.

Niki's warning bells were ringing even louder. Anya had said the same thing. *The craving's been riding me so hard for two days.* She threw her arms around their shoulders. Max brushed his cheek over hers. Lara leaned her head on Niki's chest. "Take a few hours to settle your wolves. Sylvan isn't going anywhere today. I'll call you if I need you."

Max and Lara reluctantly left and Niki called Andrew to stand guard. Then she knocked on Sylvan's door.

"Alpha?"

"Come."

Sylvan's office was lined with bookshelves on one side, another stone fireplace taking up the entire opposite wall, and a bay of floor-to-ceiling windows behind her desk on the far side of the room. The roughhewn plank floors were covered with thick earth-toned rugs, and a pair of forest green leather chairs sat in front of her dark cherrywood desk.

Sylvan leaned back in a heavy wood and leather desk chair, a laptop computer in front of her. She'd donned a plain white cotton shirt and rolled the sleeves up, but hadn't bothered to button it. The sweeping muscles of her chest and soft inner curves of her breasts glowed with a fine pheromone mist in the dim lamplight. Her eyes were more wolf-gold than blue. A rush of sex and power hit Niki so hard her sex contracted painfully. Sylvan's tussle with her earlier, the run, the hunt, might have been enough to blunt Sylvan's needs, but she was Alpha, and required more than just that vigorous physical release to vent the hormones cascading through her. No wonder Max and Lara had been suffering. Niki had been well satisfied with Anya, but Sylvan's call had her in desperate need of more. She couldn't believe the Alpha wasn't close to feral with frenzy.

"How's Misha?" Niki asked, her throat dry and raspy.

"She's not awake yet," Sylvan grated.

"Fever?"

"Not the last time I checked."

"That's good." Niki considered diplomacy and then decided that was last thing Sylvan needed from her. "You either need to stay in your den or take someone to bed."

Sylvan stood abruptly. The top button of her low-cut jeans was open, the etched muscles in her stomach tense and tight. A line of silver glinted in the cleft between her rigid abdominals. "I don't remember asking your counsel, *Imperator.*"

Niki's pulse spiked at the edge in her Alpha's voice, but she stood her ground. "You're broadcasting to everyone in scent distance. The guards can't concentrate. I'm concerned for your safety." At Sylvan's furious expression, Niki spread her arms. "I just walked in the room and the only thing I can think about is finding a female."

"Assign mated guards, then."

"None of the *centuri* are mated, you know that, Alpha." Niki sucked in a breath, forcing down the craving beginning to blur the edges of her reason. "Even you won't be able to function efficiently much longer without release. If you don't want any of the Pack, I will—"

"*No.*" Sylvan cleared the desk in one fluid leap, barely restraining her urge to take Niki to the floor as she landed inches from her. After her run with Niki, she'd headed directly to her office because it was the closest place to sequester herself. Her helplessness over Misha had left her with an uncontrollable need to dominate, an instinctive need to reestablish her claim as protector and assert her leadership over the Pack. She craved a female under her, submitting to her will. Her system was primed, broadcasting her dominance, and any unmated Were who crossed her path would attempt to submit to her. She wasn't certain she could resist, and she did not want to tangle out of frustration and anger. She was the Alpha. She had to have enough control to lead the Pack no matter how great the pressure, how unrelenting the stress. She owed it to them. "You play a dangerous game, Niki."

"You call, Alpha." Niki pressed her open mouth to Sylvan's neck and licked her, tasting the primal forest thick with sweet pine and dark passions. She quivered, her instinct to submit warring with her natural dominance. Her sex pulsed with readiness, and she moaned, rubbing against Sylvan's bare torso. She pressed her palm to Sylva's abdomen, claws extruded. "I answer. I am not playing."

Sylvan closed her eyes, shivering with the heat of Niki's mouth gliding over her throat. Niki's claws pricked her skin and her nipples tightened. Her sex flooded, her clitoris swelled, and in another second, she would take Niki. They would both regret it, not because what they might do would be unnatural, but because it would destroy *their* natural order. She skimmed both hands over Niki's shoulders and down her arms, then gently pushed Niki away. "Leave me. Now. Go."

Niki's hunter green eyes were glazed, her skin flushed and sex-shimmering. "I willingly submit. Please."

"No, you don't," Sylvan snarled. *"Leave me."*

Sylvan reached around Niki, yanked open the heavy doors, and shoved her out into the hall. After slamming and locking the door, she leapt to the lead-paned windows behind her desk, flung them open, and threw herself through. Her wolf landed soundlessly and in an instant had left the Compound, and temptation, behind.

❖

"Dr. McKennan?" The ER charge nurse knocked softly on Drake's call room door. "Are you awake?"

"Yes," Drake replied gruffly. They'd cleared the board of patients shortly after four a.m. and she'd retreated to her on-call room. She didn't expect to sleep, but she needed the solitude to sort through her riotous feelings. She couldn't get the episode with Sylvan Mir out of her mind. Whenever she recalled the ferocious way Sylvan had attacked Misha's wound, as if she could defeat the injury through sheer force of will, Drake shuddered with excitement. She understood the physiology of an adrenaline high—she'd experienced it frequently after an intense life-and-death struggle. And those few moments in that cubicle surrounded by the unbridled aggression of the Weres, particularly the Were Alpha, had been some of the most exhilarating moments of her life. What she couldn't so easily explain was how sexually aroused the episode had left her.

Hours later, the image of Sylvan's eyes glowing wolf-gold and the gleam of lethal canines against her sensuous lips made Drake's clit quicken. Lying alone in the dark, she couldn't deny her arousal and she couldn't pretend ignorance of the source. Sylvan Mir fascinated her—beautiful, powerful, viciously aggressive, exquisitely tender. Drake shifted restlessly, so agitated even her skin was hypersensitive.

"Drake?" the nurse asked again.

Drake bolted upright. God, she needed to get control of herself. "Yes. I'm sorry. I'm coming." Running her hands quickly through her hair and checking to be sure that her scrub shirt was tucked into her jeans, she pulled open the door. "Problem?"

Pam Liu glanced worriedly down the hall. "A Detective Gates is asking for you. I told her you weren't available, but she insisted on speaking to you now. Said it couldn't wait until end of shift. I'm sorry."

"That's all right," Drake said. "Where is she? I'll talk to her."

"I put her in the private waiting room."

"Okay. If you need me, come and get me." Drake stopped in the small kitchen to pour herself a cup of coffee, then walked to the far end of the L-shaped ER to the family consultation room. It was nothing more than an exam room that had been converted, by adding a round table and a few chairs, into a place where staff could speak with families of seriously ill patients. The walls were still institutional gray, the floors a nondescript patterned tile, the lights inset square fluorescents. Harsh, bare, and barren. Definitely not a warm and cheery place. The woman waiting for her looked right at home. Her face—though flawlessly featured with delicately arched black brows over midnight eyes, narrow nose, and elegantly refined bones—appeared as cold and emotionless as a magnificently carved marble statue.

"Drake McKennan," Drake said, extending her hand. "I'm one of the ER attendings."

"Detective Jody Gates," the woman said, rising to return the handshake. She was dressed in tight, tailored black pants that shimmered with some kind of metallic thread woven into the fabric, a body-hugging dark silk shirt, and black leather blazer. A round gold shield glinted at her narrow waist. Her fingers were long, strong, and cool.

"Coffee?" Drake lifted an eyebrow toward the cup she held in her hand. "I have to say, it's pretty bad."

"No, thank you."

Drake pulled out a straight-backed plain wooden chair and sat down across from the detective. She spoke to hundreds of people every week and considered herself very good at reading nonverbal cues. She couldn't get a thing from this woman who sat absolutely still, appraising *her*. She might have been looking at a painting. She sipped her coffee and waited.

"I'm investigating a report of a stabbing in Washington Park around ten p.m. last evening," the detective finally said. "I understand you treated a girl for a stab wound about that time."

"Your information isn't quite correct, Detective," Drake replied, thinking furiously. She hadn't filled out any paperwork because she hadn't actually treated Misha. She wasn't certain why the police were involved, but instinctively, she wanted to protect not only Misha, but Sylvan Mir. The reaction didn't make any sense, but she trusted her gut feelings. "I did not treat anyone with a stab wound earlier. What's this all about?"

The detective leaned forward, resting her arms on the table and folding her hands. Her voice was perfectly modulated, calm, and seemingly unperturbed. "What's your relationship with Sylvan Mir?"

"I'm sorry. If I had a relationship with Ms. Mir, I don't think it would be anyone's business. But I'm afraid I don't know her."

"You're not acquainted?"

"Not personally, no."

Detective Gates pushed a folded newspaper that had been lying next to her right arm across the table. With one efficient flip of her finger, she opened it to the front page. "This says otherwise."

The photo above the fold on the front page of the *Albany Star*, the local version of the *National Enquirer*, showed Misha lying on a stretcher in the examining room with Drake holding her down. In profile, Sylvan Mir, with canines gleaming, snarled in rage at Drake. The headline in 50-point block letters read: WERE COUNCILOR LOSES COOL—ANIMAL REGULATION, NOT RIGHTS?

"Jesus," Drake muttered.

"Would you like to amend your story?" the detective asked in her preternaturally calm voice.

Preternaturally calm. Classically beautiful. Emotionally enigmatic. Cool. *Literally.*

Drake took her time studying the detective, who stared back at her with a faint smile, her eyes fathomless obsidian pools. Finally, Drake said, "Gates. You hear that name in the news a lot these days. I don't suppose by any wild chance you're related to…"

"Councilor Zachary Gates is my father," Jody said.

Zachary Gates was the U.S. Special Councilor on Vampire Affairs. Sylvan Mir's counterpart in the Praetern Coalition.

"Does that make you a friend or foe?" Drake asked, nodding to the newspaper.

"That makes me a detective. Did the girl have Were fever?"

Drake glanced at her watch. 5:50. The sun was up. She didn't know this detective and had no reason to trust her, but she couldn't control her automatic surge of concern. "Shouldn't you…uh…be somewhere safer?"

Detective Gates smiled, a full smile that turned her from simply beautiful into breathtakingly spectacular. "I'm not dead, Dr. McKennan. Exposure to direct sunlight gives me a headache and occasionally makes me nauseous. But it doesn't kill me within a matter of minutes. It won't—not until I animate."

"So you're—forgive me if I use the wrong term—a living Vampire?"

"We prefer the term pre-animate, but basically, yes." Jody tapped the newspaper. "The adolescent in the photograph. She's a Were, correct?"

"Yes," Drake said. "Look, I really didn't treat her. I don't know what's wrong with her."

"Have you seen any other adolescents with Were fever within the last few months?"

"No. You should know as well as I they rarely seek emergency care."

"These wouldn't be Weres," Jody said, with the first sign of emotion flashing in her eyes. "These would be humans."

CHAPTER SEVEN

"What do you mean, humans?" Drake asked. The chill coming off the detective sitting across from her made the hairs on the backs of her arms stand up. If she hadn't seen the fire flickering in the Vampire's eyes a moment before, she would have thought her totally without emotion. The truth was completely the opposite—Drake finally understood what was meant by *cold fury*. She also appreciated for the first time that she was in a closed room with a predator. One just as deadly as a Were and not likely to give any warning before she struck. Drake kept her gaze steady on the detective's, ready to move if she had to.

"I don't bite," Jody said softly. "Unless invited."

Drake made an effort to relax her shoulders. It wasn't easy. Some primitive focus deep in her brain was flooding her with enough flight hormones to make her entire body quiver. "I'm sorry."

"You don't need to be. You are surprisingly sensitive for a human, but I still should have better control."

"Any better control and I really would think you were dead."

Jody's expression went completely blank, and then she laughed. The transformation was as breathtaking as the sunrise. Drake felt herself smiling, warming inside, as if she'd received an unexpected gift. She wanted to make her smile again, and dimly recognized that she didn't usually react this way, no matter how beautiful the woman. Predators often lulled their prey before striking—could Vampires do the same?

"Tell me about the girl," Jody said.

Drake shook her head, as much to clear it as to signal she wasn't going to answer without more information. "You first. Why would a human have Were fever?"

"You should ask your Were medic that. Sophia, isn't it?"

"Yes." Drake wasn't going to volunteer anything. While the detective was admittedly charming when she let down her formidable guard, Drake didn't know what she was after. Gates was subtly interrogating her, that much was clear, but Drake didn't think she was the target of the detective's suspicions. She couldn't help feeling that the Were Alpha was somehow the one Gates was after, and her immediate response was to shield her. She wasn't reacting at all like herself, which was all the more reason to be careful of what she said.

Jody Gates reached inside her leather blazer and came out with a plain white card embossed with her name and telephone number, which she placed squarely in front of Drake. "Call me if you see or hear of an adolescent female, Were or human, with Were fever."

"What about patient confidentiality?"

"It's a communicable disease," Jody replied. "You have an obligation to report it."

"I've never seen any official communiqué from the International Institute of Health or the Center for Communicable Diseases classifying it as such." Drake desperately wanted to know what she might be facing with this disease, because the ER was a battlefield, the front line where every minute could make the difference between life and death. She wouldn't be forced to stand helplessly on the sidelines while patients died because she didn't know how to treat them. This detective obviously knew something, and Drake didn't intend to be played. "Without that, my hands are tied."

"You'll have to trust me when I tell you that you'll be saving more than just the life of a single patient if you call me with anything you learn."

"Why should I trust you?"

"Because I have everything to lose. I and every other member of the Praetern races."

Drake immediately thought of Sylvan and her apprehension escalated. How big was this problem? "What are you saying?"

"Can you conceive of what it means for an entire species to suddenly be vulnerable, overnight"—Jody said with quiet lethality— "to mass genocide?"

Even as recently as the day before, Drake would have answered yes. Intellectually, she understood that the Praetern races had taken a big chance when they'd emerged from the shadows, risking that the humans who vastly outnumbered them would accept them despite their differences. Even though she'd seen the subtle prejudice directed at Sophia, she hadn't truly appreciated the extent of human distrust until she'd tried to aid Misha and Sylvan. Then *she* had been the target of suspicious looks and quiet disdain. The Weres *were* different— admittedly frightening—and yet so powerfully compelling. What kind of pressure must Sylvan feel to protect her Pack? Drake had given even less thought to the plight of the other Praeterns, all of whom seemed on the surface so much more like humans than the Weres, with their animal shapes and predatory natures. And no one really knew what to think about the Vampires. If they were dead, what claim did they have to any rights at all?

"No, I *can't* know what it means for any of you," Drake replied. "And it's precisely because I can't that I don't want to inadvertently endanger anyone."

"It's too late for that, Dr. McKennan. We're all in danger now." Jody Gates stood and pointed to the card. "If humans come to realize that Were fever is not only untreatable and lethal, but also that *they* are at risk, there will be open hunting on Weres."

"I'm curious," Drake said, pocketing the detective's card. "Why come to me? Why trust me with this?"

"Because I saw your picture in the newspaper." Jody's mouth flickered with a half-mocking smile. "And you had your bare hands on that young female's shoulders, inches away from her face. If she was infected and had bitten you, you might be dead by now. Her Alpha might easily have killed you on the spot just for touching her. But you tried to help her anyhow."

She shrugged, a gesture so eloquent Drake felt an involuntary twinge of arousal. This Vampire was the most effortlessly seductive woman she'd ever seen. Something in her response must have registered with Jody, because for the briefest instant, her eyes flamed crimson. Drake felt a tug in her belly.

"I'm a medic. I was doing my job," Drake said, steadfastly ignoring the heat kindling in the pit of her stomach.

"Then I have to believe you'll keep doing it. I didn't agree with my father when he supported the Exodus. I think he has placed our people in unconscionable danger by exposing us. But I didn't get a vote, and now it's done." Jody stopped with her hand on the door, her eyes flaring as she fixed on Drake. "It doesn't matter which species is the first target of a purge, the other Praetern races will fall. First the Weres—then the Vampires. Then the witches and the sorcerers and the farsighted and the telepaths. Which are you, Doctor—friend or foe?" Her voice dropped, grew smoky and smooth. "I'd like it to be friend."

Drake became breathless, trapped in a vortex of incredible power that caressed the very center of her being. The detective's gaze probed her mind and laid claim to her body. Heat flooded her senses and she ached for those long cool fingers on her flesh. Hungered for a touch, eager to be devoured. She saw Jody's parted lips flush crimson, the tip of her moist tongue just visible between blinding white incisors. Drake longed for that mouth on her. Every instinct pulled her forward, urged her to sink into the abyss of immeasurable pleasure. Struggling not to go to her, Drake gripped the table and her hand brushed the newspaper to the edge. Out of the corner of her eye, she saw Sylvan Mir's face in the photograph—fierce, predatory, proud. She shuddered, clinging to that image as she fought the Vampire's compulsion.

"Stop it," Drake whispered.

Almost instantly the agonizingly erotic grip on her senses released, and Drake sagged as if loosed from a powerful undertow. To Drake's surprise, Jody was breathing as hard as she was. Jody grimaced as if the loss of their connection pained her, and her incisors flashed faintly. Drake still felt like prey, but not in the usual sense. The Weres might be natural predators, but the Vampires were sexual ones. She'd just been hunted, and had barely escaped.

"It's never wise to lie to the police," Jody murmured. "Whatever Sylvan Mir is to you, it's much more than an acquaintance." She opened the door. "I'll be waiting for your call."

❖

Sylvan followed the river south, slipping through the underbrush along its banks like a sliver of moonlight flickering among the shadows. Her *centuri* would follow her trail, but they would be long minutes behind her. Her powerful muscles bunched as her legs swept over the ground in huge bounding strides. She tasted the morning on her tongue, felt the wind ruffle through her pelt. Rabbit and deer scattered at her approach, but she was not hunting. She was running. Running to burn the heat from her blood and the frenzy from her loins. Running until the exhaustion dampened desire and clarity eclipsed instinct. She ran, even though she knew her quest was fruitless. She was Alpha, and as long as she breathed she would have one purpose—to lead and protect her Pack. Nothing short of death—not injury or fatigue or the clarion call of reason—would override that most primitive drive. But she ran nevertheless.

She reached Washington Park at sunrise and made her way silently past the early morning joggers and dog walkers, warning off the canines with a subvocal growl that only they could hear. When she reached the deserted park facilities building, she shifted back to skin form. Then she keyed in a code on the side panel of a nondescript gray metal box about the size of an air-conditioning unit behind the building. The boxes were everywhere in the city, affixed to utility sheds, public works garages, electrical transformers, and water processing plants—just one more mechanical unit that faded into the background for the myriad workers who passed dozens of similar ones every day. She sorted through the small cache of clothes inside and removed a navy blue T-shirt and jeans. Since she wasn't rushed as she had been the previous evening, she took the time to pull out a pair of plain black loafers. After dressing, she punched in some codes on the electronic menu inside the door. The information would be logged in at Mir Industries, and one of her employees would replace the items within twenty-four hours for the next Were who found themselves in need of clothing.

She started walking through the park toward the capitol complex with the intention of going to the office. After a few minutes, she veered toward New Scotland Avenue instead. Her body felt pleasantly loose and limber after her thirty-mile journey and she wasn't looking forward to being caged in an office and tethered to a desk. And she was hungry. She was also penniless and without her phone. Niki would be very unhappy. Her options were limited, and since she didn't want to wait for her guards, one of whom would be following in the Rover, she decided to try her luck at catching Sophia at the hospital. She didn't think the young medic would mind taking her to breakfast.

Most Weres could disappear in plain sight, having a predator's natural ability to move without stirring the air, and she was far better than most. No one paid any attention to her when she followed a group of nurses through the double doors separating the waiting area from the rest of the emergency room. She scented another Were at the far end of the hall, but it wasn't Sophia. A young male. He stepped out from a cubicle, holding an X-ray plate under his arm. He stared in her direction, his expression questioning and uncertain. When she shook her head, he ducked his and hurriedly disappeared back behind the curtain.

Sylvan registered another scent, one she recognized, and not one that should have caused her pulse to race. Human. Female. Her thinking brain told her to turn around and leave, but her instinct urged her to follow the scent. She found Drake McKennan sitting at a small table in an otherwise empty room. Sylvan stepped inside and closed the door.

"Good morning," Sylvan said.

Drake leaned back in her chair and smiled ruefully. "I don't know about good, but it's been one hell of a morning so far."

"What did the Vampire want?" Sylvan demanded, unaccountably angry that Drake had been in close contact with a very powerful Vampire with very powerful desires. "Besides you?"

"Okay," Drake said, placing both hands flat on the table. "I've about had it with cryptic allusions and half-facts. And individuals who seem to know more about my business than I do. So it's someone else's turn to answer questions. What are *you* doing here?"

Sylvan folded her arms and leaned back against the door, unable to suppress a smile. She didn't derive any pleasure from instilling fear in others, but she was used to it. Apparently, Drake was immune. Or as she had previously suspected, naïvely brave. "I was looking for Sophia."

"Oh," Drake said, feeling foolishly disappointed and hoping her reaction wasn't apparent. Obviously the Were Alpha would want to talk to the Were medic, especially when it was clear from Detective Gates's questions that something serious was going on in the Were Pack. Just because *she* had been thinking about Sylvan most of the night didn't mean that the Were had given her a second thought. Maybe there was more to Sylvan's relationship with Sophia than Sophia had let on. After all, it was six o'clock in the morning—an odd time for the Alpha to show up. "She's not here."

"I know." Sylvan's jaw tightened and her face seemed to grow bolder, stronger, more intense. "Your turn. What did the Vampire want with you?"

"How do you know she was here?"

Sylvan growled. "I know."

"How?"

"I can smell her all over this room." Sylvan pushed off the wall and leaned over the table. "Will I smell her all over you?"

"And if you did?" Drake's throat was suddenly dry. Sylvan was so close Drake could see the gold flecks in her slate blue eyes. She could smell her, too. Wild cinnamon and burnt pine. She probably should have been intimidated, but she wasn't. And she knew instinctively that backing down was the wrong thing to do with this Were. "What would that tell you?"

"Then I would know friend from foe."

"No, you wouldn't." Exasperated, Drake stood up. She must have blinked because she didn't see Sylvan move, but in the next instant, the Alpha was standing next to her. They were nearly the same height. For the second time in less than an hour, Drake felt herself drawn in by a gaze, but this time, she welcomed the stirring in her blood. "Those terms have been going around a lot tonight. Friend. Foe. I don't even know the sides."

"Who was it? Maybe I can help you with that."

"Detective Jody Gates. And she was very interested in Misha."

"Was she." Sylvan sighed and backed away a step, needing the distance to temper her aggression. She had no reason to feel territorial about this human. Another indication that she was riding too close to the edge. She would have to do something about that, and soon.

"She asked me something else too," Drake said. "If I'd seen any humans with Were fever."

"Have you?"

"Not that I know of." Drake rubbed the back of her neck in frustration. "And that's a problem. I don't know anything. Sophia won't give me any information, because she says that's up to you." She looked into Sylvan's eyes and immediately felt the pull—the wash of heat, the tightening in her depths, the stirring of excitement. She steadied herself, refusing to look away. Refusing to give in. "So I guess

I need you to give me some answers. Because I don't care if it's a Were or a human, I intend to take care of the next one who comes in like Misha."

"You don't know what you're letting yourself in for," Sylvan said gruffly.

"Then why don't you explain it to me."

Sylvan almost smiled, wondering if this human had any idea that she had just challenged her with her steady stare, her tone of voice, her posture. If she'd been a wolf, Sylvan would have had her by the throat by now. As it was, she had to fight her wolf not to snarl and snap. Foolish brave human.

"I need breakfast." Sylvan effortlessly vaulted the table, pulled open the door, and looked over her shoulder. "Join me."

CHAPTER EIGHT

Sylvan stepped into the hall where Niki and Andrew flanked the door, having positioned themselves to see anyone approaching from either direction. She'd scented their arrival a few minutes earlier. They must have run very hard to be only a few minutes behind her. For her the long distance had been a vigorous workout—for them it would have been exhausting. They would both need to eat soon.

"Alpha," Niki murmured. She and Andrew immediately crowded close to Sylvan, brushing their bodies against her in welcome, seeking reassurance after their separation.

"Centuri." Sylvan cupped the backs of their necks, caressing gently. "Who's in the Rover?"

"I had Jonathan bring it down," Niki said, referring to one of the young dominants whom they had begun considering as a *centuri.* "I can call Max and Lara if you need—" Niki stiffened as Drake appeared next to Sylvan.

"No need to call them." Sylvan made room for Drake, creating distance between them so Niki would not perceive Drake as a threat to her. The *centuri* instinctively guarded the Alpha's personal space, not trusting anyone close to her except her mate. They wanted to be present when she had sex, but were forced to tolerate her being unguarded then because she insisted on privacy. She had no compunction in her guards seeing her naked or in the throes of sex frenzy. But she wanted her partners to feel some degree of intimacy, since she would not give them what many of them wanted: a bond. "Dr. McKennan and I are going to have breakfast. You two should do the same."

"We'll wait," Niki snapped, staring at Drake. Andrew jerked his head in agreement.

"You'll both eat," Sylvan said flatly and turned to Drake. "Where would you recommend?"

"There's a place right down the street. The Recovery Room."

"Let's go." Sylvan headed off and Drake matched her long stride.

"Your guards are unhappy," Drake said.

"They're too protective."

"Do they have reason to be?"

Sylvan shot her a glance. "Why are you so curious?"

"You interest me."

"Really?" Sylvan's brows rose. "Why is that? Or do you just have an unnatural fascination for animals?"

"Is that how you see yourself? An animal?" Drake stepped through the double doors out into the morning. She saw Sylvan take a breath as if testing the air, her eyes scanning the street in all directions. Wary. Guarded. Inborn, instinctive movements.

"In my heart, I am a wolf. What would you call me?"

"I'd call you a Were." They came to the end of the ER turnaround and Drake touched Sylvan's bare arm to direct her. Hard muscles rippled beneath her fingertips. Sylvan's skin was hot and unexpectedly silken, almost as if covered in invisible fur. Drake slid her fingers up and down without thinking. Sylvan tensed, and from very close behind her, Drake heard a growl. Niki. Irrationally, Drake wanted to ignore the warning—she wanted to keep caressing that velvet steel. Good sense prevailed, and she reluctantly removed her hand. "The diner's down this way."

Laughing quietly, Sylvan asked, "Why aren't you intimidated?"

"She's letting me know that if I threaten you, she'll hurt me, right?"

"Yes." Sylvan hid her surprise. She hadn't expected the touch, and she definitely never expected to like it. Ordinarily she would not allow a stranger so deep into her personal space, and she would never have tolerated even casual contact. But Drake's hand on her arm hadn't felt foreign or threatening. Drake's slowly stroking fingers had seemed to caress her deeper than skin. "Doesn't her aggression bother you? It does most humans."

"Could she stop her reaction if you told her to?"

"No. She's my second, the highest-ranking wolf in my Pack. Her strongest drive is to protect me. She can't do anything other than be who she is."

"Then it doesn't bother me." Drake slid her palm along Sylvan's forearm. "Here's the diner."

Sylvan glanced down at Drake's hand on her arm. "You don't want to tempt her."

"You're right, I don't." Drake wasn't sure what she was doing. She had no desire to antagonize Niki, but she resented being warned away from Sylvan. "I trust you to let her know that I'm completely harmless."

Sylvan held the door for Drake. "I never lie to my wolves."

Grinning, Drake followed Sylvan inside. The long railroad car–style diner was half full of people in hospital attire. Sylvan asked for a corner booth, and after she and Drake slid in, Niki and Andrew took the one across the aisle. Sylvan's guards sat on opposite sides of the table, at the outer edge of the bench seats where they could quickly step into the aisle and block access to her.

"Does it ever bother you?" Drake asked. "The constant company, the…surveillance."

Sylvan shook her head. "From the time we're young, we're surrounded by Pack. The pups sleep in piles. They nurse from any lactating female. Any Were in the Pack will protect any young, regardless of who whelped them. We're all connected. To be isolated would kill us."

"Do you mean that literally?"

Sylvan grew very still, so still that Drake actually had trouble seeing her, as if somehow she were no longer sitting across from her. The Alpha had gone to ground.

"How many Were medics do you have like Sophia working in the human health system?" Drake asked, trying a different tack.

"Why do you ask?" Sylvan replied.

"Because—" Drake paused to order breakfast from the middle-aged waitress who plunked heavy white ceramic mugs brimming with dark, oily-looking coffee down in front of them without being asked. When the waitress moved across the aisle to take Niki and Andrew's orders, she continued. "If it's as few as I think, then it's not enough to take care of any substantial medical crisis."

"We don't, as a rule, require medical care." Sylvan tried the coffee. "This, however, could be lethal."

Laughing, Drake took a sip. "Sophia says caffeine doesn't do anything to you."

"She may never have tried this coffee."

Drake leaned closer and lowered her voice. "Why are the police asking about humans with Were fever? I don't remember reading anything about it in med—" She grimaced. "Well, of course I wouldn't have learned anything about it in medical school, because no one knew anything about *any* of the Praeterns until just recently."

"Were fever is very rare, even among Weres."

"What is it, exactly?"

Sylvan considered her response while the waitress set plates of food in front of them. Drake was right—they did not have many Were medics. Before the Exodus, the Were medics worked in secrecy to cover up the uncommon instance when a Were was brought into an emergency room for care. Most often, this happened when a Were was involved in an accident or an altercation that led to police involvement. The police and emergency service personnel routinely brought the injured to the emergency room, but unfortunately, a Were was likely to heal their injuries halfway through treatment. Every wolf Were carried a health card that, when scanned into any database anywhere in the world, would alert a central clearing station at Mir Industries. A Were medic would be sent to intervene. Feral cat, rodent, and other less common Weres did not interact with the human population enough for accidental discovery to be a problem.

If she was facing an outbreak of Were fever, she would not have enough medics to cover it up. And if humans somehow became infected, it would be disastrous. Even so, she couldn't risk revealing too much. Until she understood exactly how widespread the problem was, she wasn't going to expose her Pack and all the other Weres to retaliation.

"Anything I could tell you would be meaningless to you."

"Look," Drake said, "we're the largest medical center in the region. Any case that looks out of the ordinary is going to be turfed to us from the local hospitals. If I know what to look for, I can triage. Start early treatment. I'll call your medics, if you want me to."

"We don't know what it is," Sylvan said, hoping that the appearance of cooperation would quell Drake's concerns. "We only know what it does. It kills nearly a hundred percent of the time, and quickly. Once the fever starts, it escalates within hours—sometimes even faster. We don't know if the fever is the cause of the cellular breakdown or the consequence, but most of the infected suffer system-wide collapse. Seizures, bleeding, endocrine storm."

"And those who don't succumb immediately?"

"Almost all become rabid and eventually die too."

Drake frowned. "What's the cause of death if not the cellular breakdown?"

Sylvan's eyes narrowed, the blue shifting to gold. She pictured Misha, struggling alone, while she stood by doing nothing. Her wolf clawed at her insides, raging at her impotence. "We execute them."

"Jesus Christ," Drake whispered. "Who decides that?"

"I do."

Drake breathed out slowly, trying to wrap her mind around the idea of killing a sick patient. Not just a patient, someone who was like family. She wouldn't have the guts.

"Still think we're not animals, Doctor?" Sylvan asked bitterly. She wasn't sure why the shocked expression on Drake's face bothered her so much. She didn't expect a human to understand the threat of a rabid wolf to the Pack. She wasn't even sure why she tried to explain.

"I think we need to find a cure," Drake said vehemently, surprising Sylvan yet again.

"Don't you think we're trying?" Sylvan snapped. "Seventy-five percent of the resources at Mir Industries go to this research." Her frustration broadcast and Niki rose abruptly, stepping toward them with a rumble. Sylvan raised her hand a fraction and telegraphed, *Stand down, Imperator. All is well.*

Niki rumbled again and slowly returned to her seat.

"Of course, I'm sorry." Drake rubbed the back of her neck. "What about humans? Similar symptoms?"

Sylvan said nothing, in total agreement when her wolf howled a warning. Some things the humans could not know, because if they did, they would surely try to destroy her and all like her.

"Should you suspect you have a case of Were fever, I and the Timberwolf Pack will be in your debt if you call us before you do the police." Sylvan stood, telegraphing Niki to get the bill. "I appreciate your desire to help us, Dr. McKennan, but I'm afraid you can't."

Drake rose as Niki put money on the table. She met Sylvan's eyes. "Thank you for breakfast. I'll get it the next time."

"I'm afraid there won't be another time." Sylvan watched Niki and Andrew pacing agitatedly nearby. Her wolf was so close to the surface, so ready to fight, she was in danger of driving her guards to lose control. She was out of time. "Good-bye, Doctor."

CHAPTER NINE

Sylvan and Niki climbed into the Rover's rear cargo compartment. Andrew got in front next to Jonathan, a wiry blond male just out of his teens who sat behind the wheel. Sylvan leaned forward between the front seats. "Drive to Nocturne."

"Yes, Alpha," Jonathan said crisply and edged away from the curb into early morning traffic.

"There aren't enough of us to protect you there." Niki's displeasure filled the too-small space.

"It's daylight. Francesca is the only one who will be awake." Sylvan glanced out the tinted window and saw Drake McKennan on the sidewalk in front of the diner, watching them pull away. Her wolf stirred, growling softly as if telling her she had unfinished business. Sylvan ignored the tug in her groin. She'd take care of that her way. Her wolf snarled.

"First the human, now this," Niki snapped. "You take chances, Alpha. We can't afford to lose—"

Sylvan bounded across the small space. If she didn't know how close Niki was to breaking, she would have forced Niki onto her back, under her. Instead, she grabbed her and pulled her close, tucking Niki's head beneath her chin. "Everything will be fine."

Niki rubbed her cheek against Sylvan's neck, breathing deeply. "At least let me come with you."

"No." Sylvan stroked Niki's hair. "I trust you with my life, with the lives of our young. Trust me on this."

"Always, Alpha," Niki whispered.

❖

Club Nocturne, a one-story, flat-roofed building with opaque black windows and flat black paint on its plywood front, sat on the waterfront in the middle of a cracked concrete parking lot with foot-tall weeds growing in the crevices. During the day, the place appeared abandoned despite a few cars and motorcycles parked haphazardly in the enormous lot. It didn't look much better at night, when a few spotlights tucked under the eaves threw just enough light to point the way to the front door. No flashing neon signs indicated that this was the most popular nighttime hangout in the city for Vampires, their blood hosts, and other beings, human and otherwise, looking for sex or more dangerous thrills. When Sylvan walked into the murky interior, a couple of human bikers in dirty denim and dusty leather perched on stools at the bar, drinking beer at eight in the morning. The bartender was Francesca's human servant—a balding ex-professional wrestler named Guy. He wore a leather vest over bare skin to show off the tats that covered his chest and arms, but mostly to display the puncture marks in his neck and nipples. Francesca or whoever she'd most recently loaned him out to had been very hungry and Guy was obviously proud of his service—the Vampire who had fed from him would have healed the punctures unless Guy had requested that they not.

"She's busy," Guy grunted. Like many Vampires, he didn't care for Weres. The two predatory species disagreed as to who was at the top of the food chain. Vampires liked feeding from Weres, claiming that the Weres' wild blood gave the Vamps a greater high and triggered more intense orgasms than human blood. Some Vampires seemed to think that made Weres prey. Considering that Weres were the only species that could tear a Vampire's heart out bare-handed, Sylvan didn't think so.

"Tell her I'm coming down." Sylvan didn't break stride as she leapt over the bar and into the alcove behind it. By the time she reached the hidden staircase to Francesca's lair, Guy must have communicated with the Mistress of the City, because Sylvan heard the faint hiss of multiple locks sliding open. Sylvan shouldered through the door and loped down the stairs into the elaborate chambers below. The door locked behind her.

Like all master Vampires, Francesca did not become catatonic during daylight hours and could usually be found at work or play in her suite beneath the club. The door to her private quarters slid open and a naked man and woman exited. The woman sagged against the man, who stumbled slightly as the pair turned and staggered away down the hall. Both wore a glazed look that Sylvan assumed was related to the fresh punctures in their necks. Francesca had been feeding, to their obvious pleasure.

Francesca lounged on a divan in the sitting room adjoining her boudoir. Like all Vampires, she was slender and painfully beautiful, with an etched porcelain air of delicacy that belied her incredible strength. Her full, rose-tipped breasts were clearly visible and barely contained beneath a diaphanous dressing gown open down to her navel. Her lustrous eyes were deep turquoise, her scarlet hair falling in artful tangles over milk white shoulders.

"What a nice surprise." Francesca had closed the door to her bedchamber, but the blood scent was rich and fresh.

Sylvan was not attracted to human blood *or* Vampire blood. She was there for one reason. Francesca would willingly meet her most urgent needs, at least temporarily, and without the risk of developing any kind of attachment to her. Theirs was a mutually beneficial relationship completely devoid of emotional complication.

"I'm sorry I gave no notice."

"You've been very busy," Francesca said, moving over to make room for Sylvan on the maroon brocade divan. "It's been months since you've been by to visit."

"I'm sure Councilor Gates has kept you up to date on the proceedings," Sylvan said. Zachary Gates might be the official face representing the Vampires to the public, but Francesca was not only the Chancellor of the local Vampire seethe, she was Viceregal of the Eastern Territory. Everyone in the Praetern Coalition acknowledged her as the power behind the throne. Sylvan sprawled on the divan, stretching her arms out along the back. "I don't want to talk politics."

"Your timing is excellent," Francesca murmured, dropping a black silk pillow with gold fringe on the floor between Sylvan's spread thighs. She knelt on it and pushed Sylvan's T-shirt up. "I was just feeding when you arrived." She looked up at Sylvan as she opened Sylvan's jeans, her lids languorous, her mouth curved in a sensuous smile. "But I hadn't finished. I've yet to satisfy my other needs." She leaned forward and ran her tongue over the ridges in Sylvan's abdomen. A fine line of rich silver pelt erupted down the center of Sylvan's lower abdomen and disappeared into her jeans. Francesca teased the satiny line that marked a dominant Were when aroused or challenged.

"I see you're ready." Francesca ran her nails over Sylvan's belly and Sylvan shuddered.

"Do it." Sylvan raised her hips and Francesca stripped her jeans down her legs. Her clitoris rose, engorged and stiff. She growled softly when Francesca fingered it. Francesca murmured approvingly as Sylvan's sex glands, the firm nodes buried in the flesh framing her clitoris, swelled in response to her teasing.

"I can't ever remember these being so full." Francesca massaged the glands with her fingertips, forcing Sylvan's clitoris to jerk. Licking gracefully along the shaft, Francesca sighed as if savoring rare ambrosia. "You're too ready for me to linger, I'm afraid."

"Don't." Sylvan's claws extended. "Just drain me."

"Oh," Francesca whispered. "I will."

Unhurriedly, Francesca parted her crimson lips, giving Sylvan a fleeting glimpse of her incisors, before she drew Sylvan's clitoris deep into her mouth. Sylvan tensed, steeling herself. With infinite care, Francesca bit down on the rigid shaft and began to suck. Her incisors pressed the sex glands into the bone beneath.

Groaning, Sylvan arched off the sofa, her claws gouging through the fabric into the wood frame. Each pull of Francesca's powerful throat ripped the fire from her blood. Her sex beat heavily between Francesca's lips, pumping her power down Francesca's throat. The Vampire scored Sylvan's midsection with scarlet nails. Sylvan panted, struggling to contain her furious wolf as Francesca pulled harder at her flesh, drinking her essence. This was not what her wolf craved but all she would permit. The physical relief was intense but not sexual—and as much pain as pleasure. Sylvan never climaxed from Francesca's ministrations, but she found some brief respite from the wild hunger that drove her. Enough so that her urges no longer threatened to plunge the Pack into chaos.

"More," Sylvan gasped when Francesca started to withdraw. Her clitoris was still rigid, her sex glands tight and aching. "Empty me."

Francesca resumed sucking, shuddering as she absorbed the potent mixture of Were pheromones and sex kinins. A minute later, when

Francesca would have stopped, Sylvan curled her hand around the back of Francesca's neck, claws extended to hold her in place. She had to release the hormones overwhelming her system, and she didn't dare risk true release with another Were. The sex frenzy could too easily become mating frenzy, and she did not want to risk activating the mate bond. Only a Vampire as powerful as Francesca could drain her enough to temper the heat. *"More."*

After what seemed like a long while, Sylvan's clitoris softened and Sylvan relaxed, lethargy suffusing her.

"Sylvan," Francesca sighed, her voice heavy with satisfaction. "Even you aren't strong enough for me to take more." She rose gracefully, parting her dressing gown along the split that ran up one side, and straddled Sylvan's bare stomach. She was slick and hot against Sylvan's skin, her clitoris a hard knot against Sylvan's belly. Undulating slowly, Francesca flicked her tongue over the pulsing vein in Sylvan's neck. "Let me drink from you. Let me make you come."

"No," Sylvan said, although she was almost too depleted to physically resist. She would never willingly submit to Francesca, but if Francesca fed from her, the hormones Francesca secreted into the deep bite would make Sylvan come whether she wanted to or not.

"I promise you pleasure." Francesca lightly pierced Sylvan's skin, the teasing bite reminiscent of a Were's during passion.

Sylvan's clitoris tightened, but she could tolerate the stimulation now. She did not want sex, but she would not deny Francesca, whose blood need after so much stimulation would be agonizing. Without blood a Vampire couldn't achieve ultimate release. "Taste me enough to satisfy yourself, but don't feed. Don't make me come."

"As you wish." Francesca, exerting more control than any other Vampire could have managed, brought herself to the brink of orgasm on Sylvan's stomach. Then with a quicksilver flash of incisors, she pierced Sylvan's neck just deep enough to start a slow flow of blood. She did not feed fully, even when Sylvan's Alpha blood sent her into wrenching orgasm. When her climax finally dwindled away, she licked the thin blood trail from Sylvan's neck and murmured sluggishly, "Take me to bed. I must sleep now."

Sylvan gently moved Francesca aside and rose unsteadily. After zipping her jeans, she picked Francesca up, cradled her to her chest, and carried her into the adjoining room. She placed her in the center of the huge circular bed and carefully covered her with a white sheet that bore crimson stains from Francesca's earlier festivities. Then she turned off the ornate crystal lamp next to the bed. Francesca would not waken until after dark.

Sylvan made her way slowly back upstairs, her legs heavy. Her hands trembled as she checked to be sure that the door to Francesca's lair had locked behind her. Guy was Francesca's only protection while she slumbered. Francesca trusted Sylvan with her life, just as Sylvan had trusted Francesca with hers.

"She shouldn't be disturbed," Sylvan said as she passed the bar on her way out.

Guy muttered something that sounded like *fucking Were* as she passed, but Sylvan wasn't inclined to fight. She wanted to curl up and sleep for the short respite she had before the frenzy rose again.

Niki was waiting just outside the door. Her eyes went to Sylvan's neck, where the bite marks were already fading. She didn't say anything as she opened the back door of the Rover and followed Sylvan in. Sylvan leaned her head against the sidewall and closed her eyes.

"Is there no other way?" Niki asked quietly.

"Not for me."

CHAPTER TEN

Sylvan woke with her face nestled against a firm, warm, naked abdomen. Fingers played through her hair. She scented safety, familiarity, Pack. Stretching, she registered another body pressed against her legs. The Rover passed over the sensors built into the Compound approach road, causing an ultra-high-pitched signal that alerted the *sentries* on the inner perimeter to an oncoming vehicle. Opening her eyes, Sylvan smiled up at Niki. "Almost home."

"Mmm-hmm." Niki's forest green eyes were mellow, content. As soon as Sylvan had fallen asleep, Niki's wolf had settled, reassured that the Alpha was secure. The awful tension twisting through her insides, howling of danger and threat, had abated. Even the sex frenzy that clawed at her for release was blessedly quiet. "How do you feel?"

"Good." Sylvan clasped Niki's wrist and brushed a kiss over her knuckles. "Thank you."

Niki rumbled in pleasure.

Sylvan sighed and caressed Andrew's shoulder where he rubbed against her thigh. Revitalized by her nap, her urges tempered by Francesca's attentions, she assessed the looming dangers. Two young females had disappeared. Misha had been attacked. Had that been an abduction attempt gone bad? Now a Vampire was asking a human medic about Were fever. Were fever and humans.

How would the human population react if news of this threat became widespread? At the very least, the negotiations in Washington would be seriously compromised, but politics were not her major concern right now. Forceful retaliation was. She doubted that many humans would be as sympathetic as Drake McKennan appeared to be.

But would even Drake take their side if she understood what was really at stake? Sylvan remembered the intensity in Drake's voice when she'd said, *We need to find a cure.* As if the fever were Drake's problem as much as hers. She'd seen the frustration in Drake's eyes when she had refused to confide in her. Frustration and disappointment. Sylvan regretted turning aside Drake's offer of help. Regretted turning *her* aside, although why that should be she wasn't sure. But she'd grown up protecting Pack secrets, and now she was responsible not just for secrets, but lives. She couldn't afford to trust anyone who wasn't Pack, even though her instincts told her that Drake McKennan was different. Had Drake been a Were, she would have had the makings of an Alpha. Fearless, focused, passionate. Sylvan's skin still carried the memory of Drake's touch. She had been right to put distance between them. Being around the human disturbed her focus, and too much was at stake for her to forget her purpose. She must protect her Pack.

Sylvan's wolf stirred, not in warning but with a message Sylvan couldn't identify. An unusual sensation. Excitement and impatience. Hunger. Not sex frenzy, a deeper craving. She shifted uneasily, struggling to connect to the wolf, to the primal, instinctual core of her being. But whatever the wolf sensed, she could not reason it into clarity. She grumbled, frustrated.

"Alpha?" Niki asked in concern.

"It's all right." Sylvan rubbed her face against Niki's smooth, hard stomach to calm her second. Niki was more closely attuned to her than any member of the Pack. When she hurt, Niki hurt. When she hungered, Niki hungered. When she was in danger, Niki stood ready to defend her. "A Vampire detective questioned the human medic this morning about Misha. She implied there were rumors, maybe more than rumors, of humans with Were fever."

Niki caught her breath. "How? If it were true, we would know."

"Possibly." Sylvan pushed upright and draped her arm around Niki's shoulders. Andrew wrapped his arm around her thigh. "But we need to prepare."

The Rover slowed to a stop. They were home. The time had come for her to do what she was born to do. Defend her Pack.

"I want to see Misha first," Sylvan said, "and then I want a war council. Find Max and Lara. And Callan and Val."

"You expect an attack?" Niki asked, eyes going sharp.

"No," Sylvan said. "We're going hunting."

❖

Drake should have gone home to sleep. She was due back in the ER in ten hours, but the early morning meeting with Sylvan left her too hyped to sleep. She couldn't stop thinking about Sylvan and deadly fevers and a newly discovered world she found as fascinating as it was dangerous. She might never have her many questions about Sylvan Mir answered, which left her feeling oddly hollow, as if she were missing out on something more important than she could even imagine. She'd have to live with the personal disappointment, but she couldn't allow her ignorance about a deadly disease to continue. She had a job to do, so she turned around and walked back to the ER.

"Mary," Drake said to the clerk in the ER file room, "could you pull all the charts on patients with a diagnosis of FUO in the last six months?"

The attractive African American woman, stylishly attired in a deep red skirt and jacket, glanced up from her computer and gave Drake a flat stare. "And you would need this when, Dr. McKennan?"

Drake grinned sheepishly. "Now?"

"Uh-huh." Mary pointed to a foot-high stack of papers by her right hand. "You know what that is?"

"Nope."

"Billing."

"Uh-huh."

"You know what happens to the money we get from billing?"

Drake concentrated. "Pays our salaries?"

"That and just about everything else around here," Mary said.

"Double caramel latte or mocha?"

"Mocha."

"Thank you," Drake said. "Is an hour good?"

Mary smiled brilliantly. "After you deliver my coffee, try checking the conference room. Sophia already has the charts. You two doing a study or something?"

"Something like that," Drake said quietly. She pointed a finger at Mary. "And you cheated."

"Oh honey, you're just easy."

Mary's laughter followed Drake down the hall as she headed to the lobby and the coffee kiosk. Sophia should be off-call now too, but she was back in the ER reviewing charts of patients with fever of unknown origin. She had to be looking for other cases of Were fever. Just curious or carrying out her Alpha's orders? Thinking back to Sylvan's unexpected appearance in the ER at six a.m. in search of Sophia, Drake assumed the latter. Angry, uncertain exactly why, she purchased Mary's mocha and threaded her way through the incoming morning crew of nurses, residents, and other staff back to the ER. She'd almost made it to the double doors with the big red sign warning No Entry when a woman with skin a shade lighter than Mary's coffee stepped into her path.

"Dr. McKennan," the woman asked in a husky alto, "how did it feel to be threatened by an out-of-control Were? Did you fear for your life?"

"Who are you?" Drake asked.

The woman looked to be in her early thirties, dressed casually in blue jeans, low-heeled boots, and a fine-knit black sweater that clung to her swimmer's shoulders and high, round breasts. She pointed to a plastic ID card clipped to the waistband of her jeans where a photo with her oval face, big dark eyes, and glossy black curls was clearly displayed.

"Becca Land. *Albany Gazette*. Did you call for security to contain the Were?"

"I don't know what you're talking about," Drake said, although she was pretty certain she *did* know. Instantly furious at the accusations, Drake cautioned herself to say as little as possible until she got her temper under control.

Becca reached into her shoulder bag and pulled out a newspaper, letting it drop open to the front page and the photo of Sylvan and Drake with Misha. The angle of the shot made it look as if a snarling Sylvan—canines gleaming—was nearly on top of Drake. Drake wondered how many people were waiting for just this kind of "evidence" to prove that the Weres represented a danger to society.

"I'm following up on a report that a number of Weres threatened the ER staff this morning," Becca said.

"Your information is incorrect. There was no threat. No danger. No problem at all." Drake keyed in the code to open the ER doors. "If you'll excuse me."

"If you care about those Weres, Dr. McKennan, you'll give me the true story." Becca looked at the paper in her hand with distaste. "Because you can be sure that rags like this are only interested in selling papers, and they don't care who suffers for it."

Drake hesitated, studying the woman who watched her with unwavering dark eyes. Friend or foe? In the course of a day she had become aware of a war in progress—battle lines had been drawn—and she was still uncertain of the sides. A strong compulsion to protect Sylvan Mir made her decision easy. "All right."

Becca held up a digital recorder. The red light blinked, indicating it was running. "On the record?"

Drake nodded. "I requested that Councilor Mir assist me in the examination of an agitated young patient. She was very helpful, and at no time was her behavior threatening or in any other way unrestrained. I never considered myself in danger and did not summon security."

"The councilor has been photographed dozens of times over the last two years," Becca said, "and she's never appeared to be anything other than completely controlled. In fact, if you didn't know, you'd think she was human." Becca shook the paper. "She doesn't look human here. What happened?"

One of her Pack was threatened—possibly dying. One of her young. Drake wondered how much more Sylvan was forced to hide every day in her public dealings. How much of herself she had to deny in order to achieve protection for her Pack. She thought of the TV images of Zachary Gates, the Vampire councilor who appeared as polished and sophisticated as any Wall Street CEO. Then she recalled his daughter's raw sexual power, the crimson flash of her eyes, and knew humans were being allowed to see only a façade—one the human world would feel comfortable with. The price of survival for the Praetern species was apparently the denial of their fundamental being.

Furious at the injustice, Drake turned and walked away. "I have no further comment."

❖

After delivering Mary's mocha latte, Drake knocked on the door to the conference room. Sophia sat at a long table with a dozen charts spread out in front of her. Her eyes widened and her nostrils flared when she saw Drake, but her expression seemed to be more surprise than anxiety.

"What?" Drake asked.

"Nothing," Sophia said quickly.

"Have you found any more cases? Or is that something else the Alpha wouldn't want you to tell me?"

Sophia straightened, her mouth tightening. "I might be a Were, but I'm also a medic. My responsibility is to all the patients. And I know the Alpha would not want me to put anyone—human or Were— in danger."

"Sorry." Drake pulled out a chair and sat down. She rubbed her face and shook the tension from her shoulders. "I didn't mean to insult your professional integrity. And I know Sylv—your Alpha—is only trying to protect your Pack."

"I think there are four cases," Sophia said softly. "No one picked up on a pattern because they were all signed out as drug overdoses."

"Not that uncommon a diagnosis in the ER population," Drake agreed. "Patient profiles?"

"All girls. Aged fifteen to seventeen."

"How many were human?"

Sophia's deep blue eyes clouded. "All of them."

Drake's chest tightened. "I need to speak to your Alpha. Can you contact her?"

"Again?"

"What do you mean?"

Sophia blushed. "Sorry. Her scent—" She lifted a hand in Drake's direction. "To us, it's very distinctive."

"Yes, well," Drake said, an unexpected ripple of pleasure catching her off balance. She liked that she smelled like Sylvan, and had no idea what to make of that. "Does everyone who comes in contact with her… carry her scent then?"

"No." Sophia frowned. "The *centuri* do, of course, but they are oath bonded to her. But I…I don't recall ever scenting her on anyone else."

"Must be because I just saw her," Drake said. "How do I reach her?"

Sophia looked uncomfortable. "I don't know. Perhaps call her office?"

"What about you? How would you…any of you, let her know of a problem?" Drake held up her hand when she saw Sophia's face blank. "Don't tell me the details. I know you can't. Just—could you send her a message from me? It's important that I speak with her."

"Yes, but I can't promise anything."

Drake sighed and pushed to her feet. "Who can?"

❖

"How is she?" Sylvan asked when Elena met her in the hall outside Misha's room.

"She's better. No fever, thankfully. The wound is trying to close, but she needs to shift to complete the healing. She tried, but she's weak and doesn't have enough control to do it voluntarily."

"I'll take care of her."

"Wait." Elena grasped Sylvan's hand.

Sylvan gave Elena a questioning look. Niki would not have permitted Elena to physically confront her, but Sylvan took no issue, as they were alone and no challenge was implied. Elena and her mate Roger were beta wolves, lacking overt dominance tendencies but far from being submissive. Their drive was to guide and nurture the Pack, particularly the young, which explained why Elena was a medic and Roger a teacher. Sylvan valued their friendship and their contributions to the Pack. "What?"

"Your energy has changed. Your call is…dampened."

Sylvan smiled ruefully. "Maybe now you'll give Roger a rest."

"There's no need to worry about my mate. He has remarkable stamina." Elena's voice was soft with fondness, but her eyes were troubled as she searched Sylvan's face. "What have you done to deplete yourself this way?"

"Don't worry. There's no danger." Sylvan stroked Elena's cheek with her fingertips. "Just worry about Misha."

"We are here for you, Alpha. If you satisfy your needs outside the Pack, you'll anger some important allies."

"I don't. Not in the way you think." Sylvan refused to be dictated to by the traditionalists in the Were Coalition who believed Alphas should only mate with those of ancient blood. Some went so far as to insist Alphas limit their sexual encounters to highbred Pack members.

Sylvan's line was centuries old—her blood stronger than any wolf Alpha outside the Russian Tundra Pack. Even the Russians would not dare challenge her overtly, but her congress with a Vampire could provide ammunition to those who secretly might wish to unseat her. "What kind of Alpha would I be if I let others decide how I behave?"

Elena threaded her arms around Sylvan's waist and rested her cheek on her chest. "Not the strong, infuriatingly stubborn Alpha we love."

Laughing, Sylvan rubbed Elena's back. "You're tired. Let's take care of Misha so you can get some rest."

Niki appeared at the end of the hall. "We're assembled in the gathering room, Alpha."

"I'll be there soon." Sylvan kissed Elena's forehead. "Open the door."

Elena pushed the door open as Sylvan shifted. She bounded into the room and onto the bed next to Misha. She loomed over the adolescent and licked her face. Misha's eyes opened and she gave a small cry of surprise before wrapping her arms around Sylvan's neck. When Misha buried her face in Sylvan's ruff, Sylvan rumbled low in her chest and called Misha's wolf. Misha whimpered, trembling as her injured body struggled to give her wolf ascendency. With age and practice the shift would become harmonious, natural, but Misha was still young, still finding her balance. Sylvan broadcast more power, reaching deep into Misha with the primal force that was programmed into her DNA and that every wolf Were was bound to answer. Misha's skin shimmered, her white and gray pelt sliding over the surface. Her back arched, her bones morphed, her cry became a howl. Sylvan curled around the shivering young wolf and gently took her damp muzzle in her mouth, telling her she was safe and protected.

Misha sighed and closed her eyes.

Sylvan waited another few moments, feeding Misha her strength, ensuring that she slept peacefully. Then she shifted back to skin and sat on the edge of the bed, softly stroking the beautiful gray and white wolf. The wound on Misha's shoulder was raw and red, but Sylvan saw no sign of the black poison.

Elena handed Sylvan her jeans. "I may need you again if she tries to shift back too soon."

"Thanks." Sylvan stood and pulled on her jeans. Her shirts rarely survived her rapid shifts, the fragments incinerating in the heat of her transition, but she usually managed not to shred her pants if she wanted them again.

"Call me," Sylvan said. "No matter what I'm doing, I'll come."

Elena kissed Sylvan lightly on the mouth. "I know. We all know."

CHAPTER ELEVEN

The windows in the gathering room were open and a breeze thick with honeysuckle and pine stirred Sylvan's hair. The scents of rabbit, squirrel, and possum rode on the heat currents, teasing Sylvan with the lure of freedom and the joy of the hunt. Hunting prey was part of the natural order, but there was nothing natural about the hunt she contemplated today. Sylvan shut the heavy double oak doors, put her hands on her hips, and surveyed her war council.

Niki lounged by the huge fireplace, her back against the stones, her arms folded beneath her breasts. Max and Andrew flanked the entry, shoulders resting lightly against the walls. Lara, her fourth *centuri*, reclined on the arm of an oversized leather chair, her eyes scanning the open windows while the fingers of her right hand played through the short, thick hair of a statuesque brunette. Lara and Val had obviously been in the midst of a tangle when summoned. Val, who like Sylvan wore only a pair of jeans, was Callan's top-ranking lieutenant and dominant enough to have been offered a place with the *centuri*. Val had declined, saying that she preferred her position with the *sentrie*. She liked spending long hours in wolf form patrolling their borders. Val could follow a days-old track better than anyone except Sylvan and could take down a full-grown cat Were by herself. On a hunt, she was merciless.

Callan, the captain of the *sentries*, slouched on the leather sofa, bare-chested in skintight leather pants, appearing deceptively relaxed. He was as tall as Max but whip slender where Max was bulky. Both had shaggy dark hair, searching black eyes, and sensuous mouths. Callan was mated and his female had recently gone into heat. He looked tired but bore the typical smug, satisfied expression of all Weres with mates in the midst of breeding frenzy.

Sylvan strode to the center of the gathering. All eyes turned to her.

"Our adolescents were attacked in a city park last night. They report their attackers were rogues. Misha was the target." Sylvan tempered her fury, needing her war council clear-headed. The mere mention of their young being attacked had them on edge, and her anger could easily stir their battle frenzy. They were seasoned soldiers, all of them, but they were wolves. Not just any wolves, but the most dominant wolves in her Pack. Their instinct was to fight. She turned to Max, who was the intelligence officer on the council. "What is our current count on the rogues?"

"We have no good accounting of their numbers," Max said. "As you know, they are largely disorganized and rarely form more than the most rudimentary Packs. Two or three living together. Many lone wolves."

"Estimates?"

"Within the urban territory? A few dozen at last count." Max frowned. "But things have been uncharacteristically quiet for several months—no petty turf struggles, no gang rumbles."

"Callan," Sylvan said, "has Fala reported anything unusual?"

Callan's mate was one of many Weres in law enforcement, a job that provided a natural outlet for Were hunting instincts. Humans couldn't detect Were scent at crime scenes, but the Were police officers could. Fala was the conduit for Were officers to report such incidents to the Pack. At the mention of his mate, Callan rubbed his chest lazily, his canines emerging and a bulge growing behind his fly.

"Focus, Callan," Sylvan barked. "You can think about breeding her later."

Callan straightened and ducked his head. "Apologies, Alpha."

Sylvan waved him off. He wasn't to blame for his instincts. There was no stronger call for a wolf than a mate in breeding frenzy, except the call of their Alpha. Callan would do his job.

"Fala mentioned the number of bodega thefts and car break-ins by the rogues have declined," Callan said. "I didn't make anything of that at the time."

"If the rogues aren't stealing for food, how are they surviving?" Sylvan said.

Niki said, "Maybe they've hired out as mercenaries or have formed a Pack."

"If there are more of them than we think," Max said, "or they're banding together, we could have a real problem. If they start preying on humans—"

"We'll be lucky if we all don't end up in cages," Val muttered darkly. More than most Weres, who instinctively feared confinement, she couldn't tolerate being restricted. She hadn't been born into the Timberwolf Pack—she was one of the rare viable offspring of a female Were and a human male. Her mother, a lone wolf, had hidden her Were nature. Fearing exposure when Val had shifted as a pup, Val's mother and her human mate had caged Val. Eventually, she had escaped and staggered, half starved, into Timberwolf territory after having run wild in wolf form for weeks. Even as an adolescent, she'd been a ferocious fighter and had damaged several of the *sentries* who tried to subdue her. Ursula, Sylvan's mother, had been forced to drag her down by the throat and thrash her until Val lay panting, her belly exposed for the kill. Then Ursula had nudged her up and taken her into the Pack.

"No one will ever take your freedom," Sylvan said quietly.

Lara leaned down and kissed Val, who closed her eyes and nodded silently.

"We need to impose order before we have humans injured…or any reports in the media," Sylvan said. Rogues congregated in warehouses and abandoned buildings, and were usually quick to run from any show of force. If the rogues were organizing, they might resist, and what had once been a nuisance could become a serious threat. Human gangs had become commonplace in the public awareness, but gangs of roving Weres? If the human population learned of the rogues, political sympathies could quickly change.

"Couldn't Misha's attempted abduction just have been sexually motivated—rogues looking for a female for sport?" Callan said.

"Maybe, but we need to be sure." Sylvan let her wolf rise and the others tensed. Niki growled. Sylvan's voice thickened with rage. "Either way, we need to send a message that our young are not targets. Tonight—Max, Andrew, and Val—you'll be with me. And we'll go hunting."

"Alpha," Niki protested, straightening and striding forward. "I should go."

Sylvan shook her head. "I need you here. You're the second."

"Let me go in your place."

"No. This is my territory, and I will make sure they don't forget again." Sylvan turned abruptly, flung the heavy doors open with a blow from her outstretched arms, and strode outside. She shifted and streaked off into the woods, heading for her den. The lassitude left from her time with Francesca still lingered, and she wanted to sleep while she could. Once she set out to hunt, there would be no rest.

❖

Becca sat at a small window table in a Starbucks on Lark Street, ignoring the pedestrians passing by the window as she transcribed her notes into her laptop. She hadn't really expected the ER doctor to give her much of anything, but she'd been pleasantly surprised when she'd gotten a genuine quote-worthy response. She glanced at the photo of Sylvan Mir and Drake McKennan, wishing she knew the true story behind that encounter. The passion almost jumped—

Her cell phone rang and she dug it out of her bag. "Becca Land."

"Were you able to determine if the wolf had slipped her leash?"

"If we had this discussion face-to-face," Becca said, "we'd both probably get a lot more out of it."

"As I explained earlier," the slightly muffled voice rejoined, "I'm not currently able to reveal my interest in the developing situation."

"What exactly is the situation?" Becca asked, fishing a pad of paper and pen out of her bag one-handed. She hastily noted the date and time.

"I thought I made that clear earlier. Humans are being contaminated, infected, *perverted* by these…creatures. And America's new darling—the beautiful, Ivy League-educated Councilor Mir—is the worst animal of them all."

Becca's skin literally crawled, because this person did not sound crazy, if she didn't actually listen to what was being said. Though indistinct, the voice was cultured and well modulated. She could imagine its owner sitting behind a desk in a multimillion-dollar high-rise office building or sipping brandy in a private club. Nothing overtly insane or extreme. But the venom curdled her blood.

"There doesn't seem to be any proof of this…contamination,"

Becca said. "If you know something, then give me a lead. Someone to talk to."

"There will be more. Soon."

"Where…"

The caller disconnected.

"God damn it," Becca fumed, scribbling madly. The mysterious caller had contacted her at five that morning, urging her to look at the early morning edition of the city rag. When she asked why, the answer was that the Weres were hiding a secret that could threaten human existence. The implication was Sylvan Mir was on the verge of losing control of her *animals*, as the caller put it.

Becca was an investigative reporter. She followed a story, no matter how slim the lead, and if there was anything at all to this story, she had a hunch it was going to be big. She sipped her cold coffee and thought about her next move. She didn't have one. But she hadn't gotten to this point in her career by sitting back and waiting for the breaks to come to her. She made things happen. She picked up her cell phone, scrolled through her contacts, and pushed a number.

"Gates," a smoky voice said. "Praetern crime division."

"Becca Land, Detective." Becca wondered how the decorated detective felt having been shunted from the elite Crimes Against Persons division to the hastily formed PCD when her father had come out as a Vampire, dragging Jody Gates into the light with him. So to speak.

"I'm busy, Ms. Land. I'm afraid I don't have any sensational news for you today."

"I'm an investigative reporter," Becca said, trying and failing not to be annoyed by the always annoying detective. Why it bothered her that she got no respect from this one detective when she had a good working relationship with other detectives on the crime beat, she didn't know.

"If you say so. I'm still busy. Goodb—"

"Wait! What do you know about some kind of Were infection getting out of control?" Becca said hastily.

Jody was silent for a long moment. "Are you telling me that *you* know something about it?"

"How big a problem is it?"

"You're fishing."

"I'm in the right pond, aren't I?"

Jody sighed. "I don't have anything for you. But if you know something, I need you to tell me."

"You see," Becca said conversationally, "the way this works is that you help me out and I help you out."

"Why would I want to do that?"

"Because we both want the same thing, Detective. We both want—"

"You want a headline with your name underneath it," Jody said, and the sting was back in her voice. "I want to prevent senseless deaths."

"You sanctimonious bastard," Becca said, losing the reins on her temper. "You don't know me or what I want."

"No, I don't," Jody said in her infuriatingly icy-calm voice. "But allow me to give you a piece of advice, nonetheless. If you keep fishing, you're likely to pull up something that you can't handle."

"Oh please," Becca snapped. "Are you trying to frighten me now?"

"If I wanted to frighten you, I can think of much more pleasant ways to do it."

The Vampire's voice slid along her spine like deliciously cool fingers on a scorching summer day. Becca tightened in places she didn't want to tighten, especially when talking to this infuriating... Vampire. She realized she was breathing a little bit faster just before she realized that a Vampire's hearing was acute enough to tell that over the phone. If she hadn't already known, Jody's throaty chuckle would have confirmed it.

"Bastard," Becca muttered.

"I'll make a deal with you," Jody said, her voice businesslike again.

"I'm listening."

"If you get a lead on any kind of unusual condition affecting the Weres, you don't go off investigating on your own. You call me."

Becca snorted. "Where's the part where I get something out of this?"

"You stay alive."

"Not good enough."

"That's a very foolish thing for a mortal to say."

"I'm not going to waste my life doing nothing because I'm afraid of dying." As soon she said it, Becca wondered why she had. The few encounters she'd had with Detective Jody Gates had been uniformly frustrating, if not downright infuriating. Somehow, being dismissed by the elegant, always calm and cool Vampire annoyed her no end. And now, she was getting very close to revealing herself to her.

"Believe it or not," Jody said, "I understand that."

Becca caught her breath. She was curious. Everyone was curious where the Vampires were concerned, and by nature, she more than most. Still, she felt an almost strange reluctance to probe, which was completely unlike her. "But why would you...I mean, dying really doesn't change things for you all that much. Does it?"

Her question came out sounding almost gentle, not like her usual in-your-face interrogation style. Gates had a way of turning her around and upside down, and Becca didn't like it.

"Being animate is not quite the same thing as being alive," Jody said quietly.

"Will you help me?" Becca asked.

"Will you promise not to take unnecessary chances?" Jody countered.

"I'm going to do my job, but if you promise to keep me in the loop...anything you have, I get it first. Exclusive. I'll let you know if I hear anything."

"And?"

Becca found herself smiling, unaccountably charmed. "And I'll be careful. No chances."

"Then we have a deal," Jody said.

"Thank you," Becca said softly. She disconnected and leaned back in her chair, knowing she was flushed and imagining cool fingers gliding over her slick skin. Shaking her head at her foolishness, she picked up her pen and focused on her notes. Such an annoying Vampire.

❖

Drake had a few extra minutes before her evening shift started, so she detoured through Washington Park on her way to the hospital from her apartment on Madison Avenue. The air held the hazy yellow glow of an August twilight and smelled like freshly mown grass. Strangely melancholic, she circled the small lake in the center of the park, watching couples stroll hand in hand or picnic with sandwiches spread out on white squares of deli paper. She tried to recall the last time she had a picnic meal. She didn't bother trying to remember the last time she'd held someone's hand. A group of noisy teenaged boys shoved past her on the winding path, and she watched them go, kings of their own small universe. She wondered if they were Weres, but she didn't think so. They didn't move with the kind of loose-jointed grace that was so typical of Sylvan and her wolves. Drake thought of Misha having been attacked in this park the night before, of the terror in her eyes, and Sylvan's tender fury. She wondered if she'd ever see the Were Alpha again.

Sylvan hadn't responded to her request to talk to her. Drake had stayed at the hospital until midafternoon, studying the charts of the patients she and Sophia suspected had succumbed to Were fever. The patients were eerily similar—so much so that the coincidences continued to nag at her mind. All girls in their mid teens, all unidentified—assumed to be runaways. Three Caucasians, one Asian. All moderately malnourished, as if they hadn't always lived on the streets. Drake knew the look. Growing up, she'd seen plenty of street kids cycled in and out of the state home—thin bodies and hard eyes. The girls had presented to the ER at intervals of about a month, which wouldn't have been remarkable unless someone had been looking for it. She wasn't surprised that no one had associated their deaths as part of a pattern. Even she wasn't entirely certain yet that it was. If the detective hadn't shown up that morning and awakened her curiosity, she might never have put the picture together.

She had so many questions, and no answers. Why these girls? And what was it that had killed them? How had they gotten infected?

Turning out of the park, she started up New Scotland Avenue. She probably should just let it go. The Weres—in fact, all of the Praeterns—had managed to survive without the intervention of human medicine and science for millennia. But these patients weren't Weres, and even if they were, she didn't care. Because she *did* care.

She followed the winding driveway to the main ER entrance, wishing she knew how to reach Sylvan. She'd left a message on her answering machine at her Council office, but she didn't hold out much hope for a response. Maybe Sophia would relay her request...

The sound of tires screeching behind her yanked her out of her aimless ruminations and back to stark reality. She jumped onto the bumper of a parked EMS van and clung to the door handle as a low, long black sedan roared past and slammed to a halt in front of the ER. The rear door opened and a body rolled out onto the pavement. Then the car roared away.

"Someone get a gurney," Drake shouted as she ran to the motionless naked girl lying facedown in the road. She turned her carefully, vaguely aware of people racing out of the ER toward her.

The girl couldn't be more than fifteen. She was so pale. White, nearly bloodless. Pink froth covered her mouth. Drake wasn't certain she was breathing. She rested her hand in the middle of a pitifully thin chest, hoping to feel respirations. The girl was hot. Burning up. Her temperature had to be 105 degrees. Her muscles were rigid. At this rate, she would seize any second.

"Get an IV in both arms," Drake snapped to the two ER techs who now knelt on either side of the girl. One of the nurses pushed a crash cart over the uneven driveway toward her. "Set up a bicarb drip and get me a hundred milligrams of dantrolene."

"Should we try to get her inside?" the nurse asked, handing Drake a pair of gloves.

Drake pulled them on automatically. "No, there's no time. Somebody get an ET tube ready. And page the Were medic on call STAT."

The tech who had been about to start an IV jerked back. "Is she a Were?"

"I don't know." Drake looked up at him. "What difference does it make? Put that IV in."

"Doctor," the nurse said anxiously, "maybe we should wait?"

The girl arched off the ground as if her body were an overtightened bow about to snap. Then she began to seize.

"Hell." Drake slid her thumb into the corner of the girl's mouth and gripped her chin, forcing her jaws to open a fraction. "Give me a laryngoscope and the ET tube."

Drake eased the metal blade of the laryngoscope between the girl's teeth, trying to move her tongue aside so she could see the vocal cords. The back of her throat was filled with thick, bloody fluid. She'd have to pass the tube blindly. Lifting a little more on the laryngoscope, Drake bent closer, the plastic ET tube held between her thumb and first two fingers. Just as she was about to slide it into the corner of the girl's mouth, the girl convulsed violently, dislodging the laryngoscope. Drake tried to cushion the girl's head to prevent her from injuring herself, and before she could even register the movement, the girl lashed out and sank her teeth into Drake's forearm.

CHAPTER TWELVE

Sylvan sent Val and Max into the park to search for the site where Misha and the boys were attacked. Misha's blood would be easy to scent, and from there, Val could track the rogues back to their lair. When in pelt, Val was only slightly smaller than Max and just as muscular from her many hours in the forest on four feet. No one would mistake the big gray wolves for dogs, but they were expert at disappearing in the shadows. Andrew parked the Rover along a darkened portion of the street bordering the south edge of the park while he and Sylvan waited for the others to pick up a trail.

Andrew had tied his thick, shoulder-length red hair back with a leather thong, and in his skintight black pants and T-shirt, he looked as delicately lethal as a stiletto. Sylvan wore tight leather pants and boots. Narrow leather bands encircled both biceps. Her bare chest glinted silver under the rising moon as her wolf prowled close to the skin. Her power filled the cab with a heady mixture of adrenaline and pheromones and Andrew growled softly, the crotch of his pants tenting at her call.

"Soon," Sylvan murmured, rubbing the back of his neck. He turned his head and brushed his cheek against her palm.

"What if they can't catch a scent?" Andrew asked.

"Fala gave us the locations of several rogue sightings in the last week. If we have to, we'll check them all. But Val will find it," Sylvan said, and as if her speaking the words were enough, a howl rose into the night. Sylvan tilted her head, listening. "They're heading east, to the waterfront. Let's go."

Sylvan directed Andrew as she followed the scent and sound of her wolves through the streets. She pointed to an overgrown lot adjoining a decrepit warehouse that had once been a receiving station for South American cocoa beans, before containers allowed offloading directly from ships to eighteen-wheelers. "There."

Andrew cut the engine and let the Rover coast to a stop. Sylvan stepped out of the passenger side and surveyed the building. Part of the roof was caved in and many of the rectangular multipane windows were broken. The sliding cargo bay door hung half off its hinges. Max and Val appeared out of the darkness, panting, eyes shining with the thrill of the hunt.

"Andrew," Sylvan murmured. "Join them."

Andrew shifted and all three wolves crowded close against Sylvan's legs.

"If you smell Misha on any of them," Sylvan said as she combed her fingers through the thick pelts of the wolves at her side, "bring them to me."

Max whined, eager to hunt. Val's heavy muscles trembled as she waited, poised, for her Alpha's command. Sylvan threw back her head and howled, an eerie, haunting cry that cleaved the night and left the darkness to bleed. She swept both arms toward the windows on either side of the cargo bay doors. "Go."

Max and Val streaked across the lot, gray shadows bounding over knee-high weeds. Sylvan raced with Andrew by her side, hitting the opening in the bay doors at the same time as Max and Val crashed through the windows and landed in the dank interior. Still in skin form, Sylvan howled again and her wolves snarled. Screams and garbled shouts erupted. Frantic footsteps pounded in the darkness. The stench of fear and sickness hung like clouds in the fetid air.

Sylvan's eyesight was hyperacute in any form, but she didn't need to see to find her prey. She scented them—acrid, panic-soaked bodies undercut with decay. They weren't just starving, they were dying. Poisoned.

"DSX," she spat. These rogues were addicted to desoxyephedrine, a variant of methamphetamine, one of the few drugs capable of corrupting Were physiology. The addiction was rapid and irreversible. When first exposed, users became hypersexual and hyperaggressive. Eventually, addicted Weres turned rabid, attacking anything warm-blooded, including humans, before spiraling into mindless psychosis.

Humans destroyed themselves with the drug. Weres became killing machines before disintegrating into burned-out husks. If these rogues were in the end stages of DSX poisoning, death would be a mercy.

Sylvan stalked into the bowels of the building, tracking her prey. Her body slashed through the shafts of moonlight filtering through gaps in the roof, and as she misted in and out of the shadows, her hunters circled the periphery, inexorably closing in on the rogues from all sides. Within minutes, she and her wolves surrounded three quivering males in their late teens.

Sylvan scented the air. "There was a fourth." She telegraphed to Val, *Go. Take him before he calls others.*

The rogues were all in skin form, so filthy their hair color was indiscernible. Cloaked in rags, bright eyed with impending insanity, they were only days from immolation. Sylvan stood over them with legs spread, hands on hips. Beside her, Andrew and Max prowled, lips curled back, warning the rogues away from their Alpha.

"Who is supplying the DSX?" Sylvan snarled.

"Fuck you, bitch," one spat and lunged for her midsection. Max caught him in midair and tore his throat out.

Sylvan kept her gaze on the last two rogues as the dead male fell at her feet.

"Tell me now or I'll let my hunters have their kill."

"Oh Jesus, it was Rex!" the smaller of the two screamed. "It was one of Rex's bitches. His bitches run it!"

"Where are they?" Sylvan demanded.

"I don't know. I don't know. He moves around all the time. On the waterfront, mostly."

The second rogue cuffed the one who was talking on the side of the head. "Shut up." He sneered at Sylvan, his features contorted with insanity. "Rex will tear your heart out and eat it, you cunt bitch."

Sylvan tilted her head, slowly scenting the air. "You smell like my wolf, rogue. No one touches my wolves."

Slaver dripped from his lips and his eyes rolled wildly. "She screamed like the weak little bitch she is."

"You trespassed on my territory and violated Pack law," Sylvan said, her voice chilled steel. "The penalty is death."

Between one breath and the next, Sylvan shifted and launched herself at the one who had attacked Misha. A streak of silver death, she caught him by the neck, the force of her body taking him to the floor. She could have killed him then, but she wanted to send a message. She backed away, circling, and gave him time to shift. He was a big rabid black wolf, his eyes frenzied, his penis swollen. Saliva hung in strings from his jaws. He rushed her, his lips pulled back and his canines slashing. One second she was motionless, the next a blur. She cut low and to the side, and his jaws clamped on empty air. Hers closed around his right foreleg, crushing it. He howled and flung his head around, his teeth snapping inches from her face. She darted away and he staggered. He was drug mad, oblivious to his injuries. Head down, growling wildly, he charged her again. Sylvan twisted out of his path and slashed his shoulder to the bone. He stumbled, dragged himself around, and crouched to strike a third time.

She could have crippled him, one limb at time, and then gutted him—leaving him to die a slow, agonizing death. But he was still a wolf, and she had made her point. She was faster, stronger, more deadly. She was Alpha. When he was almost on top of her, she leapt over him. Before he could turn and make another run at her, she vaulted onto his back and bit at his jugular. He went down, a fountain of blood arcing into the murk. Within seconds, he twitched and lay still.

Sylvan raised her head and howled. Her wolves joined her. Misha had been avenged. Justice had been served.

The remaining rogue huddled on the floor with his arms over his head. Sylvan shifted and crouched beside him. "Remember this. Tell Rex that the Alpha of the Timberwolf Pack is coming for him, and I won't be as merciful."

He whimpered. Urine stained the front of his jeans and dripped onto the floor.

Sylvan straightened and stalked away. "Throw the bodies in the river."

Outside she breathed deeply, letting the warm summer scents purge her lungs of death and decay. Her wolves would be sure the bodies did not surface until there was nothing left but bone. She took no satisfaction in the killing. She'd done what was necessary to preserve order. She ruled a species whose instincts were primal and lethal. Were justice was harsh and absolute. Her word was law, and none could be allowed to forget or flout it. If she could not personally enforce Pack law, she could not lead.

She opened the rear gate of the Rover and extracted jeans from the pile they had packed earlier. She pulled them on as the others, having shifted to skin, joined her and dressed.

"You tracked the runner?" Sylvan asked Val.

"To an empty warehouse a quarter of a mile from here," Val reported. "Wolves had been there as recently as last night. A lot of them."

"And the rogue who escaped?"

"He won't be a threat to anyone again." Val's lips pulled back in a grin. "Are we going after this Rex tonight?"

"No," Sylvan said. "I want to find out more before we hunt. Where he came from, who supplies him. How many rogues he has assembled. Where they're headquartered." She embraced her hunters, one after the other.

"Tonight was for Misha. You fought well."

❖

"I'm all right," Drake told Sophia, trying not to clench her jaws at the lacerating pain shooting up her arm as Sophia cleansed the bite. Blood oozed from the punctures halfway between her wrist and elbow, and the skin around the wounds had already turned purple. "Lori gave me an IM dose of antibiotics."

Sophia finished wrapping gauze around Drake's arm and glanced behind her at the closed curtain. "It's not infection we need to worry about. It's been less than an hour and your temperature is elevated already."

"Only a degree. That could be attributed to the trauma itself." As soon as the words left Drake's mouth, she shivered violently and her teeth chattered. Sophia stuck a thermometer under her tongue. The LCD readout registered 102 degrees.

"What will happen if I develop Were fever?" Drake asked when the rigor passed.

"I don't know," Sophia said, her discomfort obvious.

"But you know what might happen, don't you?"

Sophia hesitated, then seemed to come to a decision. "If the fever doesn't kill you, you'll turn."

"Turn." An icy hand gripped Drake's heart even as her skin flushed hotter. "What are the chances?"

"Most humans never turn."

Drake wrapped her arms around herself as another chill shook her so badly she could barely remain sitting upright. "You mean they die before they turn."

Sophia nodded miserably.

"And if they turn? Are they...okay?"

"Sometimes," Sophia said softly.

"And the rest of the time?"

"They're rabid."

"And rabid wolves are executed," Drake said.

Sophia looked away.

"I can't stay here if I might turn and attack someone." Drake heaved herself off the stretcher and her legs gave way. Her thigh and back muscles cramped and she doubled over. "Oh God. It's moving fast. Sophia—"

"It's rhabdomyolysis. You may lose consciousness soon."

Gasping, Drake said, "Can you get me somewhere I won't be a threat to anyone?"

"Yes." Sophia grabbed Drake around the waist, steadying her until the cramps subsided. "Can you walk out of here so we don't arouse suspicion?"

Drake gritted her teeth and nodded. Her vision was blurry, her body a mass of lancing pain. "But we have to go now. I don't...have long."

"If you can make it through the ER, my car is right outside."

"Let's go." Through the haze of agony, Drake could see Sophia hesitate. She forced out a word. "What?"

"You may not have a chance to tell us later." Sophia cupped Drake's face in her palm. "You have a choice. If you don't want to turn, the Alpha will be quick and merciful."

"I'm not afraid of turning. I just don't want to be a danger to anyone." Drake clutched her stomach as another spasm struck. "Tell Sylvan...I trust her. Tell her to do...what must be done."

CHAPTER THIRTEEN

S *he said to tell you she was coming for you and she wouldn't*
be merciful.

Rex's blood simmered with the desire to kill the messenger, but he needed all the spies he could recruit. The howlers—end-stage DSX addicts—traded information for drugs, and since their lifespan was unpredictable, he tried to keep them around until they were too psychotic to be useful. He had a network of spies all over the urban territory. Still other rogues, non-addicts, held regular jobs in very valuable positions like the police department and even City Hall, but he relied on his underworld informants for critical intelligence. If word got out that he killed them when they delivered bad news, his supply of information might suddenly dry up. So, instead of shredding this one's skin from his bones, Rex buried his claws in the sniveling howler's shoulder and dragged him to his feet.

"What else did you tell her?" Rex demanded, slashing the howler's cheek with his canines. Right now he was sequestered in the shadows under a highway overpass with two of his most trusted lieutenants and a handful of rogue street soldiers. He needed to find out just what the weaklings had revealed before Sylvan Mir had killed them. "What does she know about us?"

"Nothing, nothing," the howler cried. "She just killed Danny and told me to tell you…what I told you."

"And you ran straight from the killing ground to my headquarters!" The howler had staggered into headquarters screaming that the Alpha bitch and her lackeys had just killed three of Rex's street soldiers. He'd been forced to evacuate for fear the bitch would track the one she'd spared right to him. For thirty panicked minutes, his lieutenants had loaded the recent shipment of DSX, weapons, and most of the rogues into trucks. Rex had given instructions to store weapons and drugs in disparate locations in the city in case his network was compromised. Fortunately, he never disclosed anything of importance to low-level soldiers and especially not to the howlers, so his secondary outposts should be safe. Still, he needed new headquarters.

"I'm sorry, Rex," the howler sobbed. "I just wanted to warn you."

Rex raked his claws down the howler's back in fury and frustration. Why was he forced to build an army with pathetic scum, when he should have been leading an entire Pack of the strongest Weres on earth to their rightful destiny?

"Why didn't she kill you?" Rex snarled. "You smell of submissive piss. What did you promise her?"

"Nothing! Nothing, I swear, Rex! I never said anything. It was all over so fast…she grabbed Danny so fast, she was so fast…"

The howler started babbling about the bitch being so strong and so fast and Rex couldn't contain his rage any longer. He snapped the howler's neck and threw his spasming body on the ground.

"Let the bitch come," he shouted to everyone within hearing distance. "The sooner she's dead, the sooner we will reclaim what's ours."

One of the bitches tried to lick the blood running down the dead howler's back and Rex kicked her away with a booted foot. She whined and tried to wrap herself around his leg, one clawed hand grasping at his groin. He snarled at her and she cowered, her eyes feverish, her emaciated body trembling. The DSX had triggered her heat and her body was consuming itself with the outpouring of hormones that drove her to keep coupling until she was bred. But Were fertility was naturally very low, and that, combined with the debilitating effects of the drugs, made it unlikely she would conceive. If the unrelenting heat didn't kill her, the DSX eventually would. Impatiently, he signaled the circling dominants to deal with her. The four rogue dominants had been waiting for the Alpha to mount her or give them permission, and now they snarled and snapped and clawed at each other. The most dominant, a male, quickly drove the others away. The groveling female in heat crawled toward him on all fours and he thrust his heavy penis into her from the rear with a savage growl.

Rex ignored them and summoned his two guards. "I need to know whenever Mir leaves the Compound. As long as she's there, she's protected. Outside—we'll have the advantage."

A muscle-bound male with shaggy black hair snapped to attention. "Yes, Rex."

"Tomorrow, I want double the runners to move out that product."

Rex stalked out from under cover of the soaring concrete abutments and opened his cell phone. He selected a programmed number and waited.

"I told you not to call this number," a cool, modulated voice answered.

"It couldn't wait until tomorrow," Rex said. "We may have a problem."

"We?"

"Sylvan Mir led a hunting party down here tonight."

"What does she know?" Rex's supplier asked carefully.

"Possibly nothing. It might have been in retaliation for a problem with one of her females," Rex said.

"What kind of problem? Now is not the time for foolish mistakes."

"It was nothing. A couple of rogues scuffled with some adolescents."

"Our business venture?"

"My end of things is fine," Rex growled.

"I'll take care of giving the *Alpha* something to worry about other than you and your activities."

"Just be sure the shipments aren't interrupted," Rex said.

"Be careful," the icy voice said softly. "You aren't the only renegade anxious to take Mir's place."

Rex cut off the call just as a high-pitched wail was wrung from the bitch in heat. His wolf lunged for freedom so quickly and ferociously he barely managed not to shift. He wanted a female, but not one of these wretched, submissive bitches. He wanted to feel a dominant female cowering beneath his body. He wanted to break Sylvan Mir.

❖

When Sylvan's cell phone rang she checked the readout and saw the call was from Niki. "Sylvan."

"Sophia called. We have a situation."

"What is it?"

"A human female was dropped off at Albany General with what looked like Were fever."

Sylvan checked their location through the window of the Rover. "It'll take me twenty minutes to get back there. Is Sophia handling damage control?"

"I think it's going to be more than she can handle."

"Is the press on it already?" Sylvan wondered if Sophia could reach Drake. Drake had offered her assistance, and even though Sylvan didn't want to involve a human in a situation she still didn't understand, she wanted to avoid media coverage that would raise panic.

"Not that I know of, but…chances are good they'll get wind of the story. The girl bit the ER doctor who tried to treat her. Sophia says the human is already toxic. I don't know if we can keep that quiet."

Sylvan snarled. "Is it Drake?"

"Yes."

"Where are they?" Sylvan's roar brought her guards to attention.

"Sophia got her out of the hospital. I couldn't reach you right away, so I told her to bring the human here."

Sylvan's wolf raged and howled in a protective frenzy, the instinct more potent than any she'd ever experienced. She couldn't fight it, didn't even try. The bones in her face angled and sharpened, her eyes flashed gold, and her claws tore through her fingertips. Her vocal cords thickened and her voice turned to sandpaper. "Sophia's ETA?"

"Ten minutes or so."

"We'll be right behind them. Tell Elena to prepare an isolation room."

"Alpha, the chances that she'll even survive that lon—"

"Do it!" Sylvan closed her phone so violently she crushed it in her palm. She threw the useless device on the floor. Plaintive whines and growls rose from the rear compartment. Val and Max had shifted when Sylvan's wolf had ascended, and now they paced restlessly behind her.

She twisted in her seat and they both licked her face. Then she glanced at Andrew, who gripped the wheel with rigid arms, fighting not to shift. Sylvan commanded her snarling wolf into the shadows, and Andrew relaxed perceptibly. He and Lara had the strongest ability to resist the call when Sylvan's wolf ascended, which is why one of them usually drove. Any less dominant wolf Were would have been powerless to resist when Sylvan was in mid-shift. "Get me back to the Compound. *Now.*"

❖

The Rover roared down the narrow forest trail and into the Compound. A dark SUV was parked in front of the infirmary. Sophia's car, Sylvan surmised. Andrew had barely begun to slow when Sylvan bounded from the vehicle and raced toward the infirmary. Niki, naked except for a pair of black leather pants unsnapped at the waist, appeared from out of the shadows on the wide porch and planted herself at the top of the steps.

"Move," Sylvan growled, canines flashing in the moonlight, her wolf ready to attack anyone who got in her way. She'd partially shifted again, her attack hormones surging.

Niki shuddered and her skin glowed golden red. "You can't go in there like that."

Sylvan snarled and pushed Niki back with a hand in the middle of her bare chest. Her claws pressed into but did not pierce Niki's skin.

"Elena will shift, Alpha," Niki panted, the pain of holding down her wolf nearly doubling her over. She'd never felt Sylvan's fury this uncontrolled, and she'd never been pulled into the maelstrom so completely. Even when they hunted, she was able to stay in skin form if she needed to. She dropped to her knees as her bones battled to morph. A trail of red-gray fur shimmered down the center of her abdomen and dove beneath the waistband of her leather pants. "Alpha…" She gasped. "Alpha, if I can't control myself, Elena…"

Sylvan closed her eyes and pulled cool night air deep into her lungs. Once again, she battled down her wolf, by sheer force of will suppressing her most primal instincts to guard and possess. She had to see Drake, and Drake needed medical care. If her agitation and aggression caused Elena and Sophia to shift involuntarily, Drake would suffer for it. She couldn't let that happen. A frustrated rumble rose from Sylvan's chest as she finally overpowered her wolf. Niki's breathing eased and the traces of pelt receded from her tight belly. Sylvan dropped a hand on Niki's damp head. "Thank you."

Whimpering in relief, Niki tilted her head back and Sylvan cupped her jaw, her thumb brushing the corner of Niki's mouth. "Stand guard for me, *Imperator.* No one comes inside."

"Yes, Alpha," Niki whispered.

❖

Elena closed the door of the last room at the far end of the infirmary. She regarded Sylvan storming toward her and held up one hand. "You can't come in right now."

Sylvan restrained herself from physically lifting Elena aside, but the effort taxed every bit of her control. "I want to see her."

"It's not safe. I had to send Sophia out a few minutes ago." Elena backed against the door, her face blanching as Sylvan growled threateningly. Her luminous dark eyes were smudged with worry, the hollows below her bold cheekbones deeper, etched with exhaustion. "The fever is progressing quickly. The human is irrational most of the time. She's dangerous."

"She won't hurt me," Sylvan said, gritting her teeth to keep her wolf at bay. She felt as if she were being pummeled from the inside out, her flesh threatening to tear from her bones. "She hasn't hurt you or Sophia, has she?"

"We don't know how this strain of fever affects a human," Elena said, her expression imploring. "We don't know if her bite is capable of inducing fever in us. We can't risk the Alpha—"

"If it's not safe for me, it's less safe for you." Sylvan braced her arms on the door on either side of Elena's shoulders and leaned down so her face was level with that of the smaller female. "I could force you to let me in, but I won't. Elena, look at me."

Elena tilted her head against the door and raised her eyes to Sylvan's. She whimpered at the intensity in Sylvan's gaze and wrapped her arms around Sylvan's shoulders. She was tired and frightened, and she needed Sylvan's strength. Sylvan kissed her forehead.

"I need to see her. I need to understand what we're facing if this spreads to more humans." Sylvan spoke the truth, but it wasn't the entire truth. She needed to see Drake, touch her, shield her from whatever threatened her. Drake was human, but she felt like Pack. Sylvan didn't question her instincts, couldn't change the ingrained drives that ruled her life. She only knew what she must do. "The survival of our Pack depends on us containing this outbreak."

"We can't lose you," Elena whispered, her fingers digging into Sylvan's shoulders. "Misha is asking for you. She needs you. We need you."

Sylvan called her wolf and broadcast her strength and power throughout the Compound and far into the forest surrounding them. A wolf howled outside on the porch—Niki. A higher-pitched howl followed—Lara. A deeper howl, then another, and another as Max and Andrew and Val added their voices. They were joined by others until the air was filled with sound of the Pack uniting in harmony and trust.

"I will never forsake you," Sylvan murmured, her lips against Elena's temple. "But I must do what is necessary. Let me pass, my wolf."

Elena cleaved to Sylvan for a long moment, then stepped aside.

"Do not enter, no matter what you sense," Sylvan said as she stepped through the door.

A single shaded lamp burned dimly on a narrow dresser against the far wall. Beneath the window, a naked form lay bathed in moonlight. Drake's dark hair lay in wet strands across her forehead and feathered against her cheek and neck. Her jaws were clenched, her chin tilted upward, accentuating the smooth column of her neck. Her back arched as if she was straining for a lover's embrace, the long muscles in her abdomen tight, her arms and legs trembling. Her breasts, firm with small hard, dark nipples, lifted and fell with each quick breath.

Sylvan recognized the scent she associated with Drake—sharp and smoky, like aged red wine. But now there was more—a dark, tangy undercurrent that promised wild pleasures. Her clitoris lengthened, her sex glands swelled, and she growled. She smelled wolf.

Drake turned her head. "Sylvan?"

"Yes." Sylvan knelt by the bed and rested the backs of her fingers against Drake's cheek. Her skin was fiery, her eyes fever-bright. Sylvan noticed a plastic catheter taped to Drake's left forearm. "Do you know how to treat this?"

"No," Drake gasped as a cramp gripped her insides. "Told Sophia what medicines to try. Don't know…if it will work."

"Do you want to turn?" Sylvan pushed her fingers into Drake's hair, forced Drake's eyes to meet hers. "Will you accept being Were?"

"Yes," Drake groaned, gripping Sylvan's arm. "The fever might be fatal."

"I won't let you die." Sylvan had only seen a few humans afflicted by Were fever, and most died from some kind of toxic shock within a matter of a few hours. A few survived, their cells carrying altered mitochondrial genetic material, mutated during the course of the fever. Turned Weres. All but one, rabid. She had not been Alpha then, and it had not been her responsibility to order the executions. She would not do it now.

Drake shivered. "Don't let me hurt anyone."

"I won't."

"Can't fight."

Sylvan didn't know how she knew, but she knew. She could sense the wolf straining to emerge. She cupped the back of Drake's neck and leaned close to her. "Don't fight."

Drake's eyes were closing, her body beginning to shake. Convulsions.

"Drake," Sylvan shouted, gripping her neck harder. "Don't fight. Let her come. Let her come."

Drake screamed and thrashed, blood-tinged saliva collecting at the corners of her mouth. Her eyes rolled back and her jaws snapped violently, mere millimeters from Sylvan's arm. The door burst open and Niki charged into the room. She grabbed Sylvan and jerked her away from the bed.

"No," Sylvan roared, lashing out, her claws catching Niki across the shoulder. Only the smell of Niki's blood, the one wolf she trusted above all others, prevented her from ripping Niki's throat out.

Niki shoved Sylvan against the wall, rivulets of blood painting her chest crimson. "She's not worth it!"

"Get away from me," Sylvan warned, her eyes wolf-gold.

Niki dropped to her knees, wrapped her arms around Sylvan's hips, and pressed her face against Sylvan's abdomen. "No."

Across the room, Drake writhed, screaming.

"Elena," Sylvan shouted.

The Pack medic rushed into the room.

"Help her," Sylvan demanded.

Niki, driven to submit after challenging her Alpha, licked Sylvan's stomach, her fingers opening the buttons on Sylvan's fly. Her canines grazed Sylvan's belly as she dragged her mouth lower.

"Don't." Sylvan threaded her fingers through Niki's hair and guided her upright. "Go outside. Calm the others. I'll be all right."

"Please, Alpha," Niki implored. "There's nothing anyone can do. Let me kill her."

"I don't want to hurt you, but if you touch her, I will." Sylvan gently kissed her on the mouth. "I need you. I need you by my side."

Niki trembled, torn between her need to obey and her need to protect. Caught between love and duty. "When the time comes to be merciful, call on me. Let me do this for you."

Sylvan shook her head. "I will do what needs be done."

CHAPTER FOURTEEN

Detective Gates, please," Becca said when Jody's cell phone rang through to the dispatcher.

"I'm sorry," a bored voice replied. "Detective Gates is not on duty tonight. Would you like to leave a message?"

"No, thank you." Becca hung up. She'd promised Gates she would contact her if something popped in the Were investigation. She'd called her, she'd kept her promise.

She hastily dressed in a sleeveless green silk blouse, black slacks, and low heels. After double-checking her bag to be sure she had her phone, her recorder, and a digital camera, she grabbed her car keys off the small table inside her front door, hurried into the foyer, and jabbed the elevator down button.

Impatiently, she watched the lighted numerals as the elevator climbed toward the eighth floor of her waterfront condo building. Her watch read 3:05 a.m. Ten minutes had passed since she'd been awakened by a call from the man—at least she thought the muffled voice was male—she had dubbed Mr. X. He'd told her to check the hospital for a victim of Were fever. He'd disconnected before she could ask him for a name.

Fifteen minutes later she was in the ER at Albany General.

"Hi, Charlie, how's it going?" she said to the admissions clerk, an implacable thin bald man with wire-rimmed glasses who always wore a white dress shirt and creased khaki trousers. He sat at the counter in a cubicle separated from the patient admitting area by a sliding glass barrier. Becca knew the night crew in the ER better than the daytime staff because crime picked up at night, and crime was her beat. When she couldn't get a doctor to even see her, let alone talk to her—which was pretty much one hundred percent of the time—she could usually find a nurse or tech who would give her a little bit of information. Charlie pointed to the rows of orange plastic bucket seats bolted to the floor, most of which were filled with patients waiting to be seen.

"Night's been crazy and it isn't even a full moon," he said in a low voice. "Who you looking for?"

Becca checked behind her to make sure no one was in hearing distance and leaned through the window for a little more privacy. "Did you sign in any Weres tonight?"

Charlie's brows drew down, three perfect rows of horizontal lines appearing in his smooth forehead. "Most of the time that's not something they put on their admission forms."

"I know." Becca thought of the photograph in the morning paper. If a Were had been brought in with something serious, wouldn't the Alpha be contacted? "How about Sylvan Mir? Was she here?"

"You see any news vans out in the parking lot?" Charlie groused. "Anywhere she goes, the press follows like a little gaggle of geese."

Becca laughed. "I resent that."

Charlie looked over his shoulder and bent forward, lowering his voice. "The Were medic—Sophia—she came in a couple of hours ago. I've been so busy up here, I didn't have a chance to find out who she was seeing."

"Is she still here?" Becca asked.

"I think I saw her leave. Like I said, it's been a zoo."

"Who would know?" Becca asked eagerly.

"The charge nurse—Harry Fitzpatrick. Good luck getting him to give you any information."

Becca knew Harry. He was an ex-army corpsman who'd gotten his nursing degree after serving two tours in Iraq. He ran the ER like he was still there, and he wasn't going to give her anything. What she needed was a little official weight if she wanted to ferret out details about a patient. What she needed was a cop. "Thanks anyhow, Charlie."

"Sorry I can't be of more help."

"No problem." Becca walked outside to use her cell phone. She called Jody Gates's number again and got the same dispatcher. She hung up. Since Vampires didn't sleep at night, Becca figured the detective was out somewhere.

So where would a Vampire be at four a.m. on her night off? Only one place came to mind.

❖

Niki returned to her post on the porch to guard the door to the infirmary. Leaving Sylvan in danger was physically painful. Her skin beaded with sweat as her wolf savaged her, demanding to return to the Alpha's side. It took every bit of her control to stay outside, and she was barely able to restrain her aggression. Snarling, ready to fight, she whirled toward the sound of someone approaching.

Sophia stepped into a circle of starlight at the bottom of the stairs. Unlike Niki, who was still shirtless and barefoot in leather pants, Sophia wore a scooped-neck tee and low-rider jeans. A swath of smooth skin glimmered between the bottom of her tee and the waistband of her pants. Her long blond hair was pulled back in a careless ponytail, heightening the angular beauty of her features. In pelt she was a pure white wolf with striking blue eyes. Smaller than Niki, fine boned and lithe. Quick on the hunt. Niki always ran with the Alpha, but she was always aware of Sophia whenever she ran with the Pack.

"I need to go back inside," Sophia said quietly as she climbed the steps.

"No." Niki didn't move, but the dominance in her voice made Sophia stop abruptly.

Sophia let her gaze drift across Niki's face, searching but not long enough to challenge. Niki's eyes were bright with pain, the bones in her face on the verge of morphing. She was in agony, and there was nothing Sophia could do to help her. "Niki, I can't leave Elena alone any longer. I need to help her."

"It's not safe," Niki growled.

"No," Sophia said softly, resting her fingers on Niki's rigid forearm. "It isn't. Please let me go inside."

Niki trembled at the gentle touch. Her wolf stopped pacing and tilted her head, as if listening for a long-awaited call in the night. "I can't. The Alpha has ordered that no one is to go in."

"Drake will die, Niki."

"Good. She should." Niki shook off Sophia's hand. "Go."

Sophia was not submissive, not in the ordinary sense of pack hierarchy. She could have resisted Niki's command, at least long enough to argue. But she knew if she tried, Niki *would* dominate her, and at a terrible cost when her wolf was already straining to break free. Sophia couldn't bear to add to her pain, so she turned and silently slipped into the dark.

❖

The huge lot in front of Club Nocturne was jammed, and despite the late hour, cars still streamed in off the four-lane highway that formed an invisible barricade between the waterfront and the rest of the city. Becca parked on the shoulder. She didn't want to get blocked in, and she'd rather take her chances sprinting across the lot for a quick getaway than risk being stuck in her car like a land-bound turtle. Not that she had any real reason to think she'd be in danger. Nocturne was part of her crime beat and she couldn't ever remember anything seriously bad being reported at the club. As she picked her way across the cracked and uneven pavement toward the dark sprawling edifice, it occurred to her that there might not be any crimes reported because the patrons volunteered for whatever happened to them inside.

Becca was surprised to see the club nearly full, even though post-Exodus the Vampire clubs could stay open all night. Most closed at sunrise, but not this one. In contrast to the bleak exterior, the interior was elegant and upscale. The beaten-tin ceiling was easily twenty-five feet high. Wall sconces cast muted cones of light into the cavernous space, leaving much of the room in pools of shadow. Many of the scattered glass and chrome tables, leather chairs, and sprawling leather sectionals were occupied by couples or groups who appeared to be having a very good time. She tried not to stare while wending her way to the bar that ran along one entire wall, but she could hardly avoid noticing the exposed bodies along the way. A male Vampire cradled a young woman in his lap, feeding from her neck while another woman knelt beside them and fondled the girl's breasts through the open laces of her skimpy leather bustier. The girl's face was a study in sensual bliss—her head thrown back, her eyes closed, her lips parted as if waiting for a kiss. Two female Vampires caressed a man stretched out on a leather sofa as they fed at his neck and groin, while next to them three male Vampires and a human female writhed in a constantly changing configuration of arms and legs and genitalia.

"I'll have a vodka tonic," Becca said when she finally reached the shining black granite-topped bar. The bartender, a bald macho type with a glinting diamond stud in his right earlobe, a mass of tattoos on his chest and arms, and multiple punctures in his neck took his time looking her over. Becca stared at him, refusing to be intimidated by his blatant sexual appraisal.

"You look like a virgin."

"I beg your pardon?"

"You've never been bitten, have you?"

"Is that a prerequisite for getting a drink?" Becca asked.

"Sightseeing can be a dangerous pastime." He turned around, mixed her drink, and put it down in front of her. He neglected to slip a cocktail napkin underneath. "Five bucks."

Becca put a twenty on the bar and continued to check out the room. She couldn't see everyone, even if she had wanted to look carefully, but she didn't immediately spy Detective Jody Gates anywhere. She should have been disappointed, but she was oddly relieved instead. She sipped the vodka tonic. It was decent.

"Have you seen Jody Gates?" Becca asked when the bartender came her way again.

He stopped and regarded her with a flicker of interest. "Why are you asking?"

"She's a friend." Becca didn't know how open Jody was about her job in this place, and she certainly wasn't about to announce she was a reporter.

"Down the far hall on the right. She likes the room on the end," the bartender said with a malicious edge to his voice.

"Thanks." Becca wondered if he thought she was the Vampire's girlfriend, or whatever the term would be, because he seemed to take pleasure in providing the information.

She worked her way around the edge of the room, preferring not to wade through the bacchanal again, and found the hall the bartender had indicated. A series of doors opened on either side of a long, narrow passageway. She made her way as quickly as possible through the clumps of humans and Vampires and others who were neither. Most were in the midst of sex and feeding.

Becca raised her hand to knock on the end door on the right when she realized the door was ajar. Pressing lightly with her fingertips, she edged it open a few more inches. Several muted recessed lights provided just enough illumination for her to make out the figures on the bed against one wall. Figures multiple, as in three. From her angle she could see the profiles of the two women who embraced in the center of the bed. Jody was still partially dressed in dark trousers and an unbuttoned white shirt that exposed a smooth pale torso and small round breasts that might have been carved from ivory, they appeared so perfect. The curvy young blonde who writhed in Jody's arms as they kissed was naked, one thigh thrown over Jody's hips. A man pressed against the blonde's back and angled his penis into her. He slowly thrust and withdrew with metronomic regularity, as if somehow detached from what was happening to the two women.

Mesmerized by the scene, Becca suddenly felt as if all her senses were heightened. The blonde's panting whimpers were as sharp and clear as if Becca had been holding the woman herself. When Jody cupped the blonde's breast and circled her erect pink nipple with her thumb, the woman's cry made Becca's sex clench. She imagined she could smell the blonde's arousal, feel the weight of her heavy breasts in her palm and the slick wetness of her sex rubbing against her thigh. She heard a dark murmur and saw the blonde nod vigorously. Jody's mouth was on her neck now and the blonde undulated even more frantically, driving her hips up and down on the phallus buried inside her.

Becca found herself breathing hard and forcibly quieted herself. The deep murmur came again, and Becca realized Jody was asking the blonde a question. The blonde clutched a hand between Jody's legs, gripping her convulsively through the material of her trousers.

"Yes, God, yes. Bite me," the blonde wailed. "Please, do it now. I want to come."

Jody dragged the blonde's hand from between her legs and kept a grip on her wrist, holding the searching hand away from her body. When she reared back for a fraction of a second, Becca caught a glimpse of the crimson glow of her eyes and her gleaming white incisors. Her expression was one of unbridled hunger and fierce need.

Jody plunged her mouth against the blonde's neck.

"Oh, oh my God!" the blonde screamed, jerking as if electrocuted. "Oh my God, I'm coming. Ohhhh, I'm coming."

Her hips thrashed wildly, her fingers clenching and unclenching, unable to break Jody's restraining grip. The man, lost in the furor, groaned and went rigid. Becca registered the look of ecstasy on the blonde's face as her cries gave way to whimpers, but Jody was the focus of her attention. Jody's eyes slowly closed as she fed, her throat working convulsively. Her long, slender fingers trembled on the blonde's breast. Her pelvis jerked each time she swallowed. She was coming. Each time the blonde's blood filled her, she twitched with another orgasmic spasm.

Becca gripped the doorjamb, her clitoris rioting. The sounds, the scents, the sight of Jody in blood thrall were so exciting she thought she might come. She imagined sliding her hand down the pale, sculpted surface of Jody's abdomen and holding her sex while she came in fitful wave after wave. Becca's sex twitched with a rapid-fire series of near orgasms, and her legs buckled. Only her death grip on the door frame kept her upright.

Jody heard a strangled moan from the direction of the hall and dragged her mouth away from the blonde's throat. She licked the punctures closed.

"Oh, don't stop," the blonde keened, grabbing Jody's head when Jody released her wrist. She tried to pull Jody's mouth back to her neck. "It feels so good. So good. Don't stop. Take more."

"No," Jody said through gritted teeth. Her sex still throbbed, she still hungered, but she'd have to take the man if she wanted to keep feeding. The blonde had given enough, and even though Jody was certain the pair would be happy to couple again while she fed from him, she was more interested in the woman standing in the doorway. She pushed free of the blonde's grasping hands and sat up on the side of the bed, gripping the mattress while she subdued her lingering bloodlust. When she was no longer shaking with hunger, she looked over at Becca. She'd known Becca was there from the moment she'd arrived, had scented Becca's growing excitement as she'd watched. When Jody had finally fed on the blonde, she'd climaxed in the heat of blood thrall with Becca's essence flooding her consciousness. "Enjoy yourself?"

Becca gasped, her expression startled, as if she'd been awakened from a dream. "I need to talk to you."

"That's all?"

Backing quickly into the hall, Becca breathed deeply and tried to get control of her out-of-control body. Jesus, what had just happened? She couldn't believe she'd stood there watching three strangers have sex and pretty much come herself in the process. She kept seeing Jody

Gates's refined features contort with need, and then the incredible
beauty of her pleasure as she came, over and over, while she fed. Becca
had never before seen anything so powerful, and she couldn't help but
envision how it must feel to be the focus of that ferocity. Her belly
warmed to the image and she found herself struggling to clear her head
once again.

Jody stepped out of the room, her shirt neatly tucked into her pants
but still open to the waist, exposing the alabaster curves of her breasts.
"You wanted me?"

Becca quickly looked away and said unnecessarily, "The door was
open."

"We encourage participants. You could have joined us."

Becca's face flamed and she wondered if it showed in the dim
hallway. "Are you trying to shock me? Or insult me?"

"You don't look offended," Jody murmured.

"Who are they?" Becca asked, the reporter in her getting the best
of her.

Jody smiled, an indulgent, amused smile. "Just a couple looking
for an adventure. I didn't ask their names."

"And that doesn't bother you? Being used to fulfill some stranger's
sex quirk?" Becca wasn't certain why she was angry. What did she care
if that blonde had just had the best orgasm of her life and probably
given her boyfriend-slash-husband the best fuck of his while Jody took
her pleasure with strangers?

"I was hungry. I fed," Jody said, her eyes turning opaque, a
bottomless darkness that Becca found both frightening and compelling.
"I don't get sentimental about my meals."

"And the sex?" Becca whispered, remembering how alone Jody
had seemed, coming without being touched. How she'd almost done
the same.

"I'm a Vampire," Jody said coolly. "When I feed, all of my needs
are satisfied. It's as simple as that."

"If you say so."

"What are you doing here?" Jody took Becca's arm and walked
her down the hallway, warning off the Vampires who reached out with
invitations along the way with a low hiss.

"I heard there might be a patient with Were fever in the ER, but I
can't confirm," Becca said. "I thought maybe you might be able to."

"How good is your information?"

"An anonymous source. But the ER clerk told me enough to make me think it's accurate." Becca sidled around a male Vampire feeding from a human male. The man wore the same ecstatic expression as the blonde with Jody. Becca averted her gaze, but not before she saw the Vampire's hips thrust as Jody's had while she was feeding. The Vampire's hand was inside the man's fly, masturbating him.

"Is your choice of...partners...sexual?" Becca asked.

"Some of us prefer hosts of a particular sex," Jody said, "if the choice is available. If not..." She lifted her shoulder. "Blood is blood."

Becca wanted to ask more, fascinated and repelled and strangely excited, but they'd reached the main bar and conversation was impossible. The room was a seething mass of hosts and Vampires, and all the Vampires were feeding. The space was awash in sex and blood.

"What's happening?" Becca gasped.

"Sunrise is less than an hour away. The risen Vampires will need to be underground soon." Jody slid her arm around Becca's waist and made a path for them toward the door. "Come on. You should not be here this late at night unless you intend to host."

"Can't I say no?"

"Can you?" Jody slowed and, when she captured Becca's gaze, loosened the hold she'd been keeping on her hunger. Becca's eyes glazed and her lips parted, her breath coming faster. Jody's need lashed through her so swiftly her incisors bulged from their sheaths and her sex beat in time to the pulse pounding in Becca's throat. She very nearly gave in, jerking her gaze away with a snarl.

"Oh my God," Becca murmured, stumbling slightly as Jody tugged her through the crowd. She'd wanted Jody to take her. She wanted Jody inside her, and she wanted Jody to take *her* inside. To feed from her. Her whole body still ached from the intensity of her wanting. "I would have let you."

"I know, and I am still living. Even a newly risen is stronger than I am, and the room is filled with risen Vampires who must feed to survive."

"Don't ever do that to me again." Becca was furious and afraid and incredibly aroused. "I choose who I sleep with."

Jody's expression was unreadable. "It was a demonstration, not an invitation."

Becca clamped her teeth together to stifle a curse. She needed to work with this egotistical Vampire, at least for the time being. "Are you going to help me or not?"

"I'm going to do my job," Jody said coolly. She pushed through the door and dragged Becca out into the night. "You should go home."

"It's my lead." Becca jerked her hand away. "You owe me, damn it."

Jody laughed and shook her head. "I'll call you if I learn anything."

"No way. I'm coming with you."

"You'll have to wait outside while I interview the staff."

Becca started to protest, but Jody was already walking away.

"Take it or leave it, Ms. Land."

Stomping toward her car, Becca muttered, "Thanks a lot, you son of a bitch."

From across the lot, Jody called, "You're welcome."

Becca had forgotten Jody could probably hear a conversation two blocks away. She slammed into her car, the Vampire's mocking laughter ringing in her ears.

CHAPTER FIFTEEN

Drake lay naked on the bed, her body covered in a sheen of sweat, the muscles in her arms and legs standing out in rigid relief. Suddenly, her back bowed and her face became a contorted tableau of agony. Elena knelt by her side and wiped her face with an iced cloth.

Sylvan prowled the edges of the room, barely able to watch Elena touch Drake. Rationally, she knew Elena wasn't hurting her, but she was beyond rational thought. Even when her mother had been murdered and grief and rage had burned through her like an inferno, she'd been able to control her beast. Now she wanted to attack anyone who came near Drake. She stayed as far away from Elena as she could, but the more Drake suffered, the closer she came to succumbing to her primitive instincts. She'd have to drive the medic from the room soon, or risk harming her.

"She's burning up," Elena said. "Come hold her arm down. I'm going to give her a sedative to see if I can calm her."

"What's happening?" Sylvan demanded, her voice as rough as stone. She leaned over Drake and gripped her left arm, pinning it to the bed. Drake struggled underneath her, bucking and grinding, her slick torso and belly rubbing against Sylvan's bare breasts and stomach. Drake whined, her eyes glazed and unseeing. Sylvan smelled pheromones and endorphins and kinins that were not quite human and not quite Were. "She's acting like she's in heat. Is it sex frenzy?"

"I don't know," Elena said. "I've never seen a human survive this long. But I do know her muscles are breaking down and the toxins are affecting her central nervous system." Elena jerked back when Drake lashed out with her free arm, nearly striking her. She gave Sylvan a regretful look. "We're going to need to restrain her soon."

"No," Sylvan said.

"She's going to hurt herself. Or one of us."

"What about the medication to treat the hyperthermia? Can't you give her more?"

"Sophia said she's had the maximum dose. Any more and we might kill her."

Sylvan growled, her facial bones shifting beneath her skin—elongating, growing heavy and blunt. Her vocal cords thickened almost to the point where she couldn't form words. "She's dying anyhow. Do something!"

"Alpha, there's nothing we can do!"

"Her wolf can heal her." Sylvan's wild energy, bred of centuries of powerful Alphas, poured from every cell, soaking the room in aggression and wrath. Drake thrashed frantically, an inarticulate cry wrenched from her chest. Blood trickled from her nose.

Terrified, Elena grasped Sylvan's arm and tried to break her hold on Drake's wrist. "Let her go! Your call is making her worse. She's too ill to shift."

"No! She *has* to complete the transition. It's the only thing that will save her." Sylvan's claws erupted and blood scent rose in the air. Trembling with the effort not to attack Elena, she pointed to the door. "Leave us."

"What are you going to do?" Elena tried to insinuate her own body between Sylvan and Drake, even though she knew she was challenging the Alpha when Sylvan was very near to losing control. "She's dangerous, Alpha. She's very strong to have lived this long. If she manages to shift and turns rabid…"

"Go," Sylvan said in a tone that no wolf could disobey.

Elena turned her head aside and closed her eyes. "As you wish, Alpha."

"Keep everyone away, especially Niki."

Elena started toward the door, then abruptly returned to Sylvan.

"No, stay away from me." Sylvan extended her arm in warning. "Elena, don't test me."

"I'm not afraid of you," Elena murmured as she skimmed her mouth along the edge of Sylvan's jaw. "I love you. Be careful."

Sylvan buried her face in Elena's hair, holding her tightly. "I love you." She kissed her temple. "Go now."

Elena caressed Sylvan's face with trembling fingers before reluctantly leaving the room.

Sylvan slowly approached the bed and knelt on the rough plank floor. Acting on pure instinct, she slid a hand behind Drake's neck and one arm around her waist. Gently, she gathered her into her arms and skated her mouth over Drake's cheek, tasting her. Oak and dark wine and midnight in the forest. She shuddered with a surge of primitive possession. Her wolf clawed and gnashed with a fierce need to protect. She wanted to destroy whatever was inside Drake that threatened to take her away. She cradled Drake's face against her chest and let her wolf rise.

"Sylvan?" Drake clutched Sylvan's arms. "Sylvan?"

"Yes," Sylvan gritted her teeth, the frenzy tearing at her insides. She broke out in a sweat, drenched in pheromones and adrenaline. Her sex swelled, the deep-seated glands expanding so rapidly her clitoris erected painfully. She wanted to climb on top of Drake and rub her sex all over her, but something far more primal than sex frenzy drove her. She wanted to dominate her, mark her with claws and teeth. The need to claim her was a fury in Sylvan's blood. *Mine.*

Drake's face twisted in pain. She opened her eyes and found Sylvan's. She touched Sylvan's face with the lightest of caresses. "Help me. Sylvan…Alpha, help me."

And suddenly, Sylvan understood in a place deep inside, deeper than thought or reason, what she must do. She was Alpha and Drake was hers, as every wolf was hers, but more. She climbed onto the bed with Drake in her arms and held her in her lap. Broadcasting all her power, she gave the order none of hers could resist. "Come to me, my wolf."

Drake gasped, her arms and legs jerking with violent contractions. "Oh God," she screamed, "it hurts. It hurts."

Sylvan's canines erupted and a trail of silver streaked down the center of her abdomen. Her clitoris pounded, her sex glands pulsed. Her wolf was upon her. "Let her come, Drake. Free her."

Blood flecked Drake's mouth and her eyes rolled back. Sylvan held Drake tightly, feeling bones shifting beneath her hands. A glimmer of midnight pelt rippled beneath Drake's skin, but still, she did not shift.

Crimson rivers flowed from Drake's mouth onto her neck and chest. Her rasping breaths stuttered and abruptly stopped. Sylvan snarled, furious at being disobeyed. She clasped the back of Drake's neck, her claws puncturing the skin, and shook her. "You will not die! *Shift*."

Drake thrashed, screaming, lethal canines erupting and lacerating her lower lip. Short, sharp claws tore through her fingertips and she scored Sylvan's back and shoulders in a mindless frenzy. Sylvan's wolf gnashed her teeth, enraged, demanding to dominate, to claim. Sylvan flung Drake onto her back and straddled her stomach. She snarled in Drake's face.

"*Shift.*"

Drake lashed out with unexpected strength and buried her canines in Sylvan's chest, just above her breast. Sylvan's vision hazed to red. Her sex glands exploded, pheromones pumped from every cell, and she came with a roar. She doubled over in an ecstasy of pain and pleasure, Drake's mouth still at her breast. In the fleeting second before her wolf burst free, her eyes met Drake's and she saw triumph in the black-gold gleam of Drake's eyes. Howling in a fury of orgasm, Sylvan curled protectively around the midnight black wolf who shivered against her belly.

Exhausted, Sylvan panted, her limbs twitching, her hips still flexing uncontrollably. *Drake?* She nuzzled the wolf's neck and whined worriedly. *Drake, can you hear me?*

The black wolf licked her face in answer.

Sylvan sighed and rested her muzzle on top of Drake's shoulder, tucking Drake's head securely beneath her chin. The frenzy was gone. She felt satisfied, content. Drake was safe, and she would keep her that way.

❖

Niki was driven to her knees by a barrage of power that blasted from the infirmary. Then she heard Sylvan roar in agony. Sylvan was in danger. The Alpha needed her. She burst inside and raced down the hall.

Elena blocked the door to Drake's room. "You can't—"

"Move," Niki shouted.

"No." Elena braced her back against the closed door.

Driven by instinct, Niki was past reason, and Elena was preventing her from getting to her Alpha. Niki grabbed Elena's shoulders and jerked her aside. Elena cried out and blood welled beneath Niki's hands where her claws gouged flesh. Before Niki could force her way into the sickroom, she was tackled and knocked violently to the floor. She landed on her back, a knee driving into her stomach and an arm crushing her throat. An enraged male with canines flashing snarled in her face. Roger. Elena's mate.

"Roger," Elena cried. *"No."*

Niki locked on Roger's face and let her eyes go wolf. He was a beta Were, far less dominant than her. He was challenging her, preventing her from protecting the Alpha. She would kill him. She showed her canines in warning.

"Niki!" Sophia cried, dropping to her knees beside the struggling pair. She had heard the snarls and growls from across the courtyard in the barracks where she'd been waiting for word of Drake and come running. "Roger is protecting his mate. Niki, he's protecting Elena."

Niki ignored Sophia, her gaze locked on Roger. Roger didn't relent, holding the challenge. Niki's eyes burned hunter green. Roger wasn't strong enough to fight her in skin form, and he wasn't dominant enough to shift quickly. But Niki didn't need to shift—she could snap his neck with her bare hands. She gathered herself to throw him off, to kill him and restore order.

Panicked, Elena wrapped her arms around Roger's shoulders from behind and pressed her cheek to the top of his head. Her voice quavered. "Roger, darling. Release the *imperator.* Please, darling. Let her go."

"Niki, it's the mate bond," Sophia whispered, her mouth close to Niki's ear, her breath soft and warm. She slipped her arm between Roger and Niki and rubbed Niki's chest and belly. "He's not challenging you."

Niki growled. "Let me go."

"No," Sophia murmured. She licked Niki's neck. Niki tasted wild and hot, her aggression so high Sophia wanted to roll onto her back and give Niki her belly. She wanted Niki to climb onto her and take her. She tried to keep her focus on calming Niki and saving Roger's life. "I know you want to fight, but you don't *need* to. You absorbed the Alpha's call, Niki—that's what's making you wild. You don't need to fight Roger."

Niki shuddered, Sophia's caresses dulling the pain she'd been carrying since Sylvan locked herself in with Drake, putting herself in danger and refusing Niki's protection.

"Tell Roger that Elena will be safe," Sophia urged, rubbing her cheek on Niki's. She pressed her breasts gently against Niki's arm, and when Niki shuddered again, stroked her fingertips down the indentation dividing Niki's rigid abs, tracing the feathery line of pelt that disappeared inside her waistband. "You don't want to hurt him."

Sophia's lips were soft against Niki's face. So soft. Sophia's touch soothed her raging wolf. Niki sought Sophia's eyes. They were tender. Strong. "Sophia?"

Sophia smiled as Niki's eyes shifted back to forest green. "Hey. You scared Roger. Tell him it's all right."

"The Alpha—"

"I know." Sophia brushed the corner of Niki's mouth with hers. "Take care of the others first. That's what the Alpha would want."

Niki closed her eyes and turned her face into Sophia's palm, breathing her scent. Sunshine and saplings. Fresh and pure. Then she caught Roger's gaze.

"Stand down, wolf. Your mate will come to no harm." Niki's throat ached from the weight of Roger's arm. She felt Sophia's mouth on her neck, just the flick of her tongue, and the pain lessened.

Roger released the pressure on Niki's neck and slid off, kneeling beside her, his head bowed. Elena pulled him back and slowly edged between him and Niki, watching Niki carefully. She would protect her mate with as much ferocity as he had protected her.

Sophia lingered by Niki's side, overwhelmed by a powerful need to comfort her. Niki had almost been driven feral with the strain of absorbing the Alpha's furious call. Niki was suffering and Sophia couldn't bring herself to stop touching her. Her fingertips were suddenly damp and she realized Niki's skin was sex-sheened. She was caressing a dominant Were and Niki was responding to her unintended invitation. Sophia hastily removed her hand from Niki's belly and jumped to her feet.

Niki rose as Sophia retreated. She throbbed with endorphins and adrenaline, pulsing with sex frenzy, but she had other duties before she could find a female for a tangle. She turned her back to Sophia and gently cupped Elena's chin. Elena's blouse was blood streaked on both shoulders. "Are you badly hurt?"

"No. Your claws just caught me—it's nothing serious," Elena said.

Rumbling quietly, Roger pulled Elena into his arms, her back to his chest, and wrapped his arms around her waist. He buried his face in her neck.

"I'm sorry." Niki rubbed the backs of her fingers over Elena's cheek, careful not to linger and set Roger off again. He would be desperate to claim her, to assure himself his mate was safe. The smallest thing would incite him until he'd taken her. "I didn't intend to hurt you. But I have to see Sylvan."

"Niki...*Imperator*...the Alpha said no one was to enter."

Niki clenched her fists and glowered at the closed door, blood flowing onto the floor as her claws sliced into her palms. "Did you hear her? Something's wrong."

"I'm not so certain," Sophia said, carefully keeping distance between her and Niki. "I sense...calm. I think the Alpha's storm has passed."

"I don't..." Niki took a deep breath, testing the air. Beneath the lingering frenzy, she detected a scent she didn't recognize. A wolf? She shook her head, perplexed and uneasy. She went to the door. "I need to be sure."

❖

Niki heard a low warning growl as soon as she opened the door. Quickly, she stepped inside and closed the door behind her, putting a protective barrier between the Weres outside in the hall and whatever danger lurked in this room. Her breath came faster as she took in the scene on the bed. A huge silver wolf crouched over a large sleeping black one, guarding her.

Teeth bared, Sylvan growled again, her eyes glinting dangerously.

Slowly, Niki knelt down, careful not to look into the Alpha's eyes. "Are you all right?"

Yes.

Niki licked her lips, her throat dry. "Drake?"

She will be fine.

Niki wasn't convinced, but she knew better than to challenge Sylvan now.

"What would you have me do?"

I scent your frenzy. What of your need?

"I need to be here."

And I need you with me. Join us.

Drake might wake up rabid and savage her, but Niki would die before she would disobey her Alpha. She shifted and padded to the bed. Carefully, she jumped up and curled around Sylvan's hindquarters, resting her chin on Sylvan's flank. She whined and Sylvan took her muzzle in her mouth, biting gently before letting go. Instantly, the pain of the last few hours disappeared and the frenzy eased. She was by Sylvan's side, where she belonged. Niki was at peace. She closed her eyes, her belly warmed by the Alpha's heat, but the burning lower in her loins reminded her of the soft caress of a white wolf with brilliant blue eyes.

CHAPTER SIXTEEN

Becca parked in the loading zone across from the ER entrance and waited while Jody went inside to question the staff. For the first ten minutes, she watched the slow trickle of people passing in and out of the big sliding glass doors and tried not to think about what she'd just experienced at Nocturne. She'd thought she had known what to expect in the Vampire club, but she was beginning to realize there was a lot humans didn't know about the Praetern species. The more she thought about it, the more she realized how few details of their social orders the Praeterns had revealed. In her research she'd found plenty of information on Praetern business and commercial ventures, but nothing on matters of health, sex, or procreation. Maybe they thought humans would accept them more readily if they minimized their differences and emphasized their importance in the economic strata. Maybe they were right.

She hadn't been surprised by the fluid sexuality of the Vampires, but she'd been caught off guard by her own reactions. She'd always considered herself pretty adventurous, even though she'd never really gotten into multiple partners and had been exclusive with women since her teens, so she couldn't quite figure out why she got so turned on watching Jody with the human couple. Even harder to understand was why she kept imagining holding Jody in her arms while Jody fed from the blonde and climaxed in the grip of blood thrall. Becca shivered and rubbed her arms. Agitated, aroused, confused, she yanked open the car door and climbed out. She checked her watch. Fifteen minutes had passed. She paced beside her vintage Camaro. She'd give the Vampire five more minutes and then she was going in after her.

"I don't know why I agreed to stay out here anyhow. Dictatorial Vampire," Becca muttered, reaching the end of her car and whipping around to start back the other way. She collided with a stone wall and stared into the amused coal black eyes of the Vampire in question. Becca's breasts flattened against Jody's chest and her nipples hardened instantly. Becca sucked in a breath. "Where did you come from?"

Jody skimmed her hands down Becca's arms and moved her back an inch. Her eyes flickered with pinpoints of crimson, like sparks drifting into the night sky. "The ER."

"I've been watching the door. You weren't there a second ago."

"Human vision relies on detecting light displacement. If the dispersion is too rapid, nothing registers." Jody lightly clasped Becca's upper arms and massaged Becca's biceps with her thumbs. Becca's body was warm. She'd felt the heat against her chest through the thin silk of Becca's blouse. She savored Becca's scent, aware of the bloodlust stirring but doing nothing to temper it. Indulging herself by toying with a human who wasn't prepared to host was a dangerous game to play, because sex and blood were inextricably bound in the Vampire psyche. Especially hers. The older or stronger the Vampire, the greater the blending of the two. Jody was a pre-animate, but her father was one of the most powerful Vampires in existence and her lineage was ancient. Even living, her drives were strong and her power to enthrall nearly as strong as a risen Vampire's. The great arteries in Becca's neck bounded with excitement, with life. Jody's incisors slid from their sheaths.

Becca was captivated by the flames dancing in Jody's eyes. She leaned into her, her breasts and belly and thighs cleaving to Jody's slender frame. Jody's full lips parted and Becca saw a hint of fangs hidden behind them. Jody Gates gave the phrase *playing with fire* a whole new meaning.

"They're not always so visible," Becca said, drawing her fingertip over Jody's lower lip. The thought that she had excited Jody excited her. She liked feeling a little reckless. "Let me see."

"Careful what you wish for," Jody murmured.

"I told you not to enthrall me."

"I'm not."

"How do I know you're not doing something to me right now?" Becca whispered. "How do I know anything I feel with you is real?"

Jody's eyes blanked, the flat black of an endless well. Suddenly she was a foot away, not touching Becca. Becca hadn't seen her move.

"You don't," Jody said. "Haven't you heard you should never trust a Vampire?"

"Did you learn anything inside?" Becca asked abruptly, pretending she didn't miss the feel of that lithe body against hers. She resented being so effortlessly turned on and as easily rejected. The Vampire wasn't interested in her, only her blood.

Jody laughed. "Back to business, huh?"

"Don't flatter yourself. It's always been just business."

Annoyed at Becca's cool tone and determined to maintain control over the case they seemed to be sharing, Jody said, "Come to breakfast with me. I'll fill you in."

"Breakfast? You mean food?" Becca said before she could stop herself.

"I eat food." Jody's gaze dropped to Becca's mouth. "I'll *feed* later."

Feeling churlish at the idea of Jody seeking more sex, Becca said disdainfully, "The blonde wasn't enough?"

"I have a healthy appetite for some things." Jody turned and started toward the street. "Coming?"

Becca caught up to her and fell into step. The sun was already bright at six a.m. Jody put on sunglasses, turned the collar up on her white shirt, and put her hands in her pants pockets. Becca glanced at her worriedly. "How long can you..."

"Be in the sun?" Jody asked.

"Yes."

"After five or ten minutes of summer sunlight I'll start to burn—"

Becca gasped.

The corner of Jody's mouth twitched. "Sunburn—not conflagration. I'd have to be staked out in direct light for an hour or more before cellular breakdown would begin. After two hours, combustion."

"And you still walk around out here after sunrise? That's crazy," Becca said, her heart skittering painfully in her chest. "What if you get in an accident and can't reach shelter!"

"I'll have millennia to live by starlight alone," Jody said quietly. "I'll take what time I have in the sun."

Becca thought she detected a note of sadness, but she knew that couldn't be true. Gates didn't seem capable of that emotion. She saw the detective reach for the diner door to hold it open for her and got to it first. She walked in ahead of Jody and intentionally picked a booth across from the windows, but out of the sunlight. As soon as the waitress poured their coffee and left, she removed her recorder from her bag.

"Off the record," Jody said.

"That wasn't our deal."

"Our deal was I would give you something when I had something." Jody sipped her coffee, enjoying the way Becca's jaw tightened and her skin flushed a richer shade of mocha. Most humans were afraid of challenging her. In fact most would do anything to avoid engaging with her at all. Becca was an intriguing change. "I don't have anything yet except conjecture."

Becca closed her fist around her recorder and leaned across the table until only an inch separated them. "Don't play games with me, Vampire. I'm not some brainless twit who's dying to offer up my blood so you can get off."

"Are you sure?" Jody said, her voice low and seductive. "Because you certainly seemed to enjoy it earlier this morning."

"Just business, remember?" Becca couldn't remember now what she'd found so attractive about this controlling, infuriating Vampire, or why on earth she cared if the arrogant fool wanted to tempt fate and walk around in the sun. "I kept my end of the bargain. Or did I make a mistake trusting you to keep your word?"

Jody's eyes erupted into a fiery red so hot Becca reflexively leaned back.

"Careful, Becca," Jody said, her voice ice. "I'm not some harmless house pet you can tease for your amusement. Remember, I bite."

Exactly how she bit flashed through Becca's mind, and she forced the image away. "Then talk to me and I won't have to risk my virginity."

Jody's brows rose and she laughed. "I can see why you're good at your job."

"How do you know I am?"

"I follow your byline."

Inordinately pleased and chiding herself for the ridiculous response, Becca refused to react. "Give, Detective."

The waitress slid toast and eggs in front of both of them.

"Thank you," Jody said. She tore a slice of toast in half and buttered it. "A Jane Doe was dropped—literally—in front of the emergency room last night. Naked and unresponsive. She had a very high fever and almost immediately went into convulsions."

"Jesus," Becca whispered. "No recorder, but I have to take some notes." She found her pad and paper. "Go ahead. What happened?"

"Unfortunately, the girl—and it was a girl, a teenager—died despite efforts to resuscitate her."

"Was the Alpha notified?" Becca scribbled *teenager* and circled it.

"Not that I'm aware of."

Becca looked up, frowning. "Why not?"

Jody regarded Becca silently.

"What? What aren't you tell—" Becca caught her breath. "Because the girl wasn't a Were, was she?"

"I can't confirm that one way or the other. I'll need to follow up with the coroner on COD as well."

"What does it mean?" Becca rubbed her forehead with her fingertips. "If she's human, it can't be Were fever, can it? But my source said—"

"Tell me about this source," Jody interrupted sharply.

Becca sat back in the seat. "You know I can't do that."

"Male or female?"

"Honestly, I'm not sure. Even if I was, I wouldn't say."

Jody hissed in frustration. "How do you contact—them?"

"I don't. I get a phone call."

"Saying what?"

Becca blew out a breath. "That a patient with Were fever had been brought to the emergency room."

"And you don't find it suspicious that they know this?"

"Of course I do, but it could be anyone," Becca argued. "An ambulance driver. Someone in the hospital. A friend of the girl's. The point is, the call was accurate."

"Someone wants the press to know about this," Jody said, "and he, or *she*, is counting on you to make that happen. Why?"

"I don't know," Becca said. "But I'm willing to bet that Sylvan Mir does."

"Then I guess I'll be talking to her," Jody said.

"I'm going with you."

"I don't think so."

Becca reached across the table and grasped Jody's wrist. She felt as if she were gripping carved marble. Smooth, hard, cool. "I will, with you or without you. But if I go on my own, I'm not going to share."

"I work alone. And even if I didn't, you're a reporter."

"I'm an investigative reporter. I work with the police all the time. This isn't even an active crime case yet."

Jody shook her head and pulled a slim black leather wallet from her pants pocket. She placed several bills on the table. "The next time you decide to visit Nocturne, make sure you have an escort."

"I don't need anyone to protect me. Least of all you."

"You do if you're going back there again." Jody slid out of the booth and leaned over Becca, bracing one hand on the table and her arm along the back of the booth, caging Becca in. "I can smell your hunger. *I* might not take you without your consent, but there are plenty of others who would consider your being at the club consent enough."

"My consent is one thing you'll never have," Becca said, refusing to back away even though Jody's mouth was almost on her neck.

"Have a nice day, Ms. Land," Jody said.

Then she was simply—gone. Becca jumped up and searched the length of the diner, but the Vampire had vanished.

"Nice try," Becca muttered as she stormed out to the street. "You'll have to work harder than that if you want to scare me away."

Jody, watching from the shadows of a tree-shrouded second-floor balcony on the opposite side of the street, smiled at Becca's words. She didn't want to frighten her away. She wanted to taste her. But she wanted to be invited to satisfy Becca's hunger, and Becca had made it clear she would never offer.

❖

Drake knew she was dreaming when she opened her eyes in a forest glade dappled with sunshine. The world burst upon her in a kaleidoscope of scents and sounds—the rush of leaves fluttering in the breeze, the whir of thousands of insect wings, the pungent scent of wildlife and growing things. She felt so alive, such a sense of wonder, she wanted to dance. She wanted to run. She wanted to share this perfect moment, but she was alone. So alone.

She trembled, aching with a vast and terrifying sense of emptiness. She whimpered, lost and uncertain.

"It's all right," a deep, gentle voice whispered.

Strong arms clasped her tightly, drawing her against a sleek, muscled body. Drake rumbled with pleasure and she pressed her hips into the curve of the pelvis cinched against her ass. A low growl from behind her struck fire in her core and her belly knotted. Pressure ballooned in her sex and a bolt of pain exploded between her legs.

"What's happening," she groaned.

"Your body is adjusting to the change."

"Sylvan?"

Sylvan kissed the back of Drake's neck. "Yes."

Drake felt another hand caress her thigh and then a warm cheek rested on her hip. "Who?"

"That's Niki," Sylvan whispered. "We're Pack. We'll look after you."

"I feel strange. I hurt...inside. I want...I'm not sure..." Drake reached back and slid her hand down the hard abdomen curved against her back. She feathered her fingertips over a thin line of soft pelt low down in the center of Sylvan's belly and followed it to a firm ridge. She pressed and Sylvan groaned. Niki growled a warning. Drake stiffened, anger making every hair on her body stand up. She made a low threatening sound deep in her chest.

"We have to leave you for a while," Sylvan said, loosing her hold and edging away. "Your wolf needs time to find her feet."

Drake rolled onto her back, breathing hard. Niki, naked, sat up on the end of the bed. Her wary eyes never left Drake as Drake focused on Sylvan.

"My wolf?"

"You turned, Drake. I'll explain later. Right now, our medic Elena needs to see you."

"Wait." Drake grabbed Sylvan's arm.

In a flash, Niki loomed over Drake on all fours, her lips pulled back to expose her canines. Niki scraped her teeth down Drake's neck, leaving a thin trail of blood. "Release the Alpha, whelp."

"I'm sorry." Drake pressed both hands flat to the mattress and met Niki's gaze. When Niki growled she wanted to growl back. Rage swiftly engulfed her and she envisioned tearing into Niki's throat. She turned her head away, confused.

"Ease away, *Imperator*," Sylvan said, running her fingers through Niki's hair before stroking her rigid back. "She'll learn."

Snarling, Niki slowly lifted her weight off Drake but crouched nearby, still poised to strike.

Drake arched as a spasm cramped her lower abdomen. She flushed and sweat broke over her. "It's starting again."

"No, this is not the fever. Your system is flooded with hormones from the transition." Sylvan cradled Drake's jaw and rubbed her thumb over the corner of her mouth. "You'll be all right, Drake. You're Pack and we will all protect you."

"Please...can you stay?" Drake whispered.

Sylvan shuddered, her wolf strafing her soul in a fury. *Take her.* Forcing herself to leave her when what she wanted was to mark her, Sylvan rose and held out her arm to Niki. "I can't."

Drake curled on her side and watched Sylvan and Niki disappear, more alone than she'd ever been in her life.

CHAPTER SEVENTEEN

W ait for me outside," Sylvan said to Niki. "I want to run."
Niki regarded the closed door to Drake's room. "You're not going back in there?"

"Not now. She needs to be with a beta Were, someone who won't incite her dominance instincts."

"Like us."

Sylvan hadn't felt a challenge from Drake, but Niki didn't need to know that. She tilted her head toward the porch. "Go. Then we'll run."

"Yes, Alpha." Niki cast one more uneasy glance at the door, then loped off.

Sylvan followed Elena's scent to the room the medic used when she stayed in the infirmary to be close to her patients. Before she could knock, Elena opened the door. Roger stood behind her, his arms loosely clasping her hips. He was shirtless. Elena wore loose pale cotton scrubs. Both had fading bite marks at the juncture of neck and shoulder.

"Drake is awake," Sylvan said. "She's loaded with endorphins and pheromones. She almost challenged Niki."

"She *is* dominant, then," Elena murmured, absently running her nails up and down Roger's arms. He rumbled and caught her earlobe in his teeth. "Is she showing signs of frenzy?"

Sylvan remembered Drake's hand caressing her abdomen, exploring her clitoris with her fingertips. She had come instantly erect and was still fully ready to release. "She might be soon, and she doesn't understand what's happening."

"She can't. She's like an adolescent in a constant state of frenzy, but she's totally unprepared for it." Elena shook her head. "She must be in such pain." Elena gave Sylvan a cautious look. "I can prepare her, but if she really is in frenzy, she's going to need release with another Were soon."

Sylvan growled. "She's not ready."

"We don't know *what* she is," Elena argued. "She's unique in our experience."

Roger rubbed his chin on Elena's shoulder, a worried whine reverberating in his chest. "How do we know she won't attack Elena? I should go in with her."

"No, she's already confused and she'll want to dominate you," Elena said gently, reaching back to caress his neck. "I am mated, and her wolf will recognize that."

"We can't be sure," Roger protested.

"You can stay outside on the porch, where you can hear my call if I need help." Elena turned in his arms and nipped at his jaw. "You'll know if I'm in danger, mate."

Roger closed his eyes and lifted his chin so she could bite his neck. He grumbled his assent.

Sylvan wrapped her arms around both of them, and Elena and Roger crowded against her. She stroked Elena's hair and cupped the back of Roger's neck. "Drake might have the urges of an adolescent, but she isn't showing any signs of being rabid. I wouldn't let Elena go near her if I thought there was any danger."

"I'll go to her now," Elena said.

"Help her," Sylvan ordered.

"And if she shows signs of needing true release?"

Sylvan growled again, her claws jutting out. "Find her someone."

Niki jumped down from the railing where she'd been crouched, waiting for Sylvan. The Alpha stormed through the door, her eyes already wolf-gold, her torso shimmering silver. Niki focused on the two purple crescents above Sylvan's breast that hadn't been evident when Sylvan's wolf had been quieter.

"She bit you!"

"Let's run."

"Alpha," Niki cried. "She could have infected you!"

"She didn't," Sylvan snapped, striding down the stairs toward the forest.

"You don't know that. She's dangerous!"

Sylvan whipped around. "Enough!"

Niki stopped abruptly, her body quivering. "You smell like her."

"I'm covered in her scent from the transition. It's nothing." Sylvan wrapped her arms around Niki's shoulders and leaned down until their eyes held. "Save yourself for a true battle, *Imperator*. This is not your fight."

"You are my Alpha," Niki whispered.

"I am. And you are my second. The wolf of my heart." Sylvan pulled Niki close and rubbed her chin on the top of her head. "We need to find out what's causing these fevers in humans and stop it before there's open season on Weres. I need you by my side, Niki, now more than ever."

Niki brushed her mouth over Sylvan's chest, careful not to touch the bite mark. "Always, Alpha. Always."

❖

"I'm the Pack medic," Elena said, slipping into Drake's room and closing the door behind her. "How are you feeling?"

"I'm not so sure." Drake sat up with her back to the wall and tucked a sheet tightly around her hips. She'd never been particularly shy or self-conscious, but her body didn't feel like hers. When she'd first awakened with Sylvan and Niki pressed close against her, she'd been comforted. But she'd been aroused too, painfully so, and when she'd been compelled to touch Sylvan, her excitement had been unbearable. She was still intensely aroused.

Elena smelled good. And she was beautiful. Her delicate features were framed by thick, long black curls that Drake wanted to run her hands through. Elena was petite but full-bodied, with luscious breasts and hips. Drake imagined skimming her mouth over the curves of her breasts and down the center of her gently rounded belly. Her clitoris jutted out and she growled softly.

"I don't think you should be in here," Drake said.

Elena leaned back against the door, watching Drake carefully. "Sylvan says your wolf is challenging you."

"Something is." Drake laughed shakily. Her stomach ached as if she were hungry, but for much more than food. When she ran her hand down the center of her abdomen, her skin felt different. More sensitive. Her muscles were tighter, harder. Her loins twinged and she winced with another sharp pain between her legs. "I'm...I'm having some control problems."

"You're an adult Were with an adolescent's appetites and urges," Elena said calmly. "It's going to take a while for your wolf to find her balance. You're likely to respond to every Were who gets close to you at first."

"Everyone?" Drake asked. "I've never been attracted to males. Will that change?"

"Most of our young will couple freely until their late teens, when some become exclusive with one sex. You're already an adult, so you may not find the males of interest now."

"So I'll only be aroused by every female I pass?" Drake thought of Niki naked and pressed against her, but Sylvan had been the one she had wanted to touch. Sylvan's torso had been a landscape of perfect muscles sheathed in smooth skin and a tantalizing tease of silky pelt. She breathed sharply at the memory and caught Sylvan's scent in the air. Her clitoris twitched and she had an overpowering urge for sex. She stared at Elena's breasts and her sex tightened. "This isn't good. I'm not going to be safe outside of this room."

"Not everyone will arouse you," Elena said with a smile. "Your wolf will quickly come to recognize the mated females, and you won't be drawn to us any longer. You may not find more dominant Weres arousing either."

Drake immediately thought of her reaction to Sylvan, but didn't say anything.

As if reading her mind, Elena said, "The Alpha is unmated. Until she forms a mate bond, all of us, even the mated ones, respond to her when her call is strong. It's the natural response of the Pack to their Alpha."

Drake shifted restlessly, the sheet suddenly feeling constricting. The pain between her legs increased and she winced. She was terribly aroused but she didn't really think Elena was the object of her arousal. She was attractive, but Drake wasn't drawn to *her.* Not the way she had been to Sylvan. Sylvan. Another spasm shot from between her legs. "Jesus, what's going on?"

"Your body has undergone a drastic, rapid transformation. You're being flooded with potent neurotransmitters. You're sexually aroused. It's normal."

"Something doesn't feel right. There's…pain."

"Lie down." Elena reached behind her and grasped the doorknob in case Drake lost control. "I need to answer your questions."

Drake stretched out on her back. Even the sheet made her skin ache and she kicked it away.

"Touch yourself," Elena said gently.

"You want me to masturbate?" Drake turned her head to look at Elena.

"Your body needs to release."

"Is it safe…with you here? What if I…are you sure I won't become rabid?"

"You smell like a normal dominant. I'm not afraid of dominant Weres—even when we're not dominant we can reject a partner if we choose." Elena smiled. "It's why the dominants fight over us when we're in heat."

"Are you sure?" Drake trembled with the primal need to take, to claim. The urge was so strong she could barely think.

"Go ahead," Elena said softly. "You want to, don't you?"

Drake smoothed her hand down the center of her abdomen, getting used to the tightly packed muscles. Her curiosity helped her contain her excitement and she cautiously explored. When she reached the space between her thighs she cupped herself. She felt the same, only not quite. Her clitoris was positioned slightly higher, leaving it more exposed. She tentatively traced its length with her thumb and finger, retracting the thickened sheath to uncover the firm head. The shaft was thicker, harder than she was used to even when she was fully aroused. She massaged it from side to side and felt resistance, as if the central core was nearly rigid.

"What's inside?"

"Early in the development of our species, all Weres, including females, had a cartilaginous core in the phallus," Elena said. "The dominant females still have a very thin remnant. Feel lower, at the base. You'll have to press hard."

Drake palpitated two olive-sized oval masses buried deep beneath her clitoris. When she touched them her hips jerked. Exquisitely tender and pleasurable. "What are they?"

"Sex glands," Elena said. "They produce *victus*, secretions of pheromones, kinins, and other chemicals, when we are aroused. They empty when we tangle—have sex—if suitably stimulated. The emissions are unique to each Were and help identify us to potential mates. Once mated, the chemical transmitters intermingle, identifying the mated pair to other Weres."

Drake squeezed harder and her clitoris abruptly extended. The pain was sharp and swift. She sucked in her breath and yanked her hand away. The pain in her clitoris increased, piercing deep into her sex. "Is it supposed to hurt?"

"You need a release to trigger the emission of the chemicals that built up during your transition. You're overloaded with them."

Drake clenched her teeth. Her excitement was building again and she wanted sex so much her reason was slipping. "Elena. You should leave."

"Stimulate your clitoris until it's completely erect. Go ahead, it's all right."

Drake closed her eyes and grasped her clitoris, running the shaft between her fingers the way she usually did when she masturbated. She was already harder than she'd ever been but she'd never hurt like this. She felt the sheath pull back and tighten beneath the crown that ringed the tip of her clitoris. She massaged the head with her thumb and felt her sex clench inside. "I feel like I have to come, but I can't."

"Now the glands," Elena whispered.

Drake fingered the swellings, and immediately her stomach tightened. She heard a growl start in her chest. Her hips flexed and she manipulated herself faster. Her shoulders came off the bed and she gritted her teeth, the pressure was so intense. "I really have to come."

"Massage your clitoris and the glands at the same time."

Drake felt a pinprick of pain and looked down. Short dark claws extended from her fingertips. A feathery line of dark pelt shimmered down the center of her lower abdomen into her sex. "Jesus. What's happening?"

"Those are signs you're almost there. Press harder, down against the bone."

The glands turned to stone and Drake's clitoris shot upright, twitching violently between her fingers. A bolt of heat shot from her sex down her legs and deep into her stomach. She rolled onto her side and doubled up, her hips thrusting in a series of wrenching spasms. Sweat soaked the sheets under her as she moaned and writhed. When the spasms subsided, she was weak and exhausted.

"God," Drake panted. "Is it supposed to be like that?" She cupped herself. "I'm still…it's not…subsiding."

"That was only a partial release," Elena explained. "Weres need the pheromones from another Were—from a bite—to trigger a complete orgasm. Self-relief is only a stopgap. Our drive for sex is very high—second only to our instinct to protect our mates—probably because our fertility rates are low." She smiled ruefully. "Aggression and danger heighten the urge. Dominants have the highest drive of all and are always semi-aroused. They'll often require a series of releases before the drive subsides."

"I don't feel right." Drake shivered.

"I wish this could have helped more." Elena crossed the room and covered Drake with the sheet. "It needed to be this way so you'd know what to expect from your body when you tangle for the first time. You're getting a crash course in Were physiology."

"Crash is a good word for it."

Elena brushed her fingers through Drake's hair. Drake's call had been strong, and had Elena not already been mated, it would have been hard to resist her. She wouldn't have *wanted* to resist her. Drake might be dangerous if the full force of her sex frenzy was unleashed without warning. She was dominant, very dominant. "I'm sorry I couldn't make it easier for you."

Drake rubbed her cheek in Elena's palm. "It's okay. I understand." She laughed tremulously. "Thanks for the walk-through."

"Move over," Elena said.

"Why?" Drake frowned.

"You're shivering, and I want to hold you. You're a Were now. You need physical contact." She removed her clothes and leaned down to kiss Drake's cheek. "I'm going to call Roger. You need the Pack. It's not sexual."

"Am I safe?" Drake's whole body longed for a touch, but she didn't trust herself. "I don't want to hurt you and I don't seem to have any kind of control."

"Roger won't arouse you, and I'm mated, so I won't either."

"It didn't feel like that a few minutes ago."

"You need to sleep and heal. This will help." Elena lay down with her head on Drake's chest, wrapped her arm around Drake's waist, and draped her thigh over Drake's. Roger slipped into the room and settled with his front to Elena's back. He extended his arm along her hip and lightly brushed Drake's thigh.

"You might wake up with the same urges—we call it sex frenzy," Elena murmured. "We'll move away before then just in case. Don't worry."

"How long am I going to be like this? So out of control?" Drake asked, instinctively tucking Elena's head beneath her chin.

"I don't know. We've never had an adult, turned Were in the Pack before."

❖

Sylvan paced in her office. She wanted to see Drake. After her run she'd gone directly to the infirmary, and before she'd even gotten inside she'd caught the scent hanging thick in the air. The hall was so laden with pheromones, the potent neurotransmitters so dense, her skin had slicked instantly and her sex readied. The bite on her chest throbbed. Drake was in need, frenzied, and Sylvan wanted to take her. She was surprised other Weres hadn't responded to the powerful call already. Instantly enraged at the image of another Were answering Drake's need, she'd stormed to Drake's door.

Then she'd heard Drake groan and Elena's low melodious voice. She knew what Elena was doing, caressing Drake into a release with her voice. She wanted to rip the door from its hinges and wrench Elena away from Drake. She wanted to be on top of Drake with her teeth buried in Drake's shoulder, her clitoris pulsing inside Drake's wet sex. Her claws had sprouted, her canines jutted out painfully, and a streak of silver shot down the center of her belly.

She wanted Drake so much she knew she couldn't risk going near her. Drake's effect on her was too potent, too powerful. She wasn't sure she could endure another bite without claiming her completely. She'd dragged herself away, crashing through the door to the porch so violently she'd splintered the wood and knocked Roger down the stairs.

Sylvan knew what she had to do. She had to get away. Drake was newly turned and couldn't control herself. She was broadcasting her needs so powerfully the others in the Pack would soon detect her call. Drake would need to tangle frequently, possibly continuously, and if Elena was right and Drake was as dominant as she seemed, she would have plenty of Weres to choose from. If Sylvan stayed there, she wouldn't be able to keep away from Drake. Even if she managed to resist, she was afraid she might tear any Were apart who tried to answer Drake's call.

Niki!

Niki immediately came through the office door, her eyes scanning the room, searching for danger. "Alpha?"

"Call the *centuri*. I'm going into the city."

"Until we determine the source of the fever, you're safer here—"

"*Now*, Niki."

Niki's jaw set. "You think I can't tell why you want to leave? I smelled your scent on *her*, too."

"I told you I forced her transition," Sylvan said. "That's all it was."

"Fine. She's a mutt, a *mutia*, and could still turn rabid. At least send her to one of the outposts until she's safe, or until she needs to be execu—"

Sylvan growled. "Be careful what you say, Niki."

"You'd leave the safety of the Compound, put yourself in danger, before you'd isolate *her*? She's not worth that."

"Don't challenge me now," Sylvan warned.

Niki narrowed her eyes and studied her Alpha. Sylvan was shirtless, as she often was around the Compound. A narrow thick trail of silver glinted above the waistband of her black pants. Her skin glowed as if kissed by moonlight. Her cheekbones were sharply angled, the rims of her deep blue irises haloed in gold. The bite on her breast was darker, bruised looking. Something was riding Sylvan hard, but Niki didn't detect the Alpha's powerful call the way she usually did when Sylvan needed release. Something else was the cause of the barrage of pheromones besides sex frenzy. Something even more primitive, more critical.

"The bite—did the bite do something to you?" Niki asked, every protective instinct on alert.

"No," Sylvan barked roughly. "Enough of this."

Niki had to try one more time. "Rena is coming into heat. Take her. She wants you to."

"I do not want a mate." Sylvan's wolf snapped and snarled as if trying to break out of a cage, refuting Sylvan's words. Sylvan shuddered with the effort of dominating her.

"Don't mate her, then," Niki cried. "Just take her! I'm still crazy to tangle. You must need to even more. Why are you denying your nature?"

Before the words were out of Niki's mouth, Sylvan was in Niki's face. She crushed Niki against the door, her arms braced on either side of Niki's head. Her teeth were on Niki's neck, her heat enclosing Niki in an inferno. Sylvan's pelvis jerked against Niki's, her hard nipples against Niki's breasts.

Niki whimpered and licked Sylvan's jaw. "Please, Alpha."

"I love you, Niki," Sylvan whispered in Niki's ear. Then she pushed her aside and stalked into the hall, shouting to Lara and Max, "Get the Rover. I'm leaving."

CHAPTER EIGHTEEN

Sylvan went directly to her office at Capitol Plaza and instructed Niki that she was not to be disturbed. Ignoring the stack of pink message slips on her desk, she put a call through on a secure line to a private number at Mir Industries. Leo Revnik, one of MI's senior scientists, answered on the second ring.

"Good morning, Alpha," Leo said in his deep bass voice.

"We may have an outbreak of Were fever in humans," Sylvan said. "I need to know the origin."

"How many?"

"Sophia reports possibly four in the last six months."

"Is there a rabid Were on the loose?"

"If the victims were less uniform, I might think so." Sylvan explained that all of the suspected cases had been teenaged girls with similar backgrounds. "I've never known a rabid Were to have that kind of reasoning ability. Plus, most rab attacks are random, clustered in time and location, and so messy it's easy to follow the trail of bodies back to the source and neutralize the rab. These attacks seem far more deliberate."

"I take it you don't have a carrier in the Pack? A Were who survived the fever, even years ago?"

"Only one," Sylvan said carefully. "And you know that's not the source here. If there's a rabid Were, or several, they're rogues, not Pack."

Leo grunted. "You believe the focus is urban, then?"

"We have no idea where these girls are even being attacked,"

Sylvan said, unable to hide her anger and frustration. "We haven't yet tracked those who turned up in the ER at Albany General. There may be more who've never made it into the system."

"Forgive me, Alpha, but the pattern is not at all typical for the transmission of the fever. The toxin degrades fairly quickly in the rabs who survive more than a day or two. If the attacks are occurring over the time frame you suggest, either we're dealing with more than one rab or the toxin has mutated into a longer-acting form."

"So we may have a new form of fever, is that what you're saying?" Sylvan asked.

"We've always been concerned about the possibility. While it's theoretically possible, we've never been able to reproduce the phenomenon in the laboratory—"

"I'm not interested in theoreticals," Sylvan growled. "We need to stop the spread to humans and eradicate any rabid carriers."

"Can you get me blood and tissue samples from the victims?" Leo asked.

"We just became aware of the problem within the last few days. Unfortunately, not in time to have any of our personnel in the hospital system procure samples from the suspected early cases."

"When was the most recent death?"

"The night before last," Sylvan said. "As far as I know, the girl has not been identified. Her body is probably with the city coroner."

"I have a few contacts there," Leo said. "I might be able to fashion a request for a blood sample that won't arouse too much suspicion. A fresh tissue biopsy for mass spec and culture is preferable, however, and I doubt I can get that."

Sylvan hesitated, every instinct screaming for her not to reveal anything further. But she was Alpha, and her entire Pack was at risk. "We have a survivor. One of the infected girls bit a human medic. She's turned."

"And she's not rabid?"

"No."

"An adult human female turned Were," Leo murmured in surprise. "We could learn a great deal by studying her."

"She's not a lab rat," Sylvan growled.

"Forgive me," Leo said, his tone immediately conciliatory. "I'm afraid I spend too much time alone in the laboratory. My tact has suffered for it."

"What would you need from her?"

"Initially, nothing too drastic. Blood samples. A muscle biopsy."

"Surgery?" Sylvan burned at the idea of anyone touching Drake, hurting her. Her wolf reared her head, snarling.

"Only a very minor incision," Leo said hastily. "I doubt it would cause her very much pain at all."

"You said initially."

Leo hesitated. "We don't know how the turning will affect a female, especially an adult. Her eggs would be—"

"No," Sylvan said immediately, her instinct to protect Drake overpowering everything else, even her duty to Pack. That realization brought her up short and she struggled to clear her head, to think as Alpha. She couldn't, wouldn't, let personal feelings interfere with her responsibility. She refused to take a mate for exactly that reason. "She just awakened a few hours ago. She's not strong enough for anything invasive yet."

"I understand, of course. But later?"

"Perhaps." At the sound of rending wood, Sylvan glanced down at her desk. She'd gouged four deep crevices in the polished wood surface without even being aware that her entire hand had morphed completely. If she'd been in public, at a press conference, that kind of slip could prove disastrous.

"When can you get me samples?" Leo asked. "I'll start setting up for the assays."

"I'll have to check with Elena on Drake's condition. Can Sophia collect what you need?"

"Certainly."

"Good. I'll have Sophia call you if she has any questions."

Leo was silent.

"What is it?" Sylvan asked.

"You said the turned Were has only just awakened. She could still deteriorate. If she's rabid…"

"She's not rabid." Sylvan's wolf pushed hard for freedom. Her skin shimmered and a whisper of pelt silvered over the surface. She shut her eyes and forced her shift to recede. "I wouldn't put your daughter at risk, Leo."

He cleared his throat in apology. "I know that, Alpha. Sophia has good instincts. I'm sure she'll be careful. Please forgive my fatherly concern."

"Understood. I want you to rush the results, and report directly to me. No one other than Nadia and Sophia is to know about this."

"My mate and I can easily handle all the testing ourselves," Leo assured her. "We'll await the samples and run the assays as soon as we have them."

"Thank you." Sylvan ended the call and resisted the urge to contact Elena immediately for an update on Drake's condition. Drake would sleep at least a few hours after achieving a release. Thinking about Drake spending herself with Elena's help, perhaps excited by Elena's presence, threatened to unbalance Sylvan's tenuous control. She grabbed the message slips for a distraction.

Councilor Zachary Gates had left three urgent messages. Sighing, Sylvan dialed his extension in the Capitol Complex. When his secretary put her through, she said, "Hello, Zachary. It's Sylvan."

"Councilor," Zachary said in his smooth, polished voice. "Good of you to call."

"How can I help you?" Sylvan asked, more annoyed than usual with Zachary's officious demeanor. Her temper and tolerance were frayed to the breaking point.

"The coalition members thought it might be a good time to convene a status meeting."

"When?" Sylvan represented all of the organized U.S. Weres in the Coalition of Preternatural Beings. Zachary represented the Vampires, Rudy Brown the Mage, Cecelia Thornton the Fae, and Ilona Dexter the Psi. Together, the five guided their species through the uncertain political and social consequences of the Exodus. In addition to unifying their political platforms, they discussed self-regulatory policies to ensure that the actions of one species did not contradict a position of one of the others or place any species at risk. Prior to the Exodus the Praetern species had been completely independent of one another, and the new coalition was an uneasy alliance. Their board meetings often devolved into heated arguments as each species subtly jockeyed for political leverage and economic power.

"As soon as possible," Zachary replied.

"An emergency meeting? Why?"

Zachary sighed as if he were reluctant to deliver the next message. "Several of the members were concerned about the media depiction of your...ah, slip."

"My *slip*?" Sylvan growled.

"I'm sure the photograph in the newspaper exaggerated your condition," Zachary said soothingly.

"My condition."

Zachary laughed. "Well, my dear—"

"Alpha," Sylvan said in a low, dangerous tone. "Alpha Mir, Councilor Gates."

"Of course…Alpha. You know how some of the board abhor public scrutiny. In fact, if they hadn't feared their economic interests would suffer, they wouldn't have joined your father in the Exodus at all. So naturally, they're concerned about any behavior that might generate adverse public opinion."

"Would you care to speak plainly?" Sylvan said icily.

"You looked like you were about to loose your beast, *Alpha*," Zachary said, all pretense of diplomacy gone. "The Coalition cannot have a rogue leader."

"You know very well what that picture showed. One of my young had been attacked. It's unfortunate the incident was photographed, but I don't intend to apologize to the board for it."

"I quite agree. And I'm sure if you give the board a simple assurance that they have no reason to fear public reprisal because of a repeat performance, the matter will be quickly disposed of."

"I'm afraid I'm unavailable for the next several days." Sylvan wondered about Zachary's true agenda. Vampires were constantly maneuvering for territory and political power, so she suspected Zachary's ultimate goal was to achieve superiority over all the other Praetern species. However, he was an adept politician and rarely revealed his true allegiances. "I'll advise you when my schedule allows."

"I'll expect your call, then." Zachary's tone was perceptibly cooler. "I wouldn't wait too long, Alpha."

"Is that a threat, Councilor?"

"Not at all. Consider it the advice of a friend."

Of one thing Sylvan was certain. Zachary Gates was no friend of the Weres. She wondered if he might be an enemy.

❖

Drake woke alone. Elena and Roger's scent lingered, but the one that overpowered theirs and made her stomach tighten was Sylvan's. Earthy and potent—burning pine and dark cinnamon. This time she'd dreamed of awakening in a hospital with Sylvan standing over her bed. In the dream, Sylvan had said she was part of the Pack now. Sylvan's scent had enveloped her and she'd become excited. She'd wanted to vault from the bed and take her. She'd wanted to bite her. Then Sylvan had been a wolf, a great silver beast calling for Drake to shift, to run, to hunt. The rest of the dream had fractured, as if experienced through a different consciousness—the world had become sound and scent and taste. And Sylvan. Always Sylvan. Alpha.

Drake thrashed restlessly. She could tell by the angle of the light streaming through the window that she'd slept most of the day. Far overhead, a plane engine droned. Much closer, she discerned muffled conversations and a riot of overlapping bird songs. She smelled fox, rabbit, deer. She sensed other presences in the building but had no feeling of danger.

Taking stock of her body, she was immediately aware of three urgent needs—she needed a bathroom and a shower; she was very, very hungry; and she wanted sex. She glimpsed a bathroom through a partially open door on the far side of her room and decided to take care of the simplest problem first.

Walking around for the first time in almost twenty-four hours, she expected to feel ill, but she didn't. She felt—strong. Alert. Excited. The bite on her arm from the girl in the ER was gone.

She used the bathroom and started the shower. The hot water brought a flush to her skin, and when she rubbed her hand over her torso, her nipples twinged and her loins throbbed. She didn't have to touch herself to know she was tense and aroused. She could feel the insistent pulse that matched the beat of her racing heart. She rubbed both palms up and down her abdomen and thought of Sylvan's arms around her, the heat of Sylvan's hard belly against her back, the curve of Sylvan's pelvis cradling her ass. She remembered the heat of Sylvan's mouth on the back of her neck and her clitoris jumped. She squeezed her hand between her legs. She was wet and hard. Ready.

A week ago if she'd felt like this she would have masturbated, but she found she didn't want to now. She wanted more than an orgasm. She wanted...she wasn't sure what she wanted. She craved warm, sleek flesh under her hands, against her tongue. She hungered for the scent of burnt leaves and cinnamon. She envisioned straddling Sylvan's hard stomach and painting her skin with her sex, marking her. Drake's canines erupted, short claws burst from her fingertips, and a trail of fire burned down the center of her abdomen. She flashed on the image of Sylvan snarling in her face and the taste of Sylvan in her mouth. Her glands swelled. Her sex pounded. She was burning up. She had to get out of the shower. She had to get outside. She had to run. To fight, to take.

Groaning, Drake stumbled back into the room and collapsed onto the bed. She couldn't go outside. She was afraid of what she might do. Covering her eyes with her arm, she gripped her sex in her fist and squeezed, trying to force the pressure to relent. Through the roaring in her ears, she heard the door open and quickly held out her arm.

"No, don't come in here."

"It's okay," a strong, clear voice answered. "You won't want me."

Drake turned her head. Misha stood inside the door. "I don't think you should be in here."

"It's safe." Misha grinned. "I could tell from outside the door you're dominant. Too close to me to be interested, probably."

"How about too old to be interested," Drake said through clenched teeth.

Misha frowned. "You're not much older than I am. I've tangled plenty with Weres older than you."

"You have?" Drake stared at the dark-haired teenager with the luminous, mahogany eyes, thankful the teen was dressed in jeans and a barely there T-shirt. She would not have wanted to have this conversation with both of them nude. She casually pulled the sheet over her body, relieved to find that the very act of talking helped her get a handle on her rioting system. She was even happier to realize she didn't have the slightest desire to jump on Misha.

"Sure. We live a long time, remember? A couple of decades is nothing for us."

"I'm not sure I can get used to that," Drake muttered. "I'm Drake, by the way."

"I know," Misha said. "Elena said you were in the ER when the Alpha came to get me. I don't remember. I'm sorry."

"No problem. How are you feeling?"

"Okay." She turned her back and pulled up her T-shirt to show Drake. Her back was smooth and unblemished. No trace of a scar. "All healed. Thanks for helping me."

"You're welcome, but I didn't do anything," Drake said. "I'm really glad you're all right."

Misha plopped down on the end of Drake's bed and propped her chin on her fist, studying Drake unabashedly. Drake moved in the opposite direction.

"You want to tangle, I bet," Misha observed.

"I…uh…how old are you?"

"Eighteen next month." Misha twisted around and put her back against the wall, tossing her leg casually over Drake's calf where it rested beneath the sheet. "I remember when I first had the frenzy. It was really really bad. I couldn't think about anything *except* sex. Everyone thinks it's so easy being dominant, because there's usually someone around who wants to tangle." Misha made a face. "It's not so much fun when no matter what you do, you can't get it to stop."

Drake closed her eyes. "I don't think we should be having this conversation."

"Why?"

"Because I don't know what I'm doing." Drake pushed herself up on her elbows and met Misha's eyes. "Maybe you ought to be a little more afraid of me."

"Maybe you should be afraid of *me*." Misha narrowed her eyes and made a low rumbling sound in her chest.

"Don't," Drake warned at Misha's challenge, her voice dropping.

Misha held Drake's gaze for a few more seconds, then shivered and looked away. "Wow. That was intense." She cut Drake a quick look. "I was wrong. You're way more dominant than me, and the Alpha says I could be a *centuri* someday." She rolled her eyes. "If I make it through *sentrie* training without screwing up again."

"What happened in the park wasn't your fault."

"I left the Compound," Misha said softly, running the sheet through her fingers. "That was dumb. Then I let that asshole get behind me. Getting stabbed serves me right."

"You'll know better next time," Drake said.

"Damn right." Misha regarded Drake with a sidelong glance,

careful not to engage eye contact. "You know, I don't get a chance to tangle with too many Weres who are more dominant than me. You might like tangling with a dominant."

"Thanks, but I don't think so," Drake said.

"I'm not interested in mating or anything," Misha said matter-of-factly. "I mean, if you want a submissive mate, that's cool. But you wouldn't have to worry about it with me."

"I don't want to…tangle…with anyone right now. Is there any chance I can get some food?"

"You sure? Because your call is really strong." Misha slid her leg a little higher on Drake's. "And I'm really feeling ready."

"Just food." Drake jumped out of bed, preferring being naked to the continued physical contact. Misha was only doing what was natural, but Drake had no idea what was natural for her any longer. "And some clothes."

Misha shrugged nonchalantly, apparently unconcerned by the rejection, and sat forward on the edge of the bed. "The Alpha lets us hunt as long as we don't go alone. Can you shift at will yet? I can, if I concentrate."

"I can't remember shifting." Drake frowned. "Maybe I can't." The thought of not being able to shift bothered her. If she was a Were now, she wanted to be whole. She gasped as sudden pain raked through her entrails. "God, what is that? It won't let up."

"Your wolf wants out," Misha said.

"How can you tell?" Drake barely managed to get the words out around the choking pain. She leaned against the wall, not certain she'd be able to stay standing much longer.

Misha pointed to Drake's stomach. A fine line of dark pelt ran down the center of her lower abdomen. "That happens when your wolf ascends. You know—when you're challenged or in sex frenzy."

"It feels like something's trying to rip its way out of me," Drake said, rubbing her stomach.

"She probably is. Especially if you need a release, which you must even if you can't tell. You sure you don't wan—"

"Food," Drake repeated, although the urge for sex was back full force. "And those clothes."

Misha vaulted off the bed and opened the door. "Come on. I'll take you to the mess hall."

Drake followed her down the hall. Misha pointed into an alcove just inside the front door.

"Grab pants from the stack in there. A shirt too, if you want."

"Thanks." Drake dressed automatically, but when Misha held open the door to the porch, she hesitated. "Should I tell Elena I'm leaving?"

"You're not a prisoner," Misha said softly. "You're Pack."

Drake knew better than to think it would be that easy. She'd been in this situation dozens of times while making her way through the state care system. Just when she'd get settled in one place, she'd be moved because of funding cuts or lack of personnel. She'd wake up in a new place, surrounded by strangers. If she was lucky, there'd be someone like Misha, who didn't care if she was an outsider, to befriend her and explain the rules and regs. But more often than not there was no one. Even if she made an ally or two, she could always count on needing to win her place. She'd learned quickly how to do that, first with her fists, then with her brain. Now she had to learn the rules all over again, but she was in a whole new world in a body she barely recognized, with feelings and urges she couldn't control. She wondered if she'd survive, let alone ever truly belong. The clawing, gnashing sensation in her stomach started again and she winced.

Outside in the ballpark-sized courtyard between the sprawl of log and stone buildings, male and female Weres, most dressed in khaki or black BDUs, a few shirtless, came and went in pairs and groups. Some slowed and stared, a few narrowed their eyes and rumbled. Drake didn't make eye contact, but she didn't lower her head either.

"Look, Misha, maybe this isn't such a good ide—"

"Hey! Here come Alex and Jazz," Misha said.

Drake looked where Misha pointed. The two teens she remembered from the ER made a beeline for them across the hard-packed earth.

"What should I do?" Drake said quietly.

"Your wolf knows what to do," Misha said confidently.

Drake wasn't so sure. She stood still as they drew closer. Her skin felt galvanized. The hairs on the back of her neck stood up. Her loins tightened, not with the now familiar urge for sex, but with an urge to fight. The two boys stopped a few feet from her and regarded her warily, their legs spread aggressively, their shoulders thrust forward. She kept her hands open at her sides and her head up. She looked from one to the other, meeting their eyes in turn. Alex immediately ducked his head and shifted to one side, leaving Jazz facing her.

"I'm Drake," she said, watching his eyes.

"I remember you from the ER." His nostrils flared and he looked confused. "You smell like the Alpha."

Drake wondered why, but she said nothing, waiting, not moving. He slipped around behind her and she growled softly, a quiet warning. She heard a soft, plaintive whine, then the press of a cheek against her shoulder.

"I can tangle with you," Jazz whispered, sliding around in front of her, brushing his chest across her arm. He met her gaze for only a second before casting a look at Misha. "Unless you...?"

Misha shook her head.

"No, thank you," Drake said to Jazz, and he shrugged, unperturbed, the same way Misha had. "Misha and I were on our way to get something to eat. You guys want to come?"

Jazz and Alex readily agreed and fell in on either side of Misha, jostling her playfully. Drake sighed inwardly, the first hurdle cleared. They'd almost reached the long one-story building from which emanated a plethora of mouthwatering odors when someone called her name. Sophia hurried across the courtyard in their direction.

"Go ahead without me," Drake said to the adolescents. "I'll be a few minutes."

"See you," Misha called as she took off with the boys.

"How are you?" Sophia said breathlessly, scanning Drake's face.

"All right, I think." Feeling curious eyes on her as more Weres passed by, Drake pointed to a shaded area by the side of the mess hall, just at the edge of the forest. "Let's talk over there for a minute."

"I called in sick to the ER for you this morning," Sophia said as they made their way over. "I hope you don't mind."

"No," Drake said. "I'm really glad you did. I'll call later and tell them I have a personal emergency. I have plenty of leave time coming." She checked the woods behind them. Possum. Rabbit. Raccoon. Nothing threatening. She put herself between Sophia and the forest just the same. "If I can go back to work at all."

"Why wouldn't you be able to?" Sophia asked.

"It's a little too soon to be sure of my prognosis."

"You look good." Sophia tilted her head. "Your scent is healthy." Sophia's eyes widened and she caught her breath, her face flushing. "Oh."

"Please tell me you're not going to offer," Drake said.

Sophia laughed. "I gather the adolescents already did?"

Drake grimaced. "Enthusiastically."

"I can't imagine how this all feels to you right now," Sophia said.

"The weird thing is," Drake said, "part of me feels completely natural. The part that isn't trying to rip my guts out."

"She wants you to shift—I remember what that's like," Sophia murmured. "All this power bottled up inside, needing some way out and never knowing how to let it free. Never being able to make it stop. All our instincts try to surface at once, creating a huge hormonal bottleneck, for want of a better descriptor. And the only outlet for a while is sex." She appraised Drake frankly. "Sex is a safety valve. A release will help you."

"I...I don't think I'm ready." Drake didn't know why, but despite the gnawing demand for sex that tore at her like a powerful predator, she didn't *want* anyone. She swiped at the sweat trickling down her neck and thought she smelled Sylvan, but that couldn't be.

"What you're feeling is perfectly natural, you know."

"I understand—but my head and my body aren't quite in sync on all of that."

"Just so you know, a lot of the unmated Weres are going to feel your call, but no one is *compelled* to answer." She grinned shyly. "A lot probably will, though. They offer because they...well...want you."

"Have you seen Sylvan?" Drake asked abruptly. She didn't want to talk about the craving that was slicing her to ribbons, one slow, agonizing cut at a time.

"The Alpha?" Sophia shook her head. "No, but none of the *centuri* are here, so the Alpha is probably no longer in the Compound."

Sylvan was gone. Drake should have expected that, but the disappointment was still exquisite. Sylvan had been doing her duty as Alpha that morning, ensuring that the newly turned Were was not a danger to the Pack. Now that Drake was reasonably stable, the morning's intimacy with Sylvan was not likely to be repeated. The Alpha was no longer concerned with her. Drake shuddered, a howl of rage blasting inside her head.

"Ah, God." Drake stumbled back a step, sweat covering her arms and soaking through her cotton T-shirt.

"Drake?" Sophia reached for her. "What is it?"

"Nothing," Drake said, suppressing a gasp as another shaft of pain radiated along her spine. "What if she wins this struggle? The...my... wolf."

"She won't." Sophia slipped her arm around Drake's waist. "Come on. Let's get you something to eat. Your metabolism is about ten times higher than it was at this time yesterday."

"Afterwards, I want you to run a battery of tests on me."

"Looking for what?" Sophia led Drake up the steps and across the wide porch to the mess hall.

"Anything. Anything that might suggest I could turn rabid."

"I'll do it," Sophia said, "but if you were going to deteriorate, I don't think we'd see a period of lucidity like this."

"But you don't know, do you?"

"No," Sophia said regretfully. "We don't really understand anything about how you were turned."

"Then until we do," Drake said, "we have to consider me a potential danger to everyone. Maybe I should be locked up a while longer."

Sophia stopped abruptly and, facing Drake, slipped her arms around Drake's shoulders. She stroked Drake's damp hair. "We don't cage Pack members. We protect them."

Weary of the constant pain and loneliness, Drake closed her eyes and rested her forehead against Sophia's. If only she could believe her.

CHAPTER NINETEEN

A little before six p.m., Sylvan shoved aside a pile of paperwork on her desk and impatiently punched in Elena's cell number. The instant Elena answered, she demanded, "How is she?"

"Better. She's with Sophia right now."

"Sophia?" A barrage of heat shot into Sylvan's chest. She'd held off contacting Sophia about taking samples from Drake so Drake would have more chance to heal. "Doing what? I told you Drake wasn't *ready.*"

"Alpha," Elena said softly, "Sophia is a medic. She's just following up on Drake's status."

"Where are they?"

"Sophia took her to the mess hall."

The pressure in Sylvan's chest intensified and she bolted to her feet. "Drake is out with the Pack? She's a dominant in frenzy and completely untrained! Elena—what are you thinking?"

"Sophia is with her and Roger is on his way to join them, but Drake is fine. In fact…"

"What? What's wrong?"

"Drake is refusing to let *anyone* answer her call."

"She's not in frenzy, then?" The pressure in Sylvan's chest eased and she drew in a slow breath.

"I'm not sure. She's broadcasting strongly, but…it's different. *She's* different."

Sylvan's heart clenched. "Is there any sign of fever?"

"Nothing so far."

"And she seems healthy?"

"Yes, very."

"That's good. That's good." Sylvan dropped into her chair, tilted her head back, and closed her eyes. She'd forced herself to work, answering phone calls, reviewing proposals, making notations on endless minutes from endless committee meetings with half a mind. Underneath it all, she was constantly aware of the powerful urge to see Drake. To touch her. She rubbed the spot on her chest where Drake had bitten her. Her sex tightened.

"Alpha?" Elena asked uncertainly.

"What?" Sylvan replied.

"I asked when you would be back."

"I don't know."

"She carries your scent."

"An anomaly. It will fade." The bite on Sylvan's chest throbbed harder. "Tell Roger I want him to indoctrinate her. As soon as possible."

"She'll need to have a complete releas—"

"You said she's not in frenzy," Sylvan snapped.

"I know," Elena said patiently, "but *something* is driving her. Alpha, I can sense her call across the Compound, and her need is powerful. Would you have her be in pain?"

"No. Never." Sylvan closed her eyes. "I must speak with Sophia."

"I'll tell her to contact you right away."

Sylvan thought of Drake in need, surrounded by Pack who would willingly answer her call. Drake deserved the comfort of Pack, and she needed the physical release—with whatever Pack member she chose. That was the natural order of their existence, and Sylvan could not interfere because of her own irrational reactions. She was Alpha, and she owed Drake no less than the freedom every other Pack member enjoyed. She wouldn't make Drake suffer just because she didn't want anyone else near her. She would have to tolerate Drake finding her place in the Pack as every Were had done for millennia.

Elena repeated, "Alpha? Should I have Sophia call you?"

"That's not necessary." Sylvan winced at the stabbing pain emanating from the bite in her chest. "I'm on my way back. I'll talk to Sophia when I arrive."

"Of course, Alpha. I'll just tell Roger to take care of Drake, then."

"Good. Tell him...tell him to make sure she has whatever she needs."

❖

Becca's number one rule was to always follow a lead, no matter where it went, no matter how difficult the pursuit might be. Unless her mysterious caller contacted her again with more information about where and how the girls were being infected with Were fever, she had to pursue those who might know something. She had two choices— Jody Gates and Sylvan Mir. Getting an appointment with the Alpha was about as easy as getting to see the President, but Jody Gates might just be her admission ticket. So Becca did the logical thing. She followed the Vampire detective.

Jody had gone home after their breakfast that morning, presumably to sleep during daylight hours. Becca called the station house again and asked for Jody, to check her schedule. She was told the detective would be on duty at ten p.m. Just to be safe, after catching a few hours of sleep herself, she parked outside Jody's State Street town house around six and waited. A few minutes before seven, Jody emerged, walked to a sleek black Porsche, and headed east toward the river. Becca gave her a full minute's head start because she was fairly certain she knew where she was going.

Ten minutes later, Becca drove past Club Nocturne. Jody's Porsche was in the parking lot. She pulled into a far corner from which she could watch the Porsche but where her Camaro wouldn't be readily visible to someone walking out of the club. She shut off the ignition and sat with her hands on the wheel, debating going inside. The longer she sat in the car, the harder it was to convince herself she didn't want to see Jody in the throes of blood thrall—even if it was with a stranger.

❖

Moving stealthily on foot through the underbrush along the shore, Rex approached the black Town Car idling under the bridge. He waited and watched the car for a full fifteen minutes, constantly scanning the area for any sign of lookouts or possible ambush. He didn't trust any of his business associates. He didn't trust anyone. When he was certain the area was clear, he posted his own bodyguards and tapped on the rear window. The door locks snicked open and the rear door swung wide. He glanced inside. Two men with military haircuts and matching black turtlenecks occupied the front seats, their weapons trained on him through the open rear door. A middle-aged man with silver streaked black hair, wearing a two-thousand-dollar blended silk suit, sat on the far side of the rear seat. The man gestured for Rex to get in.

"Tell your men to put away their guns," Rex said.

"Of course," the man said pleasantly. He murmured something in a voice too low for Rex to hear, and the men in the front slid their weapons from sight.

Rex got into the vehicle and closed the door. "What was so important we had to meet in person? I have important business—"

"*Our* business is important," the man said with a biting edge in his voice. "Your business is running drugs."

"My profits underwrite your agenda," Rex snarled.

"And we don't need your people drawing unwarranted attention to us."

"Everything is under control," Rex said.

"Is that why the Were Alpha made a personal visit to the waterfront to dispatch a pack of rogues?"

"I can hardly be responsible for every rogue Were in the city."

"She's asking questions. It's only a matter of time before she discovers where your drugs are coming from. And where the profits go."

"She'll soon have something bigger to worry about than a few rogues overdosing on DSX."

"We can't risk further exposure." The man leaned forward, his dark eyes glinting like a cobra's in the half-light reflected off the nearby water. "Your lack of control over your underlings has forced us to escalate our plans. She has to be eliminated."

"I'll take care of it," Rex said, inwardly reveling at the chance to finally destroy his enemy.

"Do it soon, and don't make any mistakes."

CHAPTER TWENTY

At dusk, Drake followed Roger down a narrow path through the forest to a clearing by a small, mirror-surfaced lake. She straddled a fallen log and put her back against a pine, giving her a view of the lake on one side and the forest on the other. Roger, a quiet-spoken male with shoulder-length thick brown hair, milk chocolate eyes, and a wiry build, settled onto a large rock a few feet away.

"I take it you've been tasked with keeping me out of trouble?" Drake said.

"Not exactly. I am a *magister*—a guidance counselor of sorts," Roger said with a wry grin. "I work with the adolescents, mostly."

"Because they're volatile?" Drake asked.

"Volatile, unpredictable, hormonally hyped, impatient, aggressive, thrill-seeking—your run-of-the-mill healthy young Weres, pretty much."

"But I'm not an adolescent," Drake pointed out. She wasn't being argumentative, just realistic. "And I might not be healthy."

"You're not an adolescent, that's true," Roger said mildly, "but we have no indication that you're not healthy. In fact, you seem extraordinarily strong for someone who's just been rearranged at a cellular level."

"Can you tell me more about that?" Drake asked.

"It's not really my area." Roger shrugged apologetically. "I don't want to misinform you. We have scientists and medics who can explain it all better than I can. But of this I am sure—everything about you signals you're a Were."

"Everything—meaning what?"

"Your scent, most importantly, and your natural dominance. But also your instinctive behavior. You just positioned yourself so you can detect any aggressor who might approach, while your back is defended by the barrier of the tree. You just act—Were."

"How long before we can be sure I won't become rabid?"

"I don't know. None of the Packs have very much experience with turned Weres." Roger met her eyes briefly before glancing away. "The Alpha wants you indoctrinated, so she believes you're safe."

"And that's that?" Drake said mildly.

"The Alpha is law."

"I understand." And on some innate, deeply primal level, Drake did understand. She felt a connection to all the other Pack members, the hundreds she'd never met and might never know, and at the center of that expansive, intricate network of connected spirits, she *knew* the guiding unifying force. Sylvan. The Alpha. "What does indoctrination entail?"

"Making you aware of Pack rules you would have learned growing up with your Packmates—except you haven't had that chance. You *will* learn, one way or the other, but it will be safer if you know how to behave before you have to be taught."

"Safer."

"You're an adult Were," Roger said gently. "It doesn't matter that you don't understand the rules. Your behavior will be taken at face value and Pack members will respond instinctively."

"Okay. So give me the critical lessons first."

"You already know the most important one. The Alpha protects us and unites us, and for that, we give her our absolute loyalty. Every member of the Pack will fight to defend her, so you must be careful not to imply any challenge to her. Don't sit until she sits, don't touch her, don't meet her gaze directly."

"And she rules for life?"

"Unless she passes the title to a successor."

"No one ever challenges?"

"Sometimes when an Alpha is very old, a younger dominant will challenge, but it's rare." Roger looked away, his expression pained.

"What?"

"All Weres are territorial and aggressive. Ours is the largest, most dominant Pack in North America, and there are other Packs who would like to see our power diminished. They've warred against us."

"Literally? Attacked your Pack?"

"*Our* Pack," Roger said gently.

Drake nodded, but she knew her acceptance into the Pack wouldn't be as simple as Roger made it seem. She'd grown up human, she knew nothing of Pack politics or hierarchy, and she might not even be a normal Were. And right now she could do nothing about any of it except learn as much as she could and be ready to fight if necessary. "When was the attack? What happened?"

"A decade ago our Alpha and her hunting party were ambushed. She was murdered." Roger sighed. "Some fear the war is not yet over. There are always skirmishes along our borders, but no full-scale attacks in years."

"But if there were, Sylvan would be the target," Drake said, the pressure in her chest erupting on a rough growl.

"She has her *centuri* to protect her."

Drake had experienced firsthand the ferocious power of Sylvan's guards when Niki had pinned her to the wall in the ER. She respected their ability, but she couldn't shake a sudden fierce desire to protect Sylvan herself. She'd never been a warrior and had no idea what prompted the compulsion, but it was so strong she wanted to return immediately to the Compound and find Sylvan.

"How do you feel right now?" Roger asked.

Drake frowned, not following the change in subject. "Considering that I woke up in a body that doesn't quite feel like my own, not too bad."

"Do you need to tang—have sex?"

"I know what tangle means." Drake grumbled in frustration, because he was right. Until a few minutes ago, the pounding in her loins had been bearable, but now the urge for sex was painful. "I would assume you already know the answer to your question."

He nodded. "I've been aware of your call all day, but you're broadcasting much more powerfully right now."

Drake dropped her gaze down his body. His *awareness* was evident. "Sorry."

Roger grinned. "I'm mated, so it's no hardship for me."

"I've already been told this is normal, more or less," Drake said.

"Your situation is unique."

Drake glowered, changing positions in an effort to relieve some of the pressure on her swollen, aching groin. "I've been hearing that a lot."

Roger looked sympathetic. "With adolescents, the urge builds gradually around the time their wolf ascends. Their wolf wants freedom but the adolescent can't shift voluntarily, despite the pressure to do so. The result is a great deal of physiological tension that is dispelled most effectively through sexual release."

"So if I could shift, the pressure to have sex would ease?" Drake asked.

"Perhaps, at least temporarily. For a very dominant Were, which you seem to be, there is no substitute for release."

"When will I know if I can shift?"

"You already have," Roger said with surprise. "The Alpha forced your first shift and probably saved your life."

Drake's heart raced at the thought of Sylvan protecting her, and the already searing pressure in her loins built higher. She leaned her head back against the tree, closed her eyes, and tried to steady her breathing.

"The first lesson," Roger said gently, "is to accept what you're feeling and act on it."

"With anyone who offers?" Drake asked, her eyes still closed, her breath catching painfully with each exhalation.

"No. You have a choice, just as do those who answer your call."

She regarded him through narrowed eyes, her vision wavering as pain lanced through her stomach. "What if I don't want anyone?"

He frowned. "I don't know. If your body is prevented from releasing naturally, the hormonal fluxes might force a breakdown."

"Make me feral?"

"Eventually your instincts will prevail, and if you can't bring yourself to overcome your resistance to finding a release, you could lose control completely," Roger said softly.

"But I might be able to fight the urge and maintain my sanity?"

"Perhaps, but why would you want to? Why not just tangle with a willing Packmate?"

"I don't know." The pain in Drake's stomach intensified and she struggled not to double over. "I'm not sure, but I don't think my wolf would let me tangle with just any Were who offers."

Roger's brows drew down. "You can feel her? Tell what she wants?"

"She's making it pretty damn clear."

"Then who *does* she want?"

Drake shook her head, knowing instinctively she shouldn't answer. Sweat matted her hair and her skin flamed. She pulled off her shirt. Her abdomen was rigid, hard-packed muscles vibrating beneath sex-sheened skin. Her canines and claws erupted. A fine thin line of midnight pelt scored the center of her lower abdomen.

"Roger," she said, her voice deep and rough. "Get out of here."

"No, I can't leave you alone," Roger protested, but he shot to his feet and backed up.

"I don't know if I can stop whatever's happening," Drake gasped. "You need to go. *Go.*"

Roger shivered, unable to disobey her command. "I'll get Elena." Roger raced toward the forest. "Hold on, Drake. Just hold on."

Drake curled up, clutching her midsection, writhing as pain ripped and slashed through her. She was on the verge of losing the battle, and terrified of what she might become.

❖

Sylvan lunged forward from the rear of the Rover and crowded between the front seats. The Compound was just ahead. "Hurry!"

Andrew shot her a worried look. "Alpha?"

From behind her, Niki said, "What is it?"

"Just hurry," Sylvan said, clenching her jaws as the throbbing in the bite on her chest intensified. Andrew slowed and Sylvan jumped out.

Elena ran across the courtyard toward the Rover, a frantic Roger at her side.

"It's Drake," Elena exclaimed. "She's in frenzy."

"I know." Sylvan ran toward the forest, toward Drake.

"Alpha," Niki shouted, following her.

"Stay back," Sylvan ordered as she burst into the clearing.

Drake lay on the ground, moaning weakly. Sylvan tore off her shirt and dropped down beside her. Pulling Drake into her arms, she cradled Drake's face against her bare shoulder, feeding her strength through the touch of flesh on flesh. Drake's eyes were feverish, her hair soaked with sweat.

"Drake," Sylvan murmured. "I'm here."

"Sylvan," Drake gasped. "Oh, God, Sylvan, I hurt."

"I know, I know. I'll fix it," Sylvan soothed, caressing Drake's chest and belly. Drake's nipples were swollen and tight, her stomach rippling with need. Sylvan's own nipples were hard as stone, her clitoris a throbbing ridge under the fly of her jeans. Drake arched in her arms, rubbing against her, coating Sylvan's skin with pheromones. Sylvan instantly absorbed the chemicals and her canines shot out. Her glands pumped out hormones and kinins with brutal force. Her system flooded with sex stimulants and her clitoris jerked fully erect. Her control crumbled. She needed to calm Drake before she lost all restraint and took her, roughly, relentlessly. She unbuttoned Drake's pants.

"You smell so good," Drake moaned, licking Sylvan's neck. She kissed her way down the tight column of Sylvan's throat to Sylvan's chest and sucked the bruise that glowed purple beneath Sylvan's shimmering silver skin.

Sylvan's hips bucked and she growled a warning. Drake ignored her, raking her short claws down the center of Sylvan's abdomen before pulling a taut nipple into her mouth. Sylvan snarled and rolled Drake under her. She ripped Drake's pants open and cupped her sex, pressing the heel of her hand down on the glands that pulsed beneath Drake's protruding clitoris. She slipped her fingers into Drake's tight, hot depths and massaged her, inside and out.

Gasping, Drake moaned against Sylvan's breast. "Oh God, what are you doing to me?"

"You need to release." Sylvan skated her mouth over Drake's and thrust her tongue inside, tasting, drinking, claiming. She thrust harder into her sex, stimulating the internal extension of Drake's clitoris with her fingertips. Potent neurotransmitters poured into Sylvan's palm and set off a chain reaction in her own body. Her clitoris twitched and her glands pumped. She readied to erupt.

Drake clutched Sylvan's shoulders, driving herself up and down on Sylvan's hand, faster and faster. She dragged her canines over Sylvan's neck and licked the shallow scratches. "I want to come. I want to come for you."

Sylvan growled and pulled Drake's head back with a hand fisted in her hair. She stared into Drake's gold-shot black eyes. "You *will* come for me."

"Yes, God yes." Drake's legs and stomach were rigid. She gripped Sylvan's arm, her claws drawing blood, and forced Sylvan deeper inside her. She threw back her head. "Now. Please now. Make me come for you."

"Touch me," Sylvan demanded, bracing herself over Drake's body on one arm while she drove inside her.

Drake tore open Sylvan's jeans and slid her fingers around Sylvan's clitoris. Instinctively she massaged the glands underneath on every rapid downstroke. Sylvan roared as Drake forced her to empty. Her pheromones gushed, merging with Drake's, enclosing them in a sensual mist of sex hormones. The bite on her chest throbbed, kinins seeping from the puncture wounds that had reopened when Drake stimulated her.

"I have to come," Drake pleaded, licking and sucking Sylvan's chest. She scored Sylvan's back, her hips a blur on Sylvan's hand. "Please. Please. Sylvan…"

"Yes. Yes," Sylvan groaned, inflamed by the heat of Drake's mouth, drowning in her essence. *"Yes."*

Sylvan buried her canines in the soft triangle at the juncture of Drake's neck and shoulder. Mine. *Mine.*

Drake jerked at the bite and exploded over Sylvan's arm. Sylvan's hips pumped and Drake's fingers were flooded with Sylvan's hot, thick essence. But Drake knew there was more. She wanted more. She wanted something she didn't know how to name. Instinct urged her to sink her canines into the bite on Sylvan's chest, but Sylvan held her face away.

"Easy, easy," Sylvan whispered, cradling Drake against her chest until Drake's release ebbed.

Sylvan curled protectively around Drake even though Niki and Andrew would be standing guard in the forest nearby. Their clothes lay in scattered shreds on the ground. A swath of brilliant stars and a bright three-quarter moon lit the clearing. Content just to watch the silver shadows play across Drake's face, Sylvan traced the angle of Drake's jaw with her thumb and let her fingers run over the mark she'd made on Drake's neck. Her mark. Hers.

"I dreamed of this," Drake murmured, smoothing her palm down Sylvan's abdomen.

"What did you dream?" Sylvan caught her breath when Drake stroked her clitoris. She should tell her to stop, but she didn't want her to. She hadn't emptied completely. She wouldn't without the bite, and she couldn't risk another bite. Still, she was more satisfied than she'd ever been with another Were. Even when Francesca drained her to the point of weakness, she'd never had such pleasure. So she didn't protest when Drake fondled her into readiness again.

"I dreamed we hunted together." Drake kissed Sylvan's throat, and her mouth. She rolled the hard, satiny head of Sylvan's clitoris between her fingers and teased her tongue inside Sylvan's mouth. When Sylvan groaned, Drake pushed her tongue deeper. Sylvan was still hard and swollen, and Drake wanted more. She kept teasing her as she talked. "We ran together, hunted in the forest together, slept curled around one another in a clearing like this one."

Sylvan was breathing hard, her legs tight, her pelvis lifting into Drake's hand. She gritted her teeth, needing to release.

"This isn't a dream, is it?" Drake whispered, scraping her canines down Sylvan's throat.

Sylvan clasped the back of Drake's neck, preventing her from moving lower, from biting her again. Silver coated her belly. She whispered, "No. This isn't a dream."

"I want to feel you come. You want to, don't you?" Drake licked Sylvan's neck. "Tell me what you want."

"Harder. Press harder."

Drake pushed herself up on her elbow and massaged the base of Sylvan's clitoris. "Like this?"

Sylvan's face shifted, grew more angular, her eyes shimmered with gold. Her words came out on a growl. "Yes."

"Maybe like this?" Drake rolled the deep glands, squeezing gently.

"Yes." Sylvan shuddered and her canines gleamed against her full lower lip. Her clitoris twitched against Drake's palm. She was so

close. Her wolf surged, furious at being dominated and denied. Sylvan snarled and reared up, trying to force Drake onto her back. To take her, come on her. Claim her.

"No," Drake murmured gently, pressing her mouth to Sylvan's ear, holding her down with just her hand on Sylvan's sex. "Let me please you." She remembered the dream and the weight of Sylvan against her back, pinning her to the earth. She licked along the edge of Sylvan's jaw and kissed her again, circling Sylvan faster and harder. "Let me please you. Alpha."

Sylvan bucked, her claws digging into Drake's shoulder. "Yes."

"That's it." Drake squeezed Sylvan's pulsing sex tightly. "Come all over me."

"Yes," Sylvan shouted, spending into Drake's hand.

Drake pulled Sylvan into her arms and leaned back against the fallen log, stroking Sylvan's back until Sylvan's labored breathing quieted. She caressed Sylvan's stomach and gently fingered her clitoris. Sylvan grumbled lazily. "You're still hard. What do you need?"

"Nothing," Sylvan sighed, more content than she'd ever expected to be.

Drake didn't believe her, but she couldn't demand more. She had no idea of her eventual place in the Pack or if she'd even live long enough to discover it. Sylvan was the heart of the Pack, and Drake could make no claim on her. She held her, committing every detail to memory—the heat of her body, her scent, the sound of her breathing—and cherished the connection she might never have again.

CHAPTER TWENTY-ONE

Sometime after midnight, Becca finally gave up on waiting and headed for Club Nocturne. Jody was still inside and might be for the rest of the night. Following her had seemed like a good idea earlier in the evening, but at this rate, she might be sitting out in the dark until sunrise with nothing to show for it.

When nothing was happening, it was time to make something happen.

As Becca threaded her way between the cars and joined the steady stream of Weres, humans, and Vampires entering the club, her excitement grew. She could have pretended the humming in the pit of her stomach was due to her natural love of the unknown and her insatiable curiosity. Partly true. But she took pride in not lying to herself, so she admitted she was aroused by the idea of watching the Vampires feed. Their sexual hunger, so inseparably linked to their primitive need for sustenance, was raw and sensual and uncivilized. The razor's edge separating the elegant, cool exteriors Vampires projected in public from their private carnal bloodlust drew her like a potent aphrodisiac. By the time she reached the door, she was wet.

Inside, the scene was much the same as it had been the night before. Muted lights, low, pounding bass notes thudding from hidden speakers, teeming bodies in various stages of undress. Tonight, though, she took her time making her way to the bar. Already many of the Vampires were feeding, and the sound and smell of sexual gratification enveloped her in an erotic haze. A growl, deep throated and dangerous, caught her attention and she slowed next to a long, low-slung leather sofa. Two Vampires, a blond female in a skintight black sheath and a svelte, shirtless redheaded male in tight riding breeches and thigh-high leather boots, crouched over the massive body of a naked male Were. The female, her hips writhing, fed from his neck while her nails raked scarlet trails across his chest. Even in the dim light, Becca could see the shine of arousal coursing down her thighs. The male Vampire, his incisors flashing, licked an enormous erection that pumped a steady stream over the Were's darkly furred chest and belly. The Were, his features contorted into a rictus of pleasure, thrashed and roared with each violent pulsation.

Becca had a sudden, sharp image of herself reclining in Jody's arms, Jody's mouth on her neck, drinking her, while another Vampire crouched between her legs, sucking and licking her until she orgasmed. The fantasy was so potent she was instantly on the verge of coming. The female Vampire looked up from the Were's neck, her mouth a crimson promise, and smiled at Becca. Her eyes were the deep maroon of long-banked coals, and when she held out her hand, Becca stumbled toward her.

You are so beautiful. Will you let me taste you?

"Oh yes," Becca whispered, aching for the sharp, sweet bite and the ecstasy to follow. Her arousal blossomed, expanded, just a breath away from unleashing. If only she could feel that stunning mouth on her throat.

An arm snaked around Becca's waist and yanked her backward, away from the mesmerizing scene. Warm breath caressed her ear.

"I thought we had an agreement," Jody murmured.

Becca whimpered, straining toward the blonde, so ready for her. "Let me go."

"No."

Jody's voice was so cool, her body so hot against Becca's back. Or maybe Becca was the one on fire. She gripped the arm around her waist and pulled Jody's hand up to her breast, arching in pleasure as long, slender fingers trailed across her nipple. She writhed against Jody and Jody's hand on her breast tightened. When she angled her head, offering her neck, she felt two sharp points of pressure against her throat.

"Yes," Becca moaned, squeezing her hand around Jody's on her breast. "Do it. God, I'm going to come."

Jody trembled, her throat working convulsively. She wanted her. She wanted to drink her. She wanted to come with the hot flood of

Becca's essence filling every dark, frozen place within her. She ground against Becca's ass, working herself toward the peak that could only be crested with the taste of Becca in her mouth. She had to have her. The hunger was vast, endless, agonizing. She sighed languorously and stroked Becca's breasts and stomach, enjoying the last sane moments of pleasure before she surrendered to the mindless bloodlust.

"Now." Becca gripped Jody's hair and forced Jody's mouth harder against her neck. "Please."

Dimly, Jody heard the broken plea, but what registered were Becca's angry words of the night before. *Don't ever do that to me again. I decide who I sleep with.*

"God damn it." Jody grabbed Becca's arm and yanked her through the crowd toward the door, ignoring Becca's sharp protesting cries. Once outside, she dragged her across the parking lot to where she'd left her car. When she reached the car, she pushed Becca against the hood and backed away from her. Becca's expression ricocheted from hurt to perplexity, and finally, to anger.

"What the hell are you doing?" Becca shouted.

"What am I doing?" Jody raked a hand through her hair. "I *told* you to stay away from this club. Do you know how close you came to hosting Meredith *and* Philip just now? Is that what you want? Strangers fucking you when you don't have the power to say no?"

"Who are Meredith—" Becca shivered and wrapped her arms around her midsection, remembering the blond Vampire holding out her hand, beckoning her. She remembered, too, the fantasy of Jody at her neck while she orgasmed in a stranger's mouth. She sagged against the car. "My God. I don't understand. One second I was watching, and the next I was…" She looked away, humiliated, praying Jody didn't know what she'd been fantasizing.

"Meredith used your own thoughts to enthrall you," Jody said sharply.

"You can do that? See someone's thoughts…twist them around?"

Jody took a deep breath, battling her still-raging hunger. She needed to sate the bloodlust stirred by the feel of Becca in her arms, the taste of her against her lips. She needed to feed. "Some can. Especially if someone is broadcasting strongly enough. Meredith is very powerful."

Becca watched Jody pace in a tight circle. She'd never seen her so agitated. Her eyes flickered with slashes of flame and her perfectly proportioned features projected starkly beneath her pale skin. Becca remembered the insistent thrust of Jody's crotch against her ass, the press of incisors into her neck. The Vampire had been excited, close to feeding, and Becca had wanted her to. Invited her to. Now Jody was still hungry, still needing.

"I'm sorry," Becca said. "Are you all right?"

"I'm fine." Jody grimaced. "I'm old enough to control myself, but some of the others in there—the young pre-ans and newlings aren't. And old ones like Meredith just enjoy enthralling the unsuspecting. What are you doing here alone?"

"You weren't giving me anything on the investigation, so I thought I'd follow you."

"Into Nocturne?"

"It seemed like a good idea at the time."

"Not without an escort," Jody said. "Give me your word you won't do it again."

"Have you found out anything about the girl at the hospital?"

Jody hissed in frustration. She needed to get away from Becca before she gave in to the hunger twisting through her like a knife. "Meet me in the morning and we'll talk. Now I want your word you won't come back here without an escort."

"There are plenty of humans in there without escorts," Becca pointed out.

"Most of them came to host, and the rest are blood-bonded already."

"Was does that mean?" Becca asked immediately.

Jody shook her head. "It's not important. Just don't come back on your own."

When Jody turned away, Becca called, "You're going back inside?"

Jody stopped and looked back, her expression once again as smooth and as unreadable as marble. "I need to finish feeding."

Becca felt her face warm. Jody was going to find someone else to give her what she hadn't taken from Becca. She should be grateful. Not jealous. "I'll see you in the morning, then."

But the Vampire was gone.

❖

Sylvan nuzzled Drake's neck. "Better now?"

"Much," Drake murmured, realizing she had fallen asleep for the first time in what felt like days. Sylvan held her against her chest, their limbs entwined. She kissed Sylvan's throat and smiled when Sylvan rumbled deep in her chest. "How long will it last—before I start hurting again?"

"You might not get this bad again." Sylvan ran her fingers through Drake's hair. "But you should have a few hours, maybe a day at least before the need starts building."

"Why did you come to me? How did you know?"

Sylvan unconsciously ran her fingertips over the bite on her chest. "I am Alpha. I feel the needs of the Pack."

Drake pushed to her knees and pulled the remnants of her shirt out of the pine needles and loam that had been their bed. "Do you take care of every Pack member like you did me?"

"Are you asking me if I couple with all my Pack?" Sylvan asked softly.

"I guess I am. I know it's none of my business."

"I don't. Why didn't you tangle with someone earlier? Your need was strong this morning."

"Then why did you leave?" Drake was angry even though she wasn't certain why. "You knew, didn't you? That I only wanted you? Why? Why is that?"

"You're mistaken." Sylvan stood abruptly and started toward the forest. "Your wolf needs time to settle. Once she does, you'll find someone else—"

Drake grabbed Sylvan's arm and spun her around. "You don't know what I'll wa—"

A red-gray wolf tore from the forest, teeth bared, and launched itself at Drake. The wolf struck Drake in the chest and knocked her onto the ground, snarling and snapping at Drake's throat as it straddled her torso. Drake gripped the wolf's neck in both hands and tried to throw it off. She felt her fingertips tear open and sharp pain erupted in her mouth. She growled and inside, a furious raging wolf tried to burst free. Drake cried out in agony as her skin threatened to split and her bones crack. She couldn't fight the pain and the wolf both. She lost her hold on the mad wolf and just managed to get her arm between the wolf's jaws and her neck.

"Enough," Sylvan roared, ripping the wolf from Drake's body. She threw the wolf to the far side of the clearing, where it landed on its side and quickly jumped to its feet, still snarling. Sylvan dropped to her knees by Drake's side and pressed her hand to the center of Drake's chest. "You're safe. You're safe now. Breathe, Drake. Calm your wolf. I won't let anything hurt her."

Drake sucked in great gasps of air, adrenaline pouring through her blood. She settled her mind the way she did in the middle of a crisis in the ER, forcing herself to see clearly, to think past the rush of fear and uncertainty. She took another breath. And another. "I'm all right."

"You will be in a minute." Sylvan looked over her shoulder at the wolf pacing restlessly at the edge of the clearing. "Niki. Come here." When the red-gray wolf hesitated, Sylvan snapped, *"Now."*

Niki crouched low, her eyes on Sylvan, and slunk close until she was pressed against Sylvan's side. Sylvan buried her fingers in Niki's ruff and massaged her neck. "Everything is all right. Drake was not attacking me." She continued to stroke both Niki and Drake until they calmed. The red-gray wolf shivered and shook and blurred in the moonlight until Niki lay curled around Sylvan's body, her head on Sylvan's thigh. Sylvan stroked Niki's back and looked from Niki to Drake. "All right now?"

Niki nodded. Drake said, "Yes. Fine."

"Niki," Sylvan said, "I want you to find Sophia and bring her and Drake to the infirmary."

"Yes, Alpha."

"I'm entrusting Drake to your care, *Imperator*." Sylvan stroked Niki's face and Niki brushed her lips over Sylvan's palm.

"Yes, Alpha."

"Drake, are you well enough to go with Niki?"

"Anything you need, Alpha." Drake sat up and rubbed the bruise on her arm from Niki's teeth. She hadn't drawn blood.

Sylvan was suddenly at the edge of the clearing, calling, "Andrew!" Then she bounded into the forest, a streak of shining silver in the starlight.

Drake hadn't moved but she felt as if she were running. The wind rushed over her body and the scent of the forest engulfed her. She caught glimpses of moonlight glinting through the leafy canopy and sensed another body running close to hers. She shivered and the sensations faded, but did not completely disappear. Agitated, Drake jumped to her feet and strode toward the dark woods. Sylvan was somewhere in the heart of the mountains with only Andrew to protect her. Drake wanted to shift and go after them, but she couldn't. She didn't know how. Couldn't follow her instincts. Frustrated, angry, she stared into the dense wilderness, willing Sylvan to return.

"You've put the Alpha in danger. I'll kill you before I'll let you hurt her," Niki said from behind her. "I should have killed you before you turned, but the Alpha wouldn't let me."

Drake spun around. Niki stood naked in the moonlit clearing a few feet from Drake, a warrior sculpture carved of muscle and bone, primal and fierce. Her eyes glinted with shards of gold and her body shimmered against the dark silhouettes of the pines. Drake looked her in the eye. "I would never hurt her."

"You will, if you call her to you again," Niki said. "She is our Alpha. Even if the Pack accepted you as her mate, you are *mutia*. You can't bear young. You would weaken her position in the eyes of the other Alphas. Even to some in our own Pack."

"Her mate?" Drake said dully. "I don't know what you're talking about."

"She heard your call from miles away," Niki snarled. "I could smell you on her this morning. I can smell her on you now. So will the others."

"We just had sex," Drake said. "Of course I smell like her."

"No. Your scents are *mingled*. Your pheromones are blended with hers. That shouldn't happen unless your kinins are chemically fusing."

"But I haven't done anything," Drake said.

"You bit her, didn't you?"

Drake's body flamed with the taste of Sylvan. A rumble rolled through her chest and she felt a wave of possession so strong her canines protruded violently. "Yes." She fought down the surging wolf that demanded she assert her right to Sylvan. She had to understand what was happening. "But Elena said Weres bite during sex. That biting was natural."

"It *is* natural," Niki said, "for a dominant to bring a beta Were to orgasm with a bite. But only a mated wolf or one wanting to mate will bite a dominant one. And no one bites the Alpha except her mate. Ever."

"Sylvan forced me to shift," Drake said, searching for an explanation. "I didn't know. I..." She stopped, unwilling, incapable, of repudiating what she had experienced with Sylvan in that glorious moment of incredible transformation. Sylvan had been so beautiful—so tender and so powerful. Drake had needed her, wanted her, desired her. She had bitten Sylvan because she had wanted her completely, as deeply and passionately as she had ever wanted anyone. She would never let anything diminish that memory, especially if the memory was all she was ever to have. "But we're not bonded, are we?"

"I don't know," Niki said. "I don't think so, or Sylvan would not have left your side tonight, even for a few minutes. A newly mated pair are always inseparable, and the Alpha's mate is usually very possessive about letting the Alpha run with the other wolves."

"Even her *centuri*?"

"Even us," Niki said. "The Alpha's mate never completely trusts anyone to protect her."

"Then we aren't bonded yet, so she is still safe," Drake said, fighting a wave of sadness that verged on despair.

"Possibly," Niki said. "I hope so."

"Are you saying if we do bond that you'll kill me?" Drake wasn't angry with Niki. In fact, she respected her, appreciated her unwavering desire to protect Sylvan.

"If I have to, yes."

"And what will Sylvan do then?"

"She'll execute me," Niki said.

"But you would still kill me, even if it meant you would die? You love her that much?"

"She is our Alpha. I am her second." For the first time Niki looked away. "I would do anything I had to do to protect her."

"I won't let her lose her mate and her second. That would destroy her," Drake said.

"Then take another mate before it's too late—and none of us are left with any choice."

CHAPTER TWENTY-TWO

Jody slowed her car in front of the arching sixteen-foot-high wrought iron gates that spanned the driveway to her father's estate. A massive stone wall enclosed the ten acres immediately surrounding the thirty-room mansion. Beyond that, another hundred acres of woods were patrolled by her father's minions at night and by human guards during the day. She waited while the video cameras scanned her vehicle. The gates opened silently and she drove the half mile down the tree-lined driveway and parked in front of the stone staircase leading to the entrance.

Before she'd crossed the expansive patio to the front door, a willowy brunette, one of Zachary Gates's human servants, opened it. The brunette, her clinging floor-length claret gown slashed low between full flowing breasts, cocked a hip and smiled indolently.

"Hello, Jody."

"Hello, Angela," Jody said.

Angela slowly ran her tongue between her lips and slid her gaze down Jody's body. "I've missed you."

"That's unexpected." Jody stepped around Angela and started down the wide central hall. "Considering that you stopped dating me to sleep with my father."

"Oh, don't be like that." Angela fell into step and linked her arm through Jody's. "You know you weren't interested in anything serious with me."

"And you think he is?"

"He said he'd turn me." Angela ran her mouth over the edge of

Jody's ear. "Unless you've changed your mind and are ready to blood-bond me. I'd love to be just yours forever."

Jody whipped around and grasped Angela's shoulders, giving her a shake. "This isn't a game, Angela. Do you know why there are so few Vampires? Not many are born, and humans who try to turn usually *die*."

"You're always so serious." Angela tapped her blood-red fingernails against Jody's mouth. "Except when you're fucking. Then you're wild."

With a curse, Jody let her go and vaulted up to the second-floor balcony. She didn't stop to acknowledge the burly Vampire standing guard at her father's door, but shoved him aside and burst through the heavy mahogany doors into the opulently appointed office. The high-ceilinged room was lit with hanging crystal lamps. Rich brocade tapestries adorned some walls, floor-to-ceiling bookcases lined others. Marble pedestals in both far corners held priceless Chinese vases. Thick Persian carpets covered the hardwood floors. Soaring windows opposite the doorway gave a breathtaking view of the mountains—a view her father would never again see in daylight.

Zachary Gates was on the phone, and when he saw her, he murmured a few words and hung up. He leaned back in his massive leather chair and straightened the cuffs on his black silk shirt. "That was an impressive entrance."

With his thick collar-length black hair shot with silver at the temples, sculpted face, and piercing black eyes, he looked like a displaced pirate from another era. Jody knew they looked alike and was always irritated when people mentioned it. She wanted to believe that any resemblance to her father stopped at the physical.

"You said you wanted to see me. I'm here."

"Sit down," Zachary said, indicating one of the leather club chairs with a sweep of his arm. "Can I get you a drink?"

"I can't stay."

Zachary went to a circular polished wood bar in a sitting area filled with leather sofas and chairs and poured several inches of scotch into two crystal glasses. He walked back and held one out to Jody. She took it and put it down on the table next to her chair.

"How is your investigation of Sylvan Mir coming along?" her father asked.

Jody kept her expression blank. "I'm not investigating Sylvan Mir."

"Really? I was given to understand that you and a reporter—Becca Land, isn't it?—have been investigating—"

"Your information is wrong." Jody got to her feet. Whatever her father was after, she wasn't going to let Becca be drawn into his dark games. "I don't work with reporters."

"Jody," her father said with a tinge of disappointment in his voice. "We want the same things."

"No, we don't. I'm not interested in power or politics."

"You should be. You're in line to rule one of the largest families in the territory."

"I don't want to rule, and I expect you will be in power for a long, long time. You do want to be Viceregal, don't you?"

"I have no desire to challenge Francesca."

"Somehow I doubt that. Isn't that why you supported the Exodus? To gain public support when you move against her?" Jody clenched her jaw. "You needed a new power base—a public one with money and influence behind it, but I think you're wrong in hoping the humans will involve themselves in Vampire politics."

"Humans will overlook species differences if the price is right." He shrugged elegantly. "You and I don't need to be at odds. Our immediate goals may differ, but there's no reason we can't share information. For example, I was given to understand that there might be a problem with the Weres. An outbreak of some kind?"

"I am a police detective. I don't share information with anyone, especially politicians."

"So noble." Zachary smiled. "You're very much like your mother."

Jody took two steps toward him, her incisors slicing from their sheaths. "I hope so."

"You should be careful where you place your loyalties, Jody," Zachary said softly. "You're a Vampire before anything else."

"I don't need you to tell me who I am." Jody spun on her heel and walked out, her father's laughter following her.

When she drove through the gates, they swung closed and locked behind her. She drove two hundred yards along the narrow twisting road and pulled over after rounding a bend. She watched her rearview mirror, waiting for the car that had been following her to catch up. When it was almost alongside her, she flew from her car and landed with her legs spread wide in the middle of the road. The car screeched to a halt a few inches from her body. The driver's door shot open and Becca jumped out.

"Are you crazy? What is the *matter* with you? I could have killed you!"

"I don't think so."

Becca marched to within a few inches of Jody and planted her hands on her hips. "Well, I don't want to find out. Don't ever do anything like that again."

"Why are you following me?"

"Because I knew if I went home I wouldn't be able to sleep."

Jody grinned. "Why not?"

"Never mind why not. Who lives here?"

"My father," Jody said grimly.

Becca looked over her shoulder at the sprawling estate. "Nice."

"Not really."

"You promised me information."

"In the morning," Jody said with exaggerated patience.

"It's four a.m. That's morning in my book."

"I have work to do."

"At four a.m.?"

"I'm a Vampire. A lot of my sources are Vampires. We live and work at night."

"I know what you are, thank you very much." Becca rubbed her arms. She could still feel the heat of Jody's body pressed against her back. She'd remained in the car watching the club after Jody went inside, wondering what Jody was doing and who she was doing it with, imagining Jody making someone orgasm while she fed from them, coming herself while she drank. She'd made herself crazy with the images. She knew if she went home she'd give in to the fantasies and have to masturbate. Then she'd feel pitiful for being so aroused by someone whose idea of intimacy consisted of mind games and anonymous sex.

"Funny," Jody said, "everywhere I go tonight, people seem to think they know what I am." She turned and walked back toward her car.

"Hey!" Becca followed her. "Where are you going?"

"Go home. I'll call you in a few hours."

Becca grabbed the edge of the door before Jody could close it. "Look, I'm sorry."

Jody slid behind the wheel and regarded her coolly. "For what?"

"You're right, I don't know you. But I know you're a good cop. And I'm a good reporter." Becca leaned down. "You're going to talk to me in the morning anyhow. So let me come with you now."

"Are you going to keep following me otherwise? I knew you were behind me when I left the club."

Becca grinned. "So I'm not very good at it."

Jody laughed. "I'm going to the morgue. I'll meet you there."

"Why did you change your mind?"

"Can't you just be satisfied that I did?" Jody countered.

"No. I like to know the reasons why people do things."

"Not everyone wants to be known, Ms. Land." Jody gently removed Becca's hand from her door, closed it, and drove away, leaving Becca racing to catch up.

❖

After her hunt with Andrew, Sylvan returned to her private quarters to shower and dress. Niki and Lara were already waiting on the porch, having tracked her and Andrew through the forest. She sent Andrew back to the Compound although he hadn't asked to be relieved. He was excited after his run with her, and she suspected he needed a tangle.

She stood for a long time under the cool spray, waiting for her body to settle. The run and the kill had helped dampen some of her urgency to claim Drake again, but the hunger had never entirely abated. Almost as soon as the intense pleasure of her release faded away, she was ready again. She'd had to get away from Drake, satisfy her primal needs in some other way, or risk losing control completely. Drake was newly turned, still struggling for harmony with her wolf, still adjusting to the tremendous physical and psychological shock of her transformation. Sylvan couldn't expect her to understand what had almost happened out there in the forest. Drake inflamed her, called to her in some deeply instinctual way, stirred her need to guard and protect and cherish as no one ever had before. The first time she'd seen Drake, when Drake was still human, she'd been aware of the connection. Drake hadn't feared her, and even in the midst of the danger to Sylvan's young, Drake had managed to calm her. To steady her wolf.

Even Niki, who she loved with all her heart, could not touch her in the places Drake had touched.

Sylvan toweled dry and held the damp cotton against her face. She smelled Drake. The chemical mix that marked her as unique, as Alpha, had absorbed Drake's kinins and incorporated them. Drake had marked her with a bite. She had marked Drake in turn. They were very close to completing a mate bond. She was still ready, full, her wolf demanding she finish the mating. Another bite, another intense coupling when their *victus*—their essence—erupted and fused, and they would be mated. Drake couldn't know any of this, couldn't understand what she was doing. Drake's drive to release was wholly physiological, the result of her tumultuous transition. How could she willingly accept the bonding when she could barely manage the chaos within her still-evolving body? How could she possibly comprehend that once mated, she would be joined physically and mentally to Sylvan for life—and if Sylvan died, she might too. One member of a mated pair rarely survived the death of the other. Sylvan was certain her father would not have survived if he hadn't been determined to protect the Pack until Sylvan could ascend. He had begun to fade as soon as Sylvan reached maturity. He hadn't wanted to live without his mate.

She would not force such a destiny on Drake. She would not take a mate when so much of the future was uncertain. She was a target of humans and Weres alike, she knew that. Even if Drake accepted the risk, Sylvan wouldn't. A mate would make her vulnerable and the Pack needed all of her energy, all of her attention. She was Alpha. That was all. That was enough.

Distance was the only safeguard against another impetuous coupling. Drake should be all right for at least the rest of the day, and when the frenzy resurfaced, she would have to take someone else. Her need would be too strong, too powerful, for her to resist. Sylvan imagined another Were pleasuring Drake, stroking and caressing and teasing her to release—coating themselves with her essence when she erupted for them. She pictured Drake biting them, forcing them to come on her, absorbing their scent. Heat blazed through Sylvan's chest and she started to shift, her spine bowing, her facial bones shifting, elongating, claws and canines extruding, a blaze of silver exploding down the center of her body. Panting, she dropped to her knees and battled her raging wolf. She would not shift. She would not claim a mate. She would not.

Niki burst into the room, Lara right behind her. Lara, less dominant than Niki, was already in mid-shift, called by the ferocity of Sylvan's wolf. Niki's face contorted in pain as she fought her own need.

"Alpha?" Niki groaned, searching the room for signs of danger with eyes gone hunter green.

"It's all right." Still on her knees, Sylvan forced herself to straighten, although she couldn't yet stand. A sleek brown wolf now guarded the open door against intruders. Lara.

"What is it?" Niki asked, her breathing easing as Sylvan calmed and got to her feet. "I've never felt your call like that before."

"Nothing you need to worry about." Sylvan draped an arm around Niki's shoulders while running her other hand down Lara's back. She kissed Niki's temple as Lara whined softly and rubbed against her leg. "Why don't you two stand down for a while. Max can take over."

"I'm fine, Alpha," Niki said quickly.

"Get some sleep," Sylvan whispered, rubbing her cheek against Niki's hair. "We'll be going back into the city in the morning."

Niki's eyes widened in surprise. "So soon?"

"Yes." Sylvan released her *centuri* and went into her bedroom to dress.

After pulling on jeans-style leather pants, a white cotton shirt, and black boots, Sylvan walked back to the Compound in search of Drake and Sophia. She found them in the infirmary center. Drake had showered and wore clean jeans and a T-shirt. Her gaze went immediately to Sylvan, and heat curled through Sylvan's belly at the hunger in her eyes. Sophia, her blond hair loose and curling delicately around her face, sat next to Drake on a sofa by the fireplace, their shoulders nearly touching. Sylvan barely managed to keep from snarling at Sophia's proximity to Drake.

"Have you eaten?" Sylvan demanded. So soon after Drake's tumultuous transition and their heated coupling, Drake would be dangerously depleted. In her weakened state, she was more susceptible to a return of the frenzy or even a recurrence of the fever. If Sylvan had been thinking instead of half crazed with need and trying to ignore it, she would have seen to it that Drake got the proper nourishment.

"Yes, Sophia dragged me back to the mess hall," Drake said, smiling at Sophia. "I pretty much devoured everything in sight."

Sylvan rumbled and stalked to the far side of the room, turning her back until she could control her temper. Sophia had done what *she* should have done, and she ought to be grateful to Sophia for taking care of Drake. Instead, she wanted to drag Drake away from the beautiful Were. When she dampened her possessive anger enough to walk back to them, she noted the anxious way Sophia edged away from Drake.

"Thank you for taking care of her," Sylvan said, briefly caressing Sophia's cheek before resuming her pacing. She couldn't be anywhere near Drake without a painful urge to touch her.

"Of course, Alpha," Sophia said softly. "I'm honored."

Drake looked from Sophia to Sylvan, trying to decipher the unspoken. She could feel Sylvan's agitation, and she could scent her need. Sylvan prowled, a low steady growl emanating from her chest. Drake doubted she was even aware of it. Sophia was, though. With each passing second, Sophia grew more uneasy.

"Wait outside," Drake said quietly to Sophia. When Sophia hesitated, Drake smiled. "It's all right. I'd like to speak to the Alpha alone."

When Sophia cast an apprehensive glance in Sylvan's direction, Sylvan nodded curtly.

"We'll meet you in the treatment room," Sylvan said. "Go ahead."

Drake waited until the door closed behind Sophia, then went to Sylvan. She wanted to calm her, to stroke her, but she was wary of the fury riding hard just below the surface. "What's wrong?"

"Our scientists want to study some specimens from you—to understand what happened."

"Good," Drake said immediately. "I was talking to Sophia earlier—"

Sylvan snarled, her canines flashing.

"Stop," Drake murmured. Not caring about protocol or what the Pack might think or even the dangerous glare in Sylvan's eyes, she cupped Sylvan's jaw and smoothed her thumb over the corner of her mouth. "You're all I think about. Don't you know that?"

Sylvan closed her eyes and rubbed her cheek against Drake's palm. "I don't want you hurt."

"Nor I you." Drake allowed herself a few more seconds of touching her, but she knew she had to stop. Niki had said there was still time for her to break whatever bond was forming between them, and even though she knew it would tear her heart from her body to let Sylvan go, she would. If it meant keeping her safe, she'd leave. She had no idea where she would go or how she would live or even if she *could* live. Already she felt a tremendous connection to the Pack, to the community of wild spirits who filled the forest with the sounds and scents of home. For the first time in her life she felt as if she belonged somewhere. She belonged to Sylvan, but she knew Sylvan was fighting the forces that drew them together. And she understood why. Niki had made it very clear. Like Niki, she would die before she would let anything hurt Sylvan—*anything*, even her own need for her. She wouldn't allow Sylvan to put herself in danger or weaken the Pack because of her. The imperative to protect Sylvan flowed through her blood more strongly than any other need she'd ever known, even her own need to survive. Calling on every ounce of strength she had, Drake dropped her hand and moved away.

"Who are they? Your scientists?" Drake asked.

"Leo and Nadia Revnik. Sophia's parents." Sylvan's voice was rough, her eyes tracking Drake as she might follow the path of prey in the forest. "The foremost experts on Were physiology in the world. They defected from the Blackpaw Pack when Sophia was an adolescent. About the time the latest skirmish in the Pack wars broke out and my... our Alpha was killed."

"Sophia wasn't born in your Pack, then?" Drake asked.

"No," Sylvan said. "My mother allowed her family to immigrate."

"That's unusual?"

"Our Packs have been at war for centuries. Members of my Pack have had their entire lines wiped out in the conflict. Many disagreed with my mother's decision, but she was Alpha."

"What do they want from me?"

"Blood samples. A muscle biopsy, if you agree."

"Of course." Drake caught the angry flash in Sylvan's eyes. "What? What else?"

"Nothing."

Drake shook her head. "There's more, and for some reason you don't want to tell me."

Sylvan grumbled in warning.

"No. You can't protect me from this."

"I can," Sylvan snarled.

"No," Drake said gently. "I know you want to. I know what being Alpha means. I know how strongly you're driven to protect everyone in the Pack. I saw it with Misha the night we met. I think that's when I…" She caught herself before she confessed to what had to remain unspoken. She wanted to touch her so badly, but she knew she couldn't. But she had something she *could* give. She had her body and whatever was happening inside it. She could help Sylvan. Help the Pack. "You need…*we* need to know why humans are displaying signs of Were fever. We need to understand why I survived when most don't. You know I have to do this."

"Your blood. A tissue sample," Sylvan snapped. "That's all."

"What else? What else do they want?"

Sylvan was suddenly right in front of her, her body pressed tight against Drake's, her hands in Drake's hair, her mouth against Drake's ear. "You'll do as I say. I won't have you hurt."

Drake sank into the heat of Sylvan's body, her flesh molding to the hard planes and subtle curves of Sylvan's form. She drew in her scent, felt herself stiffen and throb. She licked the faint dew from Sylvan's neck and her skin sheened. "You make me so ready so fast."

"I shouldn't touch you like this," Sylvan rasped, her body vibrating against Drake's. Her claws skimmed Drake's neck. "It's too soon for you to control the frenzy."

"It's not frenzy," Drake whispered.

"I'm used to touching my wolves. I'm sorry." Sylvan released Drake, her face hardening. "You're not ready for casual handling."

Drake shuddered with the brutal sensation of being cut adrift, of being terribly, horribly alone. "I understand, Alpha."

"We should let Sophia get the samples."

"Of course." Drake's legs were unsteady, her stomach cramping.

She could hardly control the aching need to touch Sylvan. Just touch her. If she couldn't be close to her, she had to be much farther away. "Let's do it. I want answers as much as you do. I'd like to be able to get back to my life."

"Your life is with the Pack now," Sylvan said, her tone dark and ominous.

"I have another life that's just as important to me." Drake strode to the door and pulled it open without looking back, hoping Sylvan hadn't heard the lie.

CHAPTER TWENTY-THREE

Becca parked next to Jody in a nearly empty lot behind the municipal complex at Lark and Madison. The city morgue was in the basement of one of the older buildings. Jody led the way through a labyrinth of poorly lit alleys and walkways to a dark loading dock. As they climbed the narrow concrete stairs to the raised platform, Jody cupped Becca's elbow. The gesture was oddly courtly and Becca found she liked it. Flustered, she pulled away.

"You sure you want to come down?" Jody asked as she pressed the buzzer next to the heavy metal doors.

"I'm not afraid of the dead," Becca said.

Jody shot her a sardonic grin. "Even when they animate?"

"You already know the answer to that, don't you?"

"Sometimes we're drawn to what we fear most."

"Look," Becca said, "let's get something straight. I'm not afraid of Vampires and I'm not drawn to them—you—either."

"Good to know."

For some reason Jody's response irritated her, but Becca didn't have time to ponder her annoyance because the doors swung open and a giant of a man stared out at them with a belligerent expression on his face. He had to be six-ten and four hundred pounds, with a wild mane of tangled brown hair and arms and legs the size of small saplings.

"Hi, Davey," Jody said. "Is Marissa here tonight?"

The giant smiled and his face transformed from fierce to friendly. "How you doing, Jody. We've been really busy. Big pileup on the Northway." He held the massive door wide. "Marissa is in three."

"Thanks. We won't stay long."

"Who is that?" Becca whispered as she followed Jody through the twisting hallways. Their footsteps ricocheted like gunshots through the unnatural stillness. The air smelled faintly of death and disinfectant.

"Davey Gleason. He's a diener—an autopsy assistant."

"What else is he?" Becca muttered.

"You guess. Your Praetern radar's pretty good."

"Must be the company I keep." Becca thought she saw a brief smile flicker across Jody's usually composed and unreadable face, and realized she liked making her smile. "Who is Marissa?"

"Dr. Marissa Sanchez. She's the night shift supervisor."

"Does she *have* to work nights?"

Jody paused in front of another set of double doors, these with glass windows through which Becca could see a gleaming autopsy suite.

"She isn't a Vampire, if that's what you mean." Jody punched a saucer-sized red button on the wall and the doors swung open. "She just likes them."

As soon as they walked into the room, the reason for Jody's remark was obvious. The petite Latina, wearing scrubs and dictating into a microphone as she bent over a body on an autopsy table, took one look at Jody and stopped what she was doing. She pulled off her gloves and switched off the microphone, then practically ran the length of the room to meet them.

"Jody," Marissa said breathlessly, ignoring Becca as if she were invisible. "Tell me this isn't business."

"Sorry," Jody murmured, "I'm afraid it is."

Marissa ran a short sculpted nail along the edge of Jody's jaw and leaned so close her breasts touched Jody's chest. "We could save the business for after pleasure."

Becca had an overwhelming urge to grasp the finger that was slowly trailing down Jody's neck and snap it like a dry twig. If she hadn't noticed Jody subtly ease away until there was space between her and the medical examiner, she just might have. The reaction totally confused her. She wasn't ordinarily jealous even of women she dated, and that certainly wasn't the situation with the Vampire detective.

"I should be done in another hour," Marissa said with a sigh.

"Maybe you could come back then and we can have...breakfast... together." She turned to Becca with a surprisingly friendly smile. "Unless you have plans to feed her?"

"Knock yourself out," Becca said sharply and Jody laughed.

Marissa's smile was blazing. "Thanks. I hope so." She caressed Jody's arm. "What do you need? Now, I mean."

"A Jane Doe came in two nights ago from the ER at AGH. A teenager—female. Do you have a COD yet?"

"I think Kerry did that one," Marissa said, all business now. "I'll have to check the file." She glanced at Becca again. "I didn't catch your name?"

"This is Becca Land," Jody said. "She's with me."

"All right...but you do know this is all preliminary?"

"Definitely," Jody said, her voice languid and seductive. Marissa's expression softened and her eyes glazed.

"The report?" Becca said testily.

Jody laughed and Marissa blinked, as if wakening from a pleasant dream.

"Come on, then." Marissa led them into a small crowded office with charts piled everywhere, several empty paper coffee cups balanced precariously on the edge of the desk, and an open sports bag in one corner, tennis rackets spilling out.

Becca and Jody stood, since the only chairs were covered with journals, while Marissa sorted through files and finally came up with a single sheet of paper. She read it over and dropped it onto the desk. "Toxic shock is the preliminary diagnosis."

"Toxic shock," Becca repeated, jotting notes on her pad. She didn't even consider trying for her recorder. "An infectious agent? Some kind of bacteria or something?"

Marissa raised an eyebrow in Jody's direction and Jody nodded for her to go on.

"Culture results indicate no bacterial or viral agent." At Becca's look of confusion, Marissa continued, "More likely a chemotoxin of some kind."

"Chemotoxin? Like sarin?"

"Like any number of poisons."

"But something like that could be contagious?" Jody asked.

"In theory, absolutely," Marissa said. "It would depend on

the method of transfer, the half-life of the drug, the LD50—" She caught herself with a shake of her head. "Sorry—LD50 is a general measurement of the toxicity of any agent—it literally means the dose at which fifty percent mortality occurs."

Becca scribbled madly. "But you haven't isolated this…agent?"

"As I said, this is Kerry's case, but it's difficult for us to isolate an unknown agent because we don't know how to test for it. We can tell you what it isn't, but it's very hard to tell you what it is."

"Anything else that might be helpful?" Jody asked.

"I don't think so…" Marissa glanced at the chart again. "Wait a minute. You said this Jane Doe died in the ER? She wasn't an inpatient for any length of time?"

"No, why?" Becca asked.

"The external exam showed multiple intravenous access sites. Many more than would be anticipated during a simple emergency resuscitation. Hold on, let me look at the photos of the body." Marissa keyed some information into the computer on the desk and sorted through a number of images on the monitor. "A lot of these puncture sites look older than a day or two." She cleared the photos and regarded Becca and Jody with a frown. "If I had to guess, I'd say this girl had been hospitalized somewhere immediately before arriving at the emergency room."

"Thanks," Jody said. "I'd appreciate it if you kept our visit between us."

Marissa smiled slowly. "Don't I always?"

Becca was silent as they made their way out. When they reached the parking lot, the sun was just rising. Jody slid her hands into her pockets and stopped, watching the lightening sky intently. Becca waited, allowing her the private moment.

"What do you think?" Becca asked when Jody resumed walking.

"You tell me," Jody said. "You're the investigative reporter."

Becca had been up all night and, despite her excitement over the new information, was feeling bitchy. "I think Marissa is dying for you to sink your fangs into her."

"I can assure you, she wouldn't be dying. And the term *fangs* is insulting."

"You know what I mean." Becca halted next to her car. "Is she one of your regulars?"

"We used to date," Jody said. "Now she hosts for me from time to time."

"You feed and she comes." Becca knew she sounded petulant, and she was never petulant. She was just having a hard time getting the hungry way Marissa had looked at Jody out of her mind.

Jody's expression never changed. "I think we've already established that's how it works. The case?"

"Something—no—a lot of somethings don't add up," Becca said, dragging her mind back to business. "Where did the Jane Doe come from? Where was she before arriving at the ER? If she really was a patient somewhere, why not transfer her legitimately—why the secrecy? And why call me and tell me about her if you want to keep it a secret?"

"I don't know," Jody said, "but I think it's time we ask the wolf Alpha the same questions."

"When?" Becca asked eagerly. She wasn't tired any longer.

"Since my involvement isn't actually official at this point," Jody said, "it may not be all that easy. I'll call her and see if I can arrange a meeting for tonight."

"You'll call me, when you…wake up?"

"I sleep during the day, Becca," Jody said with a hint of amusement in her voice. "I don't die."

"Don't think you can leave me high and dry in this. Because I promise you, if you don't call me, I *will* hunt you down."

"Of that, Ms. Land," Jody said wryly, "I have no doubt. Have a nice day."

Becca watched as Jody walked away and couldn't help but think of Marissa's offer to feed her. She wondered if Marissa or someone like her would be there for Jody when she awakened. Just as quickly, she thrust the images and the accompanying frisson of anger from her mind.

❖

Drake, acutely aware of Sylvan a few inches away, stood in the doorway of the laboratory and assessed the sophisticated setup while Sophia talked on the phone. An operating table with three circular halogen lamps positioned above it occupied the center of the large room.

Several rows of workbenches in one corner held state-of-the-art medical equipment—mass spectrometers, centrifuges, gas chromatographs, hemolytic analyzers. Glass-fronted cabinets contained instrument packs, rows of drugs, and other supplies. An anesthetic machine was attached by multicolored conduits to oxygen and anesthetic outlets in the ceiling and a portable X-ray machine occupied an adjacent alcove. A laboratory and operating room like this required skilled personnel to staff it—Weres like Elena and Sophia who had been trained in human institutions and brought their skills and knowledge back to the Were community.

Reminded that her own prognosis was far from certain and anxious to shed any light on the disease process, Drake walked to the gleaming stainless steel operating table and sat down on the vinyl padded surface. She purposefully did not look at Sylvan, who stood with her arms folded across her chest and a tight expression on her face. Sylvan hadn't said a word on their way to join Sophia, but her agitation was palpable, impossible for Drake to ignore even if the steady low-level growl hadn't started again. Sensing Sylvan's upset only made Drake want to touch her more. Her limbs vibrated with the need to go to her, to stroke the tension from her body and soothe her worry. She wanted, *needed*, to calm her.

"I think you should wait outside, Alpha," Drake said, stretching out on her back in the hopes of appearing relaxed. "This is all just routine."

"No, it isn't." Sylvan was suddenly at the end of the table, looming over Drake with her arms braced on either side of Drake's legs. "I'm staying."

The heat of Sylvan's body wafted over Drake's like a blanket covering her on a cold winter night. Transported, she felt her face buried in a thick silver pelt, felt Sylvan's strong muscular body curled around hers in the haven of a fallen pine. Sylvan smelled of home and safety—sheltering her, guarding her, even as Drake protected her. Drake gasped at the vivid image and Sylvan's scent filled her chest, stirred her. Excited her. Agitated, full and ready, she twisted restlessly.

Sophia pocketed her cell and pushed a stainless steel cart over to the table. "I just talked to my mother about what they'll need." She smiled down at Drake. "We'll start with the simple things, and we can stop anytime you want."

"Just take anything you need."

"Tell me what you're going to do," Sylvan demanded.

"A battery of blood tests first, looking for viral components, chemical toxins, immunoglobulins, altered neurotransmitters…" Sophia shrugged. "Anything that might account for the elevated temperature." She glanced at Sylvan, as if asking for permission. "Because Drake was human, we can't assume whatever triggered the symptoms of fever was the same for her as it would be for one of us."

Drake lifted her head and focused on Sylvan, who still leaned over her. "What triggers Were fever in you?"

"Us," Sylvan said softly, her wolf-gold eyes boring into Drake's. "You're a wolf Were now. You're mine now."

Drake's chest tightened at the possessive tone in Sylvan's voice. She'd schooled herself not to care about being an outsider, not to care if she didn't belong anywhere or with anyone, and over the years, she'd come to believe those things didn't matter. She'd been wrong. She wanted to belong to Sylvan. "Us, then. What causes the fever in us?"

Sophia glanced at Sylvan, and when Sylvan nodded, she said, "Argyria—silver poisoning. The metal ionizes and produces hyperthermia and cellular breakdown. Most victims die from systemic collapse due to massive rhabdomyolysis and hemorrhage. Those who don't die shift without the ability to control their wolves."

"And become rabid," Drake finished. When that happened, Sylvan would have the rabid Were executed. She thought back to the silver fragment Sylvan had pulled from Misha's shoulder, and how close the adolescent had come to death. A fierce protective urge welled up in her at the thought of anything happening to Misha or the boys or any other Were, and she growled.

"We guard that knowledge for obvious reasons," Sylvan said quietly, rubbing Drake's leg. "Don't worry, our Pack is protected."

Drake nodded, taking comfort from Sylvan's touch. The certainty in her voice. "Since humans aren't susceptible to silver poisoning, it has to be something else."

"Yes," Sylvan said grimly. "Humans should not be susceptible to Were fever except in the very unlikely instance of being bitten by rabid Weres. Then the levels of the toxin are very high and capable of transmitting the disease—much like humans are infected by Ebola or hemorrhagic fever. That's why we execute Weres as soon as they display signs of being rabid."

"But I was bitten by a human," Drake said, "and as far as you… we…know, she didn't contract it from a rabid Were."

"Exactly," Sylvan said.

"So both she and I have contracted something anomalous. Something that might be even more dangerous." Drake glanced at Sophia. "We need specimens from one of the other human victims too."

"I know. My father is trying, but we don't want to reveal why we need the information."

"Then it's all the more important you get everything you can from me." Drake sat up and unbuttoned her jeans. Sylvan stepped back from the table and Drake pushed off her pants, unconcerned by her nudity. "Let's get the blood first, then a muscle biopsy. Use my leg for the tissue, and take several core specimens. You'll need fresh tissue preps, so only anesthetize the skin."

"That's going to be painful," Sophia said.

"I'll be fine." Drake lay back down and forced herself to relax, very aware of Sylvan pacing back and forth at the end of the table. "Sylvan, why don't you—"

"No."

Sophia wrapped a tourniquet around Drake's bicep and filled half a dozen multicolored vials with blood. After she'd labeled and stored them, she prepared a number of biopsy trocars and lined them up on a tray.

"Are you ready?" Sophia asked.

"Yes, go ahead," Drake replied.

"Careful." Sylvan grasped Sophia's arm. "Her wolf will react to the pain and Drake might not be able to control her."

"Alpha," Sophia said softly, "if you could perhaps sit next to Drake while I do this. Her wolf will know you…"

"Yes." Sylvan clenched her jaw and pulled a stool over next to the table. She draped an arm over Drake's chest and pinned Sophia in place with a hard stare. "You will stop if I tell you to."

"Yes, of course," Sophia said with a quick duck of her head.

Drake covered Sylvan's hand and looked into her worried eyes. "I'm fine. You don't need—"

"Quiet," Sylvan said gently, stroking Drake's hair. "I'm going to take care of you."

Drake didn't move at the cramping pain in her thigh when Sophia slid the quarter-inch-wide trocar into the muscle and sliced free a cylinder of tissue. Although she noted a burgeoning sense of hypervigilance, a bristling swell of aggression, she wasn't worried. She wasn't afraid of pain. When Sophia took the second biopsy, the pain escalated and she tensed reflexively. Sylvan grumbled.

"I'm okay," Drake said, stroking Sylvan's arm.

"Are you almost done?" Sylvan demanded, her eyes completely gold, the bones in her face hard-edged and dangerous.

"Just one more," Sophia said quietly. "Drake?"

"Yes. Go ahead." Drake gripped Sylvan's arm when another surge of pain shot deep into her thigh. Her claws shot out and she scratched shallow lines down Sylvan's forearm. "I'm sorry."

Sylvan leaned down and ran her tongue along the edge of Drake's jaw. Her voice was throaty and low. "I like it."

"Sylvan," Drake murmured, her clitoris pulsing hard. "Something's happening to me."

"Your wolf feels challenged. Aggression always produces a sexual response. It's normal." Sylvan wrapped her hand possessively around the back of Drake's neck.

Drake watched Sylvan's eyes flare and knew she had readied too. Sylvan's call flooded her senses. She wanted to rub against her, lick her, bite her. Voice cracking, she said, "Sophia, what else did they want?"

Carefully not looking at Drake, Sophia busied herself storing the specimens in transport containers. "They requested…bodily fluids."

"No," Sylvan snapped.

"What fluids?" Drake panted—she didn't have long before she couldn't think anymore. She hurt, she wanted Sylvan. But she couldn't—she couldn't have her. Take her. Claim her. She couldn't and she was running out of time. "What Sophia, what?"

"Buccal swabs." Sophia hesitated. "Vaginal secretions. And *victus*, if we can get you to produce a specimen."

Sylvan shot to her feet, her canines bared. "You're not making her release."

Clearly shocked, Sophia blurted, "No, Alpha, I only meant…"

"I'm sorry," Sylvan said instantly, sliding the backs of her fingers over Sophia's cheek. "I know you're just doing what needs to be done."

"I understand, Alpha," Sophia whispered.

Drake shuddered, her skin slick and hot. Sylvan smoothed her hand over Drake's chest, down her belly. She rubbed the hard muscles and brushed her fingers up and down the fine dark line in the center of Drake's abdomen. Groaning, Drake arched at the caress. "She's had enough. She's on the verge of frenzy."

"I'll go," Sophia said.

"Wait," Drake gasped. "Take the swabs. From my skin too. I'm secreting pheromones right now." Reaching down, she carefully palpated the deep swellings around her extended clitoris. She was tense, throbbing, and the slightest pressure was both painful and exquisitely pleasurable. She wanted to grab Sylvan's hand and press it between her legs. She had to get Sylvan to leave the room before she lost control completely. "I think I can get you the other, too."

"I'll hurry." Sophia quickly brushed one cotton swab over Drake's shoulder, then sampled the inside of her mouth. Finally, she handed several more swabs to Sylvan. "Alpha, if you could help her with the rest, I'll wait outside."

After Sophia hurried out, Drake said to Sylvan, "You should go. I can do it." She was barely holding on. She wanted Sylvan inside her so much. She wanted Sylvan coming in her mouth.

"You're shaking too badly to do anything right now." Sylvan slid her hand along the inside of Drake's thigh and gently opened her legs. She carefully parted Drake's sex and swabbed her. A rumble rolled from her chest. "Look how ready you are. So strong and beautiful."

"I'm sorry, I can't...I have to..." Drake closed her eyes and massaged her clitoris. Her glands pulsed under her probing fingers and she moaned. "Please go."

Sylvan brushed Drake's fingers away. "I'll do this."

Drake rolled her head from side to side, whimpering as Sylvan stroked and squeezed. "You're so good. You're going to make me come all over myself."

"No," Sylvan grumbled, leaning down to kiss her, "I'm going to make you come all over me."

Sylvan plunged her tongue into Drake's mouth, teasing and sucking and biting. Drake gripped Sylvan's shirt and shredded it, then tore open her own T-shirt. Rearing up, she dug her claws into Sylvan's shoulders and rubbed her breasts over Sylvan's. She thrust against the hand working between her legs. "If you stroke inside me, I'll come for you."

"Wait," Sylvan growled against her mouth. "Let me get what Sophia needs the first time. If I take you, I won't stop until you're empty."

"Hurry." Drake propped herself on her elbows and watched Sylvan masturbate her. "Oh yes, like that. Like that. It's close. Close now." Her hips jumped and she roared at the first shock of release. Pumping into Sylvan's hand, she fell back onto the table. Then Sylvan was inside her, thrusting into her, driving her to an even more powerful release. She came hard and immediately came again. Then she was being lifted into Sylvan's arms and her legs locked around Sylvan's waist. Sylvan's canines latched on to her shoulder and she was coming all over Sylvan's belly, flooding her, marking her.

"Don't let me bite you," Drake cried. "Oh God, don't let me bite you."

"Don't worry." Sylvan dropped to her knees, her head buried in the curve of Drake's shoulder, clutching Drake against her chest as she erupted inside her leather pants. She shook uncontrollably and her wolf went wild, howling for Drake's bite and the final release. "I won't let you."

CHAPTER TWENTY-FOUR

Niki grasped Sophia's arm and pulled her down the hall and outside the infirmary. "What's happening in there?"

Sophia wrapped her arms tightly around her middle and leaned against one of the porch columns. "I think you should ask the Alpha."

"I'm asking you." Niki crowded close behind Sophia, her mouth nearly brushing Sophia's neck. Sophia shivered, and Niki sensed need and fear and confusion. Instantly protective, she gripped Sophia's shoulders and pulled her back against her chest. "What happened? Did someone hurt you?"

Sighing, Sophia relaxed against Niki, as if welcoming the support. "No. Nothing like that. It was just...hard."

"What did Drake do to you?" Niki remembered her caution to Drake. *Find someone else to mate.* Drake had coupled with the Alpha just a short while ago, but she could easily be in frenzy again and looking for release. Release with an unmated female like Sophia. Niki rumbled with an unexpected rush of territorial hormones and her sex surged to readiness. She wrapped her arms around Sophia's waist and whispered hotly in her ear. "Did she tempt you with her call?"

Sophia arched in Niki's arms and tilted her head back, whimpering softly when Niki licked her neck. "You know who she wants."

"Who do you want?" Niki tugged Sophia's earlobe with her teeth and rocked her pelvis against Sophia's ass. "Who do you want, Sophia?"

"Please."

Sophia rubbed against her, her plaintive cries of need forcing Niki's claws and canines and clitoris to throb. Niki tried to think.

She was harder than she should have been so soon, almost as if she'd been running with the Alpha for hours and absorbing her powerful pheromones. Sophia, always so careful not to be caught in a frenzy, even when she ran and hunted with the Pack, was ready. Too ready.

"It's the Alpha." Niki sucked in a breath, understanding why they were both on the verge of full-fledged sex frenzy. Sylvan was broadcasting sex and fury. Every Were in the vicinity was probably feeling the call. "Is she all right?"

Sophia pulled away abruptly, her chest heaving. "Is she all that matters to you? Don't you even care what Drake is going through? How much pain she's in?"

"No, I don't care about a Were with the power to hurt the Alpha," Niki snarled, incensed by Sophia's need and knowing she couldn't take her. "I only care about the Alpha, and so should you."

"That's not fair," Sophia said softly, rubbing her arms as if she were cold when she had to be on fire. "I would do anything for her. All of us would, you know that." She reached out, but stopped herself before she touched Niki's cheek. "I know that you would die for her. But maybe that's not enough."

Niki growled. "It's the best I have to give her."

"No," Sophia said with a gentle shake of her head. "No, it's not."

"Don't mistake me for someone else," Niki said darkly. "I wasn't born for tenderness."

Sophia started to protest when the front door slammed open and Sylvan stormed out, shirtless, blood welling from shallow gouges on her shoulders, her face and body in mid-shift.

"The Rover," Sylvan ordered, the muscles in her throat and chest straining. "Get it."

"Right away," Niki said, signaling across the Compound to Lara, who stood at wary attention by the side of the vehicle.

Sylvan rounded on Sophia. "Drake. See to her. Take care of her."

"Of course," Sophia said. "I'm sorry if I hurt—"

"No," Sylvan said. "You did nothing wrong."

"Wait." Niki grasped Sophia's arm, preventing her from going back inside. "If Drake is in frenzy—"

"She isn't," Sylvan snarled. The lacerations on her shoulders had already closed, but the purplish bruise above her left breast remained dark and angry. She threw off Niki's arm and said to Sophia, "Go to her."

"She'll ask for you," Sophia said quietly. "What shall I say?"

Sylvan strode down the stairs as Lara pulled the Rover in front of the building. She yanked open the rear door and Niki jumped in after her. "Tell her I'm gone."

❖

"Home," Sylvan said from the back of the Rover. She needed to shower and change and leave the Compound until both she and Drake were more in control. With effort, she reversed her shift enough to retract her claws and canines. The thin band of silver pelt persisted down the center of her abdomen; her clitoris and glands remained full and hard. She closed her eyes, ignoring Niki's worried rumblings, while the Rover tore through the woods. When they reached her cabin, she leapt out and vaulted onto the porch, tearing off her pants as soon as she was inside.

She groaned as she stepped into the shower. Even the water beating against the bite on her chest was agonizing. The pain of the uncompleted bonding was so excruciating she finally gave in and curled up on the shower floor, her arms wrapped around her middle, knees drawn up to her chest. Her sex was too tense and swollen to even attempt temporary relief. Her body screamed out for Drake, and Drake alone, to finish her. Drake's bite would force her to release every unique chemical and hormone that defined her. She would flood Drake's mouth, her skin, her body until they were linked physically as powerfully as they were emotionally.

But Drake didn't want that. *Don't let me bite you!*

She'd almost let Drake take her. Another touch, another scrape of Drake's teeth on her skin, and she would have.

Forcing herself into a sitting position, Sylvan leaned back against the hard tiles, the cooling water sluicing over her chest and abdomen. Eventually the pain relented enough for her to stand, and she methodically dressed in a dark silk shirt and summer-weight raw linen jacket and trousers.

Max and Andrew waited with Lara and Niki by the Rover. Both

Max and Andrew had fresh bite marks on their necks. Niki and Lara looked anxious and agitated.

"Are you all right?" Sylvan asked them quietly.

"Yes, Alpha," they both said immediately.

Sylvan nodded curtly and climbed into the back of the Rover. "Take me to my office."

❖

Drake heard the door open and close quietly. She was lying on the treatment table again, covered with the sheet Sylvan had placed over her when she left.

"Is she all right?" Drake asked.

"Drake, I..." Sophia sighed. "It's not something for me to discuss."

Drake sat up, tucking the sheet around her waist. "I'm hurting her, aren't I?"

Sophia leaned back, her hands flat against the door. She bit her lip, conflicted. "Sylvan's mother ruled for generations. Many of us don't remember the last time we had an unmated Alpha. I'm not sure, but I think everything about mating is stronger, fiercer, for the Alpha. Her..." She closed her eyes. "She gives us everything, and we take everything. She asks only for our loyalty. It's hard for me to talk about her this way."

"You love her," Drake said gently. "So do I."

"I know."

"Do you?"

Sophia smiled. "We all would fight for her. But I've never seen anyone, even Niki, who could gentle her. She needs that."

"What she needs is a mate who will make her life easier, not harder." Drake gripped the cold edges of the steel table until they cut into her palms. "I can't seem to be around her without...*arousal* seems too mild a word for it."

"That's why we call it frenzy," Sophia said. "It's more than desire, more even than need—it's a biological imperative for us."

"But we could bond with others, couldn't we?" Drake knew she wouldn't. Couldn't. She wouldn't be able to bear it if Sylvan did, but she didn't want her to be alone, either. Sophia was right—the Pack demanded everything from her and Sylvan needed to give it. But she couldn't give forever without someone to protect and care for her. Drake swallowed around the pain in her throat. "Sylvan could bond with someone else?"

"I don't know," Sophia said. "Even if a Were survives the death of a mate, they never mate again. And I don't know of anyone who didn't complete a mate bond once the mating frenzy had begun. Why would they?"

"Surely some pairings aren't welcome?"

"Mating isn't random. It's not accidental. The mate bond is only possible when your heart and your mind and your body need only the one." Sophia shook her head, a sad smile on her face. "Sometimes we go unmated because our wolves can't recognize each other—because we've been injured or damaged somehow or unconsciously block out the call. But when each recognizes the other, no one ever denies the bond. We are born to be mated. It's the natural way for us."

"She'll be all right if I stay away from her, won't she?"

"Will *you*?"

Drake didn't answer, but she didn't think so. Roger had said she might not be strong enough to deny her need for release, her need to mate. She might lose control completely. At least if she did, she was confident Niki would execute her. Niki would not let her hurt Sylvan or anyone else. But as long as she could think and reason, she had work to do. "I'd like to meet your parents. Will you take me to the lab?"

Sophia hesitated.

"Please. I might not know anything about Were physiology, but I do about human. I might be able to help them interpret the results of my tests."

Sophia nodded. "I was going to send the specimens by courier, but we can take them ourselves. My car's outside. I'll get you something to eat while you get ready."

"Thank you," Drake said. "Thank you for trusting me."

"Of course I trust you. You're the Alpha's…" Sophia's expression softened with sympathy. "You are Pack now."

❖

"Come," Sylvan said when a knock sounded on her door.

Niki entered and closed the door behind her. "You have visitors."

"Who?"

"Councilors Gates and Thornton."

Sylvan grumbled and got to her feet, turning to look out the window. A visit from her Vampire and Fae coalition counterparts was the last thing she wanted to deal with. Her temper was too frayed for diplomacy and her wolf too close to ascending for safety. All she could think about was Drake. She wanted her again. She wanted to be inside her. She ached for Drake to suck her, make her come completely, take all she was. Her glands pumped out pheromones and kinins at a furious rate and her skin was slick with the potent combination.

"I'll tell them you can't see them," Niki whispered.

Sylvan spun and leapt over her desk, landing in front of Niki. Niki automatically ducked her head and Sylvan grasped the back of her neck, tilting her face up until they were almost nose to nose. Niki's eyes glazed hunter green, and her canines gleamed like white spikes against her blood-red lower lip. She shuddered in Sylvan's grip, her breath shallow and fast.

"And what will you tell them?" Sylvan asked, her voice low and dangerous. "Will you tell them the wolf Alpha is on the edge of frenzy? That she can't control her beast?"

"It's not true." Niki rubbed her palms over Sylvan's chest, hoping to soothe her.

Sylvan growled when Niki inadvertently caressed the bite above her breast. The bruise was exquisitely tender and all she wanted was Drake to bury her canines in it. "Open my shirt."

Trembling, Niki obeyed. The muscles in Sylvan's chest and abdomen stood out as if etched in stone and were just as hard. With a small whimper, Niki trailed her fingertips down the center of Sylvan's torso, the back of her fingers skimming the inner curve of Sylvan's breast. A fine dusting of silver marked a path to the top of her pants and would be thicker inside, framing her sex.

"You still think I have control?" Sylvan growled.

"You do," Niki said, rubbing Sylvan's stomach. "If you didn't, you would have taken me right here by now."

Groaning, Sylvan pulled Niki into her arms and cradled Niki's head on her shoulder. She rubbed her chin in Niki's hair, breathing her in, grounding herself in Pack and family. Her agony was not Niki's fault, nor Niki's burden to ease.

"I'm sorry," Sylvan said.

"No need." Niki nuzzled Sylvan's neck. "But you need to mate. You can't go on like this."

"My wolf wants a mate," Sylvan said. "I don't."

Niki took a slow breath. "You at least need to stay away from Drake. She's driving you too clos—"

"You think I don't know that?" Sylvan snarled. "You think I want to force this on her?"

"Then let me remove her from the Compound."

Sylvan gripped Niki's shoulders and stepped back, lowering her head until they were eye to eye. "You won't touch her. Do you understand?"

"Yes, Alpha," Niki said.

After a moment, Sylvan released her and returned to her desk. She sat down and ruthlessly caged her furious wolf. Then she picked up a pen and pulled a file folder in front of her.

"Send in the Councilors."

A moment later Zachary Gates strode in with the Fae Queen by his side. Cecilia Thornton was a voluptuous blonde with huge green eyes, a delicate face, a sinful mouth, and a quick, calculating mind. In her Prada suit, she looked every inch the CEO of the Fifth Avenue marketing powerhouse that she was. When she sat on the Fae throne she traded in her designer suits for gossamer gowns or sleek, body-hugging leathers. Sylvan wasn't certain the full extent of Cecilia's power, but she'd seen her reduce a traitorous subject brought before her court to an unrecognizable mass of quivering jelly—literally—with a nonchalant flick of her hand. Like all absolute monarchs, Cecilia craved power and guarded it jealously.

"Cecilia, I thought you were in Washington." Sylvan gestured to the chairs in front of her desk. "Please. Sit down."

Ever the gentleman, Zachary waited until Cecilia was seated before sitting himself. He wore his Armani well, giving the appearance of a modern-day corporate raider. Which he was. He leaned forward with an unctuous smile. "Forgive this unscheduled visit, Alpha. Since Cecilia arrived unexpectedly for business, it seemed a perfect opportunity to meet with you privately."

Cecelia crossed her legs and folded her lovely manicured hands in her lap. "Especially since you seem too busy to schedule time for the full coalition board."

"The next meeting isn't until late next month," Sylvan pointed out, wondering what Zachary would do if she took him down with her teeth in his neck, which she'd had the urge to do since he walked in the room.

"True," Cecilia said, smiling as her eyes slid over Sylvan's face. "But in light of recent events—"

"Recent events?" Sylvan said.

"The delay in moving PR-15 out of Weston's committee has some of us concerned," Zachary said. "The bill has substantial economic repercussions—and until we can assure our stockholders that our corporations are solid and secure, our margins are at risk."

Sylvan narrowed her eyes and barely suppressed a growl. "I wasn't aware that the primary goal of the legislation was to preserve your portfolio. We get reports every day of attacks on Praeterns, including homicides—because humans don't fear prosecution."

"Of course," Cecilia said, "those things are important too, but without an economic advantage, it will be far more difficult for us to convince the humans that it's important to recognize our place in the world trade structure."

"And what about the sanctity of our territories, protection for our young, our right to governing autonomy?" Sylvan shot back.

"We don't need the humans' help to preserve our societies." Cecilia shrugged. "We'll let the humans know what we want them to know. That's always been our way."

"That presumes keeping a great many secrets," Sylvan said.

"Exactly," Zachary said. "The less we call attention to our... differences...the better it will be." He glanced at Cecilia, who nodded almost imperceptibly, then turned back to Sylvan. "You might consider whether you really want to remain as visible as you have been."

"It sounds suspiciously as if you'd like to replace me," Sylvan remarked, leaning back in her chair. She decided that she didn't really want to tear Zachary's throat out. It would be messy and unsatisfying in the long run. Parrying Zachary and Cecelia's mind games actually helped her distract her wolf from her singular goal, which was to find Drake and claim her.

"Your opinions, of course, are invaluable," Zachary said, "but I think we all know that the public has the hardest time embracing the concept of others who are…part animal."

Sylvan laughed. "And you think they don't have trouble with bloodsucking Vampires?"

Zachary's eyes flared crimson for a moment, and then he smiled thinly. "On the contrary, they seem to like the side effects of blood-hosting quite a lot. As I think you're aware."

"I appreciate the concerns of the coalition," Sylvan said, although she was fairly certain that Zachary and Cecelia were jockeying for more power and didn't represent the entire board. If she were replaced by a Were who didn't have the ability to dictate policy—and no one did, other than her—Zachary and Cecelia would steamroll the coalition into going along with their own agendas. She had no intention of allowing that to happen. "But there's really nothing to worry about. Weres have coexisted with humans for millennia without being detected, and we'll have no problem continuing to coexist now that they know of us."

"Even when the humans discover that you're capable of transferring a lethal infection to them?" Zachary asked.

Cecilia sat back, a placid expression on her face, as if she were watching a mildly entertaining tennis match.

Sylvan growled. "What are you talking about?"

Zachary spread his hands. "Just a…rumor…that a number of humans have contracted a fatal condition from Weres. We all know how the humans deal with a threat of that nature—the next thing you know, they'll want to isolate you in camps, regulate your breeding, experiment on your offspr—"

"How exactly were you made aware of this rumor?"

"A phone call," Zachary said. "Actually, several of them. Of course, I immediately sought to bring this to your attention."

"And I certainly appreciate that." Sylvan stood, waging a fierce internal battle to keep her claws and her canines retracted. Zachary was threatening her Pack and she wanted to scatter pieces of him around the room. "Your solidarity…and Cecelia's"—she tipped her head to Cecelia, who gave her a slow, indolent smile—"is very much appreciated, but I can assure you, rumor is all there is to this."

Zachary rose and extended his hand to Cecelia, who rested her fingers delicately on his arm as if he were a royal consort.

"That's very comforting, Alpha," Cecilia said. "Please do keep us informed."

"Of course," Sylvan said as the pair walked out. When the door closed behind them, she snarled in frustration. Her chest throbbed and she rubbed the bite. Very few individuals knew about the human females who had contracted Were fever. Drake knew, but Drake would never betray her and the Pack. Sophia, who was loyal unto death. Someone else had alerted the Vampire—someone who was not Pack. An enemy.

Niki knocked and edged inside the room. "I'm sorry, Alpha, but while you were engaged a call came in—one I think you'll want to address."

"What is it?"

"A request for an urgent meeting with you tonight. From Detective Jody Gates."

"Zachary's daughter."

Niki nodded.

"I wonder if she's finally decided to do her father's bidding."

"The timing is suspicious," Niki agreed.

"Well, let's see what she has to say. Set up the meeting."

"Yes, Alpha." Niki hesitated, then quietly left.

Sylvan returned to the window. The sun had set, but the night sky was hazy and the city lights obscured the stars. She ached for the taste of pure mountain air in her lungs, for the feel of pine needles under her feet, for a glimpse of an endless midnight sky. She longed for the comfort of another running close by her side, their shoulders touching, their breath mingling.

She picked up her cell and called Elena. "How is she doing?"

"As far as I know, she's not showing any signs of decompensation. She's very strong."

"Where is she?"

Elena hesitated.

"Where is she?" Sylvan demanded.

"She left with Sophia this morning. They haven't returned."

"They've been gone half a day?"

"Yes, Alpha."

Sylvan cursed and broke off the call. "Niki!"

Niki burst in. "Alpha?"

"Find Sophia. I need to speak with her."

"Is something wrong?"

Sylvan leaned on her desk, her claws scraping the surface. "I hope not. She and Drake left the Compound together this morning."

Niki's eyes narrowed and she rumbled. "Sophia is with her? With an uncontrolled dominant who's likely to frenzy at any time?" She snarled and her claws shot out. "If Drake touches her, I'll kill her."

"You forget, neither of them is mated. You have nothing to say about it." Sylvan grimaced bitterly. *Nor do I.*

CHAPTER TWENTY-FIVE

Drake waited impatiently in a conference room on the fifteenth floor of a glass-and-steel building, one of many in the sprawling industrial complex that comprised Mir Industries. Sophia had left her to assist her parents with the analysis of the tissue specimens. Drake would have volunteered to help, but she was no bench scientist. She'd only be in the way, and she got the feeling that the Revnik lab was off-limits, even to those who made it through the elaborate security at the building entrance. With each passing hour, her physical and emotional agitation accelerated. The conference room, despite being spacious and airy with one entire wall of windows giving a view of the nearby mountains, felt confining. She paced, her skin tight and her limbs twitching with the need to move. To run. She wanted to be back in the Compound. She wanted Sylvan. She wanted to taste her. She wanted to mark her with her mouth and her teeth and her claws. She wanted to come on her again. She wanted Sylvan to carry her scent in every cell.

The door opened and Drake spun around with a warning growl.

"Sorry." Sophia let the door swing close behind her and stood still, watching Drake cautiously.

Drake rubbed her forehead. "No, I'm sorry. I'm just...jumpy. Anything yet?"

"We've got quite a lot of preliminary results. My parents can explain it better than I can. They'll be here in a minute."

"Great, thanks." Drake forced herself to sit down at the conference table. Her T-shirt, damp with sweat despite the air-conditioning, clung to her back and chest. She'd purposefully chosen a pair of jeans a size too big when she'd dressed earlier, but the slightest brush of denim against her center sent slivers of pain and arousal through her.

"How are you doing?" Sophia sat down next to Drake.

"I feel like I'm coming out of my skin."

Sophia gave her a sympathetic smile. "I'm so sorry."

Drake shrugged wryly. "Are you uncomfortable around me? Am I...doing anything to you? Anything objectionable?"

"No, of course not." Sophia's eyes widened. "And you're right, I *should* be more sensitive to your call. I was yesterday."

"What do you mean?"

"Nothing," Sophia said quickly.

"Please, don't keep me in the dark," Drake said urgently. "Everything is moving too fast for me as it is. I need to know as much as I can."

"It's just...I might not sense your call because unmated Weres don't respond when mated Weres are in need. It's protective—if unmated Weres responded to mated females in heat, there'd be chaos. The dominants would instinctively want to breed and the mates would try to kill them."

"What are you saying, then?"

Sophia took a deep breath. "You smell like the Alpha. You smell mated."

"I didn't bite her again."

"She bit you, though, didn't she?"

Drake shuddered and closed her eyes, the memory of Sylvan taking her so potent her body screamed for release. "Yes."

"I think your wolf wants *her*, and that's why your call doesn't affect me nearly as much."

"I feel like I'm not in charge of my life," Drake said. "There's this huge part of me that *wants* and I have no idea how to control it."

"If you had grown up Were, you would have had years to integrate your instincts. You would have gradually learned to control your needs and urges. I think you're amazingly strong to have survived the transition and for you still to be you." Sophia reached for Drake's hand. "I knew you when you were human, remember. You're still caring and brave. And honorable."

Drake grimaced. "I'm not so sure about that."

"Why don't you want to mate with the Alpha?"

"Do you think I'm the mate she needs? One the Pack would accept?"

"That's for the Alpha to decide."

"We don't even know what's happening in my body. What if there's been some kind of permanent cellular damage—a degenerative process of some kind? What if I can't shift?" Drake sighed. "I don't mind telling you, I'm scared."

Sophia squeezed Drake's hand. "We'll help you. You're not alone."

Not alone. She'd only ever been alone. Sophia's hand was warm in hers, steady and calm. Sophia's eyes were tender and soothing. Drake rubbed Sophia's hand against her cheek and was comforted.

"That's better," Sophia said gently.

"Thank you."

"You would do the same for me." Sophia stroked Drake's cheek. "I shouldn't have brought you here. You need to sleep. You've been through too much."

"I'm all right. I can't sleep. I can't stop wanting…" Drake flushed and fell silent.

"Maybe this is happening just as fast and unexpectedly for the Alpha as it is for you. Trust her."

"I do," Drake murmured, realizing she had trusted Sylvan instinctively since the moment she'd seen her tear into Misha's shoulder to rip out a lethal piece of silver. Thinking about Sylvan, envisioning her face, remembering Sylvan's hands and mouth on her brought a surge of unbearable longing and desire. "I do."

The conference room door opened and a man and a woman Drake assumed were Sophia's parents walked in. They weren't at all what she expected. Leo and Nadia Revnik were blond and blue-eyed like Sophia, and didn't appear to be much older than her. If Drake had met them under other circumstances, she would have put them in their early to mid thirties. Clearly, not only was the Were lifespan much, much longer than humans realized, but the aging process itself was remarkably slower. That alone made it imperative she not allow any further strengthening of the bond with Sylvan. If her transition wasn't complete, she was likely to die decades, if not centuries, before her.

"I'm Drake McKennan," she said, standing and extending her

hand. The Revniks, each carrying a file folder, introduced themselves and sat down across from her.

"You understand," Leo said, "until we have advised the Alpha of our findings, we can't share all the results with you."

"I appreciate that," Drake said, "although we are talking about my personal situation."

Nadia nodded. "And we're sympathetic to that." She opened her folder. "There are some things we can tell you now."

Drake steeled herself. "Go ahead."

"As you probably already suspected, there's no evidence of a biological pathogen. No identifiable bacterial toxins or viral components."

"A chemical agent of some kind, then," Drake said.

"That was our initial thought." Sophia's father passed Drake a serum electrophoresis report. "However, we've identified an elevated paraprotein as well as its degradation products in your blood. We're lucky to have gotten the specimens when we did. In another twenty-four hours, we might not have found this."

"What do you make of it?" Drake studied the printout.

"We think it's a synthesized antigen," Nadia said. "Probably one with mutagenic properties."

Drake waited, but the scientists remained silent, leaving her to work it through herself. From what little of the evolutionary history of the Praetern species had been made public, she knew Weres, Vampires, and humans had diverged very early in primate development—resulting in similarities in form but vast differences in function. Were fever was a toxic reaction to silver that produced rapid systemic cellular death. That level of destruction usually indicated disruption of critical subcellular functions. The most important job of a cell was the production of energy to sustain life, and the mitochondria were the powerhouses doing the work. Mitochondria also carried DNA, the genetic maps to any number of critical biological functions.

"The Were genes are in the mitochondria, aren't they?" Drake said. "And mitochondrial DNA is only passed from the mother, which means only a Were female can produce Were offspring."

The Revniks neither confirmed nor denied, but they didn't have to. Everything was so much clearer now. Drake remembered Sylvan's fury with the adolescent males for taking Misha out of the Compound and failing to protect her. Every female Were, and *only* the female Weres, carried the genetic material to preserve and propagate the species.

"This antigen you've isolated," Drake said, "it targets mitochondria, but for some reason mine mutated instead of destructing."

"That's our present conclusion, yes," Nadia said.

"But if someone is synthesizing this compound, why?" Drake looked from Sophia to her parents. "Surely they're not trying to create Weres? Isn't it more likely they're trying to produce a chemical weapon *against* Weres?"

"Either is possible," Nadia said. "The only thing we can be certain of right now is that all the evidence indicates this agent is almost uniformly fatal in humans. You seem to be the exception."

"Maybe," Drake said hollowly. "Maybe the degenerative process is just delayed."

"No," Leo said. "We ran your mitochondrial DNA from the muscle biopsies. Your profiles are indistinguishable from native Were DNA."

Drake's heart leapt. "Normal?"

"Structurally, yes. Whether all those gene sites are active remains to be seen."

"You mean, whether I'll be able to shift," Drake said.

Sophia shook her head. "You already have shifted."

"Yes," Drake said, "when Sylvan forced me to."

Nadia Revnik sat forward. "The Alpha forced you to shift?"

"Yes." Drake flushed. "That's when I bit her and she shifted too."

Nadia cast her husband a worried look.

"What? Isn't it normal for Sylvan to be able to force a Were to shift?"

"Yes," Nadia said, "but you were still in the throes of fever. And you bit her."

Drake's heart twisted. "You think I might have transferred something dangerous to Sylvan? That this toxin could hurt her?"

"We don't know. We might be able to tell more from your progenitor cells—to determine just how complete, and stable, a mutation has occurred," Nadia said.

"Anything. Do it."

"We'd like permission to do both bone marrow and laparoscopic ovarian biopsies," Leo said.

"Yes, of course," Drake said immediately. "We should do it now. Do you have the equipment here?"

"Wait," Sophia said. "We can't do procedures of that magnitude without discussing it with the Alpha."

"Yes, we can," Drake insisted. "You have my permission, and we need this information." She turned and took Sophia's hands. "And we need to know. We need to know for Sylvan's sake. Please."

Sophia hesitated, then nodded.

"Before we do anything," Nadia said, "the Alpha wants to speak with Sophia. Her *imperator* called here a few minutes ago looking for her."

"I'll call her now," Sophia said, rising. "May I use your office, Mother?"

"Don't you have your cell phone?" Drake asked.

"They don't work in this building," Sophia said. "Radio transmissions are blocked for security reasons. Only the land lines function." She paused. "You can come with me if you want to speak with her."

Drake wanted to hear Sylvan's voice almost as much as she wanted to see her, touch her. "No. I want your parents to harvest the specimens now. Tell Sylvan...tell her I'm all right. But don't tell her about the biopsies. I'll take responsibility for this. I need to know if I've hurt her."

"She'll be angry." Sophia glanced at her parents. "With all of us. You must scent what Drake is."

Leo said, "She is the Alpha's mate."

"No." Drake shot to her feet. "No, I'm not. And if there's the slightest possibility I'm a danger to her, I can't go back to the Compound. I can't see her again. Ever."

❖

Niki's cell rang as she climbed out of the Rover in front of Jody Gates's townhouse on State Street.

"Kroff," Niki said.

"It's Sophia. My parents said the Alpha was looking for me."

"Are you all right?" Niki asked.

"Yes, I'm fine. Why?"

"You and Drake haven't tangled. She hasn't touched you?"

"What?" Sylvia exclaimed. "No! Of course not."

"Just be careful," Niki snapped. She caught up to Sylvan and held out the phone. "Alpha, I have Sophia."

Sylvan paused on the steps and took the phone. "Is Drake still with you?"

"Yes, Alpha. She's…with my parents right now."

"How is she?"

"She seems fine."

"I want her back at the Compound *now*, and I want Elena to check her as soon as she returns. I won't be long."

Sophia was silent.

"Sophia?" Sylvan growled.

"I don't know if she wants to go back to the Compound, Alpha."

"She doesn't know what's best for her right now. I want her somewhere safe."

"I understand, but—"

"Never mind, keep her there. I'll be there in less than an hour. Tell her I'm coming. Tell her that."

"Yes, Alpha."

Sylvan tossed the cell phone back to Niki. "Let's hear what the Vampire has to say."

❖

Becca probably should have been intimidated by the group gathered in Jody's bookcase-lined study, but she was fascinated. As a group they *were* intimidating, but as individuals, they were breathtaking. She couldn't stop staring at the wolf Alpha. She'd seen photos of Sylvan Mir, heard her interviewed on television. She'd expected her to be beautiful and confident. She hadn't expected her to be so magnetic. So powerful. The Weres with her, male and female, were every bit as stunning—wild and dangerous and wary. The Alpha wore a stylish suit with a sense of studied disregard and the others, in dark military pants and skintight black shirts, looked exactly like the soldiers they were.

Jody was a mesmerizing contrast. Elegant, refined, completely contained. She was a cipher, an enigma—only her endlessly deep obsidian eyes hinted at the restrained lethality she kept so tightly leashed. But Becca knew what deadly power lay beneath her poised exterior. She'd seen the predator uncaged.

Sylvan, with her guards flanking her, stood on one side of the spacious high-ccilinged room, having declined Jody's offer to sit in the leather sofas and chairs in front of a marble fireplace.

"Something to drink?" Jody asked, indicating an antique sideboard and an array of liquor in cut-crystal bottles.

"No," Sylvan said. "I'm surprised to hear from you, Detective, and not the police commissioner. I have a good relationship with her, and she hasn't informed me of any inquiries involving Weres."

"There isn't an official investigation—yet," Jody said. "But I suspect there will be one before long. Someone wants the public to know that humans are being infected with Were fever."

Sylvan pivoted to Becca. "I take it that's where you come in, Ms. Land. Rather unusual to involve the public when all you have is speculation—although that doesn't seem to matter much to the press these days."

Becca lifted her chin. "I have a job to do, Alpha. And I have a responsibility to report the truth, especially if there's a danger to the public."

The auburn-haired female who'd been introduced as Sylvan's second growled, displaying a flash of fully extended canines. Becca slid her eyes to her and refused to lower her gaze even when the Were snarled a warning.

"Ms. Land is not the cause of your problems, Alpha," Jody said smoothly.

Becca hadn't seen Jody move, but suddenly Jody was between her and the Weres.

Sylvan looked from Jody to Becca. "How did you hear about these rumors?"

"An anonymous source," Becca said. At Sylvan's look of disgust, she added, "And no, I'm not being difficult. I really don't know."

"Whoever contacted Ms. Land may have also alerted others," Jody said. "I came across the rumor from intelligence sources monitoring anti-Praetern groups."

"Let me guess—HUFSI," Sylvan said.

"What—" Becca said.

"Humans United For Species Integrity," Jody explained. "A small but radical offshoot of some of the more civilized groups trying to block legislation on Praetern rights."

"You're kidding," Becca muttered, mentally making a note to investigate the group. She couldn't believe that her fellow humans actually thought they had the right to relegate entire species to some kind of second-class status. But then again, her ancestors had been slaves, so she wasn't sure why she was surprised.

"Unfortunately, HUFSI is not the only group, just one of the more militant." Sylvan asked Jody, "What's your interest in this, Detective? Vampires don't usually involve themselves in anything that doesn't directly affect them."

"My job is to see there are no further victims."

"Your father didn't seem particularly concerned about the victims."

Jody went completely still, the stillness of a predator just before an attack. The Were Alpha's second took a step forward, putting her even with her Alpha. She parted her lips, displaying her teeth. Jody slowly caught the guard's gaze and sent a wave of power. The Were's green eyes clouded and she grumbled uneasily, deep in her chest.

"Stand down, Vampire," Sylvan murmured.

Jody held the Were in thrall a moment longer, then shrugged with graceful insouciance. "My responsibility is to uphold the law. I don't follow my father's agenda."

"Even when the law doesn't protect your species?" Sylvan asked quietly.

"That's your job, isn't it, Councilor? To see that the law does."

Becca edged forward until Jody was no longer shielding her. "We all know there are plenty of factions who don't want to see Praeterns recognized—legally, socially, economically, or politically. Maybe that's a place to start. Who are your enemies, Alpha Mir?"

Sylvan smiled and looked pointedly at Jody. "More every day."

Becca had had enough of watching the wolf Alpha and the Vampire test each other. She expected one or both of them to pee on the carpet at any moment. "Look—none of us want to see another dead girl. That's why we either find out what exactly is killing them, and fast, or I will have to go public. Now—do we work together or not?"

Sylvan and Jody stared at her.

"What?" Becca said testily. "Was I supposed to raise my hand to ask for permission to speak?"

That mercurial smile flickered over Jody's mouth and Becca felt a rush of heat.

"It's a matter of police business," Jody said.

"It's Were business," Sylvan snapped.

"Oh, for God's sake," Becca said, planting her hands on her hips. "Can't you—make a temporary alliance or something?"

Sylvan raised a brow. Jody frowned.

"I have no reason to trust you," Sylvan said to Jody.

"And I have no reason to share information with you."

"Then we have a stalemate," Sylvan said and turned to leave.

"You know," Becca interjected, "I can get my story without either of you. I'll just go back to the ER and interview Drake McKennan again. Then I'll decide if we go public."

The wolf Alpha slowly pivoted and fixed Becca with a flat, hard stare. The Weres with her moved into a V formation behind her. Becca shivered as if a cold wind had blown over her skin.

"Careful, wolf," Jody murmured.

"Drake has nothing to do with this." Sylvan's voice dropped to a guttural rumble.

"All right, then," Becca said, pleased that her voice did not quiver. "Then *you* be my source. You can't tell me you aren't looking into these deaths."

"You are either very brave or very foolish," Sylvan said.

"She's both," Jody said.

"We don't believe the humans were infected by Weres," Sylvan said, still watching Becca. "We don't know who these human females are or where they came from. We don't know how to explain what happened to them. But we will find out."

Jody lightly grasped Becca's elbow and moved her back, putting distance between her and Sylvan. "The medical examiner thinks the girls were being held somewhere—a hospital—before they arrived at the emergency room."

"A hospital?" Sylvan said softly. "Or a laboratory?"

"Oh my God," Becca said. "You think someone was experimenting on them?"

"I don't know," Sylvan said. "I can only tell you that humans are not generally susceptible to Were fever. Whatever they have, it isn't that."

"How many are we talking about?" Jody said.

"Four suspected."

"Give me the victims' names and I'll run background checks," Jody said. "If we don't have a lead on the perpetrators, then we'll study the victims. The victimology may tell us what happened to them."

"Our medic will call you with the names," Sylvan said carefully. "Then we should talk again."

"Yes," Jody said, "and you can tell me what your scientists have discovered."

"So we have an alliance?" Becca asked.

Sylvan stared at Jody. "Agreed, Vampire?"

Jody held Sylvan's gaze for a long moment, then, with a slight incline of her head, said, "Agreed, Wolf."

"We'll be in touch." Sylvan turned to leave and Lara fell in on one side, Niki on the other.

Jody led the way into the hall and across the foyer. "I'll call you once I've run the searches."

Jody pulled open the wide stained-glass door and a windowpane shattered, raining multicolored shards onto the marble floor. Niki shouted. Becca was suddenly thrown down and pinned by a heavy weight. Someone slammed the door closed. Barely able to breathe, Becca managed to turn her head. A bright red sheet of blood cascaded across the polished marble foyer toward her face.

CHAPTER TWENTY-SIX

Becca!" Jody crouched by Becca's side, urgently running her hands over Becca's body. "Becca! Are you hurt?"

"No, no I don't think so." Becca sat up and her heart lurched. Jody's face was blood streaked and the front of her white shirt splattered with crimson. "God, Jody. You're bleeding!"

Jody shook her head grimly. "No, I'm not."

"What was it? What happened?"

"Gunfire," Jody said.

"Who—" Becca trailed off as the horrible scene came into focus. A few feet away, the wolf Alpha knelt in a spreading scarlet pool, one of the black-uniformed Weres cradled in her arms. The Were guards had formed a physical barricade between Sylvan and the damaged front door. Blood bubbled from a hole in the Alpha's shoulder and soaked her shirt, but she didn't seem to notice it. Her eyes, fierce gold daggers in a face gone feral, were fixed on the female in her arms.

Drake was awakened from her post-procedure doze by a sharp pain in her chest. She jerked upright in the recliner. "Something's wrong."

"What is it?" Sophia quickly rose from the desk where she'd been running a computer search and hurried to Drake's side. "Are you having pain?"

"No." Drake grimaced. "Yes. I don't know."

Sophia drew the sheet aside and examined the small incisions in Drake's lower abdomen where her mother had inserted the instruments to do the biopsies. "These are nearly healed. There's no evidence of bleeding. Where's the pain?"

"Not there—my upper abdomen. And my chest." Drake gritted her teeth as another stabbing pain shot through her chest. She checked the monitor on a stand next to her chair. Her EKG was steady, her pulse and blood pressure normal. "Everything looks normal. It's not me. It's not me."

"Then what—"

Drake groaned with another wave of twisting pain, this one spearing down her right side. Her claws tore through the ends of her fingertips. Her canines burst out, flooding her mouth with hot blood. She bolted to her feet. "Sylvan. Something's happened."

❖

"Lara," Sylvan said gently, "I have to get the bullets out. The bleeding won't stop until I do."

Blood streamed from the corner of Lara's mouth and gushed from a crater in the center of her chest. Her whiskey eyes held Sylvan's, calm and unafraid. She nodded, her voice barely a whisper. "Yes, Alpha."

Sylvan's chest burned with every breath, but the pain was nothing compared to her rage. Lara had jumped in front of her, had taken most of the bullets meant for her. Now her wolf, her *centuri*, was hurt, suffering, and she would not let her die. Her arm shifted and her claws, three inches long and razor sharp, glinted. "Don't be afraid. I'm here."

"I know."

Lara screamed when Sylvan plunged her claws into the wound, her eyes rolling back, her body contorting into a rigid arch. A crimson river rushed out around Sylvan's limb, adding to the midnight lake around them. Sylvan jerked out a silver bullet and flung it aside, then drove her hand back into the wound three more times.

"They hit the heart," Sylvan growled, gripping the shredded organ to stem the flow. "There's too much damage. She'll bleed to death before she can heal."

Jody dropped down beside Sylvan. "My blood can keep her alive until she heals."

"She is nearly empty."

"Then we have to hurry. Decide, Wolf."

Sylvan met Jody's eyes. "Will she turn?"

"I don't know. Possibly."

"Do it."

Jody tore off her jacket and shirt, then sliced open the large artery in the bend of her right elbow. Blood spurted out in a scarlet fountain. Jody slid her hand behind Lara's neck and turned Lara's face into the bend of her arm. Holding her, she crooned, "Drink, Lara. Drink."

Lara shuddered, her throat working convulsively as she swallowed.

❖

Becca bit her lip, wondering how everyone else could be so calm—so deadly calm. Perhaps death held a different place in the natural order for these predators, who seemed so human, but were not. The foyer looked and smelled like a charnel house. The priceless linen wallpaper was covered with great swaths of red, as if someone had flung a paintbrush dipped in blood at them. The marble floor was awash in Lara's and the Alpha's blood.

Becca didn't remember moving over to Jody, didn't remember touching her, but now she knelt in a congealing pool a few inches from Jody with her hand on Jody's back. Jody's eyes were closed and her body trembled under Becca's fingers. Her midnight hair lay in damp tendrils on her neck. Her flawless skin had gone from purest white to ashen. And still Lara drank. The only sounds were Lara's desperate swallows and Jody's rapid breathing.

"Is she healing?" Becca asked at last.

"Yes, slowly," Sylvan said, her forearm still deep in Lara's chest. "Her heart is trying to beat. Just a little more."

Jody moaned, more agony than pleasure. Becca slid her arm around Jody's shoulders and murmured in her ear, "Are you all right?"

Wordlessly, Jody nodded.

Seconds passed. A minute. Another.

"She's almost there." Sylvan withdrew her hand and pressed her palm over the wound in Lara's chest. Lara curled around Jody's arm, her mouth working feverishly on Jody's flesh.

Jody sagged and Becca barely caught her before she collapsed completely. "We have to stop this. It's too much—Jody can't give any more."

"No," Jody whispered, her head lolling on Becca's shoulder, her arm still outstretched. "I'm all right."

"You're not," Becca cried. "You're so weak. I can feel it." She shot Sylvan an imploring glance. "Please. This is killing her!"

Jody laughed weakly, her lips ice cold against Becca's neck. "You're not afraid of the dead, remember."

"Vampire," Sylvan snapped, "are you blood-bonded?"

Jody was silent. Sylvan cursed and bent over her feeding *centuri*.

"Lara." Sylvan gently cupped Lara's chin and drew her face away from Jody's arm. "You have to stop."

Lara didn't struggle, but almost instantly stopped breathing and went limp.

"Alpha!" Niki cried. "Let her drink. We can't let her—"

"Wait." Sylvan gripped Lara's shoulders and called Lara's wolf. Deep inside, her own wolf rose. Her wounds flared and burned, but her wolf was strong. She let her power flow to Lara, calling to the part of Lara that was hers and would always be hers.

Lara's body jerked and her eyes shot open, blank and unseeing. She sucked in a breath as if she were drowning. Then she shimmered and shifted. The sleek brown wolf immediately collapsed, but her chest rose and fell and her heart beat. Sylvan sighed, weak and nearly drained. Her *centuri* would live.

"Jody! God, Jody!" Becca clutched Jody tightly. "She's unconscious. What's happening?"

Sylvan passed Lara to Andrew. "Get her to the Rover."

"Yes, Alpha." Andrew gently lifted the wolf and held her against his chest.

"Max—go with him. Secure the street. Make sure the shooter is gone."

"Yes, Alpha," Max barked out, shielding both Andrew and Lara as he led the way.

"Jody's not breathing." Becca choked, panic squeezing her throat closed. "She's *dying*."

"She'll rise," Niki said. "She's a Vampire."

"No, not without a blood bond," Sylvan said. "If she dies now, she won't animate. She needs blood now before she dies. She needs to feed."

"I'll do it," Becca said quickly. "Tell me—"

"You're not strong enough," Sylvan said. "Give her to me. Hurry."

"Alpha," Niki exclaimed, "what are you doing? You're wounded. You can't—"

"I won't let her die," Sylvan snarled. "She saved my wolf."

"Then I'll feed her!" Niki shouldered her way between Sylvan and Jody. Kneeling, she tore off her shirt, grasped Jody's limp body, and pulled Jody into her lap. She opened her jugular with a quick slice of her claw and pressed Jody's mouth to the wound. With surprising gentleness, she whispered, "Feed, Vampire. Don't die."

Jody shuddered, her lids fluttering. The lure of potent Were blood drew her back from the edge of a gaping abyss. With a snarl, she lifted her head, her eyes on fire, and sank her incisors into Niki's neck.

Niki jerked at the shock, her eyes shifting to hunter green before her lids slowly closed. Moaning softly, she swayed, her grip on Jody's shoulders loosening.

"Let me help." Becca slid behind Niki and supported the enthralled Were against her chest. Niki's head dropped onto Becca's shoulder as Jody drank in deep pulls from her neck. Becca felt Niki tremble, heard her whimpering with pleasure. Jody's eyes opened and locked on Becca's, and Becca couldn't look away. The force of Jody's hunger held her captive, and Becca wanted nothing more than to satisfy her. Suddenly the black of Jody's irises flamed the color of the blood painting the room, and Niki arched violently. Jody snarled and bit deeper.

Niki roared and her hips jerked convulsively. Becca embraced the writhing Were, stunned and horrified to find herself aroused in the midst of carnage.

Sylvan twisted her hand in Jody's hair and pulled her away from Niki's neck. "Careful, Vampire. Don't drain her."

Mindless with bloodlust, Jody snarled and thrashed in Sylvan's hold.

Niki protested weakly, "Don't stop her."

Jody tried to bury her incisors in Niki's neck again. Sylvan rumbled a warning and dragged her back a few more inches.

"More," Jody growled, her chest heaving.

Becca released Niki, who curled up on the floor, her face slack with satiation. Carefully, Becca half crawled to Jody and caressed her cheek, unheeding of the dangerous incisors flashing inches from her hand. "Jody. Jody, it's all right."

"Need more."

"I know, I know," Becca murmured, stroking the back of Jody's neck. "But you can wait, can't you? You don't want to hurt her, do you?"

Jody shook as if in the throes of a violent chill and stared at Becca, recognition slowly dawning in her eyes. With a jolt, she broke Sylvan's grip and pushed away from the others. "Get away from me. All of you. Get out."

Sylvan grasped Niki by the back of the neck and lifted her upright. Supporting Niki with an arm around her waist, she said, "My Pack is in your debt, Vampire."

"You may not thank me when your *centuri* wakes up hungry," Jody said. "I need to be there when she does. When I've taken care of my needs, I'll come."

"We'll look after Lara until you arrive."

"You need to see to your own wounds, Wolf," Jody said, her gaze on the still-bleeding hole in Sylvan's shoulder.

"Don't be concerned. We're not as delicate as you." Sylvan sent a silent call to Andrew and the door opened.

"Alpha?" Andrew asked.

"Take Niki."

Andrew carried Niki outside and Sylvan followed him to the door. "Watch your back, Vampire. The shooter's still out there. Perhaps he has more than one target."

"His bullets were silver," Jody reminded her.

"Enough bullets would put you down long enough to take your head," Sylvan said. "And I need you in good health to look after my wolf."

"Don't be concerned. We are not as slow as you."

Sylvan's eyes flashed at the challenge and she smiled. "We'll see one day. Take care, Vampire."

Once the room was clear, Jody gave Becca a flat stare. "You need to leave. Use the phone down the hall to call a cab. Take a raincoat from the closet by the door to cover your clothes."

"I'm not leaving you like this. You were practically dead." Becca got unsteadily to her feet. She was soaked in blood, but she wasn't physically hurt. Jody no longer looked like she was on the verge of death, but her face was gaunt and hollow, her eyes sunken. She was dangerously weak and trying to hide it. "I know you need to feed more. Feed from me."

"I don't want you." Jody gave her a mocking smile. "Don't worry, I'll be well taken care of."

And then she was gone. Becca blinked, looking around the blood-drenched foyer. She was alone and the house was completely silent.

"Fine, you ungrateful bastard, I'll go." Becca stormed over to the antique phone and yanked the receiver out of its cradle. "But you haven't gotten rid of me."

❖

As Andrew rocketed them north toward the Compound, Max sat with his back braced against the sidewall of the Rover with Lara, nude and in skin form again, in his arms. Niki slumped beside him, slowly regaining strength and awareness.

"How is she?" Sylvan asked.

"She shifted back as soon as we got outside," Max said. "She's unconscious."

Sylvan struggled to stay upright on the bench across from him. She needed to shift, and soon, if she was going to have any hope of healing her wounds. The acid burn spreading through her chest and abdomen signaled the toxin was spreading fast. She unbuttoned her shirt and examined the bullet wound high on the right side of her abdomen, the one she had been careful not to let the others see. Had her *centuri* realized the extent of her wounds, they might have been able to overpower her and force her back to the Compound, and she could not leave Lara or the Vampire to die. The flesh around both bullet wounds was black and festered. Silver. She shivered and broke out into a sweat. The muscles in her abdomen and legs contracted violently and she fell to her knees on the floor of the van, barely catching herself with an outstretched arm. She couldn't shift here. If she did, and the fever took her, she would be a danger to them all.

"Alpha!" Max cried.

Niki shook herself and crouched down beside Sylvan, circling Sylvan's shoulders with her arm. "Alpha, you need to shift."

"Not until we reach the Compound."

"We'll be there in fifteen minutes," Niki insisted. "Please, Sylvan—shift."

Sylvan held Niki's gaze fiercely. "Secure our borders. This might have been the first wave of an all-out assault."

"Andrew," Niki called, her focus never leaving Sylvan's face. "Call Callan—tell him to reinforce our borders. General alert."

"Yes, *Imperator*," Andrew called back.

"Drake." Sylvan coughed up blood, black with silver poisoning. "Safeguard her."

"Yes, Alpha," Niki said, her eyes wild with panic.

"I love you, Niki." Gritting her teeth against the excruciating pain, Sylvan cupped Niki's face in her palm and forced herself to stay conscious until she could give what might be her last order. "Lead my Pack. Protect my wolves. When the time comes, kill me."

Chapter Twenty-seven

Leo Revnik burst into the recovery room where Drake was hastily pulling on her clothes. "Sophia, Elena just called. You must return to the Compound immediately."

"Why?" Sophia exclaimed.

"What's happened?" Drake demanded.

"There are wounded."

"Sylvan!" Drake winced as the pain in her chest exacerbated. "She's hurt, isn't she?"

"I don't know." Leo hesitated. "But you are safer here. The Alpha would not want you in danger."

Drake wanted to howl in rage. Ignoring him, she grabbed Sophia's arm. She needed to be with Sylvan. Nothing else mattered. "Hurry."

The wait for the elevator was interminable. The huge ground-level atrium was filled with male and female Weres in gray BDUs, armed with sidearms and assault rifles, streaming toward the entrances. A dark-haired female stopped them before they reached the exit to the parking lot where Sophia had left her car.

"We're needed at the Compound," Sophia explained.

"Yes, ma'am. A security team will escort you both." The female inclined her head toward Drake deferentially.

"I have my car," Sophia said.

"We are at general alert," the guard replied. "I cannot permit you to leave without protection."

"Fine, whatever it takes," Drake said, "but we must hurry."

Even as she spoke, an armored vehicle similar to the ones she'd seen at the Compound screeched to a halt in front of the door. More guards hurried inside and quickly surrounded them. Drake allowed herself to be shepherded into the rear of the vehicle.

"We'll be there soon," Sophia murmured. "How do you feel?"

"I just need to find Sylvan." Drake clenched her fists on her thighs and closed her eyes. The surface of her body burned despite the fine sheen of adrenaline-spiked hormones coating her skin. She smelled Sylvan, and her, and their unique union. She didn't know who she was or what she would become or if she would even live long enough to find out. She didn't care. She knew all she needed to know. She needed to be with Sylvan. Her every instinct, every emotion, every physical impulse told her this was true. A truth she might not understand, but could not question.

She clambered forward between the seats occupied by two male Weres, their expressions fiercely savage. "Stay on the highway as long as you can before turning onto an access road to the Compound. You'll make better time. Do you have a radar detector in this thing? We don't want to be picked up."

The male Were behind the wheel glanced at her, nostrils flaring. His eyes dropped to the level of her shoulder. "Yes."

"If anyone attempts to intercept us, try to outrun them. If that fails, run them off the road. Just get me to the Compound."

He straightened to attention and snapped, "Understood!"

❖

No one tried to stop them on their mad dash north. Perhaps local law enforcement recognized the vehicle as one of Sylvan's and passed them on. Still, the thirty-minute journey seemed endless, and by the time the Compound came into view through a break in the forest, Drake was ready to claw her way out of the back of the Rover. The gates, heavily fortified with armed guards stationed on a narrow walkway running along the top of the stockade, swung open at their approach. Their driver barely slowed as they careened through.

"The infirmary," Drake ordered. She didn't wait for him to stop but shoved open the rear doors and jumped out while they were still moving. She hit the ground running, barely noticing the jarring sensation as she landed. She'd never felt so strong, so certain of her destination. Max and Andrew flanked the door to the infirmary. "Where is she!"

"Inside," Max said, moving to block the door, "but—"

He was sixty pounds of muscle heavier than her, but she had speed and will on her side. She caught him by surprise when she turned her shoulder into him, hitting him square in the chest. He grunted and gave way. Drake slammed the door open and barreled into the building.

"Stop," Niki shouted, barring the way to a closed door halfway down the hall.

"Get out of my way," Drake growled.

Niki, her eyes hunter green, snarled a warning. She lunged forward before Drake could react and knocked her onto her back. Pinning Drake with a knee on Drake's chest, she thrust her claws into Drake's throat, millimeters short of tearing out her trachea. "You don't belong here, *mutia.*"

Drake's wolf went wild. She would not be dominated. She would not be kept from Sylvan. Acting on pure instinct, she clubbed Niki on the side of the head, stunning her for a few critical seconds. Rearing up, she grabbed Niki by the throat and threw her off. Before Niki could retaliate, Drake leapt, straddled her chest, and choked her. "You will not keep me from her."

Niki thrashed, snapping at Drake's arms, slashing Drake's shoulders and chest.

Going for the kill, Drake's claws shot out and she thrust them into Niki's neck.

Howling in agony, Niki arched and writhed. Blood jetted from the wounds in her throat onto her chest. Her agonized cry was that of a dying soul reaching out in the darkness for connection, for family, for home. For Pack.

Her cry struck Drake's heart, and the red haze of her fury evaporated. Niki was Pack. Niki was Sylvan's. Niki was hers.

"She needs me," Drake said, easing her hold on Niki's neck. She pressed down on the punctures she'd made and they immediately stopped bleeding.

"No one can help her." Tears streamed down Niki's face. "It's too late."

"You're wrong," Drake whispered, as certain as she had ever been of anything in her life. She got to her knees, letting Niki slide out from under her.

Sophia, followed by Max and Andrew, crowded around them. Sophia exclaimed, "Oh my God. Drake, your arm."

Drake stared at the arm that was no longer an arm, but a limb covered in sleek black fur and tipped with lethal claws. When she spoke, her words were thick and guttural, barely recognizable to her own ears. "What is happening?"

Niki touched Drake's face, her own features contorted with shock. "You've partially shifted. No one but the Alpha can do that."

"The Alpha's mate can," Max murmured.

"Is Elena with her?" Drake got unsteadily to her feet. Her arm ached and when she looked again, her hand appeared like her hand once more.

"No one is with her," Niki said. "She ordered us out when she shifted. We wanted to stay, but as soon as she shifted..." Niki's voice broke. "She waited too long and there are too many wounds. Too much toxin, spreading too fast." She straightened, her face a mask of sorrow. "She's not broadcasting to us. She's lost in her wolf. She's rabid."

"No, she isn't," Drake said. The place inside her that only Sylvan had ever touched resounded with life. She knew if Sylvan were gone that space inside her would become a cold, dark void that would expand until she was swallowed by darkness. If that ever happened, she would surrender without a struggle. Without Sylvan's warmth and passion and light shining somewhere in her life, she would be lost. "She's not gone."

Niki looked at her without anger, but with endless pity. "She ordered that I execute her, and I will follow her orders unto death. You will have to kill me to stop me."

"If the need ever comes, I won't stop you. You are her right hand and her brave heart. But you will not die today, and neither will she." Drake cupped Niki's jaw. "You are her second, and right now, you need to safeguard the Pack. Who is her third?"

Max stepped forward. "I am."

"Then you both know what you need to do. I am not going to let her die." Drake turned to Sophia. "Help Elena prepare an operating room."

"She won't recognize you," Niki cautioned as Drake reached for the closed door. "She'll tear you apart."

Drake paused and brushed the backs of her fingers over Niki's cheek. "She won't hurt me. But if I'm wrong, don't let her suffer."

❖

Drake eased into the moonlit room. The bed was empty. A low, ominous growl emanated from the far corner of the room.

"Sylvan?"

The growl became a snarl. The fine hairs on the back of Drake's neck stood up and her wolf stirred uneasily. Drake recognized her wolf now, her wariness, her strength, her bravery. Her stubborn refusal to be dominated. Her wolf wanted to shift. Drake wanted it. Her bones slid over one another, the pain nearly dropping her to her knees. Her muscles stretched to the point of tearing. Her sex spasmed and tears ran from her eyes. She brushed her forearm impatiently across her face. She couldn't shift. She still didn't know how to give her wolf control without losing herself.

"Sylvan," Drake said gently, lowering herself to her knees. She let her hands fall open at her sides, exposing her chest and belly to the darkened room. "It's Drake."

She had no warning—no scrape of claws on wood, no flash of silver pelt in the moonlight—before the massive beast struck her in the torso and took her down by the throat. Every instinct primed her to fight, and her canines and claws thrust out. But she didn't fight. The silver wolf snarled in her face. She lifted her chin and gave the wolf her neck.

"Sylvan, I won't hurt you. I will never hurt you."

Claws gouged into her chest and raked her belly, drawing fire and blood. The wolf-gold eyes staring into hers were filled with nothing but rage and pain, completely devoid of recognition. Blood matted the thick fur on the wolf's chest and belly. Drake's heart ached for Sylvan's pain.

Slowly, Drake raised her hand. "Let me help you. Let the Pack heal you."

The wolf pulled back her lips, her eyes narrowed, and her ears slanted back. She was preparing to attack.

"I love you." Drake stroked the wolf's powerful head. "I need you. We all need you."

The heavy muscles in the wolf's shoulders bunched.

"They hurt you," Drake whispered, gently caressing the wolf's uninjured shoulder. Her tears mixed with Sylvan's blood. "But you're strong. Your wolf is strong. Sylvan. Find her. Help her."

Drake wrapped both arms around the wolf's neck and rested her cheek against the enormous muzzle. Blood dripped onto the floor and the huge body swayed. "Fight, Sylvan. Please, love. Fight."

The wolf shook her head, whined uncertainly. Drake pushed to a sitting position and drew the great silver head to her chest, ready to beg and bargain with any power that might exist to spare this glorious creature, this brave and noble being whose fierce strength and generous heart had captured hers. She buried her face in the ruff that smelled like Sylvan and her and them together.

"I love you. Sylvan, please come back. I need you. I need you so much."

The wolf licked her neck and, with a sigh, lay down in Drake's lap. Careful of the wounds, Drake wrapped her arms even more protectively around her. "I love you."

You shouldn't have come here. Sylvan's voice, steady, strong.

Drake's tears dampened the glossy fur beneath her cheek but her heart raced with joy. *Where else would I be?*

Somewhere safe.

Drake rubbed her chin on the wolf's head. *I'm always safe with you. Will you trust me?*

Always.

Will you let me help you?

Yes.

Then the immense wolf closed her eyes and surrendered to Drake's embrace.

Niki, Drake telegraphed, *we need you.*

CHAPTER TWENTY-EIGHT

Jody pulled the Porsche into the Were Compound just before dawn. She walked around to the passenger side and opened the door. "Are you sure?"

"Of course, darling," Marissa Sanchez said. "I can't wait. Especially after you dragged me away from work but refused to let me feed you."

"This could be dangerous—she's going to need to feed every few hours." Jody had already warned Marissa that newly turned Vampires in bloodlust were insatiable and could easily kill a host. "I can find a Were to feed her."

"No." Marissa's color heightened. "You know I want this. And I trust you."

"If she needs more than you can give, I'll still need a Were to join us."

"All the better."

"I hope you arranged for coverage at the morgue—we won't be leaving here today." Jody led Marissa toward Niki, who, shirtless and barefoot, stood on the porch of a nearby building with her hands on her hips and legs spread wide, watching them through narrowed eyes. A faint dusting of red-brown at the waistband of the low-slung black pants she hadn't bothered to close matched her auburn hair.

Marissa's gaze traveled slowly over Niki's body. "Please tell me it's her."

"No," Jody said impassively, taking in the tightly muscled chest and abdomen, the strong thighs, the toned arms, the full sensuous lips. The rich taste of the Were still lingered even though she had fed from one of her human hosts after fleeing from Becca. Her bloodlust was unsated and now the memory of the orgasm this Were had induced, as hot and powerful as the essence Jody had consumed, taunted her. "No, not her."

"Pity. She's an amazing specimen."

Jody climbed the stairs and stopped one step below Niki, their eyes level. "How is your Alpha?"

"The medics are seeing to her."

"I need to speak with her."

"When she is available."

Jody frowned. "How serious is it?"

"The Alpha is not your concern," Niki said. "Especially considering she was shot on your doorstep when no one knew we would be there."

"I owe you much, Wolf, but you do not want to make an enemy of me." Jody let the hunger rise and caught Niki's gaze. Niki's forest green eyes glazed. "You would do better to give me your neck again."

Niki shivered and fought for control. She was already close to frenzy from her fight with Drake and the constant lash of adrenaline as she worked to secure the Compound's defenses. Seeing this Vampire, remembering her bite and the volcanic release that had stripped her of her last drop, made her stiffen and throb. She wanted teeth in her neck again and fire burning in her blood. Lust warred with her need to dominate and she growled, flashing a challenge.

"Some other time," Jody murmured, reading the need in the Were's eyes that echoed her own. "I am here to see to my newling."

"We don't know that yet," Niki snarled.

"She has not awakened?"

"She's been restless but still unaware."

"Good—then we can feed her as soon as she wakes." Jody drew Marissa up beside her. "Dr. Sanchez has graciously volunteered to host if necessary."

"Come with me." Niki abruptly turned and led them down the left wing and into a room lit by a single lantern perched atop a narrow chest of drawers. Wooden shutters had been closed to block out the emerging sunlight. Niki indicated the darkened corner where Lara lay under a thin sheet. "We can't tell if she's in pain. What should we be looking for?"

Jody shook her head. "If she's turned, you'll know. Her hunger will be agonizing and she'll attack any source of nourishment."

"But one of us can feed her, can't we?" Niki asked.

"How many of you have experience hosting?"

"I don't know. Some, definitely." Niki's jaw tightened. "That's why I'm here. I'll feed her."

"She'll be difficult to control, frightened. And you cannot host again so soon."

"I'm a Were. We heal and regenerate quickly."

"I know that." Jody nodded toward Marissa. "But it's better she have an experienced host the first few times. After all, it's more than just feeding, isn't it?"

"I'll do whatever she needs," Niki said with an edge. She'd never tangled with Lara, but she would give Lara her blood and her body and her throat if that was what she needed. They were *centuri*, oath-bonded to each other as well as the Alpha. "We won't lose her."

"Even if she has turned?"

Niki's lip curled. "She is ours. Vampire or Were, it doesn't matter."

"She's lucky, then." Jody studied Niki. "After sundown I can take her out to hunt. If she needs more than Marissa can give before then, I'll use you."

"I'll be ready."

Jody cupped Marissa's elbow and drew her close. "Are you?"

"Very ready," Marissa said, her eyes on Lara.

"Leave us," Jody said to Niki. "I'll take care of her."

Niki hesitated, then reluctantly left.

"She's so beautiful," Marissa murmured when Jody led her to the bed.

Lara lay motionless, her chestnut hair contrasting sharply with her pale, gaunt face. Jody slid the sheet down and smoothed her hand over Lara's chest to cradle her breast. Lara's flesh was as flawless and smooth as ivory. A faint pulse, slow and distant, beat beneath her perfect breast. Jody said to Marissa, "Take off your dress."

Wordlessly, her avid gaze on Lara's face, Marissa complied. She dropped the garment carelessly on the end of the bed and sat beside Lara.

"Is she alive?" Marissa whispered.

"Yes." Jody stroked Lara's angular jaw, running her thumb over her full lower lip. "Lara. Lara, wake up."

Lara's eyes snapped open and rolled wildly. She lurched upward, snarling, no sign of reason in her whiskey-gold eyes.

"Listen to me," Jody said firmly, grasping Lara's face in both hands, capturing Lara's gaze with hers. "You will do as I say."

Lara writhed, struggling to break Jody's grip. "Pain. Have to stop the pain."

"I know." Jody tightened her hold, her fingertips digging into the angle of Lara's jaw, forcing her mouth open. Lara's incisors slid from their sheaths and her eyes flickered like flames against a midnight sky. "Marissa, touch her."

Marissa pushed the sheet completely aside and stretched out next to Lara's naked body. She caressed the arch of Lara's hip and pressed a kiss to the inner curve of Lara's breast. Sliding her thigh between Lara's, she took a nipple into her mouth. Her eyes glazed as she sucked and stroked her, her hips undulating slowly.

Lara's face was savage as she gripped Marissa's hips, pulling her closer. Panting, she struggled to break Jody's grip. "I want her."

"Your hunger is her pleasure," Jody whispered, slowly releasing Lara. "Take what you crave. Give her what she needs."

Marissa looked up at Lara, her face dazed with desire. "Please."

Lara stared into Marissa's dark, eager eyes and then at the pounding pulse in her neck.

"I want you to taste me," Marisa whispered, tilting her head to one side. "I want to feed you."

Lara plunged her incisors into Marissa's neck. Marissa cried out, her back bowing. Jody knelt beside them, caressing Lara as she fed in wild, savage gulps. Lara thrust her thigh between Marissa's legs, her powerful hips churning.

"Oh, God, she's so strong." Marissa clutched Lara's hand and pushed it into the cleft between her legs. "Touch me. Oh, please."

Growling, Lara rolled Marissa under her and straddled her thigh. She buried her hand inside her and fed voraciously, her arm pumping in sync with the convulsive waves in her throat. Marissa clutched Lara's back, her pelvis lifting and falling, faster and faster.

"I'm coming," Marissa whimpered. "I'm coming."

Lara's hips spasmed and she released, burying her incisors even deeper.

Jody clamped her hand on the back of Lara's neck and pulled her mouth away from Marissa's neck. "Enough for now."

"No," Lara snapped, the bones in her face moving beneath her pale skin. Part Were, part Vampire. "I want her."

"You've fed enough," Jody insisted. "Feel her heartbeat—how fast, how thready. She can't give more right now. Let her rest."

Lara struggled against Jody's iron grip, rubbing her still erect clitoris over Marissa's thigh. "Need more."

"Let her take me," Marissa pleaded to Jody. She licked Lara's neck and caressed Lara's breasts with trembling hands. "Please. God. She feels so good. I'm on fire." She worked her hand lower. "She's so swollen still. She needs me."

"In a few minutes," Jody repeated. Lara needed to learn to tolerate the hunger, control her bloodlust, or she would never be safe around a host.

Lara growled threateningly. Her face contorted in fury. "I want her *now.*"

"Look at her," Jody ordered. "She gave you life. You cannot take hers. Satisfy yourself another way."

The wild hunger in Lara's eyes retreated and she braced herself on her arms over Marissa's shivering form. Gently, she licked the puncture marks on Marissa's neck until they closed. "Will you let me taste you later?"

"Yes, oh yes," Marissa cried, twisting her fingers in Lara's hair. "Oh God yes, yes."

Lara moved lower, swirling her tongue over Marissa's erect nipples until Marissa writhed. When Lara kissed her way down Marissa's abdomen, Marissa reached fitfully for Jody.

"Kiss me," Marissa begged, pulling Jody down with a hand behind her neck. "Your eyes are so hungry. Let me feed you."

"Another day," Jody whispered, kissing Marissa as Lara pressed her mouth between Marissa's legs.

Marissa jolted and came in Lara's mouth, crying out her pleasure against Jody's throat. Bloodlust carving away her reason, Jody snarled and struggled not to bury her mouth in Marissa's neck.

Before Marissa's orgasm waned, Lara rocked to her knees and

parted Marissa's sex with one hand and her own with the other. Panting, she thrust her clitoris into Marissa's center and pumped in short hard strokes.

"Oh my God." Marissa bucked in Jody's arms. "Oh God, she's making me come again."

Lara's pelvis jerked and her face contorted in rage and pleasure. Groaning, she fell onto Marissa and bit her shoulder. The bite plunged Marissa into another convulsive orgasm and Lara spent herself in a series of hard thrusts between Marissa's legs.

"God, oh God," Marissa murmured, stroking Lara's damp hair. "You're amazing. Incredible."

"I don't know what I am," Lara said bitterly, pushing herself up and off Marissa. Her eyes bleak, she stared at Jody. "I can feel you, like I feel the Alpha. What does that mean?"

"I turned you," Jody said. "We're connected."

"Was I dead?"

"Does it matter? Now you're a living Vampire."

"No." Lara pushed unsteadily to her feet. Naked, drenched in sweat and sex and blood, she said desperately, "I'm a *centuri*. I'm Pack."

"Yes, you are." Jody fixed on Lara, and Lara, moaning softly, swayed toward her. Jody kissed her. "You are also mine."

CHAPTER TWENTY-NINE

Moisture dripped into Drake's eyes and she rubbed her face against her upper arm. Her blurry vision wasn't from the sweat running into her eyes, but from the tears she barely held back. The wounds in Sylvan's chest and abdomen were like nothing she'd ever seen before. Far worse than Misha's had been. Even the worst cases of gangrene had never been so completely destructive, so relentlessly nihilistic. The beautiful wolf was dying before her eyes.

"We have to get the rest of the silver out of her," Drake said. "Now. We're out of time."

"I don't know how," Elena said desperately.

Drake and Elena had probed the wounds for an hour, trying to locate and remove the silver bullets that were poisoning Sylvan. They hadn't been able to find a single one.

"The Alpha has always been the one to do this," Sophia said from the head of the operating table where she monitored Sylvan's vital signs. "Her fever is still climbing—I've never seen one so high. If we don't do something, we're going to lose her."

The leash Drake had kept on the beast inside of her snapped. Her wolf roared to life—part of her now, not some foreign being, but an intimate, integral part. Her very essence. And her wolf knew, just as she knew, as surely as she breathed, that Sylvan was hers, and she would not let her die.

Drake didn't see Sylvan lying on the table. She didn't see the Alpha. She saw her own heart. And she saw an enemy. An enemy threatening to take from her everything that mattered. She would not surrender Sylvan to that enemy while her own heart beat. With a wild cry, she plunged her claws into the wound. The poison deep in Sylvan's body, festering and vile, drew her like the feral scent of an intruder in her territory. She attacked without mercy, defending what was hers. Protecting the one most precious to her.

She found the first bullet and ripped it free. Bright red blood bubbled out in her wake and Elena quickly pressed a clean bandage to the wound. Drake didn't hesitate, but tore into the wound in Sylvan's belly. She found a second bullet, then a third nearby.

"That's all," Drake gasped. "How is she?"

When no one answered, Drake looked up from the wounds and found Elena and Sophia staring at her with shocked expressions. She followed their stunned gazes and found that her arm had shifted again. She hadn't felt it or intended it. She should probably be frightened, but she didn't care what was happening to her. Sylvan was dying, and with her, Drake's every reason for being.

"Sylvan? How is she?"

Sophia jerked back to awareness and quickly scanned the monitors. "Her fever is coming down. So is her heart rate."

"Look," Elena said in amazement. "She's healing!"

Drake turned back to the gaping holes in Sylvan's chest and abdomen. The necrotic tissue was receding, and healthy skin and fur were growing back. The wolf was healing. Sylvan would live. Drake's vision dimmed and her legs trembled, and for a moment she thought she would fall. She gripped the table to steady herself.

"We need to get her somewhere quiet. She might be disoriented when she wakes up." Drake saw Sophia and Elena exchange worried glances. Sylvan had survived the fever, but would she emerge undamaged and in control of her wolf, the deadliest wolf in the Pack? Drake wouldn't believe otherwise. She wouldn't lose her now. "Get her ready to move. I'll tell the others."

Drake stripped off her coverings and went out into the hall. Niki and Andrew crowded around, enclosing her. They needed contact, and she realized that she did too. She slung her arms around their shoulders. Their unyielding presence steadied her.

"The Alpha?" Niki asked gruffly.

"She's healing. Now we just have to wait for her to wake up."

"Has she shifted back?" Andrew's face was creased with fatigue and worry.

"Not yet." Drake knew they all shared the same unspoken fear. A rabid wolf could not shift form. "I'll stay with her until she does."

"That's dangerous," Niki protested. "If she wakes up rabid—"

"Would you have her fight this fight alone?" Drake asked softly.

"She's not alone, she has the Pack."

Niki's eyes were tortured and Drake doubted she could survive Sylvan's loss. The Alpha and her second weren't mated, but they were bound almost as strongly. She caressed Niki's face. "And your strength will help her. Hold on to your connection to her—" Drake scanned their faces. "She needs the Pack with her. It's you she lives for. It's you she needs."

"Not as much as you," Niki murmured.

"All of us," Drake repeated. "Is the Compound secure? She'll want to know."

"Yes," Niki said, her voice stronger. "We've had a few reports of incursions in our Northern Territory, but that's not unusual. The Blackpaws test our border defense regularly."

"What about Lara?"

"She's most likely turned," Niki said, her eyes and voice devoid of inflection.

"What will happen?" Drake asked.

Niki shook her head. "I don't know. She might lose some or all of her Were traits."

"Her turning could prevent her from shifting again?" Drake couldn't imagine what that would do to a dominant Were like Lara, whose very purpose in life was to fight and protect her Pack.

"She hasn't shifted again since the Alpha called her wolf, right after she fed from the Vampire. She didn't hold her wolf long, even then." Niki hesitated, and then revealed a secret only a very few Weres knew. "Some Weres voluntarily blood-bond with Vampires. Most lose their ability to shift when they do."

"You mean they mate with a Vampire?"

"Yes." Niki grimaced. "They trade their most powerful gift to live with the dead."

"Maybe their love is stronger—more important—than even that," Drake suggested gently.

"It's not love." Niki couldn't block out what was happening in Lara's room, even though she'd retreated to another part of the building when she'd heard the human female's cry of ecstasy and Lara's roar of release. Her sex had tightened with a rush of pleasure and she was still ready. When Jody had fed from her, she'd burst more ferociously than she ever had before. The intensity was exquisite. Addicting. Even now she couldn't think of it without needing desperately to release. "The Vampire is with her now. Let me help you with the Alpha."

"Yes." Scenting Niki's call, Drake said, "Once we've moved her, you should get some sleep. And take care of your other needs."

Niki's eyes narrowed and her lip curled. For some reason, she thought of Sophia and quickly abolished the image. If she let Sophia feel her call, she could seduce her and Sophia would not resent her for it. But Sophia rarely tangled and when she did, she always chose a non-dominant Were. Niki wouldn't draw Sophia into a liaison she would not willingly have sought. Anya, on the other hand, was always willing. Niki's clitoris twinged at the image of Anya's mouth on her. "I won't be far, if you or the Alpha need me."

"I know." Drake started back to the treatment room when Niki grasped her arm.

"When she wakes up, her hormone level will be astronomical—from her injury, from the danger to the Pack, from Lara. She'll be in need." Niki grinned ruefully. "You know what I'm talking about. The same thing is happening to you right now."

Drake couldn't deny it. Her hours of fear and anxiety had kicked her entire system into overdrive. Her heart raced, her pulse pounded, her clitoris was stiff and throbbing. "Whatever she needs, I'll take care of her."

❖

Sylvan glided through the forest as silent as a ghost, following the one trail out of dozens that would lead her home. The tangy scent of aged wine and autumn leaves was familiar, comforting, exciting. She ran effortlessly, powerfully, covering ground in great leaping strides. Her heart beat with pride and passion. She was the Alpha, the leader and protector of her Pack. She would always be their heart, as they were hers. But now she did not run alone. She was whole. She was healed.

Sylvan's eyes flew open and she snarled.

"You're all right. You were hurt, but you're all right now." Drake's heart brimmed with joy. She'd fallen asleep next to a wolf and awoken with a Were.

Sylvan turned, her gaze seeking Drake's. They were both nude and their legs naturally entwined. Sylvan's nipples were tight and when her breasts brushed Drake's, heat pooled in her belly. She pressed her palm to Drake's stomach, steadying herself in Drake's heat. "Lara? The Pack? Are they safe?"

"Yes. Everyone is. Niki has seen to it." Drake slid her hands up and down Sylvan's back. She loved her muscles, her taut skin, her wild scent. "How do you feel?"

"I dreamed of you," Sylvan said, pressing her face against Drake's throat and inhaling deeply. "I followed your scent. You led me home."

Drake trembled, every instinct driving her to affirm her bond with Sylvan. She wanted her. Needed her. She had to get away from her. "You should rest now."

Sylvan grumbled a warning when Drake tried to pull away. "You're in need. I feel your call."

"I can't help it."

"Why should you?" Sylvan kissed her. "I woke up ready for you."

"Please," Drake murmured, her skin sheened with want. Her clitoris was swollen, her glands so hard she could barely stand the pressure of Sylvan's thigh between her legs. "I can't fight you any longer."

"No, you can't." Sylvan nipped at Drake's lower lip and soothed the tiny bite with her tongue. She rumbled with pleasure when Drake's mouth took hers in a hard, fierce kiss. She wanted Drake to take all she had to give. She wanted to meet passion with passion. Their tongues clashed and then gentled, whispering over and around each other as if dancing in moonlight. Sylvan caught Drake's hand and guided it between her legs. She closed Drake's fingers around her clitoris. "This is for you."

"It's not safe," Drake protested, but she couldn't stop touching her. Sylvan was so hot and hard and wet already. She knew Sylvan wasn't thinking, couldn't be, not after what she'd been through, what her body demanded now. But Drake didn't have the strength to deny her. She needed Sylvan just as badly—needed to feel Sylvan's power, vibrant and vital. "I want all of you. I won't be able to stop."

"I don't want you to stop." Sylvan scraped her canines down Drake's throat. "You're mine. I want to come on you."

"I want you all over me." Drake moaned and rubbed against her. Sylvan's clitoris swelled between her fingers. "I want you. I'm afraid— I'm afraid I'll hurt you."

"You calmed my wolf. You brought me back." Sylvan kissed Drake again, her eyes going wolf-gold. "You said you loved me."

Drake threaded her fingers through Sylvan's hair and pulled Sylvan's head back. She licked the rippling pulse. "I do. I do love you."

Sylvan cupped Drake's sex, teasing her fingertips just inside her as she pressed her palm down on Drake's clitoris. "Then I'm going to claim what's mine."

Hunger, a need more intense than anything Drake had ever known, exploded in her chest. She pushed Sylvan onto her back and dragged her mouth down Sylvan's throat to her breast. She caught a nipple between her teeth and tugged on it. "Not before I take what's mine."

Sylvan growled and her claws shot out. "Be careful, Wolf. Don't challenge me."

"Or else what?" Drake settled her chest between Sylvan's legs and circled Sylvan's nipple with her tongue. When Sylvan grasped her shoulders and tried to dislodge her, Drake shook her off and skimmed her mouth down the center of Sylvan's abdomen. "Or else what, Alpha?"

"I won't be gentle."

"I don't expect you to be." Drake licked the fine silver line between the hard ridges of Sylvan's abdominal muscles. Sylvan's clitoris pulsated against her breast, satin soft and hot. "I'm going to make you come in my mouth."

Sylvan's hips jerked. "Are you?"

"I'm going to drink you until I've had my fill." Drake pinned Sylvan's wrists to the bed on either side of her hips and raised her head to see Sylvan's face. Sylvan's canines protruded. So did hers. "Then you can do whatever you want."

"Why should I wait?" Sylvan snarled.

"Why?" Drake licked Sylvan's clitoris, slowly swirling her tongue over the head and down the rigid shaft. "You like this, don't you?"

Sylvan yanked one hand free and grasped Drake's neck, her claws pressing but not puncturing. "Yes."

"So do I." Drake sucked, careful not to push her canines into the glands near the base of Sylvan's clitoris. She didn't want to make her release right away, and she knew Sylvan wanted to. She intended to savor her. She wanted to pleasure her. She wanted to own her.

"Harder," Sylvan gasped, her body straining under Drake's. "Take me all the way in."

"Not yet," Drake murmured, toying with Sylvan on the tip of her tongue. She massaged Sylvan's stomach with one hand until the tense muscles relaxed a fraction. "That's better." She flicked at Sylvan's clitoris and quickly skimmed lower, basking in Sylvan's essence. Sylvan's legs jumped. "I love how ready you are. So fierce and beautiful."

"Drake," Sylvan growled. "Make me come."

"And so impatient." Laughing, Drake slid her fingers into her. Instantly, she was surrounded by hot, firm muscles. The internal extension of Sylvan's clitoris throbbed and she massaged the fullness gently with her fingertips. Sylvan thrashed, an ominous rumble rising from her chest. Drake licked her again. "You're almost there."

Breaking Drake's hold, Sylvan reared up and grabbed Drake's head, forcing her clitoris between Drake's lips.

"Suck me," she demanded, her face contorted with savage pleasure. "I'm ready to come."

Drake wanted to keep her that close forever, but she couldn't wait any longer either. She had to have her. She wanted the taste of Sylvan in her mouth, in her memory, in every conscious and unconscious part of her. She wanted her, needed her, body and soul. Drawing Sylvan deep into her mouth, Drake slid her hand down Sylvan's belly and massaged the base of her clitoris while she sucked her.

"Yes, now," Sylvan gasped, erupting into Drake's mouth. She came harder and longer than she ever had and still her hips pumped. More, she needed more. She needed to give more, take more. She needed to be joined. A wild raging hunger stormed through her, and she flipped Drake onto her back. "Mine."

"Yes," Drake cried, so full and so ready she wanted to scream for release. Wrapping her legs around Sylvan's hips, she reached down and opened herself. Instantly the swollen ridge of Sylvan's clitoris glided between her folds. When Sylvan thrust, Drake rose to meet her. She was so close and never close enough. "Come inside me. Can you come inside me?"

"Bite me." Sylvan's wolf-gold eyes burned into Drake's. "Bite me now."

With a strangled cry, Drake buried her canines in Sylvan's chest. Sylvan's clitoris, stiff with the rush of her orgasm, throbbed wildly in Drake's sex. Sylvan bit Drake's shoulder when she came, and Drake exploded with her.

"I love you," Sylvan gasped, collapsing in Drake's arms.

Even as Drake held Sylvan, shuddering and spent, her heart shattered. She wanted nothing more than to hold Sylvan for the rest of her life. To spend her life by Sylvan's side. But what if she was damaged, truly *mutia*? She couldn't stay with Sylvan if her presence made Sylvan a target with the other Weres, with rivals in her own Pack. Leaving Sylvan now would kill Drake, but even death could not make her regret this perfect moment. For the first time in her life she knew she was not alone.

CHAPTER THIRTY

Even asleep, Drake knew immediately when Sylvan left her. The places where their bodies had touched while they'd slept wrapped in one another were cold. Where moments before she had been content and satisfied, now she churned with want. The bite on her shoulder throbbed and she wanted Sylvan's mouth there again. Aching for Sylvan inside her again, Drake watched Sylvan lope silently away. She could not fathom how she could survive being separated from her when she already yearned for the sight and scent and sound of her.

Drake forced herself to get up. She found a stack of shirts and pants in the closet and got dressed. Her hands trembled. She was edgy, anxious, like she had been when she was first transformed, only worse. She wanted Sylvan, only Sylvan, and she wanted her with a fierceness that drove reason aside. She was covered in sex sweat, her stomach cramped and twisting. She wondered if she had a fever, if her cells were even now breaking down, releasing the mutagenic chemicals that would make her a danger to everyone around her. She'd bitten Sylvan, let Sylvan bite her. Had she infected her, put Sylvan's life at risk? She was a medic. She knew better than to ask questions when what she needed was data, and she was determined to get it. She had to know, once and for all, if she was a risk to those she loved.

She found Andrew standing guard in the hall when she left her room. He smiled a greeting.

"Have you seen Sophia?" Drake asked.

"She just came in a few minutes ago. I think she's in the laboratory."

"Thanks."

"You're welcome, Prima."

Drake halted. "I'm sorry?"

Andrew looked confused.

"You called me something. Prima?"

"Oh," Andrew said, his face clearing. His blue eyes sparkled. "I'll have to tell Roger he's falling down on his job. He should have explained all of this to you."

"Explained what?"

"As the Alpha's mate you are the Prima—equivalent within Pack hierarchy to the Alpha. The only one more dominant is the Alpha herself." He shrugged. "There can only be one Alpha, one leader. Because you are the Alpha's mate and essential to her strength and well-being, the *centuri* are bound to protect you as we would her. As will all the Pack."

Drake couldn't deny her bond with Sylvan. She wouldn't deny it. She loved her. She had claimed her. And Sylvan had claimed her. "I guess I don't have any say in all that, do I?"

Andrew grinned. "I'm afraid not." His expression grew more serious. "It's not just Pack law, or even a matter of instinct. Our entire existence is dependent upon our preserving hierarchical order. We are predators, and without a strong Alpha, our society will fail. We need her. She needs you."

"Does everyone know we're bonded?" Drake asked, wondering what would happen if she had to leave.

"Yes, we can feel your connection to the Alpha, just as we feel her. And the two of you—your scents have merged." He regarded her thoughtfully. "Can you feel the Pack?"

"Yes," Drake said. "I have since Sylvan first called my wolf, but it's much stronger now. It's like looking up into the night sky at thousands of stars and knowing that I am indelibly linked to each one. I may be standing alone, but I am never isolated, never adrift. I'm connected."

"Exactly. And the strongest, brightest guiding star is the Alpha."

"Sylvan." Drake felt a moment of rightness, as if she was exactly where she was supposed to be, doing exactly what she was born to do. Free from fear and worry for the first time in so long, she took a step forward, about to throw her arm around Andrew's shoulders. He suddenly looked panicked and jumped back.

"I'm sorry," Drake said.

"No," Andrew said hastily. "You didn't do anything wrong. I've wanted to touch you since you came out of the room. It's natural for us to bond that way. But you and the Alpha are newly mated, and newly mated dominants are even more territorial and aggressive than is usual for a mated pair. And she's the Alpha. If she smells me on you..." He grinned. "I would like to keep all my parts intact."

Drake imagined anyone touching Sylvan, and her possessive fury surged so hot and hard that she growled. She wanted Sylvan's taste in her mouth. *Now.* "I understand."

Andrew clearly sensed her need because he said quickly, "She's with Lara, if you would like me to take you to her."

"No, I know she has things to tend to. And so do I. If she's looking for me—"

"She'll know where you are. She'll always know where you are."

"Will she?" Drake said softly, wondering if she had any future with Sylvan at all.

❖

Sylvan eased into the room and took in the figures on the bed. Jody sat with her back against the wall. Her shirt was open and her breasts bare. Lara and a naked human female Sylvan didn't recognize reclined in Jody's lap, their limbs sinuously entwined. They appeared to be asleep.

"The sun is almost down," Sylvan said.

"I know." Jody stroked Lara's hair. Lara rumbled in her sleep, a typical Were sound of pleasure, and caressed the dark-haired human's breast. "Lara's sleep cycles will be erratic for a few days. She'll wake again soon, hungry."

"We need to talk."

"Yes." Jody gently disengaged and strode over to Sylvan. "Marissa will not be able to host much longer. I want to take Lara back to the city with me tonight."

"To hunt?"

"Yes. She needs to be supervised while she learns to feed."

"How long?"

Jody raised a brow. "You expect her to come back?"

"Of course." Sylvan had felt Lara wake and knew Lara was listening. "She's my wolf, my *centuri*. This is where she belongs."

"She's a Vampire of my house."

Sylvan growled. "Do you challenge me, Vampire?"

Jody met Sylvan's stare impassively. "She must feed to live. She'll be nocturnal and photosensitive. She might not be able to shift."

"Then let me die," Lara pleaded.

Sylvan swung in her direction, letting her wolf rise. "Your wolf lives. I can feel her."

"Alpha," Lara said brokenly, "if I can't serve you and the Pa—"

Sylvan vaulted across the room and gripped Lara's chin, forcing Lara's eyes to hers. "Feel my call. Your wolf *lives*."

Lara shuddered and for a few seconds, her whiskey eyes turned amber gold. Then she flinched and grabbed her abdomen, unable to stifle a cry. "I hurt. Alpha, I'm so cold."

"I know." Sylvan knelt and pulled Lara's head to her chest. She kissed her and stroked her cheek. "I know. That's why I want you to go with Jody." When Lara murmured a protest, Sylvan shook her lightly. "Until you've learned to control your hunger and how to satisfy it."

Lara raised tormented eyes to Sylvan's, tears streaking her cheeks. "I'd rather die than leave the Pack."

Sylvan framed her face and kissed her forehead. "Do you feel me in your heart?"

"Yes, Alpha."

"I hold you in mine. I will not let you go. You will return to us."

"Yes, Alpha." Laura buried her face in Sylvan's neck.

Sylvan cradled her, caressing her trembling shoulders, and looked over at Jody. "If any harm comes to her—"

"None will," Jody said with absolute certainty. "You'd do better to worry about yourself."

"Lara needs to feed," Sylvan said, feeling Lara's questing mouth hot against her throat. Gently, she eased Lara back onto the bed. Lara's eyes blazed wildly and her incisors unsheathed. Snarling, she rolled over onto Marissa, who immediately reached for her.

"You need me, baby?" Marissa murmured, guiding Lara to her neck. She moaned, her head falling back, as Lara sank into her. Her hips rolled as the rich scent of copper filled the air.

Sylvan moved away from the bed and joined Jody on the far side of the room. "Will they be safe if we go out into the hall?"

Jody shivered almost imperceptibly and dragged her gaze away from Lara's avid feeding. "For a few minutes. Then I'll have to stop her."

They stepped outside and Sylvan took in Jody's haunted look. She'd seen Francesca with the same expression too many times not to recognize it. "How much longer can you contain your bloodlust?"

"I'm all right," Jody said. "I'll feed when I get Lara back to the city."

"Such honor is unusual for a Vampire," Sylvan said dryly. "But then, we find ourselves in an unusual situation."

Jody laughed. "Your second thinks I tried to have you assassinated."

"Did you?"

"If I wanted you dead, Wolf," Jody said, "I'd do it myself."

"That's what I thought."

"Any other ideas?"

"If this had happened a few weeks ago, I would have said HUFSI was behind it."

"They have been campaigning to have all Praeterns neutered," Jody agreed, "and have come out strongly against the new Praetern rights bill."

"There are plenty of militant splinter factions who aren't going to be swayed by any ballot," Sylvan said. "They've made regular death threats."

"It's certainly possible," Jody said. "Historically, killing the figurehead doesn't stop a movement from effecting change, but fanatics rarely learn from history. You have your doubts now?"

From inside the room, Marissa cried out. Sylvan felt Lara's wolf straining for freedom and scented Lara's wild pheromones mixed with a cooler, sharper element. "She's a *centuri*. Her wolf is strong. Eventually she's going to shift," Sylvan warned. "Will you be able to handle her?"

Jody smiled mockingly. "Vampires know how to handle Weres when we feed. Who else wants you dead?"

"Someone wants to create panic among the humans and discredit the Weres," Sylvan said. "Maybe they think they'll have a better chance of doing that if they also eliminate the leadership."

"It may not just be a movement against Weres," Jody said. "There may be a much larger assault coming on all of us."

"Then it's a good thing we're on the same side."

"It's fortunate we have an alliance," Jody said smoothly. "What do you plan to do?"

"My Pack has been challenged. That cannot stand." Sylvan smiled, her canines fully exposed. "I intend to go hunting."

"I didn't report the shooting." Jody shrugged. "I am a detective, but this is Praetern business. Let me know if you need assistance."

"Just take care of Lara." Sylvan nodded. "I'll expect to hear from you soon about your search on the human victims, Vampire."

"And I'll await your report from your scientists."

"Take care of my *centuri*."

"Don't insult me, Wolf," Jody said.

"Good night, Vampire." Sylvan strode rapidly toward the adjacent wing, eager to find her mate. She'd been away from her for too long. Her wolf was restless and edgy. She didn't want her mate out of her sight. She needed to touch her. She needed to taste her again. She needed to assert her claim.

Sylvan knew before she reached the other side of the building that Drake was no longer in their room. When she encountered Andrew talking to Niki in the center of the infirmary building, her eyes were completely gold and her face honed to a knife's edge.

"You left the Prima unprotected?" Sylvan growled.

Andrew flinched. "She's in the building, Alpha."

"That's not what I asked you." Sylvan stalked him and he backed up.

"I'm sorry, Alpha. I should have gone with her." Andrew turned his head away as Sylvan crowded him up against the wall.

She slid her claws into his abdomen, just deep enough to make him shudder. With her mouth against his ear, she warned, "Don't ever do that again."

"Alpha," Niki said softly, carefully not touching Sylvan. "She's all right. We won't let anything happen to her."

Sylvan swung her head around, her canines gleaming. "She

doesn't understand Pack ways yet. She doesn't understand the dangers from outside."

"She doesn't need to," Niki said. "She's the Prima. It's in her blood."

Andrew ran his mouth along the underside of Sylvan's jaw. "We're hers as we are yours."

"Thank you." Sylvan leaned her forehead against Andrew and stroked the back of his neck, withdrawing her claws. He sighed and closed his eyes. Niki sidled up against Sylvan and wrapped her arm around Sylvan's waist.

"How is Lara?" Niki asked.

"She's alive." Sylvan draped her arm over Niki's shoulder so Niki could rest against her chest. "We'll need a temporary replacement for her in the guard. You two discuss it with Max and let me know your candidates."

"I sent Max back with Jace and Jonathan to track the shooter's scent," Niki said, referring to the twin dominants—sister and brother—who were already lieutenants and prime candidates to be elevated to *centuri*.

"Good." Sylvan's blue eyes sparked gold. "We'll leave as soon as I've seen to my mate."

"Yes, Alpha," Niki and Andrew said together.

Sylvan followed Drake's scent through the building, her impatient hunger escalating until all she wanted was Drake under her, inside her, over her. When she pushed open the door to the lab, the only thing she saw was Sophia with her hand on Drake's bare shoulder. With a roar, she leapt for them.

CHAPTER THIRTY-ONE

Drake swept Sophia behind her with one arm, blocking her from Sylvan, whose wolf rode so close to the surface that her eyes and face had partially shifted. The shimmering sheen of arousal on Sylvan's bare torso misted Drake's skin and her sex swelled, readying for her mate.

"Back away from her," Sylvan snarled in Sophia's direction, her whole body shuddering with the effort not to tear Sophia apart.

"Sylvan," Drake murmured, pressing her mouth to the bite on Sylvan's chest. She had felt Sylvan calling out to her long before she'd reached the room, had felt her power—hungry and demanding. Her own need had grown in the short time they'd been separated until she could barely remain in the lab. She'd wanted to stalk through the Compound until she found Sylvan and reminded the Alpha and anyone near her exactly who Sylvan belonged to. She scraped her teeth over the bite and Sylvan shuddered. "I've missed you."

Growling ominously, Sylvan grasped Drake behind the head and yanked her forward, covering her mouth in a ferocious kiss. Sylvan's nipples were hot and hard as diamonds as they chafed Drake's chest through her thin shirt. Drake pressed her hips into Sylvan's and raked her blunt claws down the center of Sylvan's abdomen. She drew Sylvan in, welcomed her questing tongue, her demanding mouth. The more she gave—the more she took—the calmer Sylvan became, until finally Sylvan released her mouth. Sylvan dragged her canines down Drake's neck and kissed the bite on Drake's shoulder. Heat washed through Drake and her stomach clenched.

"You have nothing to growl over," Drake murmured. "I hunger only for you."

"She was touching you," Sylvan said fiercely, her arm around Drake's waist, her pelvis tight against Drake's.

"I needed her to draw blood for some tests," Drake said, stroking Sylvan's face.

Sophia, who had quietly withdrawn to the far side of the room, said, "It's my fault, Alpha. I know better than to be alone with her now."

"What tests?" Sylvan whipped her head around, fixing Sophia with a flat, hard stare.

"We want to repeat the mitochondrial DNA analysis," Sophia said.

"Why?" Sylvan's body coiled tightly, driven by a primal force stronger than any other to protect her mate. She would allow nothing to harm her.

Drake smoothed her hands up and down Sylvan's back and kissed her neck. "I need to be sure the changes in my cells are stable. That I'm not carrying any kind of mutagen that could be a danger to you or—"

"You're *fine*," Sylvan snarled. "You're my mate. Do you think I couldn't tell if there's something wrong?"

"I'm not a born Were," Drake said gently, knowing this barrier could prevent the rest of the Pack from accepting her as Sylvan's mate, even if Sylvan refused to acknowledge the problem. "We don't know if you'll be able to sense everything about me as you would if I were *regii*."

"*I* know." Sylvan nipped Drake's chin hard enough to make Drake grumble. "You're my mate and I say you're fine."

"If you don't mind, Alpha," Drake said, digging her claws into Sylvan's ass through the denim of her jeans, "I'd like to verify that with some tests. We need the information."

Sylvan's eyes narrowed and flared molten gold, but she rubbed her forehead over Drake's and murmured, "As you wish, Prima."

Drake slanted her mouth over Sylvan's and teased her with a quick flick of her tongue inside her lower lip. "It won't take long."

"Good." Sylvan stepped behind Drake and wrapped her arms around Drake's middle, resting her chin on the top of Drake's shoulder.

Running her hands up and down Drake's belly under her shirt, she glanced over at Sophia, who was studiously not looking at them but was labeling a row of multicolored blood vials. "Go ahead, Sophia. Be quick."

"We should have the results of these and yesterday's biopsies in a few hours," Sophia said as she wrapped a tourniquet around Drake's upper arm.

"What biopsies?" Sylvan demanded.

Sophia remained silent.

Drake turned her head and gently bit Sylvan's jaw. "I'll explain in a few minutes. Let Sophia work."

Sylvan rumbled and nuzzled Drake's neck. "All right."

Smiling, Sophia filled the tubes and removed the tourniquet from Drake's arm. She gathered the vials and stepped well out of Drake and Sylvan's sphere. "I'll drive these over to the lab myself."

"Call me as soon as you get the results?" Drake asked.

"Of course."

"Lock the door behind you," Sylvan said, sliding her hand down to the button on Drake's jeans. She traced her mouth over Drake's ear and nudged Drake toward the counter with the thrust of her hips against Drake's ass. "You smell hungry."

"So do you." Drake grabbed the counter with both hands as Sylvan cleaved to her back. When Sylvan reached down into her jeans and squeezed, the sweet pressure ramped her toward release. "Maybe you should take care of that."

"I'm going to." Sylvan lightly bit Drake's earlobe.

Drake pushed off her pants and kicked them away, then spread her legs. "In me now."

Sylvan milked Drake's clitoris between her fingers, making it jump and swell. Drake groaned and Sylvan rumbled with satisfaction. "You're so hard and wet for me."

"All the time." Drake covered Sylvan's hand and directed her fingers where she needed them. "I wanted you when I woke up."

"I know. You keep me ready to burst." Sylvan shredded Drake's T-shirt and sucked the mating mark on her shoulder, letting Drake guide her caresses over her swollen sex. "Good?"

"I'm going to come," Drake said breathlessly, guiding Sylvan's fingers lower. "Please, I need to feel you."

Sylvan eased back a fraction and quickly shed her pants. Naked, she rubbed her clitoris in the cleft of Drake's ass and buried her fingers in Drake's core. Drake rolled her hips and Sylvan groaned. "I want to come all over you."

"Oh yes." Drake reached behind her and dug her claws into Sylvan's ass, tensing her muscles around Sylvan. "Your clit's so hot. Does that feel good, love? Is that what you need?"

Sylvan's hips bucked and she bared her canines, silver spreading like summer lightning over her belly. "Mine. Say it."

"Yours."

"Say it again," Sylvan panted, one hand around Drake's throat, the other inside her.

"I love being yours." Drake turned her head and bit Sylvan's lip. Sylvan thrust inside her and Drake clamped down hard on her. "I'm coming for you. Can you feel me coming?"

Sylvan pushed deeper between Drake's legs and Drake jackknifed forward over the bench, flooding Sylvan's hand. Sylvan's clitoris stiffened on the cusp of release.

"More," Sylvan groaned and bit Drake's shoulder.

Drake's ass clenched as she emptied violently and Sylvan spent with a roar. Drake's claws gouged deep trenches across the bench as her mate rode her back in a frenzy of teeth and claws, and still she felt Sylvan's call. Sylvan needed more. Sylvan needed completion. Sylvan needed *her*. A rush of furious possession arced through her and Drake swept her arm over the counter, shoving file folders and trays of instruments aside. Spinning around, she lifted onto the counter and gripped Sylvan's hips. Dragging Sylvan between her thighs, she scissored her legs around Sylvan's waist. Sylvan's clitoris slotted under hers, sliding between her folds and teasing her entrance. The pressure was so intense, the pleasure so exquisite, she immediately readied again.

"Fuck me," Drake demanded and sank her canines into Sylvan's chest.

Sylvan's wolf erupted in a fury. Hips thrusting hard and fast, Sylvan gripped the back of Drake's neck, her claws just breaking skin. Drake drove her mating bite deeper into the muscle above Sylvan's breast, forcing Sylvan into the ultimate release.

"Say it," Drake cried.

"Yours," Sylvan roared, pouring her essence into the very heart of Drake's being.

Drake clasped her mate tightly until Sylvan's last tremor subsided, then soothed the bite she'd made with her tongue. "I love the way you come for me."

"You didn't come." Sylvan rested her head on Drake's shoulder, her breath coming in shallow pants. "I'm sorry. I needed you so much."

Laughing, Drake played her fingers through Sylvan's hair. "Oh, I think I can forgive you for losing control, Alpha."

Sylvan kissed Drake's neck. "Only you could do that to me."

Drake's heart seized. She had allowed the mate bond, even though she knew she was being selfish. "I love you so much."

"Then why are you unhappy?" Sylvan leaned back and studied Drake's face, a frown marring the smooth skin between her golden brows. When Drake looked away, Sylvan gently clasped her chin and forced Drake to meet her gaze. "Tell me."

Drake smoothed her palms back and forth over Sylvan's broad, strong chest, then settled her arms loosely around Sylvan's waist. "Even if I'm completely healthy, I'm not the right mate for you."

Sylvan snarled, her canines lengthening.

"No," Drake said gently, rubbing her thumb over Sylvan's lower lip. "I'm not Pack born. The other Alphas, even some of your own Pack, will not accept a Prima who is not *regii*."

"The Timberwolf Pack will accept what I tell them to accept," Sylvan said darkly.

"Maybe. And maybe some will try to challenge you."

"Let them."

"Now is not the time for unrest in the Pack. Not now, when so much depends on your negotiations in Washington." Drake's hand shook where it rested on Sylvan's face. "Not now, when someone is trying to kill you. You need all your allies behind you. You don't need anything—anyone—to make you vulnerable."

Sylvan's eyes narrowed. "Who told you this?"

"It doesn't matter. It's true, isn't it?"

"Niki," Sylvan grumbled. "She needs to learn—"

"She loves you." Drake kissed Sylvan softly. "And you love her. Stop snarling."

Sylvan gripped Drake's shoulders and leaned close until all Drake could see were Sylvan's eyes. "Listen to me, Prima. I am the Alpha of this Pack and I choose who I mate. My wolf chooses you. *I* choose you."

"Sylvan," Drake whispered. "I can't give you young."

"You know how we breed? Roger told you?"

"No. Sophia's parents explained some of it to me yesterday." Drake shivered, thinking that she had been discussing science while someone had been lying in wait to assassinate Sylvan. "I know a dominant female can breed another receptive female. That the kinins released by the mating bite when you come contain carrier proteins that deliver the mitochondrial DNA-signature to the egg and activate it."

Sylvan smiled, a supremely satisfied smile. "Yes. Exactly what we just did. Didn't you feel me empty into you?"

Drake's hips jerked and her breasts tightened. "Of course I felt you." She ran her tongue down the center of Sylvan's throat and bit the thick muscle above her collarbone. "I can feel you inside me now. Everywhere." She laughed unsteadily. "I can hardly believe it, but I'm ready for you again."

"I'm full for you again too." Sylvan cupped Drake's jaw. "This is more than mating frenzy. Your transformation has accelerated everything. This is breeding frenzy."

"But *mutia* can't—"

"Stop." With infinite tenderness, Sylvan kissed Drake's forehead, her eyes, her mouth. "You are my mate. My instincts tell me we are breeding now. If we have no young of our own—this time, or ever, I will name a successor from among the strongest of the Pack when the time comes."

Drake caressed Sylvan's face with trembling fingers. "I can't keep you from fulfilling your destiny. You were born to be Alpha, and you should be able to see your daughter—"

"So you'll give me up to another?" Sylvan asked. "Have me breed with another fem—"

Drake's wolf burst out so quickly she didn't have time to reason or react. Her face shifted, her jaws elongated, and a thick line of dark pelt streamed down the center of her belly. Her claws raked Sylvan's shoulders. In a voice guttural with possessive rage, she rasped, "Mine!"

"Yours." Sylvan tilted her head back and gave Drake her neck.

Drake gripped Sylvan's throat in her jaws and shook her hard. With a cry, Sylvan came on Drake's stomach.

When Sylvan sagged, Drake caught Sylvan to her and kissed her. Cradling Sylvan's head against her shoulder, she whispered, "Did I hurt you?"

"You will never hurt me as long as you never leave me." Sylvan gasped as another spasm shook her. "Say you won't leave me."

"I won't. I can't." Drake leaned her head against Sylvan's. "I'll die before I leave you."

"You'll be in danger because you are my mate. The attack last night—that might be just the beginning."

"I'm not afraid." Drake's only fear was losing Sylvan, and she would do anything and everything in her power to protect her.

"I didn't think I needed a mate. I thought a mate would make me weak. I was wrong." Sylvan straightened, her blue eyes ringed with wolf-gold. Her face was calm, strong, certain. "I love you. I need you, and not just because a Pack is always stronger with an Alpha pair to lead them." She brushed the backs of her fingers over Drake's cheek. "I never knew how lonely I was until I wasn't lonely anymore. You already run with me in my dreams. Soon, we'll run together on our land, with our Pack. Say you love me. Say you will run by my side."

"I love you, Sylvan," Drake said, joy eclipsing all regrets. She would live, no matter what demons inside her or enemies outside threatened her. She would fight, because she would not leave Sylvan alone. Sylvan was hers, forever, to love and cherish and protect. "You're my heart, my mate. I will always be by your side."

Sylvan pulled her close and buried her face in Drake's neck. When Drake realized Sylvan was shaking, she stroked her hair. "What is it?"

"I need to leave for a few hours." Sylvan drew deeply of Drake's scent. "I'll be back as soon as I can."

"You just asked me to run by your side," Drake said, her mouth against Sylvan's neck. She couldn't ask her not to go. Sylvan was the Alpha. She had to lead. But she didn't have to lead alone any longer. "Do you think I will let you hunt alone?"

"It's too soon," Sylvan said. "Your wolf—"

"The fight was brought to us—yours by the Exodus, mine by a bite from a dying girl. We didn't choose the time or circumstances. If you hunt, so do I. I'm your mate. Don't ask me to be less. Not now, not when I've given you my heart."

Sylvan's eyes glowed with pride and possession. She kissed Drake hard, drawing power from Drake's strength. "I love you."

"Then let me love you."

With a nod, Sylvan grasped Drake's hand.

Niki, the Alpha called, *it's time to hunt.*

CHAPTER THIRTY-TWO

"Max and the twins have been tracking the scent since last night," Niki said as Andrew drove the Rover from the Compound.

Drake sat on the side bench with her back against the wall with Sylvan lounging on the floor between her legs. Sylvan tilted her head back against Drake's stomach, and Drake ran her fingers through Sylvan's hair, unable to stop touching her even for a minute. Like Sylvan and the others, she wore only a pair of jeans, and when Sylvan reached back and idly ran her blunt nails over Drake's bare flank, she growled softly. She knew a fight was coming and she was primed, her adrenaline pumping, a flair of midnight black pelt streaming low on her belly, her clitoris erect and throbbing. Her wolf clawed the undersurface of her skin, demanding the freedom to hunt or tangle—the two urges nearly indistinguishable in her newly transformed system.

"Have they sighted the prey?" Sylvan asked.

"They lost the scent at one of the warehouses on the river last night, but they spent all day checking similar buildings and tracking scent trails. They picked up our prey again just a few hours ago. Max reports the one we want is with half a dozen rogues."

Sylvan snarled. "The rogues have never been aggressive before."

"They're loading containers into trucks," Niki said. "Max thinks it's DSX."

"The methamphetamine variant?" Drake asked.

"Yes," Sylvan said. "Highly addictive and highly toxic to us."

"If the rogues are running drugs," Drake suggested, "they must be part of a larger trafficking ring. They need suppliers, distributors, probably police protection. With that kind of backup, they might feel untouchable. That could explain why they'd risk an all-out assault."

"Most rogues are usually too undisciplined to carry out any kind of illicit operation," Sylvan said. "Whoever is in charge is not some half-feral DSX addict."

"The assassin?" Drake asked.

"Probably."

Drake massaged the muscles in the back of Sylvan's neck. If they found the shooter, Sylvan would need to destroy him, but Drake worried Sylvan wasn't yet strong enough for a fight. Her gunshot wounds had nearly killed her. Knowing only one way to protect her mate, Drake reached deep inside herself and touched her wolf. Instantly, her skin burned and pain shuddered through her bones. She remembered her dream and the agony of shifting. She feared she wouldn't be able to shift in time to keep her mate safe, but she had to try. The pain intensified and she groaned.

Stop, Sylvan telegraphed. *You're all I need.*

I want to go with you. I want to be by your side.

Sylvan stroked Drake's leg and turned her head to kiss Drake's stomach. *Not unless you shift. You won't be safe, otherwise.*

What if I can't?

Don't worry. Sylvan tugged on the skin of Drake's belly with her teeth, then licked the small mark of ownership. *Your wolf will know when it's time.*

Drake caressed Sylvan's cheek and caught Niki's gaze as she sat opposite them watching. Niki couldn't hear what had transpired between them, but Drake could reach Niki. *If I can't go with her, I'm entrusting her to you.*

Niki jolted upright, the surprise in her eyes quickly giving way to resolve. And respect. "Yes, Prima."

❖

"Turn here," Sylvan said as she felt Max's call.

Andrew drove down a narrow overgrown path between a narrow strip of trees and the river's edge just south of the city. Across the broad expanse of water, a train whistle blew. Overhead slashes of blue-black clouds skated across the face of a brilliant full moon.

"That's the building up ahead. Stop here and we'll go the rest of the way on foot."

When they climbed out of the Rover, Drake stared up at the moon. Her skin tingled and heat balled in the pit of her stomach. Max stepped out of the darkness followed by two incredibly beautiful young blonds—the male was slightly taller than his sister, both were nude except for pants, both as perfectly muscled as a Michelangelo statue. Immediately, the three newcomers crowded around Sylvan and she stroked each of them in turn.

"What have you found?" Sylvan asked.

"There are seven inside, Alpha," Max said. "Including the one we tracked from the park across from the Vampire's lair."

"And you're sure that one is the shooter?"

"Yes, Alpha," the blond female answered briskly. "His scent is thick with silver. Blowback from the ammunition he used."

"Well done, *centuri*." Sylvan gripped the shoulders of the two young lieutenants. "Jace. Jonathan. Welcome to my guard."

Brother and sister immediately dropped to one knee and touched their foreheads to Sylvan's thighs. She caressed them briefly, then urged them up. "Max, take Jace and Jonathan and secure the rear. Andrew and Niki—with me." She spread her arms wide. "Come, my wolves. To the hunt."

Drake tried to watch the *centuri* shift, but all she could discern was a faint shimmering before their shadows blurred in a dark, hypnotic dance. Within seconds, it seemed, Sylvan was surrounded by five fierce wolves. A huge gray—Max; a lean, muscular red-gray—Niki; a svelte red—Andrew; two white and grays—Jace and Jonathan. Only Sylvan remained in skin form, and yet she seemed no less dangerous or less powerful than the animals who crowded against her.

"I'm coming with you," Drake said.

"No. I can't risk losing you." Sylvan dragged Drake forward and kissed her ferociously. "Wait in the Rover. I love you."

"Sylvan!" Drake called as Sylvan loped away, as graceful as her wolves. From deep inside, Drake heard—felt—her other self call to her, claiming her place. *Sylvan must not go alone.* Her midnight wolf was the sky to Sylvan's star. She knew her destiny and what she must do.

Drake took a step, then another, then she was running. Running free. The hot summer air danced across her tongue, carrying teasing hints of prey scurrying in the underbrush, the acrid taste of drug-frenzied rogues, the sharp tang of the *centuri*. And the powerful, hot rush that was Sylvan. Drake covered the ground in huge, bounding strides and reached Sylvan's side just as Sylvan prepared to breach the warehouse doors.

Welcome, mate. Sylvan reached down and buried her fist in Drake's ruff. Together, they leapt at the door and crashed it inward, Niki and Andrew soaring past them to land in the midst of a startled ragtag group of rogues. Most were half naked, covered in haphazard remnants of tattered clothing. Several looked and smelled sick. Three males carried automatic rifles, and as they brought the weapons to their shoulders, Niki, Andrew, and Drake launched themselves as one.

Drake didn't think. Her only imperative was to protect her mate. The guard went down with her teeth in his neck, and she shook her head and shoulders with instinctive ferocity. He went limp and she dropped him, racing back to Sylvan's side. Niki and Andrew drifted toward the shadows on either side of Sylvan. The other rogues had all run, leaving a single blond male standing in a shaft of moonlight that filtered through a broken skylight high above them. Unlike the other renegades, he looked fit and healthy. His dark shirt and pants hugged his muscular frame as if tailor-made. His sharp blue eyes were clear and filled with hatred.

"Sergi Milos," Sylvan snarled, her voice echoing throughout the cavernous space. "Your mutts called you Rex." She laughed. "You could live a thousand lifetimes and never deserve that name. But you won't have the chance."

"Just like your mother," Rex sneered. "You let your *centuri* fight for you. Now I'll kill you just like I killed her."

"You already failed." She spread her arms, displaying her unblemished torso. "Only a coward uses bullets instead of teeth and claws."

"Your Pack should be mine," Rex raged.

"Is that what the Blackpaw Alpha promised you when you led the raid against my mother? When you *ambushed* her?"

"Her guards were lucky and managed to defeat my lieutenants, or I would already be Alpha. Bernardo promised me half of your territory."

"Bernardo ordered your execution as part of the new treaty after the failed campaign against us."

"Bernardo is a weakling." Rex laughed. "As you can see, he failed to put me down."

"I won't." Sylvan growled. "You destroy your own species with drugs. You're not fit to lead anyone."

Rex trembled with anger. "When I put you down like the bitch you are, I will claim the Timberwolf Pack and all its territory."

"I accept your challenge," Sylvan said softly. "Here and now."

Rex's eyes flickered around the room. "You ambushed my guards. I have no witnesses."

Max appeared behind Rex, dragging two stunned Were guards with him. He tossed the male and female onto the littered floor. "Here are your witnesses."

"Shift," Sylvan ordered, "and bring your challenge."

With a vicious snarl, Rex's face contorted and then his body transformed. Not as fast as the *centuri* had shifted, but within a minute, a huge white wolf with mad dark eyes stood slavering a few yards from Sylvan.

Drake caught her breath, wondering why Sylvan, her face completely calm and composed, remained in skin while allowing her enemy to assume his stronger wolf form. Then with no warning, Rex launched himself at Sylvan's throat, jaws snapping. But Sylvan was no longer the standing target he had anticipated. Instead, a silver wolf collided with him in midair, grabbing his neck in her jaws as she undercut the arc of his leap. His claws raked her chest and underbelly and blood drenched her silver pelt. Drake growled, quivering, barely able to restrain her instinct to propel herself into the fray. But Sylvan was her Alpha and her mate, and she trusted her, believed in her. Drake held her ground, growling threateningly when one of the rogues would have crawled away.

Rex was heavier than Sylvan by forty pounds, but despite the blood streaming from her wounds, Sylvan's jaws locked tight, her wolf-gold eyes molten with fury. The wolves crashed to the floor, their bodies a roiling mass of muscle and blood. The air vibrated with their growls of rage. Rex tore at Sylvan's soft flank, trying to dislodge her. Drake felt the searing pain as his teeth sliced Sylvan's side. Infuriated by his attack on her mate, Drake reached out to Sylvan with her heart and mind, sending all her love and strength. *Now, love. Take him now.*

With a tremendous burst of force, Sylvan wrenched her head viciously back and forth, tearing Rex's neck open in a froth of crimson. He dropped onto his back, convulsing in her grip. Straddling his twitching body, Sylvan raised her blood-spattered head and howled in victory. She glimmered with power and pride in the moonlight.

Drake trembled with a surge of joy at her mate's triumph and joined her voice to Sylvan's. While the *centuri* echoed their cries, the rogue Weres cowered on the floor, their heads down, puddles beneath their legs. Sylvan swung her great head around, searching for Drake. When their eyes met, her pelt receded and she staggered upright. Without any thought to shifting, Drake simply rose up to meet her, her wolf quietly retreating. She took Sylvan into her arms, Sylvan's hot blood painting her breasts and abdomen. Niki crowded close to Sylvan, her muzzle drawn back in a snarl as she guarded Sylvan's injured flank. Sylvan shuddered in Drake's embrace.

"How badly are you hurt?" Drake said, too softly for the others to hear. She stroked Sylvan's back and would have cradled Sylvan's head on her shoulder if the rogues had not been watching.

"I'm all right. Already healing." Sylvan rubbed her cheek over Drake's. "I felt you with me."

"Yes. Forever. I promise."

Sylvan's blue eyes clouded with pain. "He killed my mother."

"I know. I'm sorry."

"He must have gone to ground before the order of execution could be carried out. Now she has been avenged." Sylvan sighed and draped her arm around Drake's shoulders. "Rex's masters will no doubt replace him by morning. Evil seems to be in endless supply."

"You've defeated a challenger." Drake gestured to the two rogues on their knees a few feet away, still guarded by the *centuri*. "They've witnessed your kill and others will hear of it. You've sent the message that you will defend your Pack to the death."

"I am afraid there will always be another battle, mate," Sylvan said.

"And when it comes, Alpha," Drake murmured before kissing her, "we'll all be at your side."

"As long as you are with me, I can face any challenge."

"Always, my love. Always."

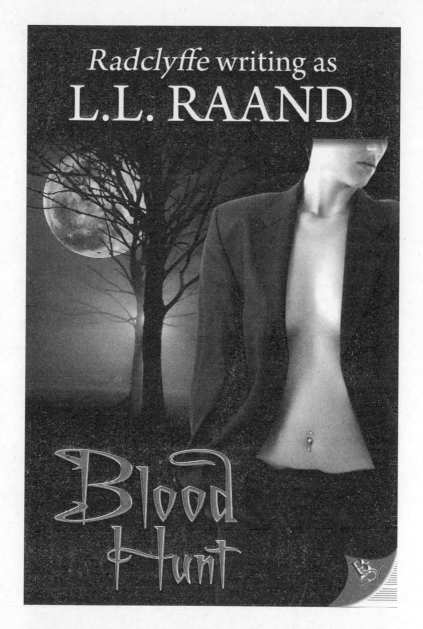

Radclyffe writing as
L.L. RAAND

Blood Hunt

Keep reading for a special preview of BLOOD HUNT,
the next book in L.L. Raand's Midnight Hunters series.

BLOOD HUNT
BY L.L. RAAND

Coming Winter 2010

Detective Jody Gates watched Dr. Marissa Sanchez orgasm in the arms of a newly turned Vampire for the third time in as many hours. Marissa moaned, her hips undulating, each time Lara pulled from the punctures she had made in Marissa's neck. Jody recognized the soft cries and urgent pleas signaling Marissa's climax, and bloodlust surged in her depths. Until recently she had been the one to feed from Marissa's neck and the one releasing the hormones that made Marissa come. She rarely allowed Marissa to host for her any longer, even though Marissa always offered whenever they bumped into each other at the city morgue or at Club Nocturne, where Jody usually sated her hunger with a willing host. Unfortunately, Marissa equated the intense physical pleasure of providing life-sustaining blood with an emotional connection that Jody, like most Vampires, did not feel. Jody might orgasm in the rush of heat and power that subsumed her when she fed, but the reaction was purely physical.

Invariably, humans, and even some Weres, came to want more from a relationship than Jody could provide. She contented herself in knowing that hosts experienced shattering orgasms while she sated her bloodlust. She had learned to move on before her blood partners sought more than pleasure.

Marissa cried out, clutching Lara's back as she rode the hand buried deep between her thighs. The allure of sex and blood saturated the air. Jody's stomach roiled and her vision shimmered. She hadn't fed since before sunrise, and now it was late evening. Her hunger was riding her hard, and the rich aroma of sex and blood threatened her control. Her incisors unsheathed as she broadcast her need. Across the room, Marissa's eyes snapped open, searching for her.

"Jody," Marissa whispered, her voice a plea. She stretched out an arm in invitation, then abruptly, her eyes rolled back and she went limp in Lara's arms.

"That's enough," Jody warned. When Lara kept feeding, Jody leapt quickly to the bed and cupped one hand beneath Lara's chin, pulling her mouth away from Marissa's neck. "Stop."

"No!" Lara whipped her head around, her eyes an inferno of red and gold. Vampire and Were. Lara was one of the wolf Alpha's *centuri*—Sylvan Mir's elite guard. A dominant female and one of the strongest Weres in the Timberwolf Pack. Just the day before, during an assassination attempt on Sylvan, Lara had taken most of a fusillade of silver bullets in the chest. Her heart had been destroyed, and even though the Alpha had torn the poisonous silver from Lara's body, Lara had lost too much blood to heal her wounds. Lara had sacrificed herself for her Alpha.

Jody still didn't know why she had offered her own blood to save the Were. She had no particular fondness for Weres. Unlike the Fae, the Mage, and the Psi, Vampires and Weres did not rely on magic and extrasensory abilities to stay alive. Vampires and Weres were predatory creatures whose survival depended upon physical power and dominance. They were more often rivals than allies.

Lara had thrown herself in the path of the bullets meant for Sylvan—any Were would have done the same. The instinct to protect the Alpha was a primal force. But Jody hadn't expected to see the wolf Alpha risk her own life trying to save one of her guards. Watching Sylvan fight for Lara's life while blood poured from multiple wounds in Sylvan's torso bore stark witness to a critical connection Jody had never experienced. No Vampire would have chanced their existence for an underling. Probably not even for a family member. So she had offered her own blood to keep Lara alive long enough to heal. Lara, however, had been so close to death she hadn't been able to replenish her own blood stores, incorporating

Jody's instead. She had turned and was now a chimera, both Were and Vampire. Lara, like Jody—like all Vampires living or risen—was dependent on the ferrous carrier compounds in human and Were blood to supply oxygen to her tissues. Without it, her own blood would slowly empty of the essential elements needed to sustain life and she would suffocate—one cell at a time.

Lara was Jody's responsibility now—hers to protect *and* control while Lara learned to satisfy her needs without killing her hosts in the throes of bloodlust. Even for powerful, experienced Vampires like Jody, the urge to absorb every ounce of heat and strength a host could provide was hard to restrain. For a newly turned Vampire, the bloodlust was so exquisitely painful, the need to feed so overpowering, they would leave a trail of bodies behind them until they were hunted down and destroyed. Jody would not allow one of her line to devolve into an animal.

Jody tightened her grip on Lara's jaw. "You will do as I say."

"I need more," Lara snarled. Her thick chestnut hair was damp with perspiration, her pale bronze skin stretched tight over knife-edged bones. The muscles in her torso rippled and a faint dusting of brown pelt exploded down the divide between her stark abdominals. Her nipples tightened into small hard stones. Lara growled. Aggression in Weres was always accompanied by sexual arousal, and she was doubly dangerous with all her drives demanding satisfaction. "I *want* her."

"She's given enough." Jody held Lara in place with the force of her gaze. "We're going hunting tonight. We'll find you another host."

"Now." Lara lunged for Jody's throat and Jody tossed her across the room. Lara crashed into the wall and fell onto her back.

Before she could leap up, Jody was on top of her. Driving her thigh between Lara's legs, she simultaneously grabbed Lara's wrists and pinned them to the rough wood floor with one hand. Lara thrashed, her incisors gleaming, her eyes blind pools of fire. Jody grasped Lara's jaw and pressed her mouth to Lara's ear.

"Don't make me kill you," Jody warned, the weight of her body magnified a dozen times by her inherent power.

Lara whimpered, the agony of endless hunger and the searing sexual need pushing her to the brink of insanity. Wrapping one leg around Jody's thigh, she ground her swollen sex into Jody. "Help me. Please. Please."

"I will." Jody relinquished her grip on Lara's jaw and pushed the flat of her hand between their bodies, skating over the stone plains of Lara's abdomen to clasp her sex. She palmed the swollen clitoris and pressed down, milking the tense glands buried deep beneath. She brushed her mouth over Lara's and commanded, "Come in my hand. Let me feel you spend, Wolf."

Lara arched like a bowstring drawn taut, only her head and heels touching the floor. Her abdomen contracted, her pelvis jerked, and she released in a howling fury of pleasure and pain. Jody held her down until the spasms stopped, her own body wracked with need. Lara was still Were enough to excite her bloodlust, but not Were enough to satisfy her. If she tried to feed from her, she would likely kill Lara and poison herself.

When Lara quieted, Jody rolled away, panting as she struggled to contain her hunger. Even had it been safe to feed from Lara, she didn't think she would have. It wasn't Lara's face she'd seen when the bloodlust rode her, but a human female she had no intention of ever tasting.

Pushing herself to her knees, Jody buttoned her shirt with trembling hands and tucked it into her pants. Lara lay curled on her side, her knees drawn up, her hips and thighs slowly flexing as her orgasm waned. Jody leaned over and skimmed her fingers through Lara's hair.

"Get dressed. We're leaving."

Jody didn't wait for an answer, but proceeded to cover Marissa with a sheet and lift the semiconscious woman into her arms. The bites in Marissa's neck were already fading, but she was hovering on the brink of serious blood loss. Marissa always did push the envelope when she hosted.

"Did I hurt her?" Lara whispered, standing now, her whiskey eyes hollow with torment and lingering hunger. She'd pulled jeans and a shirt from the closet and dressed mechanically.

"Dr. Sanchez will be fine after a night's rest and some nutritional supplements," Jody said. "Don't forget she volunteered. She wanted the pleasure of feeding you."

"The pain won't go away."

"Your body is seriously oxygen deprived." Jody opened the door and gestured for Lara to precede her down the hall to the main lobby of the infirmary. "What you're experiencing is severe lactic acid poisoning. You need to replenish the ferrous carrier compounds frequently or the pain will become debilitating. If you don't, your cells will break down and your muscles and organs will disintegrate. You'll become paralyzed, lose consciousness, and die within hours."

"Aren't I dead already," Lara said bitterly. She'd launched herself in front of the Alpha when the gunfire had started, taking the silver bullets into her own body to save Sylvan. She had done her duty and would do it again. When she would have died, when even the Alpha with all her power could not save her, this Vampire had prevented her death. But at what cost?

"No, you're not dead. You're pre-animate—a living Vampire."

"I am a wolf Were!" For an instant, Lara's wolf surged again and her eyes shifted to amber gold. The bones in her angular face sharpened. A deep rumble of warning resonated in her chest.

Jody slowed, untroubled by Marissa's weight. Although others frequently misinterpreted her tall, slender form and pale complexion as delicate, she was stronger than any human and even some Alpha Weres. Her lineage was ancient, and when she rose after death, if she rose, she would be among the most powerful Vampires in the world. At any other time she would not have tolerated Lara's display of dominance, but she didn't want to subdue her again. Lara was still too unstable, her system in chaos, fluctuating wildly between her Were and Vampire urges. Most Weres who were turned, and who survived the turning, were more Vampire than anything else. Many could never shift form again. Lara was not just any Were—she was one of the strongest Weres ever turned. Where she would fall on the spectrum, the eventual extent of her power, was unknown. She was likely to be one of a kind.

"You should thank me, Wolf, not challenge me." Jody captured Lara's gaze in her thrall. "We don't have time for this rebellion tonight."

Lara shuddered, unable to break free. Her face was luminous with pain and still she managed to speak. "When will it stop?"

"When you've fed enough."

About the Author

L.L. Raand writing as Radclyffe has published over thirty-five romance and romantic intrigue novels, dozens of short stories, and edited numerous romance and erotica anthologies. She is a seven-time Lambda Literary Award finalist and winner in both romance (*Distant Shores, Silent Thunder*) and erotica (*Erotic Interludes 2: Stolen Moments* edited with Stacia Seaman and *In Deep Waters 2: Cruising the Strip* written with Karin Kallmaker). She is a member of the Saints and Sinners Literary Hall of Fame, an Alice B. Readers' award winner, a Benjamin Franklin Award finalist (*The Lonely Hearts Club*), and a ForeWord Review Book of the Year Finalist (*Night Call*).

This is the first Midnight Hunters novel. *Blood Hunt* is coming in Winter 2010.

Visit her websites at www.llraand.com and www.radfic.com.

Books Available From Bold Strokes Books

The Midnight Hunt by L.L. Raand. Medic Drake McKennan takes a chance and loses, and her life will never be the same—because when she wakes up after surviving a life-threatening illness, she is no longer human. (978-1-60282-140-8)

Long Shot by D. Jackson Leigh. Love isn't safe, which is exactly why equine veterinarian Tory Greyson wants no part of it—until Leah Montgomery and a horse that won't give up convince her otherwise. (978-1-60282-141-5)

In Medias Res by Yolanda Wallace. Sydney has forgotten her entire life, and the one woman who holds the key to her memory, and her heart, doesn't want to be found. (978-1-60282-142-2)

Awakening to Sunlight by Lindsey Stone. Neither Judith or Lizzy is looking for companionship, and certainly not love—but when their lives become entangled, they discover both. (978-1-60282-143-9)

Fever by VK Powell. Hired gun Zakaria Chambers is hired to provide a simple escort service to philanthropist Sara Ambrosini, but nothing is as simple as it seems, especially love. (978-1-60282-135-4)

High Risk by JLee Meyer. Can actress Kate Hoffman really risk all she's worked for to take a chance on love? Or is it already too late? (978-1-60282-136-1)

Missing Lynx by Kim Baldwin and Xenia Alexiou. On the trail of a notorious serial killer, Elite Operative Lynx's growing attraction to a mysterious mercenary could be her path to love—or to death. (978-1-60282-137-8)

Spanking New by Clifford Henderson. A poignant, hilarious, unforgettable look at life, love, gender, and the essence of what makes us who we are. (978-1-60282-138-5)

Magic of the Heart by C.J. Harte. CEO Susan Hettinger and wild, impulsive rock star M.J. Carson couldn't be more different if they tried—but opposites attract in ways neither woman can resist. (978-1-60282-131-6)

Ambereye by Gill McKnight. Jolie Garoul is falling in love with her assistant. The big problem is, Jolie is a werewolf. (978-1-60282-132-3)

Collision Course by C.P. Rowlands. Tragedy leaves Brie O'Malley and Jordan Carter fearful and alone. Can they find the courage to take a second chance on love? (978-1-60282-133-0)

Mephisto Aria by Justine Saracen. Opera singer Katherina Marov's destiny may be to repeat the mistakes of her father when she becomes involved in a dangerous love affair. (978-1-60282-134-7)

Battle Scars by Meghan O'Brien. Returning Iraq war veteran Ray McKenna struggles with the battle scars that can only be healed by love. (978-1-60282-129-3)

Chaps by Jove Belle. Eden Metcalf wants nothing more than to flee from her troubled past and travel the open road—until she runs into rancher Brandi Cornwell. (978-1-60282-127-9)

Lightbearer by John Caruso. Lucifer dares to question the premise of creation itself and reveals that sin may be all that stands between us and living hell. (978-1-60282-130-9)

The Seeker by Ronica Black. FBI profiler Kennedy Scott battles ghosts from her past, deadly obsession, and the evil that haunts her. (978-1-60282-128-6)

Power Play by Julie Cannon. Businesswomen Tate Monroe and Victoria Sosa are at odds in the boardroom, but not in the bedroom. (978-1-60282-125-5)

The Remarkable Journey of Miss Tranby Quirke by Elizabeth Ridley. When love enters Tranby's life in the form of a beautiful nineteen-year-old student, Lysette McDonald, she embarks on the most remarkable journey of all. (978-1-60282-126-2)

Returning Tides by Radclyffe. Insurance investigator Ashley Walker faces more than a dangerous opponent when she returns to the town, and the woman, she left behind. (978-1-60282-123-1)

Veritas by Anne Laughlin. When the hallowed halls of academia become the stage for murder, newly appointed Dean Beth Ellis's search for the truth leads her to unexpected discoveries about her own heart. (978-1-60282-124-8)

The Pleasure Planner by Larkin Rose. Pleasure purveyor Bree Hendricks treats love like a commodity until Logan Delaney makes Bree the client in her own game. (978-1-60282-121-7)

everafter by Nell Stark and Trinity Tam. Valentine Darrow is bitten by a vampire on her way to propose to her lover Alexa Newland, and their lives and love are placed in mortal jeopardy. (978-1-60282-119-4)

Summer Winds by Andrews & Austin. When Maggie Turner hires a ranch hand to help work her thousand acres, she never expects to be attracted to the very young, very female Cash Tate. (978-1-60282-120-0)

Beggar of Love by Lee Lynch. Jefferson is the lover every woman wants to be—or to have. A revealing saga of lesbian sexuality. (978-1-60282-122-4)

The Seduction of Moxie by Colette Moody. When 1930s Broadway actress Violet London meets speakeasy singer Moxie Valette, she is instantly attracted and her Hollywood trip takes an unexpected turn. (978-1-60282-114-9)

Goldenseal by Gill McKnight. When Amy Fortune returns to her childhood home, she discovers something sinister in the air—but is former lover Leone Garoul stalking her or protecting her? (978-1-60282-115-6)

Romantic Interludes 2: Secrets edited by Radclyffe and Stacia Seaman. An anthology of sensual lesbian love stories: passion, surprises, and secret desires. (978-1-60282-116-3)

Femme Noir by Clara Nipper. Nora Delaney meets her match in Max Abbott, a sex-crazed dame who may or may not have the information Nora needs to solve a murder—but can she contain her lust for Max long enough to find out? (978-1-60282-117-0)

The Reluctant Daughter by Lesléa Newman. Heartwarming, heartbreaking, and ultimately triumphant—the story every daughter recognizes of the lifelong struggle for our mothers to really see us. (978-1-60282-118-7)

Erosistible by Gill McKnight. When Win Martin arrives at a luxurious Greek hotel for a much-anticipated week of sun and sex with her new girlfriend, she is stunned to find her ex-girlfriend, Benny, is the proprietor. Aeros Ebook. (978-1-60282-134-7)

Looking Glass Lives by Felice Picano. Cousins Roger and Alistair become lifelong friends and discover their sexuality amidst the backdrop of twentieth-century gay culture. (978-1-60282-089-0)

Breaking the Ice by Kim Baldwin. Nothing is easy about life above the Arctic Circle—except, perhaps, falling in love. At least that's what pilot Bryson Faulkner hopes when she meets Karla Edwards. (978-1-60282-087-6)

It Should Be a Crime by Carsen Taite. Two women fulfill their mutual desire with a night of passion, neither expecting more until law professor Morgan Bradley and student Parker Casey meet again…in the classroom. (978-1-60282-086-9)

Rough Trade edited by Todd Gregory. Top male erotica writers pen their own hot, sexy versions of the term "rough trade," producing some of the hottest, nastiest, and most dangerous fiction ever published. (978-1-60282-092-0)

The High Priest and the Idol by Jane Fletcher. Jemeryl and Tevi's relationship is put to the test when the Guardian sends Jemeryl on a mission that puts her not only in harm's way, but back into the sights of a previous lover. (978-1-60282-085-2)

Point of Ignition by Erin Dutton. Amid a blaze that threatens to consume them both, firefighter Kate Chambers and property owner Alexi Clark redefine love and trust. (978-1-60282-084-5)